The Dragons' Rose

By

Danielle Outlaw

Copyright © 2024 by Danielle Outlaw

Published by Hemingway Publishers

Cover design by Hemingway Publishers

ISBN: Printed in the United States

Dedication

To my Mom, whose love and support have meant everything. To my children, to show you that anything is possible. To my Brother Dj, and Sisters Nicole and Ellen — this book wouldn't have happened without your love and support. I love you all; thank you for everything. And to my friend Dave, you are dearly missed.

Page Blank Intentionally

Table of Contents

Foreword

In the beginning, there was only the God and the Goddess, two powerful beings who embodied both masculine and feminine energies. They created the stars, the planets, and all living things - from the tiniest insects to the mightiest beasts. Together, they maintained balance in the world by guiding the seasons and nurturing life and death with equal love and care.

As their creations flourished, they named their world Elara, though other races would come to know them by different names. Among these races were humans, the only ones to worship the God exclusively. His once-equal partner, known as The Mother, was now relegated to a lesser role.

But as time passed, greed and desire for power corrupted some of the humans. They started wars in the name of their one God, attempting to force all other races to follow suit. In their pursuit of control, magic became outlawed, and those born with it were forced into service by the church.

The other races - Elves, fairies, and any creature with magical or beast-like abilities were forced to hide. Eventually, they vanished completely, leaving the humans to believe they were the only race left in Elara. However, whispers on the wind spoke of a prophecy foretold a child who would unite the fractured trust between worlds and bring them back together.

Within Elara, there were many kingdoms - each with its own unique culture and landscape. Five of these kingdoms stood out as mighty powers: Almathea, Carpo, Kalyke, Bestla, and Narvi. Located on the main continent, these kingdoms grew wealthy and powerful over time - but with wealth often comes greed.

Almathea was considered to be the jewel of Elara's kingdoms. Its castles sat atop a great hill surrounded by lush forests, fertile plains, and winding streams that sustained its people. With control over agriculture and timber production, Almathea had become the wealthiest Kingdom in Elara.

Carpo, with its vast mines and gleaming jewels, held all rights over the import and export of minerals in the five kingdoms. Kalke, known for its rolling plains and esteem for scholars and architects, charged exorbitant fees for education, making it a place only the wealthy could attend. Bestla was a kingdom built upon the sea, its people skilled in fishing and shipping trade. Foreign lands seeking to trade with any of the five kingdoms were required to sail to Bestla. Narvi was renowned for its production of fine armor and weapons fit for royalty and nobility.

But as wealth and power often do, it bred conflict between the kingdoms. Eventually, war erupted and two kingdoms fell: Carpo and Kalke. Their kings perished on the battlefield, their heirs slaughtered by hired assassins. In the end, Almathea emerged victorious, claiming the two fallen kingdoms as spoils and becoming the largest of the remaining three.

In an effort to avoid further bloodshed, the kings of Bestla and Narvi signed a treaty with Almathea, agreeing to pay tribute to the ruling monarch in exchange for keeping their crowns. In this newfound unity, the three surviving kingdoms formed a church in God's name and created an army to protect their people - The Order of the Dragon.

This elite order was made up of individuals with various ranks and abilities. Those born with magic were recruited as acolytes - mages specializing in mind control, illusions, or scholarly pursuits such as linguistics and archiving. They primarily trained in Kalke and held ranks such as Prior, Seneschal, Marshal, High Marshal, and the highest rank: Grand Marshal.

Battlemages were those with a talent for destructive magic such as fire, ice, and lightning. They would typically train in Kalke before being transferred to Bestla for their final years of training. Their ranks within the order included Levies, Companions-At-Arms, Corporals, Sergeants, and the highest ranking: Sergeant Major.

Those without magical abilities were also recruited into the order as Knights. They trained in Narvi and then traveled to Almathea to be knighted by the High King. Those who wished to rise in rank from Knight had the opportunity to become a Knight Lieutenant, Knight Captain, Knight Major, and ultimately, a Knight Commander.

The Order of the Dragon held many duties - serving their people, their King, and above all else, God. It was not uncommon to see members of the order acting as representatives or ambassadors to other kingdoms. And it is here where our story begins...

Prologue

en years old and dressed in his finest attire, Cullen Branson sat quietly in the carriage next to his father. It was a grand day, one that would forever shape his future. He glanced up nervously at his father, whose stern expression never wavered. The Duke had always emphasized the importance of proper behavior and manners, especially for children.

The sun shone brightly through the carriage windows, casting a warm glow on Cullen's honey-gold hair. His short locks were neatly styled, a reflection of his well-groomed upbringing. His pale skin and striking amber eyes stood out against his dark clothing.

As they rode towards Narvi Cathedral, the sound of horses' hooves echoed through the countryside. The Duke rested his head on his hand, leaning against the carriage window. Their journey had taken several days, with stops at only the finest taverns along the way. This was tradition for their family, and Cullen couldn't help but feel a sense of dread as he could only anticipate what lay ahead at the prestigious cathedral.

Cullen's gaze flicked up to his father, taking in the man's meticulously pinned-back golden blond locks that cascaded like a river down his broad shoulders. Towering over him at six feet tall, his lean and athletic frame exuded confidence and power. The dark depths of his eyes hinted at a sharp intellect and determination. His coat was adorned with oversized, excessively padded sleeves, emphasizing his formidable build. As a Duke, the family was dressed in the latest fashions, but Cullen, at ten years old, couldn't have cared less. He preferred to keep to himself and lose himself in books.

But now he was on his way to Amalthea's Cathedral, where he would become a squire to the Order of the Dragon and eventually a knight. This prestigious training was not only physical but also heavily focused on education and discipline. Cullen would learn riding, fencing, scripture, literature, mathematics, Latin, hymns, and the Lord's Prayer. By joining the order, he would commit his life to their cause.

As he stepped out of the coach upon arrival at the cathedral, Cullen was immediately struck by its awe-inspiring architecture. The building radiated with elegance and opulence in every aspect. White marble walls reached towards the sky while grand steeples adorned the roof. Gargoyles perched along the edges of the rooftop, adding an air of mystery and wonder. Gold trim adorned every corner and statue, after magnificent statue lined its exterior, each depicting powerful angels in intricate detail. Two sets of massive doors loomed before him, painted a bold shade of red.

Mother Superior was waiting for him inside - her stern face befitting even for a nun. Cullen could feel himself being drawn deeper into this world of splendor and devotion as he crossed the threshold into this holy place.

With a regal air, the Duke emerged from his carriage, standing tall and proud. The nun approached Cullen, who seemed unsure of himself in this new setting. She let out an exasperated sigh. "So this is what we have to work with?" she muttered in a monotone voice. Her gaze shifted to the Duke, her tone stern. "If he's anything like you, we're in trouble."

"Oh, I assure you he won't be," the Duke reassured her.

The nun remained unimpressed as she turned her attention back to Cullen. "There are only two certainties in life, Your Grace: death and taxes." Her sharp eyes bore into Cullen's. "Now come along," she said briskly, leading them towards the steps of the cathedral. "Your belongings will be brought to your new room in due time."

Once inside, the Mother Superior introduced herself to Cullen as Sister Ester. She showed him around the cathedral's library, giving him permission to study or spend his free time there when his education allowed. As they walked through rows upon rows of bookshelves, reaching all the way up to the ceiling and built directly into the walls, Cullen's eyes widened in wonder. To a ten-year-old boy, it must have felt like staring out onto an endless sea of books. The nun couldn't help but feel a flicker of hope ignite within her - perhaps the Duke's son would prove to be a better student than his father, unlike the current Duke, who was only interested in learning about weapons and battle tactics and had no desire for reading or knowledge.

Cullen quickly settled into his classes at the Cathedral and formed a small circle of friends. Between studying and attending mass, confession, and prayer, he found moments of leisure in the Cathedral's peaceful courtyard. Under the shade of a grand old oak tree, Cullen would spend hours lost in thought or pouring over a stack of books. The Mother Superior often caught glimpses of him throughout her day, silently observing as he pored over each page with intent focus.

Four years passed. Cullen found himself in scripture class under the instruction of Father Mathews, a thin man of average height with round spectacles and a thinning hairline. As he paced up and down the aisle, book in hand, the priest's voice rang out to the students seated at their desks. "God's word is law," he declared sternly. "And above all else, we are taught obedience. Obedience to the laws of God and to nature."

He paused for effect before continuing on to quote a passage from Leviticus: 20:13 - "If a man lies with a male as with a woman, both of them have committed an abomination; they shall surely be put to death; their blood is upon them." One student, whom the priest always viewed as a nuisance, raised his hand and spoke up. It was clear that this child enjoyed asking embarrassing or inappropriate questions. "Why?" he asked with a sly grin, barely containing his laughter.

The priest's posture straightened as his eyes narrowed, a faint crease forming between them. His deep voice carried authority as he addressed the class of young boys; his words met with giggles and snickers. "Questioning scripture again, Nathaniel?" The students found it amusing, as children are wont to do. "But it is God's law that dictates man and woman as the only appropriate coupling for procreation, to give thanks for his many blessings." Cullen watched as the priest's usually stern face turned even more severe. "Any other form of relationship is deemed an abomination, embracing the devil and giving into the deadly sin of lust."

Cullen observed in silence as the priest strode back to his desk, setting aside his book and picking up a switch almost casually. The room fell silent as he turned around, holding the long, thick branch in both hands. It was clear that this was a subject not open for debate or mockery. "Nathaniel, please stay after class."

A ten-year-old girl with braided blonde hair and bright brown eyes dashed through the Cathedral's halls, her excitement evident in her quick steps. She wore a well-made dress adorned with delicate gold trinkets. Mother Superior caught sight of her and gave a disapproving look, causing the girl to slow down and walk more carefully. "Apologies, Mother Superior." The nun nodded in response. "He's in the garden, Princess." With a nod of thanks, the little girl continued down the hallway until she reached the archway leading out to the garden. As expected, Cullen was sitting under the oak tree reading a book. But before he could react, his book was suddenly swiped from his hands, and a familiar face was shoved towards him. "Edith!" Cullen exclaimed in surprise.

"Oh, how I've yearned for your return since you left the palace!" The Princess exclaimed with a joyful squeal. Her words were loud and cheerful, echoing off the grand castle walls. Cullen's expression turned sour, as if he had been forced to swallow something unpleasant. "But you were only six when I left! How could you possibly remember me, let alone miss me?" The Princess pouted, her bottom lip jutting out in a childish manner. "You used to play with me all the time, then suddenly you were gone. I begged Daddy every day to tell me where you went until he finally revealed the truth yesterday. And since yesterday was my birthday, I consider you my very own birthday present!" She beamed at him with a toothy grin before her face turned serious. "But seriously, I didn't want you to think that I forgot about you! And it's quite rude of you not to have written to me and told me where you were all this time!" Her tone was scolding and cross.

Cullen shifted uncomfortably, unsure of how to respond to her outburst. He had never been good at talking to people, especially the Princess. "What was I supposed to write to you about? My progress in Latin studies? Or maybe my recent fall from a horse?" He questioned with a touch of sarcasm.

Edith pouted again, "Well, that's better than nothing! You could have at least kept in touch and let me know that you were alive!" Cullen stood up and nervously rubbed the back of his neck. "Honestly, letter writing isn't my strong suit. And there was nothing much to report anyway. My father never writes back when I do."

Edith's expression turned smug as she smiled triumphantly, "Well, if you had written to me, I could have told you some news." Cullen raised an eyebrow in curiosity, "Like what?"

"Like the fact that you now have two new sisters and another one on the way!" She announced with a superior tone. Cullen's shock was evident as he processed this information. Of course, his father would not have bothered to tell him about his expanding family. It seemed that he had been cast aside and left to be raised by the church. He made a mental note to start writing letters to his Mother from now on; she would at least respond. As for Edith, she seemed like any other typical ten-year-old - carefree and bold, saying and doing whatever she pleased.

Edith grabbed Cullen's right hand and dragged him to the center of the garden, placing his left hand on her hip. "Father has me learning how to dance," she declared with determination. "He says a proper young lady must always know her steps." Then her expression turned puzzled as she shrugged, "Whatever that means." With a regal air, she declared, "And as your Princess, I demand that you dance with me." Cullen felt awkward and out of place as he tried to follow her lead, stumbling over their feet in the process. Edith became frustrated with his lack of coordination and noticed the Mother Superior observing them disapprovingly. "Why doesn't he know how to dance?" She huffed in annoyance.

The nun's face remained stoic as she clasped her hands together in front of her. "The squires here are training to become knights, not dancers, Your Grace," she spoke firmly. Edith let out an exasperated huff, "Well, they should learn both. I order you to have Cullen trained in the art of dance!" Cullen shifted uncomfortably, unsure of how to respond. "I must follow the orders given to me, not what you desire," he said hesitantly. Edith swung around; her face flushed with anger. "I will be your Queen one day and you will obey me! Besides, I've heard our fathers discussing a potential marriage between us...or at least I think so. Either way, you need to learn how to dance." Cullen couldn't hide his shock and silently prayed that she had misheard.

The nun's expression did not falter as she looked at the girl with disdain and half a mind to slap her for her arrogance. "You are in the Lord's house, young lady. You have no power here. If you dare speak to me with such disrespect again, you will spend the night copying the commandments until dawn. Is that clear?" Edith's posture seemed to shrink before the nun's stern reprimand.

"Yes, Sister," she mumbled in a soft voice.

Edith turned back to Cullen with tears in her eyes. "I just wanted to dance."

As Edith rode home in her carriage, she sat with her hands folded on top of her favorite book, lost in thought. She flipped through its pages and noticed a small piece of paper sticking out from between them. She carefully unfolded it and felt her heart flutter when she saw it was a note from Cullen. It read: 'We will dance one day, I promise.' A soft smile spread across her face as she clutched the note to her chest, cherishing the hope of a future dance with Cullen.

Chapter 1

In the Kingdom of Amalthea, new graduates of the order had arrived at the castle of the High King, King Richard. King Richard was handsome, kind, and deeply religious. He had medium-length, rusted, auburn red hair with patches of white hair. He had blue eyes and pale skin. He ruled Amalthea prosperously for over twenty years. The castle was made of illustrious limestone and marble. Tapestries, high turrets, and steeples decorated the skyline, and suits of armor adorned the halls as guards were posted at key points. The stature and the magnificence of the castle could never be put properly into words - stunning trees, sprawling gardens, fragrant flowers all around the palace and its grounds.

Families of the newly anointed knight had gathered in the throne room. Nobles from far and wide had come to see their sons knighted. One such Noble was Cavan Branson, the Duke of Amalthea itself. He was a proud, pious man, had honey-blond hair, dark eyes, and a stern but pleasing face. Bits of silver shone in his medium-length hair. He wore a dark red cloak with heavy bear fur and bits of gold thread shimmering in the sunlight. His luxurious, rich clothing signified his position.

His eldest son, Cullen, was outside the throne room with his fifty classmen. He's six foot two inches with a broad chest and shoulders. Pale skin, rich amber eyes, shoulder-length honey-blonde hair with some waves, nicely combed back and tied in a half ponytail. He had an unshaven face, a day or two at least. He'd forgotten to shave that morning since he'd been up for days, nervous about today's ceremony. Cullen was fully aware he was going to be berated by his father when he'd seen his unkempt appearance. His father was always a stickler for cleanliness.

Cullen was the eldest out of ten children and the only boy to truly top it all off. So, there was no real question about what was going to be expected of him in life. He hoped that in becoming a knight, his father would become proud of him and finally see him as a worthy son. He'd been training for ten years for this day since he was ten years old.

Cullen was pulled out of his mind's wonderings after he caught a glimpse of his Mother. The Duchess, Lilian was known for her kind and gentle manner. She had golden curls that went down her back. Her amber eyes always seemed to enchant anyone who looked into them. She wore a square neckline and a beautiful shade of lavender. The bodice was beautifully embroidered and had spectacular crystals sewn in. She wore long sleeves that draped down and folded over her wrists. She'd write to her son regularly to keep him updated on family affairs. She supported Cullen as she did for all her children in all things.

Cullen wore the Order of the Dragon's breastplate with a chainmail undercoat made of steel gauntlets and sabatons. A leather belt wrapped around his waist held an empty sword scabbard.

Two huge oak doors opened wide, and Cullen and the others stood at attention in two straight lines. He was quite a few rows back from where he could see the King waiting on top of a small staircase, a sword's hilt in both hands and a blade pointing downward. Cullen could see he wore the finest royal robes and an elegant gold crown. Christian priests entered the room, singing their prayers as incense burned in golden dispensers hung by golden chains. Acolyte priests anointed crucifixes on people's brows with holy water.

Afterward, a fanfare of trumpets filled the air as the herald stood at attention at the doorway. "NOW ANNOUNCING THE INITIATES

TO THE ORDER OF THE DRAGON! PLEASE APPROACH!" The lines of soldiers marched in, their heavy feet echoing off the ground. Cullen caught his Father's eye as he approached. His Mother gave him a gentle and encouraging smile.

One by one, each soldier was called by his name to approach up the steps and kneel before their sovereign. King Richard lowered his left hand and took the hilt of his magnificent sword into his right. Cullen couldn't hear what was said, but he could see after the King gently laid the blade on one shoulder and then the other, the man rose. Amalthea's Cardinal anointed the knight with holy water as he spoke words of prayer.

The Cardinal was an older man - late fifties, short with neatly trimmed hair. He was about five foot nine, two hundred and sixty pounds. Had baby blue eyes that showed pious arrogance. His name was Cardinal Reginald Thomas, and he was the King's most trusted advisor on religious matters. He'd served the court for over forty years and ruled over it by collecting every bit of information about Amalthea's noblest houses to use at his discretion. Even without lifting a finger, he was one of the richest in the realm, thanks to the King giving him access to all the financial books of the Kingdom's religious houses.

As the ceremony proceeded, the King's chancellor took a step, and the newly anointed knight stood up. The man threw a tunic around the knight's shoulders. It was a white tunic with a red cross on it with flames coming out of each side of the pentacle. Cullen noted that it went down to the man's ankles.

A servant handed the Chancellor a sword presented on open palms. The knight took the sword and put it in his empty scabbard.

It was now Cullen's turn. He took a nervous gulp and climbed the small set of stairs. Once he was at the second to last step, he knelt down. King Richard held his sword in hand, and a small corner smile snuck itself onto his lips. Richard prided himself on knowing Cullen since infancy. And now, seeing this young man becoming a Knight was a proud moment, to say the least. He'd always wished for a son, but his wife died in childbirth with their daughter Edith, who was now sixteen.

Richard looked at the crowd as his chest puffed out with pride, "The oath you are about to take is a sacred one," he then looked at Cullen, who was still kneeling with his head lowered. "You are to become a servant of God. To protect the weak is your most sacred duty." Cullen felt the King's blade on his right shoulder. "To protect your King and country from domestic and foreign threats. Above all, you are a servant of God and wield your sword in his name." Cullen felt the blade on his left shoulder, "Rise!" Cullen swiftly kissed his sovereign's cloak. "And be recognized." Cullen stood up and looked at the Chancellor, "Knight of the Order of the Dragon."

The Cardinal wiped Cullen's brow, forming a crucifix with holy water. "May God bless and keep you as you walk in his favor and light." He was then presented with his sword; he slowly took it and sheathed it in his scabbard. He turned around and saw the people clapping. He couldn't help but horribly blush as he looked at them all.

Afterward, there was a huge feast in the dining hall; meat, ale, and every food imaginable was there. Cullen looked around and noticed all the glitz and glamour, with roaring fires blazing from the fireplaces that were on either side of the room. Servants were tending to guests who dined at long tables and benches. The King and his family were seated at one end of the room on their own long table that extended the length of the room. They sat on intricately carved wooden thrones surrounded by elegant golden table candelabras and jeweled chalices. They were served succulent mutton in the finest tableware. The dancers entertained between the royal table, which was positioned horizontally, and the other tables placed vertically down the hall, forming five long rows with over twenty feet of space between them.

Cullen noticed the King's eldest daughter, Edith, looking at him with dreamy eyes. They had known each other since childhood. She had soft blond hair, brown eyes, and pouty lips. Cullen always thought that she was a silly and frivolous girl. She loved to wear elegant clothes, ride the finest horses and balls, and do everything else a princess was entitled to.

And Cullen was quite the opposite. He was never impressed by such things or the privileges his position brought. He was quiet by nature; he loved reading and writing, and he abhorred violence. He was desperate to become a scholar, but his father wouldn't allow it. He hoped to marry a woman who was kind by nature and, most importantly, of his own choosing.

As Cullen turned his head back, his father, who sat across from him, looked at his son, "You should feel honored to be in the order." he said, putting his eating utensils down and holding his chalice, his body adjusted to sit up straight.

Cullen looked at his father in shock that he was talking to him. Usually the man sent messengers when he wanted to convey anything to him. "I do," he answered as he cut into his decadent mutton.

The Duke took a swig of his chalice. "I'd still be serving the order if I hadn't been..."

Ten years back, the Duke was one of the highest-ranked knights of the order. However, while in service, he was badly injured, attacking a nest of religious heretics his company discovered in a nearby forest. His company ambushed them at dawn, but they were prepared in case of attack. They tied a large log with ropes to fall and swing from the trees when a tripwire was triggered. The Duke's horse broke the tripwire, and the log swung out, hitting the Duke, knocking him off his horse, and smashing him against a tree. The Duke permanently impaired his sword arm and left his left leg with a permanent limp. Such forever injuries caused him to be bitter and determined that his only son would become a knight and serve God.

Cullen watched his father drain his cup dry, "Yes, I know. I'm glad to see you continue our family's tradition." Personally, Cullen wanted a quieter and simpler life away from court. He'd hoped and prayed that his new life would give him such a life. He'd heard stories from other knights who taught him in his sparring classes that King Richard's reign was one of the most peaceful to be ever known. Most knights became dignitaries and ambassadors throughout the continent. Many grew fat, bored, and lazy before their retirement. However, Cullen had a feeling that if his father had anything to do with it, he'd be sent on the most important and dangerous missions to bring glory not only to the realm but also to his family's name.

The Duke slammed the cup on the table. He knew his son wasn't at all interested in being a knight. He desired a much quieter life of obscurity. "Don't mock me," he said with a snort, "if I had listened to your mother, you'd be out reading and going to some sort of college." Cullen noted the dismissive tone in his father's voice. "Instead, you're now serving your country, bringing honor to your family's name, and serving in god's!" Cullen leaned over the table and held his hands together. Honestly, he doubted his father would ever know what serving in God's name truly meant.

He looked at his mother, who was nothing but a kind and loving woman. She only wanted to support her children and all of their endeavors. He always loved her tight ringlet of curls that were partially swept up. He looked back at his father, "When do we go home?" he questioned. He couldn't wait to go home and sleep. The day was more than full, and he was exhausted.

The Duke gave his son a sharp look, "You won't be returning with us."

Cullen looked at his father in shock, "What?" he questioned. He felt as if someone punched him right in the gut. After all this time of living and training at the Cathedral, Cullen thought he'd finally be able to go home after the ceremony to see and meet all his sisters. He'd now started to forget his sisters' names.

The Duchess reached out and held her son's hand. "Dearest!" she said softly, understanding Cullen's feelings. All he wanted was to go home and rest before he'd go off into the world in service of the King and Country. Cullen's face grew solemn as he put down his utensils. His Mother's right hand held his left, and it seemed as though he was about to cry, shrinking more with each passing moment.

The Duke scoffed at such a display of tenderness, "Come now, you can't coddle him anymore." He told his wife, who promptly withdrew her hand and placed both in her lap. The Duke didn't even look at his son as he cut into his meat, "Your belongings have been transferred to the barracks of the order. They're here on the castle's grounds, so you won't have to go far." Cullen snorted, shaking his head in frustration, "You never slept there; you always came home and left when a message from the palace came."

The Duke then gave his son a firm look, "As a knight, you are to live in the barracks till you serve a total of ten years. After that, your family arranges a marriage, and you live with your spouse and home until you are summoned. That is the way of it."

Cullen sat in shock. The news hit him like a rock on the head. He ran his right hand through his hair, trying to process the information. "Why ten years?" he asked.

"Because it proves God favors you and your line," his father answered, "No sense in getting married and having an heir if you're going to die in a year or less. Wives die in childbirth, babies too, if you're not here to-"

"I don't care!" Cullen snapped as he folded his arms, giving his father a sour look, his hands balled into fists. He was tempted to punch his father in the jaw, but even with his impediments, Cullen knew he wouldn't win against his father - a trained soldier and former captain of the order. "You're the one who made me become a knight, made me -"

"I made you a man!" the Duke snapped and slammed his right hand on the table. He did not like to be questioned by anyone, especially his son. It took him a moment to regain his composure before he took a bite of meat and reached for his chalice again. "Also," the Duke continued. From the tone of his father's voice, Cullen knew this wasn't something he'd like. "I've talked to the King personally." Cullen realized there were future plans ahead of him. "I have arranged for you to marry King Richard's daughter, Edith."

Cullen's jaw dropped, feeling he'd been the wind knocked out of him. "What?" He bit his lower lip to stop himself from shouting. He looked to his left before looking back at his father. "I don't want to be married to a princess, let alone Edith!" he shouted under baited breath. The very idea of marrying Edith made his skin itch. She had a nasty, jealous streak that he never found charming or befitting a lady of her station.

The Duke gave a hard look, "You will do what is best for your house! After your ten years of service, you will marry, and there is no one better than Edith. It will elevate not only you but all nine of your sisters as well."

Cullen's face hardened as he stood up from his seat. "I'm already doing what is best for this house! You made sure of that! You say you want to raise this family and the prospects for my sisters by marrying me to Edith, in truth, the only person it truly elevates is your own self." he growled in a snide tone before turning and walking away.

As he left, Cullen wasn't paying attention to where he was going. He bumped into a woman and instinctively grabbed her by the shoulders. "God help me, I apologize! I didn't see where I was going." Cullen stammered and saw that he'd bumped into Princess Edith.

The Princess giggled, placing the tips of her left hand to her lips. "Clearly"

Cullen immediately bowed, "Princess, please forgive me!"

Edith gave an eloquent curtsey, delicately holding the hem of her dress and lowering her head. Cullen noted the soft velvet fabric dyed a soft powder blue. She wore a delicate golden crown upon her brow with a teardrop diamond dangling at the center.

Edith had a delicate and pure beauty that caused Cullen to blush horribly. The Princess raised her eyes to meet his. "My lord knight, I congratulate you. God has truly favored you this day."

Cullen blushing even more, placed his right hand behind his head. "Thank you, your Highness," he began, only to be interrupted by the princess' giggles. "No need to be so formal. We've known each other since we were children."

Edith looked at the musicians. They played a lite and cheerful song. "Shall we dance?" She questioned as she took Cullen's hands into hers. Normally, it was the men who asked for dances in polite society, but knowing Cullen, Edith knew he'd never ask. She had known about Cullen's shy nature since they were young. Cullen had taken dancing classes, as any noble gentleman would, but he had two left feet.

"But...I" Cullen stammered.

Edith placed Cullen's left hand on her hip, and he awkwardly attempted to lead the Princess across the floor. The entire court watched the two dance. Edith beamed as she looked into Cullen's amber eyes. "I know it'll be quite some time before we can get married, but I know the wait will be worth it!"

Cullen looked into the princess' eyes. "Don't you?" she asked. A cold pit formed in his stomach as he struggled to find words. Instead, he puffed out his chest and continued to dance with the Princess, desperate not to step on her feet too much.

King Richard as he beamed with pride in seeing his daughter so happy. He'd been watching the two from the crowd. The Duke walked over to the King, seemingly satisfied with their children dancing together.

A sound of approval escaped the King's lips, "It seems the two are a good match."

The Duke nodded, "They should be; they've known each other since childhood." he remarked, arms folded as he looked at his friend. "So it's agreed then, after ten years, the two will be wed?"

Richard clasped his hands behind his back, "Actually, I have different plans." The two looked at each other. "I have an assignment that needs to be taken care of, and I've chosen your son to take care of it."

"And what would that be?" the Duke questioned, sitting in a chair next to the King.

Richard sighed as he picked up his chalice, "There's a heretic not far from Bestla, we suspect in the forests...again." The Duke grabbed a nearby chalice. He quickly brought it up to his lips. That forest, that damn forest! It always gave him a bitter taste in his mouth. No amount of wine could ever wash it out. "I want your son to find this heretic and neutralize her."

The Duke raised his right brown, "A woman? Are your spies certain of this?" he questioned as he looked at his friend. Most heretics were found to be women, preaching as if they had the authority of any priest who had been blessed by the church to preach the holy word. For some reason, these preachings caught on like wildfire, especially with the poor. To hear even one syllable was subject to the harshest punishments for any who were caught. So great secrecy had to be taken to arrange such gatherings, usually at night and in the thickest and most dense part of the wood. The Duke had half a mind to counsel the King to burn down the woods completely, but he also knew that if they did, the heretic rats would just find another place to gather, so there wasn't much point to it.

Personally, he'd never heard what was said among these people, but from what he heard in the King's council meetings —of which he was a part, alongside other nobles and the Cardinal—it was clear that the heresy was dangerous. From letters sent to the Cardinal and shared with the council, they had learned of whispers and private teachings of the Mother, who would one day give birth to the child of God and bring forth God's true and holy word. This word foretold a union of two worlds, where magic would once again connect with their own and flourish. Such teachings would never be tolerated in the Kingdom and would be dealt with swiftly.

The King lowered his cup, "After that, I will see that your son and my daughter will be married upon his return." The Duke liked the sound of their houses joining so quickly.

However, the Duke's expression grew concerned, "Are you sure he can handle such a mission?" The King gave a nod, "I won't be sending the boy alone." he assured the Duke.

Meanwhile, Edith looked at Cullen with dreamy eyes and gave him a gentle smile. "Are you happy to be home?" she questioned. Cullen was already struggling to remember the dance steps; he was not eager to add conversation into the mix. He nodded slightly, "Yes, but I won't be going home, not truly. My father just informed me, I have to live in the orders barracks. I was hoping to see my sisters and rest for a few days before moving --"

"It means we can see each other more often." the Princess giggled, "I asked Father especially because I think we should get to know each other better before we are wed."

Cullen's foot accidentally slipped onto Edith's left foot. "Sorry!" he quickly apologized, even though it wasn't entirely an accident.

Edith had everything planned out in her mind. They'd marry in a lavish white wedding, with her holding a bouquet of white roses and lilies. Her hair swept up into a loose bun adorned with flowers and jewels, and a tiara on top of her head as she wore a beautiful white dress. Cullen would wear silver armor, polished to a shine that glinted in the sunlight. They'd have many children and rule the Kingdom together.

Cullen, on the other hand, was wondering when the dance would be over. The two gently turned, their palms touching as they made circular motions, switching hands as they did so. Cullen placed the other hand behind his back as she twirled. He caught sight of his father and the King talking, laughing, and watching them as if their worlds were soon to be bound together. As he looked around, he began to feel like a rat in a cage; it made his skin itch. Looking back at Edith, he noticed she looked like she wanted him to mount her, claim her, and, in doing so, make him hers.

The King looked at the two as he leaned to the right, his elbow on the arm of his chair and his index finger resting on top of his upper lip. He watched as the music stopped, and both Cullen and Edith bowed to one another. Cullen then ever so gently kissed the princess' hand before he stepped away and walked into the crowd. He sensed the Cardinal leaning over to the King and whispering into his ear, watching the two rather in a hurry.

)0(

The Order's quarters were in a distant section of the castle. One would dare say it was a castle of its own. It had tapestries and banners hanging from the rafters. Nuns lived with the walls as cleaners, cooks, singers, and organ pianists within the chapel. Priests were advisors, chaplains, and teachers. They also sent and received messages from other strongholds of the order. That way, they could keep apprised of what was going on all over the land.

As Cullen and other newly appointed knights were escorted by an old nun with a lantern, the halls seemed dark and empty. As he looked around at the stone walls, lit torches, and eerie silence, he understood why his father loved it so much. He knew the place inside and out. His father told him everything about what the building contained and where - a map of schematics of the place in his letters. He knew the location of each and everything and how to get to it. He knew about the living quarters, the chapel, the armory, the kitchens, every place. He knew, for example, they were headed to where his room was going to be. He knew when he entered that the Nuns and Priests were now observing "The Great Silence," which meant that this was a time that no one was to talk and to commune with either God or the Mother, where prayer was believed to be heard the most. To hear what the spirit had to say and guide.

Cullen was the last to be shown his quarters. Once there, he opened the door, and stood for a moment, then looked back at the nun who walked away, taking the light with her. Cullen sighed as he resolved to his new life. He struck a match and lit a candle. He took off his armor and put it on an armor stand about three feet from his bed, between his bed and the door. He opened a pack given to him by the nun when they arrived at his door and changed into a simple white velvet tunic to wear at night in his quarters. His room was an eight-by-ten cell; well, it felt like it anyway. A modest bed and a shelf for books. A small shrine of the Mother with a simple dress and long veil resting on her head and draped on her shoulders. Her hands held out in mercy and love. Cullen looked at the trunk that had been left on the bed. He opened it and smiled. His Mother had packed all his favorite books, poetry mostly, and a few of his old shirts.

Cullen picked up a particular book. Its leather was exceedingly worn, and its binding was a hair's breadth away from falling apart. It was a book his mother read to him all the time as a child. He put it on the shelf along with all the rest of his books, then turned to look back at the trunk and was stunned to find his mother's rosary.

It was pink quartz for the Hail Mary beads with ten beads in each strand, which represented a decade. Five decades made the top of the rosary and red resin roses for the 'Our Father' beads between each of the strands, four in total. The center was made of pure silver and that of the Holy Mother; one rose bead was below it, along with three pink quartz crystals, one more red rose, and a large silver crucifix at the bottom.

Cullen immediately picked up the beads and kissed them. He then put his right hand on his trunk to close it but saw another book.

The book was fresh leather. As he lifted it up, he could smell the freshness of the book. Slowly, he opened the book and saw that all the pages were blank except the first page, written in his Mother's handwriting. It read:

Follow your heart, darling. This journal is meant to be your companion. Write your journeys, your loves, whatever your heart desires. Follow your heart, and you can't go wrong.

With the beads in hand, Cullen sat on his bed and smiled at the journal. Lying in his bed and looking at the ceiling, he covered his face with his hands for several moments before taking a long, slow, and deep breath. His hands slowly slid down and away from his face. "God, if you're listening, please help me make my family proud." he prayed in his heart.

Chapter 2

Not far from Belfast, two men rode on majestic horses through the rolling green countryside; one of them was a middle-aged man. His handsome features were framed by a mane of raven black hair with strands of silver woven through. His skin had a dusky glow as if he had spent most of his days under the warm sun. His chocolate brown eyes were accentuated by a faint layer of black eyeliner, adding an air of mystery to his gaze. Light stubble adorned his strong jawline, hinting at a ruggedness beneath his polished appearance. He exuded strength and nobility, every inch the battle mage he was known to be. A teasing smile played on his plump lips, causing women to swoon and his friends to roll their eyes in amusement. He wore leather armor over a crisp white tunic emblazoned with a bold red cross, cinched at the waist with a sturdy leather belt. As a battle mage, freedom of movement was essential.

Beside him rode another man dressed in flowing white robes of an acolyte adorned with the same red cross symbol. His flawless tan skin shone in the sunlight. He walked with confidence in his worn leather sandals. A red sash was tied around his waist, adding a touch of color to his otherwise monochromatic outfit. His neatly trimmed beard added to his regal appearance, while his swept-back hair gave him a stylish yet practical look. Thick layers of eyeliner emphasized his piercing blue eyes, giving them a smoky allure. He carried himself with an air of entitlement as if he were born into luxury and privilege.

As they neared their destination, an inn nestled among the trees, they dismounted their horses and tied them to a sturdy post outside. The cool night air nipped at their exposed skin as they made their way inside. Rubbing their hands together for warmth, they stepped onto the cozy interior, its warm glow welcoming them. Making their way to the bar, the battle mage ordered a mug of ale before finding a table for them to relax and unwind after their long journey.

The battle mage caught the barkeep's eye "Ale Please." he said confidently.

The barkeep stood behind the counter, cleaning a mug with a dirty rag. His gaze lingered on the two patrons who had just walked in, and his expression was one of judgment and disapproval. The acolyte's eyes narrowed at the man's look. "Are you deaf? My friend here ordered an ale."

The barkeep was average height and his large belly protruded over the counter. His face was bloated with gout, his teeth were yellow and crooked, and his brown beard was unkempt. He sniffed disdainfully as he looked at the two men. "You're from the Order of the Dragon, aren't you? I thought your lot didn't partake in any indulgences," he said suspiciously.

The acolyte smirked. "If you had seen half of what we have - fabled beasts, heretics spewing blasphemy from their deranged lips - you would understand why a drink is sometimes necessary." He gestured emphatically with his hands, demonstrating the intensity of their experiences. "Ale is the least of our desires for consumption."

The battle mage chuckled and placed a hand on his friend's shoulder. "Dorian," he said fondly. He always admired Dorian's talent for storytelling.

"You'd need a drink to sleep at night too!" the acolyte finished triumphantly. The barkeep threw his rag over his shoulder and reached for a pitcher of ale, pouring it into a mug and setting it down in front of Dorian. The look on Dorian's face showed serious misgivings about not only the cleanliness of the mug but also its contents.

The man furrowed his brow as he looked at Dorian incredulously. "Is that...eyeliner?"

Dorian rolled his eyes and dropped his left hand onto the counter with a sigh. "What kind of a ridiculous question is that?" he asked, exasperated. It seemed like they had encountered yet another closed-minded individual who couldn't handle freedom of expression or personalization, especially when it came to men. Dorian was well aware that most men didn't place much importance on hygiene or self-expression, but for him, it was a priority. He refused to smell like rotting meat and look like a beggar from the docks of Bestla just to conform to societal norms.

Dorian's nostrils flared with anger as his blood began to boil. "Can you believe it, Amant?" he seethed, gesturing towards the fat, over-the-hill barkeep who had dared to criticize their fashion choices.

The barkeep's face contorted into agitation. "What kind of name is Amant anyway?" he retorted.

It was clear that the barkeep could sense a strong camaraderie between Dorian and his companion, but only his imagination could conjure up what kind of relationship they had. As Dorian took a deep breath through his nose, attempting to calm himself, he fixed the man with a sharp gaze. "It's a name that only those with sophisticated wit and understanding would understand," he replied, gripping the sticky surface of the bar with both hands. "I highly doubt a low-born, illiterate bumpkin like yourself would ever comprehend such a word."

Before the barkeep could gather enough courage to ask if he was being called stupid, the battle mage quickly downed the rest of his ale and slammed the glass down. "Time to go, Dorian!" his companion exclaimed, placing a hand on his shoulder and pulling him back.

Giving them both suspicious and judgmental looks, the barkeep inquired, "What kind of queer look are you two going for? And what kind of name is Amant?"

Taking a step closer, the battle mage placed several coins on the counter. "Actually, it's not Amant at all. It's Maxwell. Thank you for the dirty ale, we'll be on our way," he stated before grabbing Dorian by the shoulders and pulling him off the stool, fighting to drag the acolyte towards the door.

Maxwell had to use all his strength to drag Dorian, who was still flailing his arms as he gave the barkeep an intense glare as he screamed about tearing out the man's throat. Despite his best efforts to restrain Dorian, Maxwell knew there was still a possibility for a physical confrontation if they didn't leave quickly. He kicked open the door with his right foot, using his arms to support Dorian's weight as they stumbled out of the inn. After a few moments, Dorian's rage began to subside and he turned to Maxwell, still flushed from anger. "I mean, honestly, what kind of person is allowed to judge someone's fashion choices?"

Maxwell gave a wry smile as he crossed his arms. "A narrow-minded one, Dorian," he replied before turning to walk away. "And now that you've so eloquently pissed off the local innkeeper, we need to figure out where we're going to sleep tonight. I was looking forward to a possible bath."

Dorian rubbed the back of his neck sheepishly. "I'm sorry, Amant. I didn't mean to..."

"You never mean to, Dorian!" Maxwell laughed, shaking his head. "But I've learned to accept it." He smiled warmly at his friend.

Dorian stepped in front of Maxwell and bowed dramatically, holding out his arms. "And for that acceptance, I thank you."

Just then, a young messenger ran up to them - a boy no more than thirteen with messy dark hair and pale skin. He wore the uniform of their order and carried a bag slung over his shoulder. "Keynes and Abreo?" he asked breathlessly.

Maxwell nodded. "Yes?"

The messenger handed him a rolled-up piece of paper and quickly scurried off. Dorian watched as Maxwell broke the wax seal and read the message. "What is it now?" he asked, folding his arms impatiently.

Maxwell looked up at him with a serious expression. "We have new orders."

Dorian let out an exasperated groan. "Wonderful!" he exclaimed in a sarcastic tone.

)o(

A heavy, insistent knock echoed through Cullen's room, jolting him awake. His heart raced as he struggled to sit up, his messy hair falling in front of his eyes. Another knock sounded at the door.

"What?" Cullen groaned, shielding his eyes from the blinding morning light that streamed in through his window. His window faced directly east, making it the perfect target for the sun's piercing rays. "AHHH!" Cullen yelped as he realized this, shaking his head and trying to get a grip on reality.

"The Knight Commander requests an audience with you," a voice called from outside. "You better hurry; he doesn't like to be kept waiting."

Cullen stumbled out of bed, still blinded by the light. "Sir? Is everything alright?" he asked, mentally making a note to put up some curtains so this wouldn't happen again. But before he could finish his thought, the voice responded.

"You should put up some drapes!" it suggested.

"I gathered that," Cullen grumbled as he finally managed to sit on the edge of his bed.

"Well hurry up," the voice urged before footsteps could be heard walking away.

Once dressed, Cullen made his way to the Knight Commander's office at an eager pace. The man was tall and imposing, with grey hair and a weathered face that spoke of years spent on the battlefield. "So you're the Duke of Amalthea's son, are you?" he questioned as he eyed Cullen critically.

Standing at attention, Cullen gave a crisp nod. "Yes sir," he replied.

"Good, your father was one of my best friends," the Knight Commander said with a hint of sadness in his voice. The words did not inspire confidence in Cullen - after all, his father was known for being cold and ruthless rather than kind and compassionate. He couldn't help but wonder if his new superior was cut from the same cloth.

Taking a deep breath, Cullen waited as the man slowly circled around him. "I have a job for you," he finally said, coming to stand in front of Cullen. "I have arranged for you to meet an acolyte and a battlemage on the road near the Cesileon forest. Once you meet up with them, your task is to go to Bestla. We have been hearing whispers of a heretic spreading forbidden gospels and slandering the Mother. As your father's son, I trust I don't need to explain your duty once this heretic is found."

Cullen's heart sank at the mention of his father again, but he quickly pushed those thoughts aside and focused on his duty. "Of course not, Knight Commander," he replied, pressing his right fist to his left breast in a show of respect. "I will fulfill my duties to the fullest."

The Commander nodded approvingly before motioning for Cullen to leave. "A few reminders before you go," he added.

Cullen turned back, already feeling overwhelmed by the weight of responsibility on his shoulders. "Yes sir?" he asked.

"This mission may take weeks or even months, during which time you may be tempted by the pleasures of flesh," the Commander warned in a grave tone. Cullen blushed deeply – conversations regarding such matters were rarely discussed except by his religious teachers. He knew that men were only allowed to lay with women, and any deviation was considered a sin punishable by torture and death.

"The Order does not forbid you from seeking companionship with a woman, but if you are found to be with a man, both your career and life will be forfeit," the Commander continued sternly.

Cullen nodded understandingly as his superior patted him on the shoulder. "Good. And with you being engaged to the Princess, I'm sure you will save yourself for your wedding night," he added with a sly grin.

Cullen's face turned red like a turnip. He could barely manage a stuttered response. "Y-yes sir," he squeaked, quickly giving a salute before hurrying out of the room.

)o(

The lush, emerald-green forest was alive with the sound of birds singing and sunlight filtering through the treetops. The melody of a flute drifted softly on the breeze, played by a male elf clad in supple brown leather clothing that allowed for graceful movement. His handsome face was framed by dark locks pulled back into a long ponytail, revealing deep, stormy grey eyes. Twin elvish blade swords crossed his back, a testament to his skill as a warrior.

As Tahl'rail's flute echoed through the forest, he smiled and dangled one leg off the branch he perched on. His keen ears caught another sweet voice joining in harmony with his tune. He played louder, hoping to attract the source of the beautiful vocals.

When he opened his eyes, Tahl'rail saw an ethereal elven maiden riding on a snow-white horse beneath his tree. The mare radiated a soft glow, her mane and tail billowing in a gentle wind. The She-Elf had long locks of snow-white hair cascading down to her lower back, intricately braided to accentuate her natural beauty. Her piercing blue topaz eyes sparkled like gems against her milky white skin and pouty lips. Her slender figure exuded grace and elegance, adorned with delicate white face paint that started at her cheekbones and trailed over her nose before branching out into intricate patterns across her cheeks and chin. Three thin white lines under her lower lip added to the mystique of her appearance.

The white tunic hugged Amalia's slender frame, the fabric draping and folding at her waistline in an intricate pattern. A black leather corset cinched her waist, the laces tied tightly to accentuate her figure. Her leather skirt fell just below her mid-thigh, revealing a flash of smooth skin with each step. Leather bracers adorned her arms, starting from her mid-forearm and extending to her fingers, leaving them bare to the elements. A long strand of leather wrapped around her hand, weaving around the bracer and securing it in place. Her boots were made of supple leather, reaching up to her calves with delicate buckles adorning the sides.

On her head sat a silver circlet adorned with a rainbow moonstone that shimmered like a galaxy of stars. The stone was as clear as a glass, shaped into a four-inch half-moon. Attached to the circlet were five-point deer antlers, concealed by Amalia's flowing hair. This headdress was a symbol of royalty, marking Amalia as a high-elf princess.

Amalia's pointed elven ears peeked out from her hair, adding to her ethereal beauty. Her delicate features were like something out of legend, making it difficult to look away from her radiance.

She was not alone, surrounded by an entourage of elven soldiers in elaborate leather armor adorned with gold and silver thread embroidery. Their hair was neatly pinned back in a half ponytail, their steeds outfitted with matching leather bridles and saddles. Two soldiers rode behind the Princess while one flanked each side of another figure - King Avron himself.

The King's long blond hair seemed to glow in the sunlight as it was neatly pinned back from his face. He wore a crown made of golden branches and leaves, signifying his status as ruler of their Kingdom. His warm blue eyes held a hint of weariness but also a glimmer of kindness. His flowing tunic was made of the finest fabric, expertly tailored to allow for ease of movement. The sides were cut to reveal leather pants and thigh-high boots.

Tahl'rail gracefully jumped from his perch on a nearby tree branch, landing on his feet before bowing deeply to the King and Princess. "Your Majesties, it is an honor to receive you in my presence." Amalia's eyes shone with warmth and curiosity as she looked at Tahl'rail, while the King maintained a stoic expression. Clearing his throat, King Avron addressed the young elf. "Rise,

Tahl'rail. What is your report?" he asked, appearing eager to move on from this interaction. Tahl'rail tucked his flute behind his belt as he straightened up and gave a respectful nod. "The wood is quiet, Your Grace. There have been no new reports from any of our borders. However, I have sensed a change in the air - whether that means the wood has decided to open itself to the outside world again or if..."

The King let out a tired sigh, his brow furrowing as he spoke. Tahl'rail's gaze shifted to the Princess, who looked back at him with wide, doe-like eyes. He couldn't help but notice every detail of her delicate features - the subtle curve of her thick black eyelashes, the poutiness of her rosy pink lips. In that moment, Tahl'rail felt a sense of calm wash over him, something he had never experienced before. He was always restless and unable to settle, but gazing upon the Princess seemed to soothe his soul.

Turning his horse to the left, the King motioned for Amalia to follow suit. "Come," he said, "We need to-"

"Actually," Amalia interjected, "I need to return home and assist my mother with the upcoming Imbolc ritual." The King nodded understandingly. "Of course. Shall I escort you back?" he asked, his concern for her safety evident in his tone.

"I will do it, your grace," Tahl'rail offered eagerly. "You have more important matters to attend to and cannot be delayed."

The King gave a nod of approval. "Very well, I entrust you with seeing the Princess safely home. It is only a mile or so." With that, he and his entourage rode off, leaving Amalia and Tahl'rail alone.

As they made their way back to the palace, the two couldn't help but smile at each other like love-struck teenagers. Amalia dismounted her horse gracefully and walked alongside Tahl'rail, still holding onto the reins. To her surprise, she felt him take her right hand in his own.

Their fingers intertwined as they walked side by side, their faces flushed with a mixture of excitement and nervousness. Amalia bit her bottom lip as she stole glances at Tahl'rail, causing him to stop in his tracks. A moment later, Amalia did the same.

In a tender gesture, Tahl'rail's hand gently caressed her cheek as he whispered, "You are so beautiful. How did I get so lucky?"

Amalia blushed, feeling butterflies fluttering in her stomach. Every time Tahl'rail looked into her eyes, they seemed to sparkle with adoration and affection. His fingers trailed down to rest under her chin as he pulled her closer, their lips meeting in a soft and sweet kiss.

To Tahl'rail, Amalia's lips were like petals - soft and warm against his own. She wrapped her arms around Tahl'rail's shoulders and neck, her fingers tangling his hair as they both deepened the kiss. She could feel his body pressed up against hers, igniting a fire within her that she had never experienced before. As their passion grew, Tahl'rail's hands gripped onto her hips firmly as she jumped into his arms, wrapping her legs around his waist.

It felt like time stood still in that moment as the two lost themselves in each other's embrace, reveling in the warmth and love between them.

Tahl'rail held his beloved with all his strength, pressing her body firmly against the rough bark of a towering tree. Amalia's small hands clutched the back of Tahl'rail's head, pulling him closer as he trailed gentle kisses along her neck. Her cheeks flushed with desire as she tilted her head to the side, allowing Tahl'rail complete access. A soft moan escaped her lips, mingling with the sound of rustling leaves and the distant chirping of birds.

The hardness in Tahl'rail's pants grew more urgent by the second, spurred on by the passionate movements of Amalia's body against his own. He couldn't wait much longer to claim her, but he knew it wasn't an option as a low-born elf. No, if he wanted Amalia as his wife, he had to do things properly. Their bodies burned more with each passing moment, and their hearts beat faster.

Tahl'rail couldn't resist rubbing himself against Amalia, thrusting his hips with increasing force until she was pressed hard against the tree behind her. The rough bark scraped at her back as they moved together in a primal dance, the fire in their bellies growing stronger.

As Tahl'rail's arousal built to a fever pitch, he finally fell to his knees, and Amalia followed suit, sliding onto his lap. He held her tightly against his chest, determined to keep her safe from harm. But even as he did so, Amalia pushed him backwards, moving her hips in perfect rhythm with his own.

Their bodies moved together like two halves of a whole, inching towards the glorious release they both craved. Tahl'rail felt Amalia grip him for stability while she moaned out loud in pleasure.

"I love you so much, Tahl'rail," she cried out.

"And I love you," he responded, sitting up and wrapping his arm around her.

Their lips crashed against each other with an intensity that left them both breathless. Tahl'rail could feel Amalia's fingers digging into the nape of his neck as their tongues danced together in a fiery symphony.

"My love for you knows no bounds," Tahl'rail whispered against her skin, his hot breath sending shivers down her spine.

The two lovers continued to share passionate kisses and caresses, their desire for one another not knowing when to stop. In this moment, they were the only two people in the world, lost in the depths of their love and consumed by the fire that burned between them.

"AMALIA!"

The sharp call of her name caused Amalia and Tahl'rail to jump in surprise, their heads snapping around to see Amalia's father, the king, riding towards them on his horse with a look of fury in his eyes. Panic shot through their bodies like a cold chill. The King's steed charged at them, causing them to quickly separate. Tahl'rail dodged out of the way just in time as the horse reared back, trying to crush him underfoot.

Amalia's heart raced with fear as she brought her fingertips to her mouth, her eyes wide with terror. She begged her father to stop, pleading for mercy. Tahl'rail was lucky enough to avoid being trampled as he somersaulted backwards and landed on his feet, narrowly escaping the hooves of the raging horse. He quickly scrambled up and leaped into a nearby tree for safety.

The King let out a roar of rage as he drew his sword from its sheath at his belt. "I'm sorry, my King, but I love your daughter!" Tahl'rail declared bravely.

But the King wasn't having any of it. His eyes burned with fire as he looked up at his daughter in the tree. "Love her? You love her enough to defile her purity!" he seethed, swinging his sword angrily through the air. Tahl'rail held out his right hand in defense, bracing himself against the tree with his left hand.

"I have taken nothing from her! She is still pure!" Tahl'rail insisted firmly. "I wish only to marry your daughter and give her a wonderful life!"

The King turned to look at his daughter, seeing the love she had for this man who was not of noble birth. He hesitated for a moment, then shook his head. "You are not worthy of her!" he growled at her. He could see the love in his daughter's eyes and couldn't deny it.

Without another word, the King dismounted from his horse with a mighty leap. Tahl'rail looked up and saw the King flying towards him, ready to strike. The two were so skilled with their swords that their movements were almost too fast to see.

The clash of blades echoed through the air as they fought with deadly precision. Both men knew that one mistake could be fatal. But Tahl'rail had one advantage - he was not fighting out of anger.

As they battled, the King grabbed hold of Tahl'rail's hair, causing him to spin around and attempt to stab the King in the neck with a dagger. The King blocked the blow with his arm brace just in time, narrowly avoiding a fatal wound. In that moment, he realized he could not afford to make any mistakes.

Their movements were fluid and graceful, like water flowing together in perfect harmony. Tahl'rail reached for his second sword, but the King cut the leather strap holding it in place, causing it to fall to the ground. Despite the setback, Tahl'rail continued to fight fiercely, arching his back to dodge an attack from the King's sword held high above his head.

The King began to struggle to keep up with Tahl'rail's speed and agility. It seemed as though he was fighting a ghost - one who could anticipate his every move without fail.

As the King towered over Tahl'rail, his grip tightening on his sword, the younger man's eyes darted to the ground where the other sword lay. Without hesitation, he launched himself downwards using a nearby tree branch as a springboard. His determination to end this fight was evident in every move.

Tahl'rail was known for his speed and agility, but even he was surprised by the lightning-fast punch that landed square on the King's face. The sound of breaking bones echoed through the clearing as the force of the blow sent the King skidding several feet across the ground. Amalia's heart raced. She ran to Tahl'rail's side, wrapping her arms around him in relief. He was huffing and puffing, his left arm tightly wound around her waist.

As they both turned their attention back to the fallen King, their relief quickly turned to dread. He hadn't moved an inch and Tahl'rail could feel a cold pit forming in his stomach. Slowly, he walked up to the body while Amalia stood back with her hands pressed to her trembling lips.

"Father? Father, please get up," she pleaded softly, trying to will movement from her beloved parent.

But as time passed, no sign of life came from her father. Amalia looked up at Tahl'rail with tears streaming down her face. With just one look in his eyes, she knew that her worst fears were coming true. Her father was gone.

Tahl'rail kissed her forehead before turning to assess the situation. It was only then that he noticed the reigns of the King's horse lay abandoned on the ground. Turning back to Amalia, he gently took her hand and led her towards the horse.

"We need to leave," he told her firmly, knowing that they couldn't stay here any longer.

Amalia looked at him with confusion and pain in her eyes. "What do you mean? We can't leave my father like this. We can't just run away!" she cried out, overwhelmed with a mix of emotions.

Tahl'rail placed his hands on her shoulders and spoke sternly, "Lia! We have to leave before it's too late. I will be put to death for this, and you know that. But if we leave now, we can have a life together. Isn't that what you want?"

Amalia was torn. A hundred thoughts raced through her mind as she looked at Tahl'rail, knowing he was right. He had fought for his life, but in the end, it would still lead to his execution. She couldn't bear the thought of losing him too.

"Lia?" Tahl'rail's voice broke through her thoughts, waiting for her answer.

Amalia took a deep breath, her heart racing as Tahl'rail's words sank in. She nodded slowly, knowing he was right and they needed to leave immediately. Her eyes never left her father, who was lying on the ground, motionless.

Tahl'rail released Amalia from his grasp and went to retrieve their horses. He brought hers over and handed her the reins before mounting the King's horse himself. Amalia followed suit, but couldn't help stealing glances at her father. The forest was just beginning to open up before them, and it both excited and frightened her.

"How are we supposed to blend in? We don't know what kind of world will be on the other side," Amalia asked, turning to Tahl'rail with worry etched on her face.

"We have to try," he replied firmly. "If we don't, we'll always be on the run and never truly safe." Amalia knew he was right and nodded, determination setting in.

With a few clicks and kicks of their horses, Tahl'rail led the way into the forest, with Amalia close behind.

)O(

Cullen descended the grand staircase that curved down to the sprawling courtyard of the castle's expansive grounds. Adjusting the straps on his right gauntlet, he noticed the Master of the Stables waiting for him.

The man was thin and worn from years of service, but he had a wise look about him.

"Come with me, Sir," he said, motioning for Cullen to follow.

Cullen trailed after him into the stables where a magnificent white stallion awaited them - it was a Friesian breed, its elegant stature and powerful build exuding strength and grace. Its long mane brushed against the ground as it tossed its head in greeting, its equally lengthy tail swishing behind it.

Cullen was struck by the horse's beauty as he approached it. "This is...incredible," he murmured in awe.

He stood in awe of the horse before realizing that it was meant for him.

"All knights of the order receive their own horse, but our Knight Commander has given me specific instructions to give you our finest beast," the stable master explained with a hint of admiration in his voice.

Cullen couldn't help but feel a twinge of guilt, knowing he was only receiving such a grand gift because he had been promised to marry the Princess. He placed a hand on the horse's head and sighed, realizing that this would be his new life - as a knight and soon-to-be husband to the Princess.

)o(

Cullen rode confidently on his magnificent white stallion, making his way towards Cesileon Forest. A small pack was thrown over the horse's saddlebag, containing all of his belongings for the journey. As he traveled down a simple road, he couldn't help but notice the curious stares from passersby. Small children gazed at him with awe and fascination while women seemed to be taken aback by his rugged good looks. Men, on the other hand, paid him little mind.

Cullen leaned over to pat his steed's neck, pondering what to name it. "You need a name," he mused aloud.

The horse gave a low nicker in response as if in agreement. Cullen looked around at the scenic surroundings for inspiration. "How about Samuel?" he suggested, but the horse shook its head.

"Maybe Michael?" Again, the horse didn't seem too keen on the name.

Cullen sighed, feeling defeated. "I'm not very good at this," he admitted to the horse, "I couldn't even come up with a decent name for my dog...just ended up calling him 'Dog'."

After a day of riding, Cullen knew he was nearing his destination - Cesileon Forest. The sound of a beautiful melody drew his attention as he approached the forest's edge. Under the shade of towering trees sat two men dressed in similar attire; one played a lute while the other read a book - both were members of the order.

Maxwell greeted Cullen with a warm smile as he continued to strum his lute. "It seems our new friend has arrived," he remarked.

Dorian glanced up from his book to get a look at Cullen before speaking in a sarcastic tone. "Fresh off the order's leading strings too," he remarked, rolling his eyes. "Wonderful."

Cullen dismounted from his horse and introduced himself. "I'm Cullen Branson, pleased to make your acquaintance," he said with a polite nod.

Maxwell gently set his ornate lute aside, its intricately carved designs glinting in the sunlight. "I'm Maxwell Keynes of Narvi, a pleasure to make your acquaintance," he said with a warm smile. "This is my companion, Dorian Abreo of Kalke." Dorian closed his book with a flourish, revealing a crest on its cover that signified his noble lineage. "Yes, my family has a long history as Viscounts of our city," he boasted proudly.

Cullen shifted uncomfortably, unsure of how to respond without offending Dorian's prideful nature. He cleared his throat and rubbed the back of his neck, "It's nice to meet you both."

Dorian closed his book with a snap and stood up from where he had been seated on a nearby tree stump. "Well, let's not waste any more time. We have heretics to find," he said dismissively as he took hold of his horse's reins and mounted it. Maxwell followed suit, and Cullen did the same quickly, eager to get on their way.

As they rode through the winding forest trails, Maxwell chuckled lightly. "It seems we have a bit of a shortcut through these woods that will cut our travel time to Bestla in half," he announced confidently.

Cullen couldn't help but feel grateful for this stroke of luck. He was all too eager to arrive at their destination sooner rather than later.

Dorian eyed Cullen's impressive horse with curiosity. "My my, what do we have here? I've never seen an Order member riding such a fine beast," he observed with thinly veiled envy.

Maxwell gave Dorian a sly grin as he replied, "Jealous are we?" Dorian gave a disdainful snort before spurring his own horse forward to lead the way. Maxwell turned to Cullen with a twinkle in his eye, "He's quite something, isn't he? Does your steed have a name?"

Cullen gazed fondly at his magnificent stallion and nodded, "Seraphim." he replied with pride.

)o(

Through the dark, looming trees of the forest, a trail of deep red blood led to where the body of the King lay. The sound of small creeks and rustling branches could be heard above as if the forest was mourning their leader's loss.

A tall male elf descended silently from the trees, his agile movements betraying years of training and skill. His skin, pale milky white, stood out against the vibrant green of the forest. He stood at an impressive six feet with pouty lips that seemed almost too perfect to be real. Long, raven black hair cascaded down his back in braids before being tied into a high ponytail, revealing the full extent of its length down to his waist. His outfit was made out of the finest leather, accentuating his lean and muscular frame. On his back, he carried a bow and quiver filled with arrows at the ready. But it was his eyes that held the most intrigue - a milky white film covering what would have been piercing blue eyes.

In the elven world, this male would be considered one of the most beautiful beings alive. Golden paint adorned his striking features, following along his defined cheekbones and leading to five small white dots above each one. A thin line of gold trailed down his nose with a medium-sized dot placed between his brows and a delicate crescent connecting them. He exuded an aura of power and grace radiating from every inch of his being.

As he moved through the forest floor, his fingers grazed the ground until they came into contact with something solid. Upon closer inspection, he realized it was a leg belonging to the fallen King. Gently placing his hand on the ruler's back, he called out to his fellow warriors: "THERE HE IS! I FOUND THE KING!"

A small band of warriors appeared from within the trees, all elves just like him. A female elf with long black hair tied back in a ponytail rushed to the King's side, carefully turning his body over. She looked back at her comrades with pained eyes and stated, "He's been killed by intruders to our forest." The male elf, known as Thamyris, could hear the tears in her voice.

But he knew the truth. He shook his head, "No, he wasn't killed by intruders." The female elf looked at him with confusion and disbelief, "Then who? Could it have been one of the other tribes?" she asked. Thamyris sighed heavily and replied, "No, it was Tahl'rail - one of our own." As his words sank in, the female elf let out a choked sob, mourning not only the loss of their King but also the betrayal within their own community.

"What?" said shocked voices.

The male elf's fingers continued to move along the King's body. His face showed concern as another elf squatted down. He looked at his friend, "What is it? What are you seeing?" Thamyris had a unique ability to see past events by touching a person or an object. Scenes flashed before his eyes that weren't too detailed. It was mostly shadows since he couldn't see anyone's face. His imagination had to fill in what someone looked like since he used touch to make sense of his world. Thamyris could see what the king saw, Tahl'rail and Amalia in an act that looked like consummation. Thamyris held up his head with an interesting look on his face.

What do you see?" the male elf questioned again.

"They were in love."

"Who?"

"The King caught Tahl'rail and my sister together." Everyone went into shock as they listened and hung onto every word. "Tahl'rail was challenged for taking my sister's honor."

The female elf looked at everyone and said, "So...Tahl'rail won?" She looked at the others, "Tahl'rail won against the King?" she questioned in amazement and shock. Thamyris gave a nod, "Yes, and they ran."

Chapter 3

he rhythmic thunder of horse hooves echoed through the forest, each beat kicking up clouds of dirt and leaves. Tahl'rail and Amalia rode with urgency, their horses galloping at full speed towards an unknown destination. As they raced through the ever-changing landscape, Amalia could not help but notice the subtle shifts in the once-familiar forest. The trees seemed to twist and bend in new ways as if welcoming them into a different realm.

"What's happening? The forest looks completely different!" Amalia exclaimed, her eyes darting around in confusion.

"I told you the forest is opening up to us," Tahl'rail replied with a grin. "I don't know where we'll end up, but I have a feeling it will be safe."

In that moment, both riders felt a surge of excitement and freedom wash over them. They were no longer bound by their former duties and expectations; they could finally make their own choices and live life on their own terms.

Amalia's gaze turned to Tahl'rail, and she saw him in a whole new light. He was no longer just a warrior; he was now a potential husband, father, and provider. Tears welled up in her eyes as she realized the limitless possibilities of their new world together. But as quickly as joy had filled her heart, fear gripped her stomach like cold fingers. Would she ever be able to return home? See her family again? And then came the most terrifying thought of all - what about the dragons?

"The dragons..." Amalia whispered, unable to control the panic rising within her.

Her horse whinnied loudly, sensing its rider's distress, and skidding to a stop. "THE DRAGONS!" Amalia suddenly screamed, pulling hard on the reins.

Tahl'rail's horse also came to a halt as he looked at Amalia with wide eyes. "We have to go back!" she cried, her role as the Priestess of the forest suddenly coming back to her.

Tahl'rail's face mirrored Amalia's fear as he realized they had let their guard down in the midst of the excitement and had forgotten about their most important responsibility. Without hesitation, Amalia turned her horse around and raced towards the forest with Tahl'rail close behind. They prayed and hoped that they would make it back before it was too late, but deep down, they knew that the forest was gone, and they were now stranded in a new and unknown land. No matter how fast they rode, they could not outrun their fate.

Amalia reigned in her horse, tears streaming down her face as she trembled with fear. Panic threatened to overwhelm her, but the comforting presence of Thal'rail by her side gave her some solace. Thal'rail turned his horse around upon hearing her sobs, his expression filled with concern and tenderness. Gently, he lifted Amalia's chin. They both knew the gravity of their mistake and the consequences it could bring. But despite it all, they were free now – free to love, to roam, and to create a life for themselves.

Thal'rail turned his horse around upon hearing her sobs; his expression filled with concern and tenderness. His words were like a balm to Amalia's panicked mind. She let out a shaky breath and looked into his calm, confident eyes.

Together, they ventured deeper into the woods, exploring their new home and getting accustomed to the unfamiliar surroundings. Amalia could not help but notice that on the edge of the forest was a break in the trees. Curiosity overtook her as she dismounted her horse, kneeling behind a bush to get a closer look. Tahl'rail watched her with a confused expression before joining her.

As they peered through the bushes, they saw a bustling town filled with humans going about their daily lives. The sight was both exhilarating and terrifying for Amalia – she had never seen humans before and wanted to know more about them, but she also feared their potential hostility towards her and Thal'rail.

Feeling a tap on her shoulder, she turned to see Tahl'rail signaling for them to retreat. Slowly, they made their way back to their horses and mounted them again. Tahl'rail led them deeper into the woods, determined to find a more secluded area.

Amalia could not help but feel a twinge of sadness – she had been excited to explore this new place and meet new creatures, but now they had to hide. Tahl'rail found a thicket that forced them to dismount and guide their horses through it. The branches scratched at Amalia's arms, the light struggling to penetrate through the dense cluster of trees.

Finally, Tahl'rail stopped at a small clearing where they could rest and tie up their horses. Amalia took in her surroundings – the sunlight filtering through the tree leaves, the chirping of birds in the distance, and the feeling of being deep in nature. Amalia was hesitant at first but eventually tied her horse's reins around a nearby branch. Despite the circumstances, she felt grateful to be here with Thal'rail by her side.

Amalia's eyes scanned the dense forest, her brow furrowed in concern. "Here? Are you sure?" she asked Tahl'rail skeptically. He nodded confidently, his long black hair swaying with the movement.

Tahl'rail hesitated, turning his head to survey their surroundings. The dense forest canopy above cast shadows all around them, the only light coming from a sliver of the moon peeking through the trees. "Just for tonight," he finally said, his voice low and cautious. "We'll explore more tomorrow. It's better if we're somewhere that's harder for people to get to...to ensure our safety for now." He struggled for the right words to describe the creatures they had just encountered. "Mortals?" he settled on, knowing no other term to use.

Taking in their surroundings, Tahl'rail noticed the dryness of the forest floor, with plenty of kindling and firewood easily found nearby. They quickly gathered enough to create a ring of stones and Amalia expertly used her fingertips in a twisting motion to ignite the wood into crackling flames. The warmth was a welcoming sensation against Amalia's skin as she rubbed her hands together. Amalia could not help but marvel at the abundance of resources in this unfamiliar place.

Tahl'rail brought back two rabbits he had quickly caught with his light-footed movements. With expert precision, they skinned and gutted the animals before skewering them over the fire to roast. With dinner roasting on skewers over the fire, Tahl'rail sat back and took in the peaceful scene before him. The flickering flames cast dancing shadows across Amalia's face as she rested her head on his shoulder. While in that moment, he realized how much he could easily adapt to this uncomplicated way of life - with the woman he loved by his side, an abundance of game in the forest, and the natural instinct to build a shelter for their protection. Perhaps one day, they would even have children to complete this idyllic dream.

As they waited for their meal to cook, Amalia began to hum a gentle tune, her mind drifting to thoughts of a future with Tahl'rail. A home, a family, a full life... it all seemed within the reach in this magical place. Without conscious thought, they intertwined their fingers together, their hands fitting perfectly like two pieces of a puzzle. Amalia's eyes fluttered open as she felt Tahl'rail's head nudged hers gently. She met his gaze and was struck by how the firelight illuminated every inch of his handsome face. His warm smile made her heart skip a beat as she noticed the playful spark in his stormy eyes. In that moment, everything else faded away as they got lost in each other's company. Tahl'rail's left hand gently took Amalia's right, their fingers interlaced together. Amalia closed her eyes as she gently laid her right shoulder against Tahl'rail's left. The soft crackle of the fire and the sweet smell of meat roasting filled the air, creating the perfect backdrop for their newfound independence.

After several minutes, Amalia felt Tahl'rail's large, calloused hand release hers and then gently cradled her delicate chin. They looked into each other's eyes for several minutes. Before they realized it, their lips had met into a slow and tender kiss. As the moments passed, Amalia's right hand held Tahl'rail's cheek. Their kisses grew more confident and passionate as they both embraced one another. Tahl'rail could feel his body responding to the soft press of Amalia's breasts against his chest as he held her in his arms. The touch of her smooth skin and her alluring scent filled his senses. He wanted to consume every inch of her, to lose himself in her completely.

As their desire for each other intensified, both felt a fire ignite deep within their stomachs, their skin flushed with heat. Tahl'rail reluctantly pulled away from Amalia's lips, trailing gentle kisses down her neck until he reached her exposed breasts. His touch was slow and deliberate, igniting a fiery passion within them both. His touch was slow yet deliberate, sending shivers down Amalia's spine. They both felt their cheeks flush and their hearts race as they gave in to the pleasure. Amalia leaned her head back, surrendering herself to the pleasure she felt. It was a freeing feeling to know that no one could stop them from being together, from expressing their love in its purest form.

With careful hands, Tahl'rail gently removed each piece of clothing from Amalia's body, his cheeks turning a rosy hue as he admired her bare form. Amalia blushed herself, feeling slightly embarrassed by his intense gaze. But Tahl'rail's touch reassured her, his lips gently caressing her delicate neck. "You are my world," he whispered. Hearing his words and feeling his breath caressing her neck made Amalia feel just how beautiful she was in his eyes.

She could not help but smile at his words, wrapping her arms around herself out of embarrassment. But Tahl'rail would not allow it. He gently urged her to let go and bask in all her glory. As they continued to embrace and kiss passionately, Tahl'rail lifted Amalia into his strong arms and gently placed her on his lap, causing her to straddle him. Her skirts rustled with movement as his hands gently caressed her outer thighs.

With trembling fingers, he struggled to undo his own clothing while keeping his gaze locked on hers. Amalia blushed as she felt something hard in between her legs. Tahl'rail blushed as he looked at Amalia with a mixture of nervousness and desire. Amalia's right hand reached up to caress his cheek, knowing just how much this moment meant to both of them. Feeling Tahl'rail become increasingly eager and aroused, Amalia reached up and lovingly stroked his cheek. With a passionate kiss, she reassured him that she was ready for them to become one.

Morning arrived and Amalia woke up nestled against Tahl'rail's warm body. She smiled as she ran her right hand over his chest, feeling content and fulfilled in their intimate connection. Tahl'rail stirred awake, putting his left hand to shield his eyes from the sunlight streaming through the trees. Amalia stood up and began to get dressed, lacing up her corset for the day ahead.

Tahl'rail's yawn caught her attention. She turned to see him retrieving some rabbits that he had hung in a nearby tree to keep them safe from predators. But as she watched him prepare breakfast, her mind started to wander to the village they had stumbled upon and the possibility of exploring it. This world was now theirs, and she felt a strong desire to learn more about it. But Tahl'rail noticed her gaze and shook his head, focusing on skinning the rabbits instead. He reminded her that they needed to figure out this new world first before venturing out into it. Amalia sighed but knew deep down that he was right. They could not hide forever, but for now, they needed to be cautious.

As they sat down to eat, Amalia could not help but think about all the things they needed to learn - the nature of this new land, its inhabitants and potential dangers, and how they could make a life for themselves here. Tahl'rail also knew the importance of gathering information, but he believed it was wiser to stay hidden for a while longer before exploring their surroundings. Nevertheless, Amalia's curiosity and thirst for knowledge remained strong, a reminder that they were not alone in this world and needed to adapt in order to survive.

Amalia looked around the dense forest, taking in the towering trees that blocked much of the sunlight. Rays of light still managed to filter through the thick canopy, casting dappled patterns on the forest floor. The filtered light also created a peaceful atmosphere. As a Priestess, she had a heightened sense for all things in nature - she could feel the ancient energy of the forest, the presence of animals even if they were hidden from sight, and the faint remnants of magic still lingering in the air. Her mother had often told her stories about a time before this forest existed, but Amalia could not remember why.

She hoped Tahl'rail would be more open to exploring this new world they found themselves in. But she also understood his desire to keep them safe after their recent journey. After breakfast, Tahl'rail set out to clear a larger space for their campsite, using one of his swords to cut through overgrown brush and struggling trees. He knew without enough sunlight, these plants would not thrive anyway, and it was better to use them as kindling or firewood. He also planned to make a small tent for shelter and would need to hunt for larger animals to provide skins for Amalia to sew into blankets and a tent canvas. He was not skilled at sewing, but he could provide her with plenty of materials as he contemplated what kind of animals might be found in this new land.

As Tahl'rail worked, Amalia heard the sound of running water nearby and decided to investigate. She knew they would need a source of fresh water, and it would also help them locate where they were in relation to any nearby villages or towns. As she followed the sound of the stream, she could hear birds singing and smell the distinct scent of water. The foliage thinned out as she walked, allowing more sunlight to illuminate her path. After about a mile, Amalia came across a small waterfall that led into a larger river. Her eyes lit up with excitement, and she quickly made her way back to camp.

Upon her return, Tahl'rail was nowhere to be found. She assumed he must have ventured out to find more suitable wood or food. Feeling adventurous, Amalia decided to explore the forest further and see if she could locate the nearby village she had seen earlier. As she approached the edge of the woods, she realized her pointed ears might cause trouble for them in a human settlement. She quickly brushed her hair over her ears to hide them and took a deep breath before stepping into the daylight and making her way toward the village.

She walked through the bustling streets. Amalia could not help but feel a sense of unease. She was used to the tranquility of nature, and this crowded, noisy place felt overwhelming. Her senses were assaulted by various smells, some pleasant and others not so much.

She was confronted by a beggar reaching out for alms. He was covered in tattered clothing, emanating a pungent smell of bodily waste and grime. Amalia's heart went out to him as she saw how desperate his situation was. She squatted down and took his hand in hers, her elvish words flowing gently over him like a calming breeze. The man was taken aback by her sudden presence and asked what she was doing. Without answering, Amalia released his hand and continued on her way. The man watched as she walked away, unaware that his boils had miraculously disappeared thanks to Amalia's healing touch.

But someone had taken notice: a corpulent man dressed in lavish silks that clung to his protruding belly. His thinning hairline glistened with grease, and he wore a thick gold chain around his neck, the weight of it pulling down on his sagging skin. His name was Naromu, and he had been browsing a stall of ripe fruit when his greedy eyes caught sight of Amalia's unique clothes and intoxicating beauty. His gaze then turned downwards, fixated on her bare feet, covered in dirt and grime from the long journey. The beggar's face was familiar to him, having been stationed at this very spot for years. After an accident in which a blacksmith's shop collapsed onto him, crushing his legs and leaving him crippled, he resorted to begging at the market for survival. People were repulsed by his disfigured face and avoided his outstretched hand, leaving him with little chance of earning any coin for food.

As the fat man continued to stare at Amalia, she was admiring her surroundings with wide-eyed wonder as if she had never experienced village life before. Her long silver hair shone like moonlight against her milky skin. Before the man could make his move towards her, another man grabbed her left wrist, pulling her away from the delicacies of the market. It was Tahl'rail, his wild mane of hair covering his pointed ears just like Amalia's.

"Lia, what are you doing here?" Tahl'rail growled in a low, agitated tone as he pulled her close to him. His sharp eyes darted around the busy market, scanning for any potential threats. "I can't believe you'd do something so dangerous. Has anyone seen you?" Amalia shook her head, "No, no one really. Just that crippled man." Tahl'rail's grip tightened on her wrist, his unease evident in the tension of his muscles. The fat man watched as the two left in a hurry, trying to be discreet as they disappeared into the nearby woods.

Gasping for breath, Amalia struggled to keep up with Tahl'rail's brisk pace as he pulled her deeper into the thick forest. She stumbled over roots and rocks, her bare feet aching from the rough terrain. "Tahl'rail! Tahl'rail slow down!" she pleaded, struggling to catch her breath. Tahl'rail abruptly turned around, his usually handsome face twisted with fear and anger. "Do you have any idea how frightened I was? I turned my back for one moment, and you were gone!" Amalia could see the genuine concern in his eyes, and it made her heart ache.

"I heard water," she explained, trying to justify her actions. "I followed it until I found a spring. We needed fresh water, so I thought it would be wise to check it out." Tahl'rail let out a sigh of relief at seeing that she was unharmed. "But why did you go to the village?" he asked sternly, demanding an explanation.

Amalia fidgeted nervously under his intense gaze, searching her mind for a valid reason. "I wanted to see it," she finally admitted with a sheepish smile. "I've never been to a village before, and I was curious. I'm sorry if I worried you." Tahl'rail's expression softened at her apology, but he still gave her a disapproving look. "You know better than to wander off without telling me, "He scolded gently. Amalia bowed her head in shame, feeling guilty for causing him such distress. "I'm sorry," she repeated sincerely.

Tahl'rail let out a heavy sigh, feeling his anger dissipate as he embraced Amalia. His long, dark hair cascaded down onto her shoulder, tickling her skin. "I'm sorry for being so cross, I was just scared," he murmured, his voice soft and apologetic. Amalia's small hands found their way around his waist as she nestled her head into the crook of his neck, finding comfort in his embrace. Suddenly, Tahl'rail's pointed ears twitched as he heard voices approaching. Without hesitation, he grabbed Amalia's right hand and swiftly pulled them both up into a nearby tree, seeking cover from whatever danger may be approaching. Amalia's heart raced with fear and uncertainty, but she trusted Tahl'rail to keep them safe. She could feel his body tense against hers as they waited in silence, hoping that whatever had caught his attention would pass by without noticing them.

The round man, accompanied by his group of six men, made their way into the dense forest. Tahl'rail had noticed the man watching them in the village and now they were being followed. Sensing danger, Tahl'rail turned to Amalia and gestured for her to stay quiet and be cautious. Tahl'rail signaled Amalia to head towards the safety of a nearby thicket. She nodded as she made her way towards it, careful not to make a sound. Tahl'rail descended from the tree with silent grace, determined to follow and protect them. As he stalked through the dense underbrush, he kept a vigilant eye on the group ahead. The fat man stopped suddenly and spun around, barking orders to his men.

"I don't know where they've gone, but find them! That girl is unlike anything I've seen before, and she'll fetch a hefty sum." Tahl'rail gritted his teeth at the mention of selling Amalia for coin. No way was that going to happen while he still breathed. He motioned for Amalia to stay put as he climbed up onto a branch, ready to attack if necessary. His hand instinctively gripped the hilt of his sword, longing to slice through the fat man's throat or roast him like a pig over an open fire.

The fat man's gaze scanned his men, "Split up and search, they have to be somewhere nearby!" But before he could make a move, a faint sound caught his attention. It was the snap of twigs and heavy footsteps approaching. Tahl'rail's ears perked up, and he listened intently as the noise grew louder. Suddenly, Tahl'rail's heart stopped as he heard Amalia let out a bloodcurdling scream as the branch she was perched on gave way, sending her tumbling to the ground. Without hesitation, he unsheathed his sword and prepared to face any danger that threatened the love of his life.

"Amalia!" Tahl'rail roared in fury and fear as he darted towards her limp form. The fat man and his lackeys laughed with cruel amusement at her fall, but their grins quickly turned into sneers when they saw Tahl'rail charging towards them with unbridled rage in his eyes. He was ready to defend Amalia with every ounce of strength he possessed. Nothing would stop him from protecting her, not even death itself.

Tahl'rail's blood boiled at the sight of the man with dark hair and a shaggy beard gripping onto Amalia. The man ignored the pain in Amalia's injured leg. Amalia was repulsed by the man's foul breath close to her face. Without hesitation, Tahl'rail unsheathed his second sword and lunged towards the assailant, plunging it deep into his gut and slicing open his belly before pulling it out in one swift motion. The man dropped to the ground with a thud, writhing in agony as Tahl'rail turned towards the others. "Let her go!" he roared, his swords dripping with blood and fury. The remaining men backed away in fear, knowing not to cross this fierce protector. "I won't ask again."

Tahl'rail's vision blurred and blackened as a sudden sharp pain exploded in the back of his head. He heard Amalia's screams, shrill with terror, cutting through the darkness as he struggled to regain consciousness. With a groan, he finally came to, only to be met with searing agony throbbing throughout his skull. As his eyes adjusted to the dim surroundings, he realized he was tied to a tree, his arms stretched painfully above his head.

But it wasn't just him who was bound. His heart twisted in fear as he saw Amalia on the ground next to him, her hands also tied above her head to a short stake. Amalia's terrified screams echoed in his ears when the bearded man loomed over her, gripping her jaw in a vice-like grip. Tahl'rail's blood boiled at the sight, and he thrashed against his restraints, shouting for the man to release her.

"Stay away from her, you bastard!" He roared, fighting against his restraints.

The bearded man sauntered over with a sly grin, taking in the scene before him with obvious enjoyment. He gave a low chuckle as he slapped Tahl'rail hard across the face, sneering at her words of protest. "You should learn how to control your mouth," he taunted. "A mouth like that can get you into trouble...and her most of all."

Fury burned within Tahl'rail as he watched helplessly while Amalia fought against her bindings. But it turned into pure horror when the bearded man kicked her legs open, and their intentions were made clear. Amalia frantically tried to summon fire from her fingers to burn through the ropes while Tahl'rail struggled with all his might against the tight knots. Amalia screamed and thrashed, fighting against her captors with all her strength, but it was no use. Tahl'rail's blood ran cold as he saw tears streaming down her face and heard her cries, pleading for him to save her. With a desperate surge of adrenaline, he strained against the ropes once again, roaring with rage and desperation.

Amalia glared at them both, her fear evident in her trembling body. "What do you want from us? We were not bothering you!" she pleaded, struggling against her bonds. But it was too late. The bearded man kicked her legs open, revealing her worst nightmare. With renewed desperation, Amalia tried to summon fire from her fingertips, but the ropes held tight. Tahl'rail let out a guttural roar as he fought against his own bindings. "Don't you dare touch her! I will kill you if you harm her!" he threatened, his voice strained and hoarse. The veins in his neck bulged as he strained against the restraints, his determination to protect Amalia evident. Suddenly, a sharp blow to the back of Amalia's head sent her spiraling into darkness. When she came to, she found herself surrounded by three men with evil intentions. One of them wielded a thick stick while another punched Tahl'rail forcefully in the stomach, knocking the wind out of him. The bearded man knelt between Amalia's legs and ripped off more of her clothing as the other two men eagerly watched on. Panicked and helpless, Amalia screamed and thrashed against her restraints, praying for someone - anyone - to come and save them.

Tahl'rail gasped for air, his chest heaving as he finally managed to fill his burning lungs. With a snarl on his lips, the bearded man sneered at the elf, his eyes taking in every inch of Tahl'rail's bound and helpless form. "You're a lucky man to have something so pretty," he taunted, reaching out to touch Amalia's delicate face with dirty fingers. Fueled by rage and desperation, Tahl'rail strained against the ropes that bound him, feeling the threads cut into his skin as he fought to break free. But as the man turned his attention back to Amalia, fear crept in. He had to act fast.

With nimble fingers, Tahl'rail retrieved a small knife from his brace and carefully positioned it between his trembling fingers. Every second felt like an eternity as he sawed through the ropes, determined to make these men pay for what they had done. As the ropes fell away, Tahl'rail knew exactly how he would make them suffer. His vision blurred with fury as he imagined cutting off their limbs one by one, starting with the one hovering over Amalia. A twisted smile spread across his face at the thought of feeding that man his own severed cock before ending his miserable life. But before he could put his plan into action, a loud shriek filled the air. Amalia's head jerked out of the man's grip, and he responded with a vicious slap that left her cheek stinging. In one swift motion, he ripped her top off, revealing her trembling form underneath.

Amalia fought with all her might, screaming and kicking as her heels scraped against the dirt. But two men were closing in on her, their depraved intentions clear. The leader grabbed her throat and forced her legs apart, each movement causing sharp pain and shredding what little dignity she had left.

A deafening thud echoed through the clearing as a stick struck the back of the man, knocking him off Amalia. It was the fat man, his beady eyes gleaming with malicious intent. "SHE'S NOT FOR YOU LOT!" he bellowed, a twisted grin spreading across his face. "She's going to fetch a pretty penny if we make them believe she's still pure!" At that moment, the ropes binding Tahl'rail's wrists snapped like twine, and he lunged at the bearded man, fueled by rage and desperation.

But before he could reach his target, another man with blonde hair intercepted him, causing him to spin around and lash out with his dagger, striking the man in the jugular. Blood spurted from the wound as the man fell, gurgling to the ground. Tahl'rail wasted no time as he snatched one of his swords from an assailant and swiftly dispatched him, leaving a trail of carnage in his wake. As more men came running towards them, drawn by the sounds of chaos and screams, Tahl'rail realized they were all in cahoots with the fat man. With swift agility, he leaped into the trees, using every branch and leaf for cover as he darted through the foliage with unmatched speed.

But even as he fought back against their relentless pursuit, tears streamed down Amalia's cheeks as she struggled against her bonds, her skin bloody and raw from her desperate attempts to break free. Her feet scraped against the ground as she fought to stand on wobbly legs.

Tahl'rail's eyes burned with cold fury as he caught sight of another man charging towards him, brandishing an axe. Without breaking his fluid movements, he thrust his dagger out behind him and impaled the attacker before soaring back up into the safety of the treetops. But just as he was about to disappear into the canopy, a barrage of ropes flew towards him, snaring his limbs and dragging him down to the ground.

With all his strength, Tahl'rail managed to cut one of the ropes before more were thrown over him. A man rushed towards him, swinging a stick that connected with his skull and forced him to his knees. Another man snatched his dagger from him and hurled it back towards the bearded man, who caught it in his throat with a sickening thud. Despite the pain and fear coursing through his body, Tahl'rail refused to give up. He would not let these monsters continue their depraved actions any longer. Meanwhile, Amalia's wrists continued to bleed profusely from the bindings cutting into her flesh, her cries for mercy falling on deaf ears.

As the man stood up and grabbed an axe, Tahl'rail could see the hatred in his eyes as he sneered at him. "We're going to teach you some manners, you scrawny shit!" With a fierce glint in his eye, Tahl'rail met his gaze head-on, refusing to show any sign of weakness or submission. But as the man dragged him roughly by the hair and started hacking off his long locks, Tahl'rail could not help but fill up with fury. He fought against the ropes with renewed vigor, determined to break free and make these men pay for their heinous crimes against him and Amalia.

The fat man knelt beside Amalia, gripping her jaw tightly as he leered at her. "So does she," he chuckled darkly. "I'm going to make a fortune off of these two! I'll be able to retire after this!" Tahl'rail's screams of rage echoed through the clearing as he struggled against his restraints. "You'll all pay for this!" he roared, fueled by a burning desire for vengeance.

The fat man towered over Tahl'rail, his cruel eyes filled with cruel satisfaction, his greasy face twisted with a sickening smile as he watched Tahl'rail's unyielding gaze fixated on his beloved Amalia. Despite being bruised, battered, and humiliated, Tahl'rail's love for her burned brighter than ever, fueling a raging inferno within him. He would make these vile men pay for what they had done to his love, relishing every agonizing death. His eyes never wavered from Amalia, the only light left in his darkened world.

But suddenly, the fire in Tahl'rail's eyes was extinguished as the fat man slit his throat without mercy. He knew that Tahl'rail would never submit and become a mere slave. As the blood spilled out of his body and he grew weaker by the second, the men callously dropped him into the dirt. With Tahl'rail dead and lying on the ground, the other men approached Amalia, cutting her bindings and setting her free. She lunged towards Tahl'rail's lifeless body, tears streaming down her cheeks as she cried out in anguish. But before she could reach him, she was forcefully pulled back and restrained by the men. They laughed at her futile attempts to break free as they mercilessly bound her wrists with rope.

"You'll fetch a pretty price, my dear," sneered the fat man as he leered at Amalia with greedy eyes

As she struggled against them, the realization hit her like a ton of bricks - she was now just another commodity to be sold and used by these heartless monsters. And in that moment, she knew that death would have been a merciful release compared to the fate that awaited her.

Chapter 4

amalia's blood-curdling screams echoed through the dense forest as fear consumed her entire being. Her body convulsed violently, causing her to stumble over her own feet as she was dragged along by her captors. With every step, Amalia could feel the sharp blades of grass and twisted tree roots desperately clinging to her, as if the forest itself was aware of her danger. Suddenly, a medium-sized tree root snaked its way around her ankle, tripping and sending her crashing to the ground with a bone-chilling scream. Naromu spun around at the sound; his expression twisted with anger and disgust at the sight of Amalia being dragged so carelessly. "You idiots don't know a damn thing!" he bellowed at the men, his voice laced with venomous rage. One of them turned to face him, panting heavily. "You try getting her to move! This damn forest is like a maze, we can barely walk ourselves!" Naromu surveyed his surroundings and realized that this wasn't just their regular forest - it was alive, and it was fighting against them. He turned to Amalia, who was still screaming in terror, and barked out accusingly, "You're the one controlling this, aren't ya?"

Amalia's heart pounded in her chest as she looked up with a tear-streaked face at the man towering over her. The forest was trying to offer her some kind of protection. And Amalia knew to trust in the kindness of this forest. It seemed to be fighting to protect her, as her very presence seemed to have awakened it from its long slumber. "I didn't do anything," she stammered, her voice trembling in fear, trying to reason with the man who held her captive.

Naromu's eyes narrowed as he barked orders at two of his people to retrieve his cart in Bestla. "We're not going to get far this way," he grumbled. Amalia watched them disappearing into the dense foliage, their bodies contorting and squeezing between trees and bushes. She shivered in fear and confusion. She couldn't fully comprehend what was happening or how she could escape this dire situation. Desperate thoughts raced through her mind as she considered calling upon ancient beings and powerful magic for help.

Meanwhile, Naromu rummaged through a burlap sack and produced a set of iron shackles. With a cruel smile, he approached Amalia while one of the men held her shoulders so she couldn't run. The ropes were removed from her wrists, and the moment the cold metal touched her skin, Amalia screamed in agony as if it were burning her flesh. The sound echoed through the forest, mingling with the sizzling noise of Naromu locking the shackles tight around her wrists. His eyes narrowed as he looked at her with disgust. "What is that?" he growled, his grip tightening on the chains. Amalia's sobs turned into wails as she cried out, "T-the shackles...they're made of iron!" The pain was unbearable, searing through every nerve in her body. But even worse was the realization that she was now completely helpless under Naromu's control.

Naromu's dark eyes narrowed as she struggled to find the words, her voice trembling with sobs. "Iron...it hurts people like me!" she cried out, her anguish echoing through the thick canopy above. The chains around her wrists cut into her skin. Naromu surveyed his surroundings, trying to gauge the time of day, but the dense foliage blocked out any sunlight. As roughly as he could, Naromu grabbed the chains tightly, causing Amalia to stand and walk with him. Her heart racing with terror, she followed him, unsure of where they were headed. Naromu stepped on a few gnarled roots to help hoist Amalia's arms above her head before securing the chains on a sturdy branch. She was left standing precariously on her tiptoes, feeling helpless and trapped. Another man approached and meticulously cut away the tree's roots, making sure Amalia couldn't even think about escaping. All she could do was cry for herself and the wounded tree that had been sacrificed to keep her captive.

As she hung there, watching the men set up camp and hearing their conversations about others who had gone to fetch a cart, Amalia felt a sense of hopelessness wash over her. The man who had been leering at her before now seemed even more sinister as he gathered wood for a fire and searched for his flints. The prospect of spending a long night in this place with these cruel men filled Amalia with dread.

Naromu and the men huddled together, seeking warmth in each other's presence. It was an attempt to keep themselves warm from the biting cold. Her hands were still held over her head as she hung from a low-hanging branch. The cold seeped into her bones, making her shiver uncontrollably. Every now and then, the flickering flames from the nearby fire offered only brief moments of warmth, teasing her with a hint of respite before disappearing again. She watched the men drink some kind of strong-smelling liquid from their flasks. Their cheeks turned rosy and their moods became more cheerful. It was clear that there was something more potent than elvish wine passing their lips.

A sense of unease washed over her when the man who had been leering at her earlier got up and walked towards her. She felt like a trapped animal, her skin crawling as he approached her with slow, deliberate steps. Amalia felt like a thousand spiders were crawling down her back as he approached.

"No, no!" she begged, trying to push him away.

But he was too close now. She twisted and struggled, desperately trying to free herself from him as he kissed her roughly. Amalia wrenched her head away from him, feeling disgusted and violated. But when she refused to give him what he wanted, he slapped her across the face with a vicious sneer.

"Bitch!" he spat.

Refusing to let him see her tears, Amalia gritted her teeth and braced for another blow. But when she peeked through one eye, she saw him turn his gaze towards Narom with a knowing smirk on his face.

"How do you know she's pure?" he taunted. "She had a gent with her!"

Naromu's eyes narrowed to slits of fiery fury as he sensed the direction of the conversation. In one swift move, he rose to his feet and strode over to the man, a storm brewing in his gaze.

Without hesitation, he unleashed a punishing slap across the man's face, causing him to stumble back in shock and rage. The air got thick with tension as Naromu stood tall and unyielding, facing off against the man with unbridled defiance burning in his eyes. Amalia's heart thundered in her chest as she watched them exchange heated words, fearfully wondering what would happen next.

"I won't say it again," Naromu growled menacingly. "She's not yours to have. And her purity means nothing to us. We'll sell her as if she is pure regardless." Amalia held her breath as the two men locked gazes, a dangerous and charged energy filling the space between them. She could see the veins in the man's neck protruding with anger, but Naromu remained immovable, unafraid of any repercussions. With a dismissive click of his tongue, the other man turned and walked away, leaving an intense and unsettling silence in his wake.

Amalia's body hung limply from the branch, her senses dulled by the crackling embers of the dying fire. But as she drifted in and out of consciousness, the sharp sound of snapping twigs jolted her back to reality. She groaned as she saw the man approaching again, his eyes burning with a sickening lust. Before she could even react, he punched her square in the face, knocking her out cold.

When Amalia came to her senses, she felt the hands of the man who had assaulted her on her face, roughly kissing her. In a moment of horror, she realized what was happening and jerked away, only to be met with a brutal slap that left her cheek stinging. The men surrounding her laughed as they ripped off her clothes, their hands grasping at her body like hungry animals. She tried to scream, but another hand covered her mouth, muffling her cries for help. She looked up to see the man's face leering at her, his breath reeking of alcohol and lust. The man grabbed her throat and forced her legs apart while another squeezed a pressure point on her thigh, rendering her unable to fight back. As one man finished using her, he carelessly let go of her, and she dropped to the ground, causing immense pain in her arms. Another man eagerly took his place, biting and squeezing at her breasts as he lifted her up into his arms and roughly thrust himself inside of her.

Amidst the excruciating pain and violation, Amalia realized with horror that she was bleeding - a cruel sacrifice for these cruel men's pleasure. Amalia's lithe build and small stature gave the men the impression that she was a virgin, which was safe in Tahl'rail's keeping. They laughed and jeered at her suffering, reveling in their power over her body. Despite her cries and protests, they continued to take turns defiling her until she finally lost consciousness from the agony. Two more men closed in on her, their eyes gleaming with malicious intent.

As she drifted into darkness, Amalia prayed for someone to save her from this nightmare. Little did she know, Naromu had already turned away from the scene as he left the men to their pleasure. He was going to walk back to Bestla and retrieve his cart for himself.

But the horror was far from over. Another man stepped forward eagerly, untying his pants as he eyed Amalia like a predator stalking its prey. He gripped her right leg tightly and thrust into her with such force that she thought she would be torn in two. The pain was excruciating, and she screamed for them to stop, but they only laughed at her struggles.

It wasn't until the man behind her bit squeezed her breasts so violently that the sheer agony caused her to lose consciousness. When she woke up again, Amalia realized with despair that these men were going to continue taking what they wanted from her until there was nothing but a broken shell of a woman left. And there was no one to save her from this nightmare.

Amalia's body convulsed in constant pain as the man continued to violate her, his hands leaving bruises on her pale skin as he laughed sadistically. Even with tears, hot and bitter, that streamed relentlessly down Amalia's face as she lay unconscious, she could feel the pain in every pore, a searing agony that coursed through her body like molten lava. She couldn't escape it, even in her mindless state, as the bastard continued to ravage her with every thrust of his member. Now, the other men joined in, masturbating and ejaculating over her broken body while the man relentlessly pounded into her. She could hear their laughter, a sick symphony to accompany her agonizing screams.

With every thrust of his vile member, he laughed with sadistic pleasure. He sliced at her delicate flesh with a sharp dagger, relishing in her cries of anguish. And as if that wasn't enough, the other men joined in on the perverse act, taking turns defiling her and ruining what little innocence she had left. When he was finally done, he pulled out with a groan, his penis covered in blood and evidence of his vile act. "That was amazing. Virginal pussy is truly the best," he boasted to his companions, who eagerly took their turns with Amalia.

Amalia felt their foul breath on her skin, their hands pawing at her bruised and battered body. They were getting off on her pain and suffering, and it sickened her to the core. Her wrists were bleeding from the shackles that bound her to this hellish nightmare. The cold iron cut into her flesh like a hot knife. But it was nothing compared to the pain she felt inside as each man took what they wanted from her - her innocence, her dignity, and ultimately, her self-worth.

As the third man approached, Amalia tried to fight back, but she was no match for his strength. He violently penetrated her and she screamed in agony as he pounded into her with brutal force. Her legs shook uncontrollably as he thrust deeper and harder, tearing apart any remaining shreds of hope or sanity. She wanted to die. She wanted this nightmare to end and for the pain to stop consuming her every fiber. But these monsters showed no signs of stopping.

As the hours passed by, each man continued inflicting more agony upon her. Beating her until she couldn't even recognize herself anymore, humiliating her beyond belief. At one point, Amalia's mind started to detach from her body. She couldn't bear the pain any longer, so she retreated into a place where it couldn't reach her.

Tears poured endlessly from her eyes as he finished and withdrew from her trembling form. But the horror was far from over as they continued to mock and humiliate her, throwing food at her and fondling her abused body without mercy. Her mind reeled with a desperate desire to escape this hellish nightmare.

After hours of using and abusing her, one man finally announced his departure with a chilling statement: "The wife will be missing me." Now Amalia was left alone with two others who showed no signs of stopping. Amalia's mind and body were shattered beyond repair. Her fingers clawed desperately at the bindings as she prayed for her death.

The other two remained, their faces twisted with cruel satisfaction. In that moment, she knew there was no escape. No hope of rescue or salvation. All she could do was endure this hell for as long as they saw fit.

)o(

Namoru stumbled out of the dense forest, his clothes torn and bloody from the thorns and branches that seemed to reach out and grab him at every turn. The half-waning moon was rising in the sky, casting an eerie glow over the town. Exhausted and frustrated, he made his way to his first stop, which was the local tavern. His footsteps were heavy. Upon entry, he found his two hired men drinking and flirting with two maids who were clearly uncomfortable on their laps. Namoru stormed over to them, reeking of sweat and frustration.

"What are you idiots doing? I asked you to bring back the cart!" he bellowed, grabbing one of the maids of a man's lap before smashing his ale mug across his face. The other man slurred in protest but quickly passed out on the dirty tavern floor.

"It got dark too fast! We just wanted a quick drink before bringing back the cart," one of the men mumbled before vomiting onto himself.

Namoru scoffed and tossed a few coins at them. "You're both fired. Take your pay and get out." He turned and left without another word, heading towards the market.

He made his way to the market and noticed the homeless man who Amalia had recently healed, sleeping on the side of the road with his cup which held a few coins in it from kind samaritans. Naromu couldn't resist and swiftly stole a handful of coins before continuing on his way. He reached his cart - a rickety open-top carriage with a crate leaning against it - and climbed onto the seat. With a snap of the reins, he urged his horses forward and away from the town. As they passed by the homeless man again, Naromu heard him stirring and shaking his empty cup in disappointment with tears in his eyes. It didn't affect him and he continued on, counting his stolen money with a smug smile on his face.

)o(

The first light of dawn crept over the horizon. Naromu returned with his cart and found Amalia's body hanging limply from a tree branch. His heart clenched in fear that she may be dead; he leaped off the cart and ran to her. The sight that greeted him was enough to ignite a fire of fury within him. Her once delicate features were now marred by bruises and blood, her hair tangled and disheveled. "What did you bastards do?" he bellowed in rage, his eyes scanning her broken form. His gaze fell upon her blackened eyes, evidence of a broken nose. "You bloody bastards ruined her!" he screamed at the group of men who stood nearby. His face turned as red as a ripe tomato, "You ruined her beauty! No one is going to buy her looking like this!"

No one had ever seen Naromu so enraged before, his normally hot temper reaching a whole new level. "I let you have your fun and this is how you repay me?" He turned to face Amalia again and saw that she was still breathing, giving him a glimmer of hope. With a shake of his head, he motioned for the men to take her down and put her in the box.

Watching as they approached her, Naromu felt a twinge of guilt for allowing this to happen. One man lifted her from her hips, causing her to cry out in pain as her arms slid off the branch. They carried her to the cart. Amalia's arms hung limply, finding some relief after being held above her head for so long. But the agony she felt in those moments could not compare to the emotional pain she was enduring.

Once inside the crate, Amalia found herself curled up in a ball with her knees against her chest, sobbing uncontrollably. She heard the lid of the box close over her and the sound of nails being hammered, sealing her inside it. Each pound felt as though a nail was being driven into her heart and soul. She wept silently, knowing that this would be her fate from now on - locked away in a box, a mere possession to be bought and sold at will.

Naromu clicked his tongue and snapped the reins, urging the cart forward towards Bestla, their cart creaking along the bumpy road. Amalia's heart ached with fear and pain, knowing she would have to face whatever horrors these evil men had in store for her. Despite her desperate attempts to repair her torn and tattered clothing, Amalia could not salvage any sense of modesty for herself despite the hopelessness of the situation. She was left vulnerable and exposed, a stark reminder of the horrors she had endured.

"We'll see if we can secure passage to a wine auction," Naromu said, his voice calm but determined. Amalia prayed for her wounds to heal quickly for them to make any decent coin and escape this nightmare. The sound of the horses' hooves echoed through the forest, their rhythmic beat providing a small comfort amidst the chaos and desperation.

Chapter 5

Maxwell rode as the head of the group, his horse's hooves pounding steadily against the dirt path. The sun beat down on their backs as they traveled, the heat making Dorian squirm uncomfortably in his saddle. Cullen, who had only recently been released from his family's protective grasp, fidgeted awkwardly in his seat, trying to find a comfortable position. Dorian couldn't help but notice how inexperienced and out of place Cullen seemed, fresh off his father's leading strings and thrust into the world of the order.

"So," Dorian finally spoke up, startling Cullen, "why did a Duke's son like yourself choose to join the order? I highly doubt it was for the thrill of adventure," he said with a bored tone.

Cullen remained silent, keeping his eyes fixed on the road ahead. He had no desire to discuss being forced into joining the order by his ambitious father, who saw it as a way to bring fame and glory to their already powerful family name.

Dorian flashed a sly smile, always having a knack for reading people. "Or perhaps it was to impress a fair maiden or bring honor to your family?" he taunted, knowing these were often the most common reasons for knights to join the order.

Cullen shot Dorian a sharp look, silently confirming that he had hit the mark with his assumptions. Dorian couldn't help but feel a sense of pride at his accuracy. "Of course," he mused, waving his hand dismissively, "you wouldn't be the first one driven by such motivations. Countless members of our Order have joined for similar reasons." He paused and closed his eyes briefly before continuing, "I was simply curious if you had a more original reason for joining."

"And do you?" Cullen challenged, raising an eyebrow skeptically. It seemed hard to believe that anyone would join the order out of pure curiosity or for the sake of fun or boredom.

Dorian's gaze flickered to Maxwell, who rode stoically at the front of the group. "Our dear battlemage..." he said, indicating Maxwell with a nod, "joined because he was only a second son with no real purpose in his family's hierarchy. If needed, he could easily be recalled back to serve in their armor manufacturing business." Dorian's tone held a hint of admiration for Maxwell's cunning decision.

"His family owns all the mines and quarries that provide the metal for making armor?" Cullen asked incredulously.

Dorian shook his head, a small smile playing on his lips. "Not quite. They own the mines and send the raw materials to workshops where they are refined and forged into usable metals." It was clear that Maxwell had seen and experienced much in his time with the order. At forty years old, he still had a youthful vigor that also bore the weight of years of service.

In truth, Maxwell was a bastard child born out of an affair between his mother and a wealthy man from a neighboring province seeking to buy metals for making steel armor plating. When it became apparent that he did not resemble his mother's husband in any way, he was quickly given to the church and subsequently joined the order. Dorian was one of the few members who knew this information about Maxwell's past since they had worked closely together over the years, and it was hard not to learn someone's history in such close quarters.

Cullen's eyes narrowed as he looked at Dorian curiously, the corners of his mouth downturned in suspicion. "And what? You joined for the money?"

Dorian gave a sly smirk, his dark eyes glinting with mischief. "Well, I can't deny it's one of the many perks," he replied nonchalantly, his voice smooth and confident. Cullen couldn't help but feel annoyed by Dorian's cavalier attitude.

"But sadly no, my family doesn't approve of magic or anyone who practices it," Dorian continued, his tone turning cold and bitter. He urged his horse to pick up its pace, leaving Cullen to follow suit and walk alongside him.

"Any others?" Cullen asked, trying to maintain some semblance of politeness despite Dorian's condescending tone. But before he could finish his sentence, he was suddenly struck in the face by a low-hanging branch.

Dorian let out a hearty laugh, clearly amused by Cullen's misfortune. "Maybe I'll tell you sometime if you're lucky," he teased, giving Cullen an unsettling look that made him shiver. It was like being stared at by a predator eyeing its prey. Clearing his throat awkwardly, Cullen changed the subject in an attempt to make conversation. "Is this your first assignment too?" he asked politely.

Dorian chuckled, the sound insincere and mocking. "God no," he replied smugly. "Lord Keynes and I have been traveling extensively for ten years, fulfilling the Lord's work all over the continent." There was a hint of bitterness in Dorian's voice as he spoke about their supposed mission from God.

"We're outcasts," Dorian added with a smirk.

"Outcasts?" Cullen questioned incredulously. "Why?"

Before Dorian could answer, Maxwell interjected sharply. "All you need to know is we're too valuable for the Order to let go. So they send us out on 'assignments' to keep us occupied." His tone was cold and distant as if he was used to this kind of treatment from the Order.

Cullen knew it was common knowledge that each sect of the Order would give assignments to their members at their respective headquarters. But what Dorian and Maxwell were saying was highly unusual. "If you don't return to Kelke or Bestla, how do you receive your assignments?" he asked, his curiosity getting the better of him.

"All our missions are sent by messenger," Dorian answered with a dismissive wave of his hand. Cullen couldn't shake off the feeling that there was more to their story than they were letting on, but for now, he filed it away in the back of his mind.

Their conversation was cut short when Maxwell abruptly stopped his horse and looked up ahead. "What's wrong?" Cullen asked, following Maxwell's gaze.

"There's a body on the road," Maxwell replied gravely.

Dorian raised an eyebrow in disbelief. "A body? You must be mistaken, Amant." But Cullen could see the concern in Dorian's eyes as he dismounted his horse, prompting Cullen and Maxwell to do the same. Something strange was happening on this seemingly ordinary assignment, and Cullen couldn't help but feel a sense of unease creep over him.

Cullen's senses were on high alert as he scanned the area, his hand instinctively grasping the hilt of his sword. The hairs on his nape raised like pointed needles as he approached a lifeless body lying face down in the dirt. Maxwell squatted down to examine the corpse while Dorian circled around to inspect the wounds. Suddenly, Dorian's sharp intake of breath caught their attention. "What is it?" Cullen asked, joining Dorian on the other side of the body. Dorian pointed to the man's pointed ears, a clear sign that he was not human. "He was brutally murdered," Maxwell stated with a grim expression, pointing out multiple stab wounds and a slit throat. The trio looked around and saw more evidence of a vicious fight -

ropes cut and scattered, blood splatter on the trees, and more bodies strewn about.

They barely had time to process what they were seeing before arrows came flying from the trees, causing their horses to panic. Dorian immediately turned towards the source of the attack, his hands conjuring wisps of light to illuminate their surroundings. As more arrows flew towards them, Cullen took charge and shielded his companions with his shield while wielding his sword. "We don't want to fight!" He shouted out into the chaos.

But then Thamyris appeared, armed with two daggers, moving so quickly that Cullen could barely keep track of him. As they fought off their attackers, Maxwell spotted another elf aiming for Dorian from a nearby tree. Without hesitation, Maxwell rushed forward and pushed Dorian out of harm's way before unleashing a small ball of ice towards the assailant.

But their enemies were relentless, and soon they were outnumbered and overpowered. Maxwell used his powers to burn one of their attackers' faces, causing him to scream in agony before being taken down by an arrow aimed at Maxwell's head. Cullen's attention was drawn to a female elf who seemed to be leading the attack. Her bow pointed directly at him. "This ends now!" She screamed, her eyes filled with rage and determination.

Cullen and the elf's swords clashed in a fierce battle, their blades ringing like church bells. Fueled by rage, Dorian stepped between them and raised an enchanted scepter that glowed with blinding light at its tip.

"Stop this madness!" Dorian yelled, his voice cracking with emotion. He raised a hand adorned with a crackling scepter, its blinding light illuminating the tense scene."Don't you dare lay a hand on him!" His eyes burned with fire as he stared down the elf. Dorian's face flushed red with rage and eyes blazed with fire. Any slight move from either fighter and Dorian would unleash destructive magic upon them both.

The elf, taken aback by Dorian's sudden appearance and power, narrowed her eyes in defiance. "Drop your weapons!" she ordered, her voice dripping with venom. Cullen immediately obeyed, dropping his sword and shield to the ground. The tension in the air was palpable as two other warriors drew their bows, and another helped the injured elf to his feet.

Maxwell held out a calming hand towards Dorian. "It's alright, my friend," he said soothingly. "We must stay calm." After a tense moment, Dorian reluctantly lowered his hands.

As they stood facing each other, both sides finally got a clear look at their supposed enemies for the first time. The elves appeared savage and primitive to Dorian's refined tastes - long pointed ears, painted faces, and simple clothing of leather and cloth adorned with braids. But they also saw something familiar in their features – they too had pointed ears like the dead man. It was clear that these strangers had never encountered humans before.

A majestic red-tailed hawk perched on Thamyris' shoulder, causing him to turn and survey the group of men before him. His gaze landed on Cullen, then moved to the other two accompanying him. "My kin are not old enough to have encountered your kind before," he stated, pointing a long finger towards the ground, "but I have. And in that knowledge, I am aware of what you are capable of. The dead body of my fellow elf will bear witness to this truth."

"So what now? You're going to kill us?" Dorian retorted with a snide tone. Cullen looked at the man with the hawk, his curiosity piqued. "What are you?"

Thamyris turned his head in the direction of Cullen's voice. "We are elves, if you must know." Cullen noticed something the others hadn't - Thamyris was blind. "You're blind," he stated, prompting Dorian and Maxwell to also realize this fact.

"How can a blind man...I mean, elf," he corrected himself, "fight like that without sight?" he questioned, trying to hide his admiration for the elf's fighting skills. Thamyris straightened his posture, exuding confidence and pride. "My blindness is not a weakness."

The group of captured men followed their captors without a word. After what felt like hours, Cullen finally took notice of their surroundings. They were walking under a dense canopy of towering trees that seemed to stretch endlessly into the horizon. Occasional rays of sunlight filtered through the leaves, casting dappled light onto their path. Eventually, they arrived at a massive set of intricately carved doors nestled within one of the largest trees.

As they entered, they were met with an opulent interior that resembled a grand castle built within the living tree itself. Elegant stairways extended up towards higher levels while pillars carved from wood mimicked the trunks of trees. Wooden and stone bridges spanned over a babbling stream that wound through the sprawling space, illuminated by the soft glow of fireflies in ornate lanterns. Other elves bustled about their daily lives within this enchanting abode, using long branches and vines to move between different living spaces. In the center of it all sat a throne carved into the tree, fit for a queen.

After traversing through a network of pathways, they finally arrived at another set of grand doors adorned with intricate carvings. Suddenly, they were shoved roughly onto their knees, catching themselves with their hands. Cullen lifted his head to see a stunning woman standing before him. Like the others, she also had long pointed ears, but her hair was as white as fresh snow and her eyes glimmered an icy blue. She wore a regal circlet made of gold and silver with two crescent moons flanking either side of a full moon, crafted from glittering moonstone. Pearls and crystals hung delicately from large deer antlers on either side, connected to the circlet. Her robes were long and flowing, shimmering with shades of blue and silver, cinched at her waist by a slender silver belt.

The woman standing before them was adorned with intricate silver tribal paint, creating elegant patterns across her cheeks and over her nose. A crescent moon glistened on her forehead, its points reaching upwards towards the heavens. Three smaller silver dots were placed within the crescent, adding to the mystical aura surrounding her. "Where is my daughter?" she demanded.

Her question hung in the air as the three companions exchanged curious glances with each other. Cullen finally spoke up, his voice laced with confusion, "Who is your daughter?" Before he could finish speaking, he felt a sharp blow to the head.

"Don't be disrespectful to our beloved Queen Corianna!" scolded the woman, who seemed to be in charge.

Quickly realizing their mistake, Cullen and his friends lowered their heads in deference to the queen. But she raised a hand to stop her companion, an elf named Eline, from attacking further. "Stop, Eline," she commanded softly.

Eline obeyed and stepped back, still eyeing the humans warily. "I know of your kind, humans," said the queen in a calm yet authoritative tone.

Cullen met her gaze and spoke earnestly, "My lady, we have never been here before. We don't even know how we got here." The queen studied him for a moment before using her hand to signal for them to rise - a gesture they did reluctantly. Maxwell sensed compassion in the queen's eyes as she looked upon them. He could see that she was troubled by the disappearance of her daughter.

Meanwhile, Thamyris, one of the queen's sons, folded his arms and eyed them with suspicion. "These humans know nothing of us Mother - our ways or history... or even their own history, for that matter," he remarked coldly. The queen calmly held out her right hand to silence her son. "This forest is as old as time itself," she informed them. "It has no name, nor shall it ever. It is known simply as the Enchanted Forest."

Dorian, who had been observing the interaction closely, finally spoke up. "You and your people are truly elves?" he asked, his gaze shifting from the queen to Thamyris. "I've read about your kind," he added, making a point to show that not all humans were ignorant of past histories.

The queen gave a small smile at his words. "I gather your people only tell of us as legends," she stated softly.

Dorian sighed and nodded, "Mostly. Any book I could get my hands on said there was a war between man and elves. The elves abandoned the battlefield on the eve before the final decisive battle that would have determined everything and disappeared from the continent - presumed dead, I'd wager. It's never explained why or how."

The Queen gracefully motioned with her right hand for the men to rise to their feet. She led them into a grand room adorned with magnificent murals on the walls. The first mural they approached depicted a powerful man with deer antlers and cloven hooves of a fawn for feet, his muscular form exuding strength and gentleness.

The men were awestruck by the moving murals. They watched in wonder as a woman with long, flowing hair gazed lovingly at the man who held her tenderly in his arms. "Long ago, our world worshipped the God and the Goddess together. They brought balance to all things - the seasons, the world, and the sexes. One could not exist without the other. Together, they created and guided all races, and we lived in harmony."

The Queen turned back to face the men as she moved to another mural. This one showed humans turning away from the other races. "As mankind evolved, they stopped believing in the God and Goddess. Instead, they believed in only one male deity and an enigmatic female known as the Mother. They built their churches and demanded that all other races follow their ways."

Maxwell stood with his arms folded, listening intently. "And the other races refused?" he asked confidently.

The Queen's gaze rested on him before she moved to another mural. It depicted humans mercilessly whipping, killing, and burning members of other races. "Yes," she answered somberly, "they refused to give up their love for the God and Goddess. And so they were tortured, interrogated, or killed. But eventually, they rebelled against the humans, with me as their leader."

"You led the rebellion?" questioned Cullen, blushing under the Queen's gaze. Thamyris, who had been leaning against the doorway, stepped forward and answered for the Queen. "No, I led them. My mother was a figurehead for our cause."

The Queen turned to face the men again, her eyes filled with sadness. "On the eve of the final battle, the Goddess appeared to me and revealed another way." Thamyris leaned against the doorway with his right shoulder, one foot crossed over the other. The Queen moved to the last mural, which depicted the Goddess in the sky above a lush forest. "She showed us this forest and told us how it pained her to see her children fighting and dying in her name."

"In whose name?" asked Dorian, his arms folded skeptically. "Theirs or ours?"

The Queen's hand fell to her side. "Both," she answered honestly. "They go by many names and forms, and they hear all those who pray to them."

Dorian's eyes narrowed, struggling to comprehend this truth. "Let me make sure I understand correctly," he said, his voice tinged with disbelief, "You're telling us that our God is one and the same as yours?"

The Queen nodded regally. "Yes, and in their name, they refused to see their children fighting over what to call them. So they opened this forest to all who wished to love them as they were." She said, gesturing towards the last mural. In it, a magnificent forest sprawled under a starry sky, with figures of various races gathered within its borders.

"There are more than just elves and fairies here - there are orcs, goblins, minotaurs, and countless others. But our forest was not meant to remain in one place forever. It travels wherever it is needed most, waiting for the day when all of the God and Goddess' children can reunite and live in peace." She gazed mournfully at the mural depicting all races living in harmony within the enchanted forest.

Dorian's voice was laced with suspicion as he questioned, "So the forest reappeared here and someone else entered, killing one of your own and taking your daughter?" His right thumb and index finger held his chin in contemplation. Maxwell's eyes were fixed on Dorian, intrigued by the situation. "If that's true," he said slowly, "seeing someone like the princess would be truly exotic." He let out a heavy sigh, closing his eyes in frustration. "I hate to say it but I fear these men wouldn't just take her. They'd parade her to every town, looking to make a profit off her."

Eline stepped forward, determination in her voice. "Send us into the world, my Queen. We'll find Amalia and bring her back!"

The Queen raised a hand to silence Eline, shaking her head sadly. "No, Eline. You saw what these humans did to Tahl'rail. He was one of our best warriors." Her voice trembled with emotion.

Cullen piped up, curious about this Tahl'rail figure. "Who is Tahl'rail?"

The Queen's gaze fell upon the young knight, her eyes filled with sorrow. "He was one of our people's greatest warriors and my sister's beloved," Thamyris replied gravely. The others looked at him in shock. "We found you all admiring your handy work before we encountered you," Thamyris added, gesturing to their weapons. "We brought him home in hopes of finding Amalia soon."

Cullen could see the pain and anguish in the Queen's eyes and he felt a surge of determination within him. "We will find her," he promised firmly.

"What?" Dorian exclaimed incredulously, looking between Cullen and Maxwell.

Cullen met his gaze steadily. "We will find your Princess and bring her home."

Maxwell's eyes widened in realization. "But how will we find an elf in a world full of humans? We have no trail, no leads on where they might be going or what they might be doing to..." He trailed off as he caught sight of the Queen's sorrowful expression and realized that his words were not helping.

Cullen turned to face Dorian and Maxwell, his voice filled with conviction. "We are ambassadors of the Order of the Dragon. It is our duty to help those who cannot help themselves. We owe it to this poor girl to save her and bring her home."

Dorian and Maxwell exchanged a look, realizing that this may be their only chance to leave the forest with their heads intact.

Dorian let out a resigned sigh. "Fine. We will embark on this quest to find your Princess," he said with a shrug. "It can't be any worse than our original assignment, at any rate."

The Queen's gaze shifted between Cullen, Dorian, and Maxwell before finally resting on her son, Thamyris. "You will accompany these men, my son." She turned to leave the room, but not before casting one last glance over her shoulder at Thamyris. "There may still be hope for our world and our people yet."

Thamyris' eyes widened in shock as he looked at his mother, unable to finish his sentence. He pointed with his left hand at the group of men, clearly expressing his disapproval. The Queen gave him a stern look that silenced him. "Your elven ears possess abilities that they do not," she explained, "it will aid them in finding Amalia. As well as seeing through Kethinar's eyes."

Without another word, Thamyris stormed off, leaving the Queen to address her guests. "You may stay here for the night as my personal guests. I insist that you rest before continuing on your journey tomorrow."

Cullen bowed respectfully and placed his right fist over his heart. "Thank you, Your Majesty. We are here to assist you in any way we can."

Eline led the men to another room, announcing that it was time for dinner. Maxwell couldn't help but ask where they were going, to which Eline simply replied, "Dinner." They were guided into a grand dining hall illuminated by chandeliers made of deer antlers and candles adorning every surface. The dining table was long and elegant, set with fine plates, chalices, and delicate glass wine pitchers. The chairs were ornate and luxurious. Cullen had never seen such opulence before. The decor had an otherworldly quality to it. The ceiling seemed to be enchanted, changing colors and patterns according to the movement of the sun and moon outside.

At the moment, it emitted a beautiful dusk-like light with shades of blue, purple, pink, yellow, and orange. Faint stars twinkled in the distance, adding to the magical atmosphere. As they took to their seats, Dorian noticed a small stage where three elves played enchanting music on harps and violins.

Cullen couldn't help but feel a bit out of place in such a grand setting, but he couldn't deny how delicious the food was. The mutton was tender and flavorful, the vegetables crisp and fresh, and the fruits juicy and ripe. Baskets of various rolls were placed between the diners, offering an array of options.

He found himself sitting across a stunning Elf maiden with long black hair, sapphire blue eyes, and milky white skin. Her slender fingers delicately held her cutlery as she ate, her pouty lips giving off a faint hint of high cheekbones. "My name is Tiatria," she responded to Cullen's unspoken question.

Flustered, Cullen blushed and stammered, "I-I didn't say anything." Tiatria smiled knowingly. "Your thoughts were quite loud," she chuckled. "I can hear them."

Maxwell jabbed Cullen in the side with his elbow as a warning. "Be careful," he whispered, "she can read minds."

Tiatria giggled at their exchange and began to eat her meal gracefully.

After dinner, the men were escorted by a male elf to an underground chamber. Heavy wooden doors creaked open to reveal a series of hot springs. Steam rose from the pools, creating a dreamlike atmosphere.

Dorian let out a sigh of relief as he stepped into one of the springs. "Finally," he exclaimed with a content smile. "Some luxury." Without hesitation, he stripped down and submerged himself in the warm water. After a few moments of blissful relaxation, Dorian resurfaced, leaning against the edge of the spring with a coy smile on his face as he playfully flicked water at his companions.

"The warm, inviting waters beckon to you, Amant," Maxwell called out with a smile as he gestured towards the hot springs. Cullen looked at him curiously, "What does that mean?" Maxwell chuckled and replied, "I'll explain another time. For now, let's just enjoy this small luxury we have." Cullen followed Maxwell to the pools, taking in the sights and smells of their surroundings. The air was thick with the scent of flowers and herbs, a refreshing change from the musty castle halls they had been confined to for weeks.

As Cullen began to undress and join Maxwell in the spring, he couldn't help but notice the harsh scars covering his back. What could have caused such severe wounds? And why did he deserve them?

They settled into the steaming waters. Cullen couldn't help but feel a small sense of camaraderie with Maxwell and Dorian. "How long have you two been partners?" he asked, trying to make conversation.

Maxwell smiled and flicked his fingers through the water absentmindedly. There was more to that question than Cullen could ever know. His face flushed slightly as he glanced over at Dorian, giving him a sly smile before replying, "Why do you want to know?"

Cullen was taken aback by Dorian's response. "Well, if we're going to be working together, shouldn't we get to know each other more?" he questioned.

Dorian simply shrugged and replied, "All you need to know is that once our assignment is complete, we won't be seeing each other again."

Maxwell could see the confusion and disappointment in Cullen's eyes, so he decided to speak up instead. "I think what

Dorian means is that we were only assigned together because you are a newly appointed knight. He and I happened to be nearby and were familiar with the area, so we were chosen to ensure the success of your assignment."

"But why won't we work together again?" Cullen probed further.

"Because we will all be given new assignments," Maxwell explained. Cullen nodded, still not fully understanding this aspect of their jobs.

"Is that a common thing for knights?" Cullen asked, trailing his fingers through the hot water and feeling its soothing effects on his muscles.

Maxwell leaned back against the edge of the spring, resting his arms above the water. He watched as Dorian relaxed into the water, a contented smile on his lips as he laid a towel over his eyes. Maxwell turned to look at Cullen, asking with genuine interest, "So are you excited to join the Knights?"

Cullen's expression turned solemn and he sighed, "Not really. My father enlisted me when I was just ten years old after he was badly injured and could no longer serve himself. But my true passion lies in writing and in poetry honestly."

Maxwell could sense there was more to Cullen's story, but he didn't pry any further. Instead, he watched as Cullen gazed into his own reflection on the water's surface, likely thinking about his looming marriage to Princess Edith once their assignment was completed. The thought alone made Cullen's stomach churn with dread and anxiety.

)o(

Thamyris' eyes burned with fury as he confronted his mother, the Queen, in her opulent cathedral. "Father's death was a result of his own foolishness! He challenged Tahl'rail without considering the consequences," he spat, his voice dripping with venom. His mother turned her head slightly, gazing out the cathedral window with tears in her eyes. "Did you touch him?" she asked, her voice trembling with fear and desperation. Thamyris shook his head in confusion. "Yes, I touched him. That's how I know what happened. Father caught Tahl'rail and Amalia together, and it drove him into a blind rage."

Tahl'rail was fully aware of his father's wrath and knew that anyone who dared to lay a hand on his sister without permission would meet a swift end. But his father had underestimated Tahl'rail's strength and determination. Ever since their escape into the woods, the king had become obsessed with keeping their people safe at any cost, even if it meant sacrificing their elvishness.

"What about Tahl'rail? Did you touch him? Did you see anything about your sister?" The queen pressed, her voice filled with desperation.

Tahl'rail sighed deeply, feeling the weight of responsibility weighing heavily on his shoulders. "No, I haven't touched him. I don't know anything," he admitted reluctantly. The queen's tears streamed down her face as she stared out at the moon, a symbol of hope and guidance for their people. "Go to him," she whispered brokenly. "Find out the truth, and then we can begin our search for Amalia."

Thamyris nodded, his heart heavy with the urgency and concern in his mother's voice. He left her chambers, the rich tapestries and gilded furniture fading into darkness as he made his way through the palace. His fingers brushed against the cold stone walls, guiding him towards Tahl'rail's location. Thamyris couldn't help but wonder what had happened to his beloved sister. The thought of her in danger or hurt sent a chill down his spine. He knew his mother was on edge, her once regal demeanor now replaced with frantic worry. With her husband dead and now her daughter missing, it was enough to drive anyone to the brink of madness. Thamyris quickened his pace, determined to find his sister and bring her back safely to their grief-stricken family.

Chapter 6

as Thamyris stepped into the courtyard, different heavy smells filled his nostrils, mixed with the scent of rosewood flowers: moon lilies, star jasmine and stargazer lilies. The sweet aroma of flowers made an attempt to mask the tragedy that had taken place. The funeral pyre for his father had been constructed in the center of the courtyard; once lit, its flames would reach high into the sky. The mournful cries of his people would echo, adding to the solemn atmosphere.

Thamyris approached a male elf who was wrapping the body in linen. The elf was taller than any elf at six foot five inches and what he estimated was two hundred and fifty pounds. Long shoulder-length auburn hair that seemed to have streaks of sunlight running through it flew wild and freely. It fell in gentle waves around his shoulders and framed his strong jawline. He had soft but piercing amber-brown eyes, and he looked at his Prince with concern. Most elves said his gentle eyes added a touch of softness and warmth, which contradicted his rough exterior. He had a sun-kissed tan, a testament to his time spent in the wilds. He wore large leather bands around his biceps, highlighting a touch of strength and masculinity. He wore a leather corset that hugged his body beautifully. It showed off his broad, perfectly toned and chiseled chest without being overly bulky and was form-fitting.

Thamyris could sense the heavy, palpable weight of grief that hung in the air, etching itself onto every elf's anguished face. Though his sightless eyes could not see the tears streaming down their cheeks as they worked, he could feel it in their slow and deliberate movements. The very atmosphere seemed to be mourning with them, clinging to every breath and movement like a shroud. They all knew Thal'rail since their childhood. He was deeply admired among them – hence, his loss was felt by all. As Thamyris stood there, a faint scent reached his nose - one of leather and earth mixed with a hint of something sweet and floral. It was a familiar smell, one that only one elf possessed. "Where is Tahl'rail, Ásbjǫrn?" he asked, his voice barely above a whisper. Ásbjǫrn had been Thamyris' friend since childhood and never once thought of Thamyris' blindness as a disability - instead, he saw it as an opportunity for strength and wisdom to shine through. He was also a priest in the temple of Cernunnos, where they both sought solace in times of sorrow, finding comfort in the tranquil beauty of nature that surrounded them.

Ásbjǫrn's head snapped up at his words, tears glistening in his Amber brown eyes. He could see the pain and exhaustion etched across his Prince's handsome face were a reflection of the turmoil inside him, visible for all to see. The dim lighting from the setting sun cast shadows across his features, highlighting the creases and lines that spoke of a life filled with struggle.

"He's here, my prince," Ásbjǫrn said, his low and powerful voice resonating through Thamyris' body like a soothing balm. His hand, warm and calloused from years of training as a warrior, rested gently on Thamyris' back, guiding him towards the grand table where Tahl'rail lay.

With an innate understanding of Thamyris' abilities, Ásbjǫrn knew not to touch his skin directly when using his gift of reading people through touch. Instead, he carefully directed Thamyris towards the partially covered figure lying before them. As they drew closer, Thamyris could feel a sense of anticipation building within him, causing his fingers to tremble with anxiety.

"Is he wrapped or unwrapped?" Thamyris asked anxiously, unable to contain his curiosity any longer.

"His head is unwrapped," the elf answered quietly from behind him, his voice laced with concern and caution. The air around them seemed to thicken with tension as they prepared to uncover the mysteries cloaked within Tahl'rail's still form. The weight of responsibility settled heavily on Thamyris' shoulders as he braced himself for what was to come.

With trembling fingers, Thamyris slowly moved up Tahl'rail's battered body until his fingertips reached his friend's face. Memories of their time together flooded Thamyris' mind - flashes of laughter and camaraderie within moments of intense pain and suffering at the hands of his enemies. The horror and grief washed over him like a tidal wave, threatening to consume him in despair as he saw humans manhandling his beloved sister. Unable to hold back any longer, tears streamed down his face as he stumbled back in shock, unable to comprehend the sight before him.

Ásbjǫrn rushed to Thamyris' side as his knees buckled and he fell onto his butt with a thud. Ásbjǫrn knelt beside the devastated Prince. His strong hand gently rested on Thamyris' back, offering comfort and support in this moment of anguish. "Your grace, are you alright?" Ásbjǫrn's voice was filled with concern and worry, mirroring the emotions etched on his features. As other guards and advisors rushed to their Prince, Ásbjǫrn held out his hand, signaling for them to stop. "It's alright! I have him!" His words were spoken with unwavering strength and determination, a beacon of hope amidst the chaos surrounding them.

Thamyris stumbled around in stunned silence, his mind swirling with a torrent of emotions as he struggled to process what had just happened. His legs felt like jelly, refusing to support him as he tried to stand up. Thankfully, Ásbjǫrn's steady arms caught him and helped him regain his balance as he rose to his feet. They made their way back towards Thamyris' mother, who anxiously awaited them; he felt like every step was an effort. His heart raced with fear and confusion, still reeling from the shocking scene that had unfolded before him.

Finally reaching his mother, Thamyris collapsed onto the ground, his body shaking uncontrollably. His mother knelt beside him, her grip on his knees tight and desperate. The terror on her face mirrored the chaotic turmoil inside Thamyris' mind. "What did you see?" she pleaded, her voice trembling with fear and desperation. "Please, tell me what happened to my daughter!" Her words hung in the air like a thick fog, enveloping the scene in a sense of foreboding.

Taking a deep breath, Thamyris braced himself as he began to recount the harrowing events that had transpired before him. Every detail resurfaced as he spoke, reliving the terror and horror all over again.

)o(

After indulging in the rejuvenating hot springs, Cullen and his companions were each escorted to their own lavish individual rooms. Cullen's breath caught in his throat as he took in the magnificence of his surroundings. The room was grander than any he had ever seen, even larger than King Richard's. A magnificent bed, intricately carved from white oak, stood proudly in one corner. Its ornate carvings depicted scenes of mythical creatures and brave warriors. A luxurious canape hung over the bed, adding an air of elegance to the space.

Cullen took in every detail of the room - the dresser filled with neatly folded clothes, the wardrobe closet stocked with fine garments, a velvet-upholstered lounge chair, a small table with a pitcher and basin for washing up. But it was the window at the end of the room that caught his attention. As he pulled back the sheer drapes, he gasped at the breathtaking view before him. From this height above the trees, he could see all of Amalthea and even glimpses of other kingdoms in the distance.

High above the treeline, Amalthea spread out below him. At certain angles, he could even catch glimpses of neighboring kingdoms. Just as he was admiring this wondrous sight, a loud rumbling shook the earth beneath him. He could not help but wonder what could have caused such a disturbance.

Curiosity getting the better of him, Cullen turned from the window and decided to explore this wonderful castle, if one could call it that. It was made from the inside of a massive tree. He walked out of his room and set off down the corridor and stairs. However, despite his best efforts, he soon found himself hopelessly lost within the vast palace. He wandered aimlessly through various halls and rooms, marveling at their opulence. He stumbled upon a vast chamber filled with statues and paintings of ethereal elven women.

Each statue was exquisitely crafted, capturing the unique beauty of its subject. However, one particular statue caught Cullen's eye. This woman was depicted as the Mother, with arms outstretched and holding a large bowl of water on a simple stand. Her serene expression and graceful features drew Cullen in, beckoning to him with a gentle smile.

Just then, a beam of moonlight shone down from an opening in the ceiling and illuminated the statue. As if by magic, the light transformed the water in the bowl, creating a perfect reflection of the full moon that was currently shining above them. Cullen could not help but wonder if this woman had a name among her people.

Suddenly, a soft laugh echoed through the chamber, causing Cullen to turn around in surprise. To his amazement, he saw Tiatria standing behind him, a secretive smile playing on her lips as she held her hands behind her back. She gazed at the statue for a moment before speaking in a hushed tone.

"Danu," she said simply.

Cullen furrowed his brow in confusion. "What? Who is Danu?"

Tiatria smiled knowingly. "The statue. You were wondering if she had a name."

As Cullen approached her, Tiatria turned to face him fully. "She is the Goddess Danu," she explained. "The deity of all magic."

Cullen's mind reeled with this new information. "Is Danu your Goddess as well?" he asked.

Tiatria gave him a small smile, her eyes sparkling with ancient knowledge. "Danu is just one of her many names."

"How many names does she have?" he asked.

Tiatria's voice echoed softly through the grand hall as she walked among the statues, her fingers lightly tracing the delicate features of each one. "These are the different representations of our goddess," she explained to Cullen. "Each one embodies a unique aspect of her being."

Cullen followed Tiatria's gaze and marveled at the intricate stonework that depicted the goddess in all her forms. The statues ranged from ethereal beauties with flowing gowns to fierce warriors with weapons raised high. But what struck him most was the diversity among them - some had long hair and some were bald, some were muscular some slender, some had wings while others had tails. It was a reminder that their goddess was free from human ideals or expectations.

"What does she do? Does she have any powers?" Cullen could not help but ask.

Tiatria smiled knowingly as she turned to face one particular statue. "Our goddess is represented by the three phases of the moon," she began. "The waxing moon represents the Maiden, embodying beauty, fertility, and innocence. The full moon represents the Mother, representing nurturing love, creation, and the cycle of life. And finally, the waning moon represents the Crone, symbolizing aging with grace, transformation, and wisdom."

Cullen listened intently, fascinated by this perspective of a powerful and multi-faceted female deity. To honor and celebrate all aspects of womanhood, it was a stark contrast to what he had been taught about women being solely vessels for men's needs.

"Are there statues of your god?" he asked Tiatria, curious to see how their version differed from his own.

With a kind smile, Tiatria took his hand and led him to another chamber within the temple. This room was just as grand as the previous one, filled with statues of elven men in various poses and attire. In the center stood a striking statue of an elven man with stag-like horns, his lower half adorned with fur and cloven hooves. His hands were folded against his chest, exuding both strength and compassion. Cullen couldn't help but be drawn to this depiction of their god.

"I saw a perfect image of the moon in the goddess' bowl. Why doesn't it appear on him?" Cullen asked, noticing the lack of lunar symbolism on the god's statue.

Tiatria smiled, her eyes glittering with knowledge. "The moon represents our goddess, while the sun represents our god," she explained. "When the sun shines upon his horns, it creates a ball of light between them - symbolizing birth, growth, and the raw power of nature. Our god is the very essence of the changing seasons and all that is tied to it."

Cullen wondered if his own father would understand or appreciate this view of nature and divinity. He knew that in his father's eyes, anything deemed heretical or contradicting church teachings would be destroyed without hesitation. But as he looked around at this enchanted place and listened to Tiatria speak, he could not help but feel a sense of enchantment and awe wash over him. It was a reminder that there was so much more to life and faith than what he had been taught.

He felt a heavy weight of disappointment settle in his chest as he thought about his father's plans for him. His father, always more concerned with maintaining their family's reputation and status, had arranged for Cullen to marry Princess Edith of Amalthea. Despite being promised to such a high society, Cullen found himself dreading the thought of spending his life with someone so shallow and materialistic. She was beautiful, but her beauty seemed to pale in comparison to the vibrant and genuine aura of Tiatria, who stood by his side holding his left hand without him even realizing it.

Cullen's eyes were drawn to Tiatria's piercing blue eyes, like staring into the depths of the ocean on a stormy day. In that moment, all thoughts of his father's expectations faded away and he found himself captivated by the elf standing beside him. He felt a sense of ease and calm wash over him, as if he had been drifting out to sea and finally found solid ground again.

"How did you find me?" Cullen asked softly, still entranced by Tiatria's presence.

"I heard you calling for help earlier," she replied with a gentle smile.

Cullen blushed at the thought of her hearing his cries for help but also felt grateful that she had come to his rescue. As they walked towards an archway that led out of the forest, Tiatria offered her right hand to guide him back to his room.

Cullen's mind raced with conflicting thoughts as they walked together - thoughts of his engagement with someone he had no desire to be with, thoughts of his inappropriate attraction towards Tiatria, and thoughts of her seemingly magical abilities.

"Do you read everyone's mind?" Cullen asked curiously.

Tiatria chuckled, "No, just those whom I am most curious about."

As they emerged from the forest into a clearing, Cullen was awestruck by the sight. The trees and bushes seemed to illuminate themselves with a kaleidoscope of colors, each taking its turn to shine. Tiatria watched with amusement as Cullen's childlike wonder took over.

"Fairies," she explained as little orbs of light flew up into the air around them. "Each fairy is a different color, representing one of the four elements - fire, air, earth, and water." But there was a fifth element that Cullen had never heard of - spirit.

"How many elements are there?" he asked with genuine curiosity.

"Five," Tiatria replied.

"But you only named four...what's the fifth?" Cullen pressed for more information.

"Spirit," Tiatria answered with a gentle smile. "And it is said that white fairies represent this element, the purest of all. They are rare and only appear to those with the purest of souls."

Suddenly feeling drawn to her even more than before, Cullen gazed at Tiatria in awe. And for a brief moment, he wondered that her presence here was not merely a coincidence but perhaps something more magical at work.

)o(

Maxwell's eyes widened as he took in the grandeur of his quarters. The bedroom was palatial, with high ceilings and ornately decorated walls. He had never lived in such luxury before, having spent most of his travels cramped in small rooms with just enough space for a bed and a trunk. The emptiness of the room felt particularly poignant without Dorian by his side. Throughout their years of travel, they could only afford shared rooms with one or two beds if they were lucky. Most often, they were stuck with twin beds, making it difficult to get a good night's sleep. Inns rarely offered discounts to members of the order, assuming they were well-off due to their affiliation with the crown. But in reality, most were living on meager stipends and whatever donations or treasures they received from those they helped.

As Maxwell explored his new room, he noticed a balcony attached to it. Curious about the sound of drums and male voices singing in a foreign language, he stepped out onto the balcony. In a small clearing below, there was a formation of rocks arranged in a half circle, with a large gold statue of a God perched on top of a nearby cliff. The intricate details of the statue were mesmerizing - the God sat upon a rock, holding a bow at rest. A pile of rocks acted as reinforcement for the cliff behind it, while an altar made of stone and bone stood just six feet away. Wooden poles adorned with windchimes made from bone, leather, and wood completed the scene.

Maxwell could not help but notice how different this part of the city was compared to the rest. It exuded a raw, primal energy that represented nature's masculinity. Never had he seen such a place - was it a temple? A sacred site for rituals and worship? His gaze then fell upon Thamyris in the center of it all. The elf's hair was unbound, cascading down past his buttocks. He wore a headdress adorned with antlers and leather pieces with dangling beads. A hawk's cry pierced through the air, causing Maxwell to look up and spot Kethinar - Thamyris' hawk - circling above them in approval.

As Kethinar landed on Thamyris' shoulder, Maxwell could not help but take in the sight before him. The elf was shirtless, revealing a slender yet toned frame with firm muscles. He still wore his leather pants, but his feet were bare. From his vantage point, Maxwell could see that the elf's body was taut and well-defined. It became clear to him that the elves were performing some kind of ritual - perhaps for war, purification, or prayers for safe travels. It was a beautiful and sacred scene to witness like getting a glimpse into the private spiritual practices of another culture.

Unbeknownst to Maxwell, Thamyris had been sent to this temple by the Queen to calm his mind on Ásbjǫrn's advice. The music and ceremony seemed to soothe his soul as he took deep breaths and let go of the traumatic memories that plagued him.

From the humble hut nestled against the steep, rocky cliff emerged a massive grizzly bear. Maxwell's heart raced as he watched in awe, expecting the elf to flee in terror. But to his surprise, the elf stood tall and unafraid before the magnificent creature. As it approached, the bear seemed to exude an air of regal power that Maxwell had never witnessed in any other bear. And as it drew closer, its sheer size and strength were almost overwhelming. Yet, instead of attacking, the bear suddenly reared up on its hind legs with a fluid grace that was both mesmerizing and terrifying. Its fur began to glow with a dazzling white light, nearly blinding all who were fortunate (or unfortunate) enough to witness it.

When the light abetted, Maxwell realized the bear really was not a bear; it was another elf, that too, a magnificent one. Before Thamyris was another elf, it was Ásbjǫrn. Unexpectedly, Maxwell was impressed by the elf's weight and size, to say the least. He wore his large leather bands around his biceps, highlighting his strength and masculinity. No shirt! He showed off his broad, perfectly toned, and chiseled chest. He wore a pair of long brown leather pants with ornate markings around the waist. He seemed not to be wearing any shoes, perhaps to feel the cold surface of the earth under his toes.

Understanding Thamyris's blindness, Ásbjǫrn softly extended his hands, offering them for the elf to hold or touch as he pleased. Thamyris' fingers brushed against Ásbjǫrn's rough, weathered palms, evidence of years spent laboring in the wilds of the forests. The contrast between their hands was striking; a sense of warmth and understanding flowed between them despite their differences in appearance. It was a simple gesture that spoke volumes about their connection. Donning a headdress adorned with regal antlers and intricate face paint, Ásbjǫrn exuded an aura of wisdom and ancient knowledge. The patterns on his face seemed to shift and change as if imbued with magic. Maxwell could feel the potent energy radiating from the elf and could only imagine that he held a revered position as a priest or shaman among his people.

The drums echoed through the air, their hypnotic rhythm filling every corner of the wood; a palpable energy thickened the atmosphere. The priest raised a wooden bowl to the sky and began singing in a language unfamiliar to Maxwell. Even Kethinar joined in with his own soaring cries, adding to the ethereal quality of the ritual.

The male elves danced wildly to the primal beat of the drums. They adorned their heads with fearsome deer skulls and painted their bare bodies. Their voices carried on the wind, merging with the haunting song of the priest. As the drums grew more intense, the priest dipped his fingers into the bowl filled with a deep red substance - perhaps paint, wine, or even blood - and made markings on Thamyris' chest.

With each passing moment, Thamyris appeared to sink deeper into a trance-like state, his head tilting back as if drawn towards the radiant moon above. This foreign yet mesmerizing ritual left Maxwell in awe, wondering if these were common practices among the earliest inhabitants of Elara. Did humans also partake in such ceremonies before discovering God and Mother's love?

Lost in thought, Maxwell made his way to Dorian's room and knocked on the door. After receiving no response, he cautiously entered and quickly realized that Dorian was not there. Frustrated, Maxwell sighed and rubbed his chin in contemplation. Where could Dorian have gone? Was he scheming an escape plan? A voice behind him answered his unspoken questions, "Your friend is in the library."

Maxwell turned his gaze towards the hallway and noticed Thamyris leaning against the wall. His right hand rested casually on his hip while a small smile played across his lips. In the dim light, Maxwell could not help but admire the flawless complexion of the elf. It seemed to take on a faint luminescent glow, almost as if it were made of moonlight itself. The intricate red markings on Thamyris' chest caught Maxwell's eye, resembling ancient runes or symbols of some sort. Strands of hair fell in front of Thamyris' eyes, adding to the mysterious allure of his appearance. Maxwell noticed that even the facial paint seemed to have a subtle shimmer in the dark. And when Thamyris' sight met his, Maxwell felt like he was being enveloped by their intense gaze. Despite being blind, there was a certain magic in Thamyris's eyes that Maxwell had never seen before.

As much as he wanted to keep staring into those captivating eyes, Maxwell forced himself to break away and clear his throat as he left the room.

"Thank you," he said politely while passing by Thamyris.

"Are you always in the habit of spying on other people's rituals?" Thamyris asked with a hint of amusement in his voice.

Maxwell stopped in his tracks, feeling his cheeks heat up from embarrassment. He gave a nervous smile and crossed his arms, trying to appear nonchalant. "How did you know?" he asked cautiously, narrowing his eyes at Thamyris.

"Kethinar saw you as he circled around," Thamyris revealed calmly, "Whatever he sees, I see as well."

Maxwell marveled at this seemingly magical ability, which explained how Thamyris could navigate through life despite being blind. But he knew that was not the real reason Thamyris had caught him observing their ritual.

"Is there any harm in observing another culture's religious proceedings?" Maxwell asked, trying to divert the conversation.

Thamyris' eyes narrowed, seeing through Maxwell's clever attempt to avoid the question. He could sense the human's discomfort and knew he wasn't being entirely honest about his reasons for observing. After all, it was unheard of for someone from Maxwell's world to tolerate or even show interest in their rituals. Thamyris himself had been persecuted for his beliefs before. But after years of serving the order and witnessing firsthand the atrocities committed in its name, Maxwell could not bring himself to blindly follow their teachings anymore. In his heart, he knew that true service meant following one's conscience and doing what was right, regardless of traditions or dogma.

Maxwell observed Thamyris with curiosity. He marveled at how the elf effortlessly navigated through the palace without any need for sight, his movements graceful and sure. In contrast, Maxwell felt like he was stumbling through a maze, constantly bumping into walls and furniture. "How do you do it?" he asked in amazement.

Thamyris smiled knowingly, his annoyance for humans evident in his expression. "This is my home," he replied simply. "I know every corner and crevice." He continued to walk ahead, descending a sweeping staircase and causing Maxwell to watch in awe.

Chapter 7

Dorian stood in what appeared to be a vast library, filled with rows upon rows of towering bookcases made of rich oak wood and adorned with intricate carvings of twisted and gnarled branches. His fingers grazed the spines of ancient tomes as he eagerly searched for knowledge. To learn in such an esteemed and mysterious place was a tempting prospect that Dorian could not resist.

As Maxwell joined him in the library, he found Dorian engrossed in a particular book, his left hand tracing the titles on a nearby shelf. "A bit of nighttime reading?" Maxwell quipped as he approached him, then leaned against a nearby bookcase and crossed his arms.

Dorian turned to face him, holding a thick tome in one hand while the other moved along the spines of various books on a shelf. "Did you know that the elves possess the earliest known histories of our land?" he said with fervor. "They have recorded everything from the beginning, including rituals and holidays celebrated by all races."

Maxwell leaned against a nearby bookcase, arms folded across his chest. "Like what?"

Dorian's excitement grew as he flipped through the pages. "Well, there was Beltane, for instance."

"Beltane? What is that?"

With a mischievous smirk, Dorian began to explain. "It's when the God and Goddess consummate their union during what we call, May Day festivities. Legend has it that God dies several months later during Mabon, in which he gives his body to the land. In doing so, his body gives the nourishment the land needs to see us through the final harvest before winter comes. By leaving his seed within the Goddess it ensures that he may be reborn anew."

Maxwell scoffed in disbelief. "Born a new? How is that possible?"

Dorian's grin widened. "The elves believe that there is life after death and one can be born anew. And the God's death and rebirth only compounds that belief all the more."

Maxwell could not help but be entertained by Dorian's passion and knowledge. He was undoubtedly one of the most skilled archivists and historians in Kalke, able to decipher forgotten languages and reveal long-lost secrets of dark magic if pressed.

"So how do we mortals celebrate this union?" Maxwell asked with feigned disinterest.

"That's the best part," Dorian answered, "we celebrate it by engaging in wild and passionate lovemaking wherever possible - in the forest, fields of wheat, barns - you name it! It was said that during Beltane, it was hard to tell which child belonged to whom. And any child born on the closest day to the new God's birth was considered blessed."

Dorian snapped the old leather-bound book shut with his left hand, its pages worn and yellowed with age. He held out his right hand to Maxwell, shaking his head incredulously. "Can you believe that such a thing even existed, Amant?" Dorian's eyes sparkled with excitement as he spoke. "That's why some humans possess magic remnants of ancient elves and other magical beings."

Maxwell chuckled wistfully, envisioning a world where people lived freely without the constraints of organized religion. "Sounds like they had more fun in those days," he mused. "Not like now, with all the restrictions and rules enforced by the church." He shook his head, imagining a life where people celebrated and indulged in earthly pleasures without the fear of divine retribution.

With a dramatic flourish, Dorian used his index finger to point at Maxwell. "But that's why it's frowned upon now," he declared passionately. "We're forced to fight for our lords in God's name as a penance for this supposed sin!" His face lit up as he grabbed another book from the shelf, eager to share more knowledge with Maxwell.

"And look," he exclaimed, flipping through the pages of a thick tome, "there are books full of spells and rituals! Magic was once openly practiced by all, not just reserved for the elite or deemed 'forbidden' by the church!"

Maxwell wrapped his arms around Dorian's waist from behind and rested his chin on Dorian's shoulder. "As fascinating as this is, my love," he whispered in Dorian's ear, "it's time for bed." Dorian turned to face him, a look of irritation crossing his features. "I can't sleep now," he protested fervently. "There are still so many books left to read!" His voice trailed off as he gazed longingly at the shelves upon shelves of ancient tomes.

Maxwell could not help but smile at Dorian's passion and dedication to learning, even if it meant staying up all night to finish. "I'm afraid you won't have time," he gently reminded him. "We need to leave at first light."

Dorian twitched his nose in annoyance - he hated it when someone doubted his abilities. "I only have one more bookcase to get through," he insisted stubbornly.

Maxwell's eyebrows shot up in pure surprise, his mouth dropping open in shock. "What? There are hundreds of books here, you cannot have read them all! It's not possible!" His eyes roamed the towering shelves surrounding them, filled to the brim with dusty tomes and ancient manuscripts.

Dorian's lips curved into a small smile, his gaze never leaving the pages of the book he held in his hands. "It is possible, trust me. I cannot leave this place without delving into every history, every bit of magic, or every piece of knowledge that can be found within these walls. I must learn it all!"

Maxwell could not hide his confusion as he struggled to comprehend how Dorian could accomplish such a monumental task with such ease. Despite spenidng many years together, there were still some secrets that Dorian kept close to his chest only. As an Acolyte, he had been trained in the art of speed reading and gathering information quickly. He had also learned spells that allowed him to absorb knowledge from any book he touched, making his quest for knowledge even more efficient.

As Maxwell watched Dorian return to his book, completely lost in its words and teachings, he knew there was no way he could pry him away from the shelves. When Dorian was this focused on learning, nothing could break his intense concentration except for reaching the final page and reading the last word. With a sigh, Maxwell turned and made his way back towards the stairs, leaving Dorian lost in the pages of history.

The warm glow of flickering firelight danced across Maxwell's face as he rested against the castle wall. His gaze was drawn to a somber scene unfolding before him. Stepping out of the grand structure, he emerged into a wide-open space, feeling small in comparison to the vastness of the night sky above. Two colossal fires roared in the center of the courtyard, their flames hungrily consuming funeral pyres. As he approached, he could see the Queen standing with tears in her eyes, her expression heavy with grief.

Cullen caught sight of the glowing light from the burning pyres as he ascended the stairs with Tiatria by his side. Curiosity piqued, he followed Maxwell's gaze and walked towards the spectacle. The soft strains of mournful hymns filled the air, tugging at everyone's heartstrings with a sense of sorrow. Thamyris stood near his mother, his face painted with red symbols and adorned with an impressive set of elk antlers. Beads and braids decorated his hair, giving him an almost ethereal appearance.

His face was stoic, and Cullen could not help but wonder if he was secretly mourning inside. Perched on Thamyris' shoulder was Kethinar, the bird tilting its head from side to side as if trying to take in every detail.

Tiatria stood behind Cullen and Maxwell, bowing her head in respect for her fallen King and kin. Tears rolled down from her eyes as she felt overwhelming sadness and pain wash over her. But as she glanced at the humans gathered there, mourning their own losses, a glimmer of hope sparked within her. Perhaps there was still a chance for their race to overcome their struggles and thrive once again.

Cullen knelt before the Queen and Thamyris, representing the Order of the Dragon. He struggled to hold back his tears as he spoke. "On behalf of our order, we offer our deepest condolences for all that you have suffered," he said with a quavering voice filled with genuine empathy.

"Well, well," said Dorian with a smug smirk, causing Maxwell to turn and look behind himself. "It seems our little soldier is growing up." Maxwell paid no attention to Dorian's words. It reminded him of his youth when he believed in the clear-cut boundaries between right and wrong before life showed him the blurry lines and gray areas.

)o(

The peaceful stillness of the night was broken only by the distant symphony of chirping crickets and the sparkling stars scattered across the inky sky. All creatures slumbered soundly, wrapped in the comforting embrace of darkness —all except for Thamyris, perched atop a grassy knoll near a grand oak tree. His intense gaze was fixed upon the crackling fire he had expertly built, its flames dancing and swaying in the gentle breeze. Their warm light cast playful shadows that seemed to dance along with the serene music of the forest. By his side, perched proudly, his faithful companion Kethinar, a regal red-tailed hawk, on a sturdy branch. He had just finished his meal of a plump mouse, his sharp eyes glinting in the firelight.

This was Thamyris' secret haven, a place where he could escape and ponder everything - from thoughts of his beloved sister, Tahl'rail, to the daunting tasks that lay ahead of him – join humans of all things in an attempt to find and save his sister. With his father's death, he had been appointed as the new High Priest of Cernunnos' temple, and now he carried the weight of spiritual responsibility of others on his shoulders.

Lost in thought, Thamyris' pointed ears twitched at the sound of approaching footsteps. "Looks like you're losing your touch Ásbjǫrn," he called out into the darkness with a smirk. Turning his head to greet his old friend as he emerged from the foliage of the wood, Thamyris settled back down next to him with a wry smile. "I hear you'll be setting off with these humans come morning."

The words hung in the air between them, heavy with both excitement and uncertainty. Tomorrow, Thamyris would embark on an adventure unlike any other, one that would test his abilities and shape the destinies of all forever.

Thamyris released a heavy sigh, his heart sinking at the thought of embarking on this journey with a group of humans. "Yes," he replied wearily, knowing that this was his duty as prince or perhaps as king if his mother wished it.

Ásbjǫrn's lips twisted into an amused smirk as he observed Thamyris' reluctance towards human companionship. "Do you require the assistance of a bear to aid you on your journey?" He offered jokingly.

Despite his lingering anxiety, Thamyris could not help but let out a small chuckle at his friend's sense of humor. "No, my friend," he replied, trying to suppress a smile. "But I do need someone to oversee the temple in my absence."

He lowered his head and ran a hand through his hair, feeling frustrated with the weight of responsibility placed upon him since his father's passing. "As the new high priest, it is my duty to ensure that the temple runs smoothly, even when I am away. And I trust no one more than you, Ásbjǫrn."

The surprise in Ásbjǫrn's eyes was evident as their gazes met. "I am honored, your Grace," he stammered out, bowing slightly. "I will do my utmost to fulfill this role to the best of my abilities." Thamyris smiled warmly, placing a hand on his friend's shoulder. "I have no doubts about that."

Using the sharp, keen gaze of Kethinar, Thamyris observed his friend with great interest. He noticed the subtle flush of color on Ásbjǫrn's cheeks and the agitated energy radiating from him. It was as if he were a predator, ready to pounce on his prey but unsure of what exactly it was that he desired. "Is something troubling you?" Thamyris asked in a gentle tone, studying Ásbjǫrn's eyes, which seemed to flicker constantly between him and the edges of the forest. It was no secret that Ásbjǫrn had a deep connection to nature, his heart and soul yearning for the wilds of the forest. There were times when he would vanish for days, weeks, or even months, seeking refuge and freedom among the trees and creatures who called the forest their home. For Ásbjǫrn, nature was a delicate balance of light and darkness, both essential for the well-being and harmony of the world.

With a quick flick of his pale amber-brown eyes, Ásbjǫrn diverted his gaze and stammered in flustered embarrassment, "No! No, your Grace." He mentally scolded himself for allowing his gaze to linger on his prince for too long. The soft light of the fire danced across his sharp features, casting shadows and highlights that only added to his ethereal beauty. Trying to regain composure, Ásbjǫrn rose from his seat with the grace and fluidity of a cat, turning back to face Thamyris. His long, auburn hair cascaded down his broad shoulders like a waterfall. "Nature beckons me to wander once more," he explained with a deep bow that seemed almost rehearsed. Thamyris felt a warm hand rest gently on his shoulder, and he looked up to see the towering form of Ásbjǫrn. The elf's massive muscular frame cast a shadow over him, but Thamyris found comfort in the protective touch. He could feel the heat radiating from Ásbjǫrn's body, an ever-present warmth that had always been there since they were children. "Return to us swiftly and unharmed," Ásbjǫrn murmured, giving Thamyris' shoulder a gentle squeeze before releasing it. His voice was low and resonant, like the rumble of thunder in the distance. "I shall miss you."

Before Thamyris could reply, he felt the familiar weight of a bear paw replaced Ásbjǫrn's hand. As they bid their farewells, Thamyris could not help but feel grateful for the unwavering friendship and loyalty of both his companions. Their relentless support had carried him through countless trials and adventures, and he knew he would miss them dearly during his time away. But he also knew that their bond was unbreakable, and no distance could ever weaken it.

As he heard Ásbjǫrn walking away and into the night, Thamyris suddenly heard screams piercing the night's peaceful silence. It was Maxwell in his room, thrashing violently in his sleep, screams tearing from his throat. In a swift, Dorian burst into the room, finding Maxwell drenched in sweat with one hand clawing at his face while his body contorted in terror. Without hesitation, Dorian rushed to Maxwell's bedside and gripped his thrashing hands firmly, trying to stop him from harming himself.

"Wake up, Maxwell! Wake up!" Dorian shouted urgently, trying to break through the chaos of Maxwell's nightmare. But Maxwell only sobbed harder, tears streaming down his face as he fought against Dorian's grasp. Finally, he jolted awake, gasping for air with Dorian's comforting arms around him, rocking him back and forth gently.

"It's alright," Dorian whispered soothingly, holding onto Maxwell tightly. He looked down at Maxwell's tear-stained face, his voice trembling as he begged Dorian not to tell anyone what he saw. "I don't want him to know! I don't want him to know!" he cried out.

Dorian's heart ached for his friend as he gently hushed him and stroked his hair with one hand. "It's okay, I won't say anything. He'll find out soon enough anyway," Dorian reassured him. But all Maxwell could do was cling to Dorian, his sobs slowly subsiding as he took comfort in his friend's presence.

"Let's just focus on you for now," Dorian said softly in an attempt to calm Maxwell. Together they sat in each other's shadow, lost in the darkness of the night and the pain of their shared secrets.

)o(

Princess Amalia was trapped in a wooden contraption, her limbs twisted and contorted into painful positions. Her head hung to the side against the rough wood, sunlight peeking through the cracks and casting eerie shadows on her tear-stained face. She whimpered, turning her head as if searching for something or someone. "Help me, Sir Knight, help me.." she cried out in a raspy voice, tears streaming down her dirt-streaked cheeks towards the floor.

Cullen jolted upright in bed; small sweat beads drenched his body as he struggled for air. His hand flew to his forehead as he tried to process the intensity of his nightmare. The image of Amalia trapped and crying haunted him, leaving him shaken and disoriented in the darkness of his room. He knew he had to act quickly before it was too late.

)o(

As dawn broke through the canopy of the trees, Cullen and others had assembled in the courtyard. The Queen's eyes pierced every man's very soul. "Before you depart from us," the Queen began in a stern tone, "I must impress upon you all the vital importance of this mission. My daughter is not just a Princess." Her words hung heavy in the air.

Dorian let out an exasperated sigh, knowing exactly where this was going. "They never are," he muttered under his breath, rolling his eyes. The Queen's face remained neutral as she turned to look at Dorian. "She is a Priestess of Danu, and as such, she has certain responsibilities."

"Such as?" Dorian prodded.

Suddenly, the ground began to shake violently, causing several individuals to lose their footing and fall. With impressive speed and agility, Maxwell and the others extended their arms in an attempt to stabilize themselves. Cullen stumbled but quickly regained his footing. After several moments, the ground settled, and silence filled the air once again.

The Queen let out a weary sigh before speaking again. "The earth tremors that have been occurring...they are caused by dragons."

"Dragons?" Dorian gasped in shock, his eyes widening with disbelief. "Real dragons?"

"Yes," the Queen affirmed with a nod. "There are many types of magic within this forest. Our goddess Danu is the mother of it all, and we tend to all her creatures – including the dragons. Princess Amalia is our High Priestess of Danu and also the Keeper of the Dragons. But because of her absence from the forest, the dragons will soon awaken from their prolonged slumber."

Dorian looked at the Queen, his hand absentmindedly stroking his chin in thought. "I would imagine that the sudden awakening of dragons would pose a significant danger to everyone in the vicinity."

"How many dragons are we talking about?" Maxwell interjected.

"Four," the Queen replied. "The first is Nimriar, the fire dragon. He slumbers in the fiery lands of the south. The second is Cadmus; she sleeps within the great lakes of the west. The third is Haku, who rests in the highest mountains where the air is thin."

"Wait a minute," Cullen's voice trembled with fear upon hearing this and a pit formed in his stomach. "You're saying there are four dragons, and we have to face them all?"

The Queen's tone was grave as she answered, "If my daughter is not returned to this forest before they fully awaken, not only our kingdom but your lands will also be in grave danger."

Cullen's heart raced as he stood before the Queen, unsure of what was to come. Her eyes seemed to hold all the secrets of the world, and her voice echoed with power and wisdom.

"Our lands? How do they know... " Cullen began to ask but was quickly interrupted by the Queen.

"Because the forest has opened not just for you but for them too," she explained, her tone firm yet gentle. "You need to leave, and soon." She gestured to her two attendants, Tiatria and Thamyris, who stood on either side of her like loyal guardians.

"These gifts will help you on your journey," the Queen said with a warm smile, turning her attention to Cullen. "I see many things in your future, young man. Your road will be hard fought and will test you many times over."

Cullen's eyes widened as the Queen presented him with a blood-red cloak. Two delicate silver chains hung from its edges, giving it an otherworldly appearance. She placed it upon his shoulders, the weight of it comforting and reassuring. "This cloak is made from the finest material, able to withstand even dragon fire," she explained with a gentle smile. "And its chains are fashioned from Mythril, unbreakable and resilient."

Cullen's heart pounded with exhilaration, holding the incredible gift before him, one that would protect him from even the most dreaded of creatures in all the land. The Queen's eyes sparkled with pride and awe as she turned to Thamyris, who presented Cullen with an exquisitely crafted shield. Made of Mythril, a metal renowned for its indestructible properties, the shield glinted in the sunlight like a precious gem. Cullen's hands shook slightly when he reached out to touch it, not believing his luck. He could already imagine facing down any foe with this powerful weapon by his side.

"Thank you, your Majesty," Cullen said in awe and gratitude.

Next, the Queen approached Maxwell with a smile on her lips. Thamyris came forward with two elven swords in hand - their blades curved slightly and decorated with intricate designs. "These swords are imbued with magic and will submit to any element you call forth," the Queen explained. Maxwell's eyes widened in wonder, and he respectfully accepted the swords, bowing his head in thanks.

But it was Dorian who received perhaps the most prized gift of all - a book bound in dark leather and adorned with gems and stones. "To you, I give the Book of Sapientia," the Queen announced with pride. "Anything you wish to know about a potion, a spell, any piece of knowledge will be yours." Dorian's face lit up with excitement and gratitude as he held the precious tome in his hands.

Before the Queen turned to leave, Cullen mustered up some courage and approached her. "Your Majesty," he began, his voice trembling slightly. The Queen turned to him with a raised eyebrow, indicating for him to continue.

Cullen's throat felt tight as he tried to find the right words. "I have something to ask of you," he finally managed to say.

The Queen's expression softened as she regarded him kindly. "Yes?" she prompted.

)O(

Thamyris strode confidently towards Maxwell and Dorian, flanked by Seraphim Cullen's majestic white horse. The animal bowed its head in recognition as Maxwell lovingly rubbed its forehead, eliciting a contented groan from the creature.

Dorian stood with his arms folded across his chest, a smirk playing on his lips. His gaze turned towards Thamyris as their footsteps drew closer. He then looked at Maxwell, hinting at mischievous thoughts. The elf was outfitted in sleek leather armor, a quiver and bow strapped to his back, and a sword and dagger secured at his waist. But perhaps the most striking feature was the simple yet elegant labradorite pendant hanging from a Mythril chain around his neck.

As they approached, a loud cry echoed through the air and Kethinar, Thamyris' faithful hawk companion, landed gracefully on his master's shoulder. "When do we leave?" the elf questioned, causing both Dorian and Maxwell to turn their heads inquisitively.

Breaking the silence, Dorian finally asked the one question that he had been dying to ask. "Alright, I'm just going to ask," he began hesitantly before blurting out, "How are you able to see? I mean, really?"

"DORIAN!" Maxwell exclaimed, reminding his friend to tread lightly.

Dorian turned to face him with an innocent expression. "What? I have been dying to know since we met! I must know!"

With a deep sigh, Thamyris explained his unique ability that had always fascinated people.

"I was born blind. My father used magic on Kethinar's egg every day until he hatched. The bond between us is so strong that I am able to see through his eyes."

Both men were awed by this revelation, their expressions showing it clearly. But their questioning did not stop just there as Maxwell prodded further, "And when you touch people?"

Thamyris simply used his right hand to gesture for Kethinar to perch on it before gracefully launching the bird into the air. "When I touch people, I can see glimpses of their past experiences, but without Kethinar's eyes, it's mostly just shadows and blurred images," he explained, hoping that would satisfy their curiosity.

Just then, Thamyris' keen ears picked up the sound of approaching footsteps. It was Cullen, the Queen and Tiatria -

dressed in similar leather outfits with staffs and weapons at their sides. The two guards gaped as they saw Tiatria holding the reins of not one but two magnificent unicorns.

Maxwell also could not contain his surprise as he blurted out, "What is all this?" while Dorian stood next to him, equally amazed.

Cullen gazed at his companions with steely determination. "I have requested her Majesty's permission for Tiatria to join us in our search for the Princess," he announced. Dorian and Maxwell exchanged curious glances, unsure of what this could mean. Was this some sort of romantic endeavor? They could not be sure.

Cullen turned to Tiatria, his eyes filled with admiration. "Her ability to read minds could prove invaluable on our quest," he explained. "She will be able to detect any falsehoods or hidden information as we gather leads about the missing Princess. We must use all resources available to us."

Dorian smiled at this, pleasantly surprised by Cullen's cleverness. "Well played, my friend," he conceded, feeling a twinge of jealousy. As the self-proclaimed brains of the group, it stung a bit to have someone outsmart him so easily. Maxwell, on the other hand, was impressed by Cullen's quick thinking and strategic approach.

The Queen smiled serenely at their exchange. "I have given Tiatria and my son special pendants that will conceal their true identities from humans," she revealed. Dorian raised an eyebrow inquisitively. "So, will they appear human?" he queried. The Queen nodded in confirmation. "Yes, it is for their own safety."

Maxwell's gaze shifted to the unicorns grazing nearby, a mix of curiosity and uncertainty in his expression. "And what about those creatures?" he asked, gesturing towards them with a slight raise of his hand. The Queen's smile grew even wider as she observed their innocent ignorance. "Unicorns are pure magic, the very embodiment of it," she explained. "They only reveal themselves to those with the purest hearts. To others, they appear as regular horses."

Maxwell nodded understandingly before walking over to his horse and gracefully mounting it. "We should get moving," he stated firmly. "The sooner we find your daughter, the better." Thamyris mounted his own unicorn, with Kethinar perched on his right shoulder. Cullen was about to mount his horse, Seraphim, when the Queen held out a small pouch. "The forest may close again at any time," she cautioned. "This pouch contains special dust that, when thrown into the wind and accompanied by the word 'open,' will reveal a hidden gate for you to enter."

Cullen gratefully accepted the pouch and secured it to his belt. Nodding in thanks, he promised the Queen confidently, "We will bring her home safely."

With a final nod from the Queen, Cullen pulled on Seraphim's reins and followed Maxwell and the others. They rode off into the unknown depths of the Cesileon Forest. In a matter of moments, the lush greenery and majestic trees vanished behind them, and they found themselves back in familiar surroundings.

Chapter 8

Maxwell confidently led the way through the dense Cesileon Forest, the trees towering overhead and casting dappled shadows on the forest floor. Kethinar followed closely behind; his senses heightened as he searched for anything that could be of interest to Thamyris. Cullen, lost in thought, occasionally stole glances at Tiatria, who walked ahead of him. Her ethereal beauty captivated him, but he shook his head, determined to rid himself of such impure thoughts. He did not want to give her the wrong impression or disappoint his Mother.

As they continued on their new mission, Maxwell could not help but feel anxious about the added complications it brought to their original one. They needed to find this heretic and determine the truth of the charges against them before dealing with it accordingly. However, the longer they took, the more irritated the King and Cardinal would become. Their mission had to take priority, but with the pressing matter of dragons looming over them, it was hard to focus. Things were not looking good for any of them.

Maxwell turned back to see Cullen talking to Tiatria. He could not help but smile at the sight of the elf playing with three tiny balls of light, a serene expression on her face.

"What are you doing?" Cullen asked curiously.

Tiatria's fingers danced around the orbs, creating mesmerizing patterns. "They're fairies," she replied with a hint of mischief in her voice.

Cullen tilted his head in confusion. "I thought fairies were hidden in the Enchanted Forest like all the rest?"

A mischievous smile tugged at Tiatria's lips as she explained, "Normally you're right, but fairies always follow unicorns." Just then, one of the tiny balls of light flew up towards Cullen's nose and burst into a dazzling display, revealing a small fairy made of pure light with delicate wings. She playfully kissed Cullen's nose before disappearing back into the ball of light and returning to join her fairy companions. Cullen couldn't help but blush at the unexpected gesture. Seeing him blush caused Tiatria to laugh in delight. She found humans to be quite amusing and their behavior rather curious, even after hearing Cullen's thoughts.

Cullen's mind became a jumbled mess of thoughts and emotions as he tried to process what had just happened. He could not deny that there was a strange sense of magic and wonder surrounding Tiatria, and he found himself drawn to her increasingly each day.

Maxwell kept to himself; his thoughts consumed by the task at hand. Meanwhile, Dorian was completely self-absorbed, only thinking about fashion and dreaming of more luxurious surroundings. Tiatria found herself drawn to Cullen, always eager to hear his kind words or see his adoration for his mother. It touched her heart to see such a devoted son, desperate to prove himself to a father he hardly knew.

"Branson!" Maxwell's voice cut through the air, causing Cullen to look up from where he had been lost in thought. Maxwell motioned for him to join them, and with a nod from Tiatria, Cullen rode over to their side.

Maxwell wore a mischievous smile as he spoke to Cullen. "I can tell you're attracted to our young female companion." Cullen's face flushed bright red, much to Maxwell's amusement. "It was quite obvious from the start," he continued, glancing at Cullen out of the corner of his eye. "You've been smitten since the moment you saw her."

Cullen's eyes darted around nervously, trying to come up with an appropriate response. "I assure you," he stammered, "that I will not let my feelings distract me from my duties. I will carry them out with utmost dedication." Maxwell simply smiled, clearly not bothered by Cullen's admission. "Love has a way of complicating things, whether we want it to or not."

Cullen returned the smile warmly, curiosity shining in his eyes. "Have you ever felt this way about a woman before?" he asked. He did not have many people to turn to when it came to matters of the heart, certainly not his distant father or the strict Mother Superior.

Maxwell lowered his head and shook it with a small smile on his lips. "No, I can't say that I have," he confessed. "My line of work doesn't allow much room for love." Dorian's eyes widened in shock and disapproval, his brow furrowing as he shook his head.

Cullen looked at Maxwell with confusion. "But the soldiers of our order are allowed to marry after ten years of service, right? You've served double that time."

Maxwell could not contain a snicker as a half-smile crept onto his lips. "Double, huh?" His voice was laced with amusement, suddenly feeling years younger in the moment. "Are you absolutely sure about that?" he questioned, watching as a cold pit settled in Cullen's stomach. Struggling to find words to repair the damage, Cullen shook his head vigorously. But Maxwell did not take offense; in fact, it only amused him more. "You see, only knights are allowed to marry within the Order," he explained, gesturing between himself and Dorian. "Battlemages and Acolytes like us are not permitted such luxuries. It's seen as a curse. Our magic passed down to our children." He glanced over at Dorian, who offered a nod of agreement.

Cullen felt the color drain from his face as he absorbed this information. It left him speechless and unable to find words to express the injustice of it all. He could not understand why individuals like Maxwell and Dorian, who had devoted ten years of loyal service to their Order, were denied the opportunity for love and family. Would not allowing them to marry means adding more skilled members to their ranks?

"But I've come to learn that love takes many forms, and they are all equally beautiful," said Maxwell, smiling warmly at Dorian. It was the most Cullen had ever heard him speak, and he found himself enjoying it.

Meanwhile, Thamyris brought his unicorn to a stop, causing Tiatria's mount to do the same. "What is it? What do you see?" she asked curiously.

Maxwell, Cullen, and Dorian stopped as well, watching as Kethinar flew up into the air and began following a trail of some sort. Thamyris dismounted gracefully and knelt down on one knee, reaching out with his hand to touch some tracks left behind by a passing vehicle. "I see a portly human man dressed in expensive clothing," he reported. "There are two, possibly three men riding alongside him, guarding a cart with a large crate in the back."

Cullen's head snapped up as he pieced it together. "That must be the Princess," he realized with a sinking feeling. "She was taken in that crate."

Nodding in agreement, Thamyris pointed towards the northwest where the tracks led. "They headed off in that direction."

Maxwell turned to face the direction indicated by the elf, his expression grave. "That's Bestla," he confirmed.

Dorian felt relieved. "We were originally headed there anyway; now we can take care of two tasks at once."

Maxwell's brow furrowed thoughtfully. "Yes, but let's not forget our top priority: bringing the Princess back safely to the forest before those dragons cause any further destruction.

Thamyris impatiently snapped the reins to his mount and rode off, his heart racing with urgency. He could not afford to waste any more time if he wanted to save his sister from a potential tragedy. Tiatria's majestic unicorn effortlessly kept pace with the prince. Its mane and tail streamed behind her like a banner in the wind while the other horses struggled to keep up. Catching a unicorn was like trying to capture the wind itself - a feat that only Thamyris seemed capable of accomplishing.

As they galloped through the forest, Dorian's voice rang out in frustration. "Bloody hell! Will these horses ever slow down?" He urged his own steed to go faster, determined not to fall behind. But suddenly, they came upon a group of unexpected obstacles - elves who had stopped in their tracks. Cullen and the others frantically pulled back on their horse's reins, narrowly avoiding crashing into them. "Are you bloody insane?" Dorian scolded, glaring at the reckless prince. But Maxwell simply smiled as he announced their arrival. "We're here."

Dorian turned his head and saw that they had reached the outskirts of Bestla. He let out a snort of annoyance as he took in the sight before him. "Wonderful," he muttered sarcastically before turning to Thamyris with a pointed stare. "Not to be a complete bastard, but..." His words trailed off as Thamyris shot him a cold look in response. "Never mind," Dorian mumbled under his breath, resisting the urge to slap some sense into the stubborn Prince.

Tiatria was struck with awe at the bustling city of Bestla. The streets were filled with merchants selling all kinds of wares while colorful banners and flags flew overhead. The buildings were made of limestone and stood at diverse levels, giving the city a unique and grand appearance. But amidst all the activity and beauty, there was one overpowering scent that Thamyris could not ignore - the overwhelming smell of fish. His heightened senses, a result of his blindness, were often a curse in situations like these.

As they rode through the city, Kethinar's cries from above caught Thamyris' attention. It was clear that human cities had changed greatly since he last visited one. In the past, they were simple and rustic - made up of wooden huts and open fire pits for cooking and gathering. But now, they boasted sturdy buildings made of wood and stone, evidence of progress and development.

Cullen's voice broke through Thamyris' thoughts, questioning their purpose in this city. "What are we doing here? Can't we find an inn?" Maxwell turned to survey the area before answering with a grim expression. "There is a slave market at the end of the docks." Cullen's shock was evident as he exclaimed, "Slavery? I thought it was illegal on the continent! Even the Cardinal denounces it as a sin!"

Dorian halted his horse and gave Cullen a serious look. "How naive can you be?" he scoffed. Feeling foolish, Cullen looked away in embarrassment.

But Maxwell's words held more weight as he addressed Cullen directly. "Clearly, your father did not teach you about the harsh realities of this world." He sighed and lowered his head before continuing in a grave tone. "Cullen, you must understand something - there is an ugliness to this world and brutal truths that cannot be ignored. The Cardinal may publicly decry slavery, but it still exists in the shadows of this world. As a member of the order, you will face things that you never thought possible. You must steel your heart for whatever may come." Cullen nodded solemnly, taking in Maxwell's words with newfound seriousness as they continued down the docks.

Cullen and his companions trudged through the bustling streets towards the docks, their feet beating a steady rhythm on the cobblestones. As they approached an old wooden barn at the end of the docks, a putrid stench hit them like a wave, causing Dorian to quickly cover his nose and mouth with a handkerchief. The overwhelming combination of sweat and feces threatened to make him lose his breakfast, but he fought back the urge with all his might.

Cullen's stomach churned with disgust as he surveyed the scene before him. Wooden cages lined the room, filled with half-starved and beaten bodies that were barely recognizable as humans. The putrid stench of filth and despair hung heavy in the air, making his eyes water. On a raised platform at the front of the room, a man paraded a group of chained slaves like prized cattle.

"ALL RIGHT GENTS!" the auctioneer bellowed, pulling one of the slaves forward, his neck shackled with a six-foot chain. The slave was a shell of a man - balding, filthy, and dressed in rags. "HERE IS A NICE SLAVE, TRAINED UP NICE AND DOCILE!" The auctioneer snarled at the slave, demanding more vigor. Dorian could feel bile rising in his throat as he watched the dehumanizing display.

As bids began to fly between buyers, Dorian lifted his hand in a challenge. "Three coins!" he called out, surprising his companions, who looked at him in shock. Maxwell questioned him, but Dorian only gave an enigmatic smile. "If I win, we can gather information about the other slaves here." His plan was met with approval and even envy from Maxwell.

Meanwhile, Cullen turned to Tiatria and asked if she could hear anything useful amidst all the chaos. She shook her head, clearly distressed by the overwhelming noise and voices flooding her mind. "Yes and no," she replied, struggling to block out the multitude of sounds.

But Dorian was determined to win this auction and get answers. "Ten coins!" he declared confidently as the crowd fell silent. The auctioneer scanned the room before announcing, "Ten coins, any other bidders?" With no response, he declared the sale final.

Dorian grinned triumphantly at his victory. "Wonderful! Now let's get some answers."

Dorian charged forward, shoving aside anyone who dared to get in his way until he reached the cashier's counter. With an angry sneer, he pulled out his money pouch only to find it nearly empty, holding only five measly coins. He turned to Maxwell, desperation etched on his face. "How much do you have?" But Maxwell could only raise his hands in defeat. "I told you not to spend all our money earlier, but did you listen? No!" Dorian's gaze then fell on Cullen, eyeing him with a mixture of hope and resentment. "What about you?"

Cullen reluctantly opened his own full money pouch and handed over a handful of coins. Dorian snatched them greedily and spun around to face the cashier with a false smile plastered on his face. "Here you go!" The cashier eyed them skeptically, immediately recognizing them as members of the Order. "You lot from the Order, aren't you?"

Dorian gave a sharp nod, meeting the man's suspicious gaze head-on. "And aren't you just the one who happily accepts our money?"

The man shrugged nonchalantly and held out his hand for payment. Dorian begrudgingly handed over the coins and the man scribbled something onto a slip of paper before handing it back to him. "Go outside through the side door and present this paper. They'll give you what you purchased."

Outside, the stench hit them like a punch in the gut as they were greeted by rows of people locked up like cattle in cages. Dorian marched towards a man with a cruel look on his face, gripping tightly onto a leash that was attached to a battered-looking slave. His new purchase. Kethinar settled on Thamyris' shoulder, preening his feathers while keeping a watchful eye out for any potential danger. As Thamyris discreetly scouted for any valuable items, Dorian watched with satisfaction as his new slave was brought forward, obediently following the commands of his aggressive new owner. "What's he doing?"

Dorian spun around, a sudden feeling of unease creeping over him as he saw Thamyris wandering aimlessly. His mind was clouded and distracted, his gaze darting around until it landed on a group of men who were leering at Tiatria. She could feel their eyes on her, making her skin crawl with discomfort. One of them approached her, his breath reeking of alcohol as he spoke in a slurred voice, "Aren't you a pretty little thing? I've never seen someone like you before."

Tiatria's heart raced with fear as she sensed the man's predatory intentions. "I can tell," she said nervously.

Cullen appeared beside her, glaring menacingly at the man. "Is everything alright, my lady?" The man seemed taken aback by Cullen's aggressive stance. "This lady and her fancy companion don't seem to belong here," he sneered.

Cullen straightened his posture, his eyes hardening. "We are their escorts; they're searching for a friend."

As Dorian observed the exchange, his gaze fell upon the new slave they had just purchased. Upon closer inspection, he realized that this person was not just any ordinary slave. "Oh, dear God," Dorian thought to himself, "this one is a mere breath away from death's door."

Meanwhile, Thamyris walked down the docks with frenzied determination. As he knelt and pressed his hands to the ground, he was overwhelmed with hundreds of images flooding his mind. It took him several minutes to filter out the ones that were unfamiliar or insignificant. Finally, he saw visions of Amalia being pulled out of a crate and paraded around like an object for sale. Men grabbed at her dress and admired her ears, treating her like a prized possession instead of a human being. Thamyris channeled his inner energy as he searched for her, striding eagerly until he reached an empty boat slip. With a snort of frustration, he could sense that she had been taken onto a boat.

Maxwell suddenly appeared behind Thamyris, startling him out of his thoughts. The elf was visibly agitated when Maxwell gripped his biceps forcefully. "Where did the boat go?" Thamyris demanded, pointing to the now-vacant slip.

Maxwell gazed at a man who was sitting at a nearby dock post, munching on a questionable-looking apple. "Did you hear the man?" His piercing gaze made the man uneasy. "How would I know? I only keep track of what is on those boats!" he retorted, gesturing towards the shabby and rundown slave ships lined up along the dock. "Not anywhere else," he added hastily before turning back to his food.

Tiatria's eyes locked onto Cullen, her voice fierce and trembling with anger. "He's lying," she hissed through clenched teeth.

Maxwell released Thamyris once he was sure the man was stable, then approached their captive with a dangerous fire burning in his eyes. "I'll ask you one more time," he growled, barely containing his rage.

Dorian rushed to Maxwell's side when he saw a vein throbbing on the back of his neck. He placed a firm hand on his friend's shoulder, trying to calm him down. "This isn't the way, look around," he pleaded, gesturing to the armed men watching them closely. Tiatria eyed the tense scene before turning away and walking off. Dorian stepped forward and took hold of their new servant's neck shackle.

"Let's get moving," he said sharply.

Soon enough, they found themselves in a dingy tavern. It was not the most high-class establishment, but at least there were no rats scurrying about. Thamyris sat hunched over with Kethinar perched on his shoulder, seemingly on edge. The bird scanned the room for any potential threats as they settled into long wooden tables with benches.

Dorian kept an eye on their new servant, who was devouring his food like a starving animal. Across from him, Cullen watched Tiatria intently as she spoke with Maxwell, who had returned from getting them all ale. As he sat down at the bench and slid mugs towards each of them, he noticed Thamyris lost in thought.

Tiatria glanced over at Thamyris and offered a gentle reassurance. "We'll find her," she said softly.

Maxwell's attention turned to them, curiosity etched onto his face. "What did you discover?"

Tiatria looked at Thamyris, whose expression was somber and distant. She placed her hands on the table, trying to focus and piece together the man's thoughts. "He was lying," she said with frustration, narrowing her eyes in concentration. "He mentioned a merchant's special cargo...something about Malania." Her brow furrowed as she struggled to make sense of it all.

Cullen reached across the table and gently took her hand, a small smile appearing on his lips. "Don't be so hard on yourself," he murmured reassuringly.

Thamyris rested his head on his hand, lost in thought. Maxwell slid a mug towards him, silently asking him to share what he saw. The weight of their mission seemed to press down on them, each one feeling the weight of their own fears and doubts. "What did you see?" he asked quietly.

Thamyris sat up ramrod straight, his body tense and his breaths coming out in sharp huffs. "I saw my sister being ripped from her imprisonment," he growled, frustration and anger evident in his voice. "She was paraded about like a trophy for all to marvel at before being dragged onto the missing ship that sailed out of port." Maxwell's expression shifted to one of concern for Thamyris; it must have been incredibly painful for him to be separated from his sister without any knowledge of her whereabouts. The weight of uncertainty hung heavy in the air as they both contemplated the unknown fate of Thamyris' beloved sibling.

)o(

Amalia's heart pounded with fear as the fat man hauled her out of the crate and gripped her wrist with a vice-like grip. She could feel his rough hands digging into her skin, propelling her forward with an unnerving determination. "We have to make you presentable for our buyers," he growled, a sickening grin spreading across his face. Amalia's mind raced with horror at what those words could mean. Panic rose in Amalia's chest as she realized what was about to happen. She would be sold like a commodity, used and discarded by these despicable men.

With a violent shove, the fat man threw her into a tiny room that reeked of stale sweat and dirt. Buckets of freezing water rained down on her, drenching her already filthy body and causing her to cry out in shock and pain. Amalia watched as her bodily dirt turned the dirt and grime on her body into a muddy river. With shaking hands, she clutched at the tattered remains of her clothing, weeping as she remembered the life she had before these cruel human men ravaged it.

Memories flooded her mind - Tahl'rail defending her from humans, their peaceful life shattered by violence and greed. Rage ignited within her, fueling a primal power that had long been suppressed.

The fat man watched in terror as Amalia's physical form began to change before his very eyes. Her once beautiful features twisted into something feral and terrifying.

Her eyes blazed with red light as they transformed, becoming stark red with reptilian slits for pupils. A guttural scream escaped her lips as spikes erupted from her skin, ready to unleash the power of the southern border. "I invoke the power of the southern border! The element of fire, doom, and wrath!" Her voice thundered with ancient magic, commanding the very elements themselves to obey her will.

In fear for his life, the fat man raised his trembling hand as hot winds whipped around them, rocking their boat violently. Waves crashed against the decks as the winds grew stronger, carrying with them the fierce roar of a dragon: Nimriar had answered Amalia's call for vengeance.

A deafening roar erupted as the ground beneath them began to convulse violently, throwing everything and everyone into chaos. The air filled with screams as chandeliers crashed down, tables flipped over like toys, and big chunks of the ceiling fell down upon them with merciless force. It seemed that all hell broke loose and there was no escape from this wrath.

)o(

The Queen stood in the forest, gazing out the window with a heavy heart. She could not shake the worry and fear that consumed her as she thought about her daughter and her fate. What did these abductors want with her? As she paced back and forth by the window, tears streamed down her cheeks and hands trembled with fear and grief. She had already lost so much - her husband, Tahl'rail, and now...her precious daughter. Why was this happening? Why now? What cruel game were the gods playing? The more she thought about it, the more she wondered if these events were occurring because the gods realized there needed to be a change. However, she couldn't figure out why it had to be now.

Suddenly, a violent tremor rocked the ground beneath her feet, causing her to desperately cling to the windowsill for support. The Queen's gaze snapped towards the forest, where hundreds of birds were frantically fleeing from the treetops. But their frantic cries were drowned out by an earth-shattering roar that pierced through the air, freezing the blood of everyone who heard it.

As the shaking intensified, dust particles rained down from the ceiling, which was held up by the branches of the tree. They seemed to spread across the ceiling like spider webs. The shaking was causing the wood of the branches to split and crack. "No! No! No!" she cried out as she fell to the floor. "Danu! Cernunnos! Gods, please help us!" Her pleas were met with no response as several guards rushed to protect her with their magic, and the ceiling collapsed around them. Tree branches broke off and started to fall onto the floor. The Queen threw up a shield as a heavy branch broke off and was about to fall on her. Her guards quickly blew magic to her shield, but the branch was colossal. With the earth shaking, they found it hard to keep the shield up till the floor cracked open and shifted, causing several to fall. More debris fell around them all.

One of the guards grabbed the Queen's hand and started to pull her away from the branch which finally hit the floor and held his actual guard's shield to protect them from falling debris. They were only a few feet away from the exit. A few soldiers ran to assist but more branches fell, hitting them. With the shield over their heads, the guard and the Queen didn't see another massive branch breaking off, and this time, it landed on top of them.

Being summoned out of anger and frustration, the forest floor violently split open, allowing the molten lava to erupt from within its depths. The ground shook violently as lava heat caused flames to spark and engulf everything in its path. Animals fled for their lives while trees cracked and splintered in the dry, hot wind brought on by Nimriar's arrival; the ground shook from the dragon climbing up the earth's walls. The dragon's massive claws emerged from the earth's crust, gripping it as it pulled its colossal body upwards. Its deafening roars echoed throughout the forest. It soared over treetops, setting everything ablaze with each beat of its scaly, bat-like wings. The dragon was a monstrous and remarkable sight having massive claws tearing through branches as it flew higher and higher into the sky.

)o(

Within moments, Nimriar flew over Bestla. He breathed a blazing hot fire that seemed to spill out like molten lava. Building rooftops went up kindling, and people seemed to melt and disappear the moment the fire was spilled onto them. The fire flew through the streets even walls catching it. The dragon's massive wings flapped, causing boats in the harbor to throw themselves backward or to capsize. As the beast turned, it roared, causing the air to become dry and trees to crack as people lost their lives.

Inside the tavern, Dorian was holding Maxwell in his arms as they leaned against a sturdy wooden beam. He held his right hand aloft as he held his scepter, shielding them from falling debris.

People shrieked outside as the dragon's fire spilled upon them and on the docks. Slave ships burned with occupants still aboard. The shabby warehouse went up in flames. It was horrific to hear the screams of the slaves burning alive. It would have made anyone with a shred of decency would have felt their blood turn to ice. Nimriar landed on what was left of the dock's warehouse and blew fire up into the air and then into the streets.

Nimriar's massive body was a spectacle to behold, with blood-red scales that reflected the glowing flames around him. His bat-like wings stretched out, displaying their impressive span, and the membranes between them were a lighter shade, like a stained-glass window. His claws, sharp and deadly, sunk into the crumbling wooden building he perched on, causing the wood to splinter and crumble.

The beast's eyes burned with fury as he surveyed the scene of death and destruction before him. His massive frame shook with rage and his growls echoed off the walls, sending shivers down the spines of those still alive. Saliva dripped from his jaws like molten lava, scorching and scalding anything or anyone it touched.

"WHERE IS MY PRIESTESS?" his voice boomed, causing the air to vibrate with its intensity.

Cullen and the others exchanged terrified glances as they heard the horrifying screams outside. As Cullen turned towards the door, he saw flames engulfing the streets, the doorway itself caught in a blaze. Without hesitation, Tiatria grabbed two large jugs of water and rushed forward, hurling them at the fire with all her might.

With a fierce determination, Tiatria then summoned all the water within her being and willed it to seep out of the wooden walls, sizzling as it met the flames that threatened to consume them. Her hands moved in a swift circular motion, commanding the liquid like an extension of herself. With a final precise stroke, she sliced through the air with her hand like a knife, causing the water to hit the fire with such force that it immediately extinguished the raging inferno.

But their relief was short-lived as Cullen's eyes caught sight of heavy beams still on fire above them. If those gave way, they would be crushed beneath the collapsing roof. Ignoring the chaos of people fighting to escape, Cullen saw Tiatria holding her temples as she seemed to be paralyzed because of the noises. He could see the tears in her eyes. With debris raining down around them and Tiatria not paying attention, she wasn't able to draw out screams and frantic thoughts of those struggling to survive. Each cry was like a dagger piercing her mind, threatening to overwhelm her.

Without hesitation, Cullen sprinted towards Tiatria amidst the chaos and danger, dodging frantic people fighting for their lives and leaping over falling debris. Tiatria's ears were ringing with screams and panicked thoughts, overwhelming her senses and nearly causing her to buckle under the pressure. Just then, Cullen reached out and grabbed her wrist, his face filled with tears and desperate fear for survival. In that moment, Tiatria could see everything in his eyes - love, determination, fear - urging her to keep fighting for their lives.

Thamyris burst out of the tavern; the thunderous flapping of Kethinar's wings echoed in his ears. The dragon's massive form loomed in the sky above, but the elf was undeterred. He gripped his bow tightly, muscles straining as he sprinted at full speed towards his target. With a swift leap from a nearby wooden cart and then a lamp post, Thamyris launched himself into the air.

As he flew, he pulled back on the bowstring, feathers tickling his fingertips. The tip of his arrow glowed with a blinding white light, drawing power from the sun itself. With a fierce battle cry, Thamyris let go of the string and released his arrow towards the dragon.

The projectile whistled through the air, a deadly missile aimed straight for the dragon's neck. As it struck its mark, causing the beast to roar in pain, Thamyris held his breath and prayed to the Horned God Cernunnos for success.

But the dragon was not defeated yet. As Thamyris prepared for another shot, Kethinar turned to face him with glowing eyes of fury. Undeterred, the determined elf drew back his bow once more and took aim at his opponent. "Grant me strength, great Cernunnos," he whispered fiercely while unleashing another arrow towards the dragon's heart.

With a fierce determination, Thamyris drew back his bowstring, feeling it's weight increase as it channeled the blazing rays of the sun into the arrow until it became a blinding beacon of light. As he released the arrow, its speed and force were so great that it pierced through the dragon's tough hide with ease, causing Nimriar to roar in both rage and pain. But the beast was not alone, for Maxwell and Dorian emerged from the tavern, quickly taking action. Maxwell conjured massive shards of ice with his hands, each one as large as a grown man, while Dorian used his scepter to unleash a blinding light that disoriented both the dragon and Kethinar, who was flying overhead.

As Nimriar flew straight towards Thamyris, Maxwell launched his ice shards at the dragon's underbelly, but they shattered upon impact against the beast's hot and impenetrable skin. Realizing their magic had an insignificant effect on the raging creature; Maxwell pulled out his new weapons - blades that glowed with an ominous blue light. Just as the dragon opened its massive jaws to breathe fire upon them, Dorian unleashed another blinding light that caused Nimriar to turn away in pain. The sudden burst of light blinded Kethinar as well, causing Thamyris to crash onto a nearby roof before tumbling down to the ground.

With a guttural growl, the dragon swooped down towards Thamyris, its jaws gaping open in anticipation of tearing him apart. But just as it was about to strike, Kethinar flew overhead; he screeched as he folded his wings, his talons stretched out as they gauged at the dragon's left eye. Nimriar thrashed his head about as he snapped his jaws, trying to crush the bird with its massive jaws. Once the hawk saw Thamyris was alright, he flew off, leaving Nimriar to try and regain his bearings; he searched for Thamyris but could not find him amidst the chaos. Letting out another earth-shattering roar, he flew off, spewing fire until disappearing into the clouds above.

Maxwell sprinted towards Thamyris, who was doubled over and groaning in pain. Blood dripped from a gash on his forehead as he struggled to sit up. "Are you alright?" Maxwell shouted over the sounds of chaos and destruction. Thamyris nodded as he waved him away with an impatient flick of his fingers. Frustrated and embarrassed by his fall, Thamyris tried to push himself off the ground.

But before he could do so, Dorian appeared next to them. "Where are the others?" Maxwell demanded, his voice thick with worry. The two of them quickly scanned their surroundings, the remains of the tavern now reduced to a chaotic mess of wood and debris.

"CULLEN!" Maxwell bellowed, fear creeping into his heart as he was suddenly engulfed in a cloud of dust and smoke. He coughed and gagged, struggling to see through the haze as he frantically searched for any sign of their missing comrade. With renewed determination, the two worked together to clear their path through piles of broken glass, jagged beams of wood, and any other obstacles in their way. Every second felt like an eternity as they raced against time to find their friend before it was too late.

Dorian's voice was laced with frustration as he threw his arms up in exasperation. "We did it, Amant. We actually killed the Duke's son and had him in our grasp within a week." Maxwell's heart pounded with fear as he frantically searched for his companions in the darkness. Two lives were on the line, possibly lost forever. He cast aside anything in his way, digging deeper and faster as terror crept into his mind.

"Stop wasting time and dig harder, Dorian!" Maxwell barked out in desperation.

But as they continued to search, Dorian gasped and fell to his knees. Maxwell's gut twisted in dread at what he might see when he turned around. "What is it?" he asked, his voice trembling.

Dorian wiped the face of his slave, now lifeless. "He's dead," Dorian sighed heavily. "At least he had a decent meal before joining God and his angels." With a heavy heart, Dorian made the sign of the crucifix and closed his eyes in a moment of silent prayer. It was a rare display of compassion from someone who had witnessed unspeakable horrors during their years on the road.

Maxwell could not hold back his tears as he continued to dig, revealing more bodies of those who were not fortunate enough to escape. The weight of innocent lives lost weighed heavily on him, fueling his frantic movements.

"CULLEN!" Maxwell cried out again, his voice cracking with emotion. "WHERE ARE YOU?" His cries echoed through the air, pleading for any sign that his dear friend was still alive.

Chapter 9

Suddenly, the ground began to tremble, and bits of debris fell from the ceiling, showering Dorian and Maxwell with loose earth. With cautious movements, they scrambled to dig through the piles of rubble, desperate to find their companions. As they cleared away the dirt and rocks, a blood-red cloak came into view. Maxwell's heart skipped a beat as he recognized it as Cullen's cloak. "I found Cullen's cloak," he informed Dorian, his voice trembling with emotion.

Dorian could see the fear in Maxwell's eyes as they both hesitated to uncover what lay beneath the cloak. Bracing themselves for the worst, they continued digging until finally, Cullen emerged from the rubble. Maxwell could not believe his eyes as he saw his friend coughing and covered in dust but alive. He quickly reached out to help him sit up, patting his back and tousling his hair in relief. "You made it!" Maxwell exclaimed with a laugh as Cullen struggled to catch his breath and coughed up bits of dirt.

Cullen wasted no time in getting up, frantically digging through the dirt and debris. To everyone's surprise, he uncovered Tiatria, who was also coughing and covered in dust. Dorian pulled Cullen back and helped him stand up while Maxwell assisted Tiatria. They all stood together amidst the chaos, brushing off bits of debris from her hair and clothes. Tears streamed down her face as she looked around at her friends, grateful to be alive.

Maxwell turned to check on any remaining survivors, but after thorough searching, he concluded that they were the only ones left under the rubble. When he turned back to his companions, he could see that Cullen was covered in dust and had a few scratches, but overall seemed relatively unharmed. "Are you both alright?" Maxwell asked with concern.

Cullen nodded before explaining what happened: "Yes, I had Tiatria go under the table, but when I saw the roof caving in, I shielded her with my body and put my shield on my back to protect us."

Dorian could not help but smile at his friend's bravery and quick thinking in the face of danger. He could not have asked for better companions to have by his side.

A triumphant smile spread across Maxwell's face as he held out his hand, beckoning Cullen to join him. It took a moment for Cullen to realize what was happening, but when he did, he extended his own arm, and the two warriors clasped forearms in a strong display of camaraderie. "Good work, Knight!" Cullen beamed at his friends, feeling proud of their success. "Let's get out of here and see if we can help anyone else," suggested Dorian.

As they emerged from the tavern, they were met with a scene of chaos and destruction. Ash rained down from the sky, thick smoke blanketed the ground, and cries of despair could be heard in the distance. People ran frantically, trying to escape the devastation that had befallen their town. Through the clouds of smoke and fire, figures could be seen huddling together for comfort and support. Cullen coughed and wiped dust from his eyes as he surveyed the wreckage. "Where's the church? The priests may be able to offer aid to those in need," he said urgently.

Maxwell nodded in agreement, his voice hoarse from inhaling the acrid smoke. "It's a good place to start," he replied, his eyes scanning the horizon for any sign of the holy building amidst the chaos.

Dorian waved his hand in front of his face, attempting to ward off the choking smoke. "If it's still standing," he added grimly. "This ash is making it hard to see anything beyond ten feet."

Cullen nodded in understanding as he continued to cough. He silently wondered about this heretic business that was plaguing their town. Tiatria, who had been watching and listening intently, was puzzled by this word - Heretic. She sensed from the tone of their voices that it was not a good thing, but she had no understanding of its meaning. She could not help but feel curious about this church they spoke of - it held significant importance in their lives. Was it like the temple she knew from her own people?

Thamyris approached the group, using his bow to guide him as he swept the ground with it. Tiatria held out her arm for him to touch her sleeve; his face showed. "Are you alright?" he asked softly, not noticing her wide-eyed expression.

Tiatria gave a small nod, "Yes," she answered quietly, still trying to make sense of everything around her. As they walked through the town, they saw homes destroyed, bodies lying in the streets, and everything covered in a thick layer of ash. It was like a suffocating blanket that clung to every surface and person. In some ways, it seemed like a blessing - shielding them from the horrors that lay beneath. But Tiatria could not shield herself from it all when she saw the true severity of the destruction. She gasped and quickly covered her mouth with her hand, turning away from the gruesome scene before her innocent eyes. Cullen placed a comforting hand on her shoulder, causing her to lean against his breastplate for support. Cullen himself could not bear to look for too long - charred bodies beyond recognition, skeletal hands reaching out in vain for help that would never come. It was a sight that would haunt them all for years.

Dorian gazed at Thamyris, his curiosity piqued by the intricate markings adorning the elf's face. "I can't help but wonder, what do these markings signify? I have noticed that all elves have them, but none as detailed as yours. And do all elves possess the same powers as you? I've never seen anyone wield a bow with such precision or an arrow fly with such skill. Blind or not, it's impressive."

Thamyris let out a heavy sigh, meeting Dorian's gaze. "Only my sister and I bear such elaborate markings. It marks us as the Priest and Priestess of our God and Goddess."

"I heard the dragon call for the Priestess or something similar," chimed Cullen from beneath the pile of rubble he was buried under. "So, it was your sister then?"

Thamyris nodded solemnly. "Yes, my sister is the Priestess of Danu, blessed with gifts of creation, love, compassion, and dominion over all her children. She has the power to awaken the dragons at her will and command their might. However, their time has not yet come, so she keeps them slumbering."

"So, if your sister is the Priestess," Dorian realized, "that makes you--"

Thamyris stopped walking abruptly, his blind eyes piercing into Dorian's soul. Even without sight, his intensity caused Maxwell to shudder. "I am a High Priest of Cernunnos," Thamyris clarified, listing off his duties with a hint of frustration. "My role includes protection, strength, guidance, wilderness survival...and yes, sexuality." Dorian could not resist smiling at this newfound benefit in their religion. "But most importantly, I am responsible for maintaining balance and harmony in our world alongside my sister. As you witnessed with me earlier, when things become unbalanced..."

He trailed off as they continued walking towards their destination. Dorian folded his arms, deep in thought as he asked the elf, "You mentioned that the dragons will only awaken when needed. What does that entail?"

Thamyris gazed up at the sky, where the distant cries of Kethinar could be heard. "Legend speaks of a time when our forest will face great danger, and only the power of the dragons can save us. Until then, they slumber. But my sister must have summoned one, believing she is in grave peril and that we are unable to protect her."

Silence hung heavy amongst the group as they processed Thamyris' words, sending shivers down their spines. It was not until Maxwell shook his head and resumed walking that they continued on.

The church sat atop a hill, surrounded by an eerie graveyard. Damage from the dragon's attack was evident, with the roof and monastery connecting to it both bearing scars from its fiery breath. As they approached, the Bishop emerged with a small entourage of priests and monks behind him. He was an old man with thinning silver hair, piercing blue eyes, and a stern expression etched onto his face. His luxurious robes and cap were crafted from fine silken velvet, and his cross gleamed with gold and a sparkling amethyst at its center.

The Bishop's hands trembled as he held them out in front of him, "Thank God you have come!" His voice was filled with both relief and fear. With a firm grasp, he shook Maxwell's hand, his eyes darting up to the sky repeatedly. "The devil has descended upon us!" he gasped, pointing frantically to the darkening clouds above. "It's that heretic! The devil himself has come to kill all of God's faithful! He is here to show his support for the one who has done this to us!" The Bishop's gaze turned to Maxwell and the others, a desperate look in his eyes. "With the Order now present, I expect we can finally put this heretic's head on a spike!"

Maxwell stood tall with arms folded as he shifted his weight from his right foot to his left. "All in due time, Your Grace. First of all, that dragon was the cause of a separate issue entirely," he explained calmly as he removed his right hand from its resting spot on his forearm. "Secondly, we must find and judge this heretic ourselves before any action can be taken." The Bishop looked slightly put off by Maxwell's calm demeanor but nodded in agreement. "But most importantly, are you or any of your people injured?" Maxwell asked with a genuine concern in his voice.

The Bishop spread his hands in a gesture of surrender, bowing his head slightly. "No, luckily God saw fit to spare us."

"Excellent," said Maxwell with a nod. "I want your people to go to the town and offer aid."

The Bishop nodded eagerly, regaining some sense of purpose. "Of course, the church offers succor to those who fall under God's grace."

Maxwell knew that this might be his only chance to gather information from the Bishop about the heretic they were seeking. He also knew the man would be holding back, not wanting to appear too eager for coin in exchange for information. "Do you know where this heretic preaches?" he asked, cutting straight to the point.

"Yes," said the Bishop, pressing his fingers together and pointing downward. He could not hide his excitement at the opportunity to share his knowledge. "There is a ravine about three miles from here."

Dorian, standing with arms folded behind Maxwell, spoke up with impatience in his voice. "Do you have any other information that may help us find this heretic? Three miles is quite a distance to search blindly."

The Bishop shifted uncomfortably but quickly replied, "My spies tell me this heretic is a woman, by the name of Eve." He could not keep the pride out of his voice as he spoke of his intelligence-gathering abilities.

"A woman?" Dorian chuckled, unable to contain his amusement. "Here I was thinking it was some monster convincing women to eat their own babies." His sarcasm dripped from every word.

A look of disapproval crossed the Bishop's face. "It is disastrous for a woman to think she is capable of understanding and spreading God's word! No woman could ever comprehend it!" Tiatria could see the genuine belief in the man's eyes and felt a twinge of anger at being viewed as inferior because of her gender.

"Why are women not allowed to speak your God's word?" she asked curiously, challenging the Bishop's beliefs. "Shouldn't all people, regardless of their gender, have the right to praise and spread His message?"

The Bishop's gasp echoed through the room, his face contorted with shock and disbelief. How could a woman of her obvious stature not know the gospels? "Are you completely ignorant, girl?" he boomed. "How can you not know the word of God?" The Bishop's hand twitched, itching to seize the girl and have her whipped for her insolence. Tiatria noticed the tension in the air, but she was not afraid. She knew that if this man laid one finger on her, he would quickly lose it.

Cullen gave an agitated look towards the Bishop. He knew better than to speak out of turn, but he could not help defending Tiatria. "Not everyone, everywhere has heard the word of God, your grace," he said calmly. The Bishop's steely gaze locked onto Cullen, clearly not appreciating his tone. But Cullen continued, undeterred. "She and her companion hail from a foreign continent."

The Bishop's eyebrow raised in surprise at this revelation. "I expect an education is soon to follow then?" he asked, more as a statement than a question. Tiatria felt a wave of disgust wash over her as she heard every vile thought running through the Bishop's mind - thoughts even he seemed to struggle with. She turned away and walked off, unable to stand being in his presence any longer. Cullen wanted to go after her, but he knew he could not leave until his business with the Bishop was concluded.

"Are you Knight Branson?" The Bishop questioned, causing Cullen to look back at him. "Yes, yes, why do you ask?" he answered back, trying not to slap the man as the urge crossed his mind. Cullen watched the Bishop pull a letter out of one of the pockets from his robe. He handed it to Cullen, "This came for you this morning; it's from the palace."

Cullen flipped the letter over to see the wax seal on it and saw it was from Edith. He recognized it from all the letters they shared as a child. Cullen caught a sly smile from Dorian, which caused him to reply, "Don't read too much into it. I'm willing to bet she's writing to tell me that her dance instructor made her dance with someone she didn't like or something." he said in a bored tone.

As Tiatria walked down the path with her arms folded tightly across her chest, the wind gently blew against her back and caused her long hair to sway behind her like a dark veil. Her sharp, elven ears caught the sound of someone weeping in the distance, and without hesitation, she ran towards it. She found a woman sitting on the side of the road cradling a small child, no older than five years old. The child's arms and legs were severely burned, and the woman looked at Tiatria with pleading eyes. "Please, help her," she begged.

Tiatria quickly assessed the situation and noticed a nearby cart of cabbages that had been broken and scattered on the ground. Without hesitation, she ran over and grabbed several leaves before returning to the injured child. The woman watched in amazement as Tiatria gently peeled off the damaged leaves and tossed them aside. Then, she spotted some aloe plants nearby and ordered a passing man to gather some for her. As soon as he returned with the aloe, Tiatria expertly squeezed out the gel from the leaves and smeared it onto the cabbage leaves, using her delicate fingers to spread it evenly. She then wrapped the leaves around the child's severely burned arm with great care, being careful not to cause any more pain. With a soft glow emanating from her hands, Tiatria used her healing powers to bind the leaves together and aid in the healing process.

As the others made their way down the road, they noticed Tiatria delicately wrapping the last leaf on the little girl's injured leg. The elf looked up at the woman with a gentle smile, her sapphire eyes filled with compassion and understanding. "Her wounds should be healed by the time the leaves wither away," she reassured the tearful mother. "Thank you, milady," the woman whispered gratefully. As Tiatria rose to her feet and turned to greet her friends, she was met with curious smiles and grateful gazes.

Dorian spoke up first, his voice laced with admiration. "I believe your good deed has not gone unnoticed, my dear." Tiatria turned around to see a crowd of injured villagers making their way towards her. She could feel their thoughts of hope and desperation, pleading for her help.

"Are you a healer?" an old man asked as he reached her.

Tiatria hesitated, unsure of how to respond. This was not her world, and she had no formal training in healing. But Thamyris stood beside her, his presence calming and reassuring. "I believe you are the only one who can help these people," he said quietly before walking away from her. Tiatria looked up at the prince, his stoic expression giving nothing away. With determination in her eyes, she turned back to face the sea of injured, determined to do whatever she could to alleviate their suffering.

Maxwell and the others quickly sprang into action, helping the villagers recover and tend to their wounded while also burying the dead. Tiatria tended to as many injuries as she could, starting with the most severe cases first.

Despite her best efforts, over half of those she tended to did not survive their injuries. However, Tiatria stayed by their side until they passed on, singing soft melodies to ease their pain. With one hand holding theirs and the other gently stroking their hair, she could hear their thoughts fading until the light left their eyes. Tiatria's heart ached with every loss. By the time night fell, campfires were lit throughout the city since most of the buildings were too damaged to be inhabited. In between tending to the wounded, Tiatria took breaks by the warm fire, staring into the flames as she processed the events of the day.

Maxwell approached Thamyris, who sat by one of the fires with his forearm resting on his knee, lost in thought. In each hand, Maxwell carried a bowl of soup. He sat down next to the elf on a wooden box and offered him a bowl. "Here, food is scarce. You should eat while you can," he said with a small smile.

Thamyris moved his hand out of habit until his pinky grazed the bowl, feeling its warmth. But then he pushed it back towards Maxwell. "I'm not hungry," he said quietly.

Maxwell noticed a hint of sadness in Thamyris' voice and looked at him sympathetically. The firelight danced in Thamyris' eyes, reflecting his inner turmoil. "We were all hoping to find your sister here and bring her back home safe," Maxwell said as he rubbed the back of his neck. "But it seems that was not meant to be."

He locked eyes with Thamyris before continuing, "But we won't give up. We'll keep searching until we find her." Thamyris remained stoic but then gestured towards Maxwell with his head. "Besides my mother, my sister is the only person who has ever loved me for who I am. She never saw my blindness as an impairment," he explained. His words caught Maxwell off guard, and he felt himself flush under Thamyris' gaze.

"Do you know what it's like to have someone who loves and accepts you for all that you are?" Thamyris asked, his voice soft but filled with emotion.

Maxwell lowered his head, letting out a heavy sigh before digging his feet into the soft dirt beneath him. Thamyris could sense the inner turmoil rising within Maxwell as he struggled to find the right words to say. As Maxwell sat with his hands folded in his lap, Thamyris was unable to see the subtle tremble in them. "Dorian," he said softly, catching Thamyris' attention. Thamyris looked towards him, and a glimmer of tears appeared in Maxwell's eyes. "Dorian is the only one," Maxwell continued, his voice breaking. Hearing Maxwell so vulnerable brought a surge of sympathy and understanding to Thamyris' heart.

As Thamyris leaned closer from his seat, reaching out to help, Maxwell smiled weakly, refusing to ask for assistance. He was determined to maintain his independence. But in the end, it was Maxwell who scooted the bowl of food closer to Thamyris' outstretched hand, allowing him to grasp it for himself. Thamyris' ears twitched at the sound of movement, but he remained silent, focusing on eating.

Maxwell spoke again, "He's the only one who has ever truly accepted me for who I am." He gazed up at the sky, lost in memories. "My family tried but couldn't, so I was given the Order as an infant." He took a deep breath before continuing. "Growing up, I hoped that God would love me just as I am." A small smile appeared on Maxwell's face as he thought of Dorian. "But then Dorian showed me that not only does God love me, but there are people who can too - the right people," Maxwell spoke softly, pausing to take a deep breath. "And how devastating it is to lose them."

Thamyris shifted in his seat, leaning closer towards Maxwell and without hesitation, reaching out for his hand without hesitation. Caught off guard by this gesture of comfort, without hesitation, Maxwell intertwined with the elves as they shared a moment of understanding and comfort. Thamyris felt relieved as images and feelings flooded his mind - things he never expected to see or experience with someone else who understood him.

After a few moments, Maxwell gently pulled away and placed his hand on Thamyris' shoulder in a gesture of support. "Eat up," he said kindly. "We leave in the morning."

Meanwhile, Dorian trudged down the road covered in dirt and sweat from assisting with burials at the nearby graveyard. As he brushed off his arms and clothes, he noticed Maxwell hunched over Thamyris, his hand resting on the elf's shoulder. Dorian's eyes narrowed in suspicion as he wondered what kind of conversation could lead to such intimate physical contact.

As Maxwell walked away, Dorian approached him with a critical gaze. "What was all that about?" he asked pointedly. Maxwell met his friend's gaze with a somber expression. "He was telling me what it's like to miss the only person who truly accepts him," Maxwell replied, his voice heavy with emotion. Dorian watched as Maxwell walked away to eat his dinner, casting a quick glance at Cullen as he went around serving bowls of soup to those in need.

Tiatria's muscles ached and her slender fingers trembled as she finished tending to the wounded. Her heart was heavy with sorrow and exhaustion after hours of healing and comforting those on the brink of death. The flickering flames of a nearby fire caught her attention and seemed to call out to her. Cullen watched in silence as she made her way over and sank down onto the ground next to the comforting warmth of the fire. Its warmth and crackling flames called out to her weary body.

Cullen watched in admiration as Tiatria made her way over to the fire, her movements graceful and fluid despite her weariness. She sat down by the fire, rubbing her hands together before holding them out to the flames. She was desperate for solace from the bitter cold that had seeped into her bones. As if summoned by magic, a steaming bowl of soup appeared in front of her face. Her tired eyes widened in surprise as she turned to see Cullen sitting next to her.

"Last bowl," he said with a small smile, gesturing towards the soup.

Tiatria's lips curved up in a grateful smile as she took the bowl. The fragrant aroma of the soup filled her senses, and she could not help but let out a satisfied sigh as she began to eat. Helping the dying and wounded had taken a toll on her, both physically and emotionally. "Thank you," she murmured, feeling a pang of hunger ripple through her stomach.

"How are you holding up?" Cullen asked gently, breaking the comfortable silence between them.

Tiatria lowered her bowl into her lap and gazed at her reflection in the warm broth. "It's hard," she admitted with a heavy sigh.

"Hearing their thoughts...their final thoughts." Tears welled up in her eyes, threatening to spill over. Her voice trembled as she spoke of the weighty burden she carried, "Their prayers to God, pleading for mercy, salvation, or just simply slipping away without realizing it." Cullen's expression turned somber as he placed a comforting hand on Tiatria's shoulder. His heart went out to her; no one should have to carry such a heavy burden alone.

"You must think I'm foolish," Tiatria murmured, feeling vulnerable and exposed.

But instead of agreeing or dismissing her, Cullen surprised her by leaning in and gently kissing the top of her hand. "I think you're brave," he said, his warm honey-colored eyes filled with admiration. "It takes a special kind of courage and kindness to aid and comfort those who are suffering."

Tiatria's breath caught in her throat as she looked at him, feeling touched and understood. "You humans are mortal creatures," she said softly, breaking the intense gaze between them. "Death must be something you've grown accustomed to. It must be so easy for you to face such things."

Cullen shook his head, his eyes serious and sincere. "No death is ever easy or familiar," he said firmly. "But it's part of life, and we learn to face it with grace and courage. Being immortal, this must be a shock for you."

Cullen's words hung in the air, the crackling of the fire the only sound breaking the tense silence between him and Tiatria. Her sapphire blue eyes, like an endless ocean, searched his face for any hint of dishonesty. She was taken aback by his knowledge of her kind – that they were immortal beings, never having to let go of anyone they loved. It was a concept she had taken for granted until now.

"You seem well-informed about us," she commented, her grip on his hand tightening slightly.

Cullen shifted uncomfortably, rubbing his neck as he avoided her gaze. "Dorian told me," he confessed, blushing deeply at being caught in his lie. "He thought I should know a few things about elves."

Tiatria's curiosity peaked. "What else did he tell you?"

Cullen cleared his throat before reluctantly admitting, "That you are capable of living thousands of years due to your connection with the earth's deepest magic. That some are born with special gifts."

A small smile played on Tiatria's lips as she looked into the dancing flames in front of them. "And that we are skilled warriors, swift and agile in battle."

Everything had changed since Tiatria and Thamyris entered Cullen's world. The way women were viewed, their religion – everything was different. She turned to face Cullen, seeking honesty and answers in his warm brown eyes.

"I think it is time for you to teach me about your people's religion," she stated calmly, "since I have shared mine with you."

Cullen nodded solemnly, knowing it was time for her to understand more about his beliefs and culture. But where to start? He had never been one to openly discuss his faith, but since arriving in this new land and encountering a new race with their own religion, it seemed necessary. Taking a deep breath, Cullen began to explain. "First, we believe in a God who reigns supreme over our world."

"Your God rules alone?" Tiatria asked, her eyebrows raising in surprise. "I'm guessing he must be quite lonely."

Cullen hesitated before responding, unsure of how exactly to answer her question. "He's not exactly alone," he finally said, struggling to find the right words. "God doesn't have a wife like the God has the Goddess. But thousands of years ago, he favored a woman who called out to him in prayer. She was a mother desperately asking God to save her gravely ill child. Her prayer was so pure and sincere that God granted it and saved her child. In gratitude, he gave her the power to bring comfort and heal those who were ill. Over time, she became known as The Mother."

Tiatria couldn't help but feel perplexed. The woman sitting before her possessed the extraordinary ability to heal and comfort the sick and dying, yet she was not considered on the same level as Cullen's God. "So, this Mother figure was once mortal?" she asked, trying to understand.

Cullen nodded hesitantly. "Yes, but she did not ascend to become God's wife."

Tiatria furrowed her brow in confusion. "But why not? If she were a powerful healer, wouldn't it make sense for God to choose her as his consort?"

Cullen shook his head. "He'd given her healing powers and was able to save her own child. But by saving her child, word got out, and others came to her seeking her gifts. She was happy to give it, of course, but it earned her the title of The Mother since she cared and comforted all who came to her. In granting her this gift, he felt he'd given her enough."

"But wouldn't having her as his consort bring even more comfort and solace to all who seek her aid?"

Cullen shrugged, clearly repeating what he had been told and believed. Tiatria sighed, too tired to argue with him at the moment.

"Why do men view women as stupid and incapable of understanding?" she suddenly blurted out.

Cullen's expression hardened. "Women are not viewed as capable as men in our society. It is our duty, as men are favored by God, to protect them." He seemed almost frustrated by this truth.

Tiatria narrowed her eyes in suspicion. "Then why did your priest say I could never understand the word of God? I have a deep understanding of everything the God and Goddess have taught my people. Why am I suddenly deemed incapable?"

"Because he is a Bishop," Cullen interrupted, looking uncomfortable. "They often have narrow-minded views about the world."

Tiatria sensed that Cullen was not being entirely truthful. She knew that women were seen as inferior by men, especially those in positions of power like nobles and members of the church. Women were expected to marry and bear children without being taught anything beyond the basic commandments. The church itself had been taken over by ambitious men, twisting it to fit their own beliefs.

"What are these commandments?" Tiatria asked, gazing into the fire as she leaned back wearily. Cullen's anxiety spiked, afraid that she would be able to read his mind.

"They are spiritual laws given by God for your people to follow so they may enter heaven after death," he replied nervously.

A spark of understanding ignited within Tiatria as she saw the control and manipulation at play in this religion. She realized then why Cullen's priest had said she could never fully understand the word or ways of God – because she was a woman deemed unworthy by societal standards. Cullen stopped realizing that this was not helping the situation to help Tiatria understand or like his religion. Now that he said it all out loud, he understood how shallow and demeaning it all sounded towards women.

Tiatria's brows furrowed in confusion as she questioned the concept of rules in death. Her voice trembled with disbelief, "When one soul dies, do they not simply go to their final resting place? How did you come to know these rules and who established them?"

Cullen's hand absentmindedly scratched at the back of his head as he searched for the right words to explain. He took a deep breath and looked intently at the curious elf before him, her desire for knowledge evident in her unwavering gaze. "The Archangel Michael brought them," he began.

"The Archangel?" Tiatria interrupted, her eyes widening in wonder.

Cullen nodded, "Yes, think of it as a powerful being similar to a fairy but with large white bird wings. They serve as protectors for God and carry out his will."

The elf's curiosity only seemed to grow as she asked more questions, "So this Archangel came to your land and shared these commandments with you?"

"In a way," Cullen replied, "the Archangel Michael descended with two large stone tablets carved with God's laws."

Tiatria fell silent for a moment, processing all the information. Finally, she asked, "What did the commandments say?"

Leaning forward, Cullen used his right hand to prop himself up as he spoke with reverence. His left thumb and index finger formed a circle as he recited the words etched into his memory.

"Thou shall have no other gods before me.

Thou shall not make false idols.

Thou shall not misuse the name of our Lord God.

Remember the sabbath day and keep it holy.

Honor your father and mother.

Thou shall not kill.

Thou shall not commit adultery.

Thou shall not steal.

Thou shall not bear false witness against your neighbor.

Thou shall not covet your neighbor's wife."

Tiatria's face displayed a mix of shock and disbelief at the number of rules. Cullen could not blame her; it was a lot to take in all at once. He could not help but feel a twinge of guilt as he thought about how these commandments would apply to their current situation. Would they be punished for breaking them, even if it were to survive?

As he looked around at the survivors huddled together around the fires for warmth, Cullen struggled with what to do for them. He could not shake off the feeling that they did not deserve this fate, no matter how many of God's laws they may have broken.

Feeling emotionally drained, Cullen glanced over at Tiatria and saw that she had fallen asleep against his right arm. The events of the day had taken their toll on her, and she lacked the strength to keep her eyes open any longer.

Cullen's gaze then fell upon his nap sack next to him. Reaching inside, he pulled out his journal and set it on his lap before retrieving his quill and ink. Opening the book, he removed the ink cap and dipped his quill into the dark liquid. Carefully placing the tip onto the page, he began to write, just as he had done during his journey to meet with Dorian and Maxwell.

He wrote about his hopes for their adventure before being shackled to Edith. And then again, reflecting on their time spent in the forest and as guests of the elven queen, where he learned about forgotten beliefs and different faiths. He wrote about finding beauty in new and foreign things. And now, as he sat in the aftermath of tragedy with death surrounding them, Cullen wrote once more in his journal. This time, recording all that he had witnessed and experienced – lives lost, horrors seen – in the hope of preserving their story for future generations.

As the fire died down to embers, Cullen carefully closed his journal and packed everything back into his bag. He did not want to disturb Tiatria, who was sleeping peacefully with her head against his shoulder. He gently adjusted his left hand against Tiatria's head to ensure she would not wake as he stood up to pick her up with both arms. As he looked around the campsite, he noticed a bedroll laid out a few feet away from them. With tender care, Cullen carried Tiatria over to the bedroll and knelt down with a soft thud. He carefully laid Tiatria onto the bedroll. He then took off his cloak and draped it over her sleeping form.

Cullen then held the letter Edith sent him, he broke the wax seal and unfolded the paper.

My dearest,

Cullen rolled his eyes as she was already writing in such terminology. Usually, it was dear Cullen. He started to wonder what else was going to change at an alarming rate once he got back.

Father already has the tailor making my wedding dress, also my quadrille instructor is having me learn a new dance for our wedding. You'll have to learn your part upon your return. Be prepared for your feet to hurt as you'll be practicing it till you get it right.

Cullen was right; she was going to put that into a letter.

I'm sad to report my maid accidently ruining my favorite pair of lavender shoes by dropping them in a wet puddle. I sent her to her room without any supper as punishment and had the money to replace them out of her pay.

Cullen rolled his eyes as he took a heavy sigh; he was starting to grow anxious as he continued to read with reluctancy.

Also, I have been working on the menu of our wedding feast and choosing the horses to pull our wedding carriage away. Also, my father is deciding which of our vacation homes we can live in after we're married. Father says a newly married couple should get to know each other with privacy for a while. I think he's hoping it will help us to produce children quickly if we don't have the pressures of the palace.

Cullen nearly choked on his saliva as he read the words *producing children.* Even though there was more to read, Cullen's skin was starting to crawl. He felt getting married when being told to was hard enough, but to have children as fast as possible was too much. Even though they have known each other for years, it was only through pen. Cullen rather get to know Edith first, and that would take several years at least. Children could always come after that, but knowing his father, he'd be immediately pressured to fulfill his husbandly duty. To have Edith produce little princes and princesses as fast as possible and as much as possible. Without another thought, Cullen threw the letter into the fire.

Cullen then tore out a page from his journal and dipped his quill into his ink. He looked back at the letter, seeing the last of a list of name suggestions slowly being consumed by the flames before he brought his attention back to the task at hand.

Edith,

You know I don't write very well in these things. However, I don't think you need to starve your maid for soiled shoes, don't you have like twenty other pairs? Or make her pay for a replacement pair for that matter. I don't know when or how soon I'll be back from this assignment, so I think getting such a jump on the wedding preparations is a little premature. Also, I think children can wait about five to ten years, honestly.

Cullen

The fire nearby crackled softly as Dorian approached Maxwell, who was sitting by the dwindling fire, finishing his soup. He sat down next to him and sighed heavily, "That bloody Bishop still thinks that dragon is the devil-made flesh." Maxwell set his bowl down and rubbed at his tired eyes. Sleep had been evading him lately, and he was feeling the effects of it. But even though he did not care much about what the Bishop thought, it was probably for the best that he continued believing the dragon was some evil creature rather than trying to comprehend the truth. "It's probably better that way, Dorian. Trying to explain everything would probably be too much for anyone to handle. Their minds might just turn to mush like custard," he said with a wry smile.

Dorian returned the smile and looked at Maxwell with concern in his eyes, "Why don't you get some rest? I'll keep watch." Maxwell almost protested but knew he could not argue with Dorian's logic. As he looked around, he saw that all the other bedrolls were taken, and he did not want to kick someone off just so he could have some comfort. Resigned, Maxwell sat up straight, folded his arms across his chest, and shut his eyes. Dorian knew that Maxwell could sleep in this position without any trouble but also knew he would wake up feeling stiff in the morning. But for now, it was the best they could do.

Chapter 10

The gentle nudge of Maxwell's finger on his shoulder jolted Dorian awake, causing him to sit up startled. "I wasn't asleep!" he quickly assured, looking around in confusion. He found Maxwell standing next to him, his index finger pressed to his lips in a gesture of silence.

Rising from his spot on the ground, Dorian followed Maxwell to where their horses were tethered nearby.

As they made their way to their horses, the darkness of night still enveloped the area, thick with the sound of crickets chirping. With a quick glance at Maxwell, Dorian whispered, "Where are we going?" His companion's expression was serious as he secured the saddle girth on his horse. "We need to find the heretic and determine if she truly poses a threat or not. I thought it is best to take care of this before we have to continue our search for the princess in the morning." Dorian knew that Maxwell was right and couldn't help but groan as he mounted his own horse, dreading the inevitable confrontation.

They rode out swiftly and quietly, following the southern edge of the forest that would lead them to the ravine where the heretic was rumored to be hiding. In the dim light, Dorian raised an eyebrow and asked, "What do you make of the prince?" Maxwell seemed to be caught off guard by the question before responding thoughtfully, "I believe he is deeply wounded by past losses – family and friends taken by humans who were already abhorrent in his eyes. His people were forced to hide in this enchanted forest and now he must leave it behind in order to find his missing sister." Dorian probed further, knowing that Maxwell could see right through him. "What's bothering you?" he asked nonchalantly.

After a moment of hesitation, Dorian finally voiced his thoughts: "I think the prince may have a crush on you." This caused Maxwell to look at him incredulously as if he had gone mad. "Are you insane? What would give you such an idea?" Dorian did not want to mention the brief hand-holding incident, but it was too late. "I saw him hold your hand," he blurted out.

Maxwell pulled on the reins of his horse, his face blushing with embarrassment. "That's what you're basing this off of?" Dorian felt equally flustered and explained, "I've never seen a man as aloof and guarded as that elf. He actively pushes people away and avoids getting to know anyone. But when it comes to you, he talks to you and even holds your hand." Maxwell shook his head, trying to suppress his irritation. "Dorian," he started, looking back at him with stern eyes. "I don't know what you think you saw, but he's angry and alone. And whether he admits it or not, he's scared." As Maxwell's words sank in, Dorian realized that perhaps jealousy was fueling his suspicions, but he couldn't bring himself to admit it just yet. "Then why is he so rude to Cullen and me?" he questioned, gesturing with his right hand. "There's no reason for him to -" Dorian stopped mid-sentence as the realization dawned on him. The expression on Maxwell's face confirmed everything.

Cullen was naive and sheltered, completely unaware of the harsh realities of the world outside. And the prince was a snob who was used to being surrounded by others who were just like him, elves. Maxwell was more familiar with Dorian and all of his charms and flaws, and he wasn't fazed by any of it since he was used to all of it. Also, being older, Maxwell was quieter, didn't push others, only guided when it was needed.

Dorian let out a sigh and kicked his horse into a slow walk. "I hate you sometimes," he muttered under his breath, shooting a sideways glance at Maxwell, who urged his own horse on with a chuckle. "And sometimes I hate being right," Maxwell teased back with a grin. Their lighthearted banter provided a brief reprieve from the tension and apprehension of their mission.

The crackling bonfire cast bright sparks into the night sky, drawing a large and diverse crowd. Some stood in tattered rags, others adorned in ornate clothing and jewelry, while some fell somewhere in between. Maxwell and Dorian had donned dark, hooded cloaks to blend in as they weaved their way through the throngs of people. Suddenly, Dorian caught sight of a mysterious figure standing atop a stack of wine barrels. They were also cloaked, hiding their faces from view. As the murmurs of the crowd subsided, the figure raised their hands to signal for silence. Even from this distance, it was clear that the figure was slim and graceful. In one swift motion, they threw back their hood to reveal long, flowing blonde hair and pale skin. But before, Dorian couldn't make out the color of their eyes, but he could tell the speaker was a woman. After a moment, the woman began speaking.

Dorian's keen eyes noticed that she was an elf, but oddly enough, no one seemed to bat an eye at her presence. It was strange to see an elf preaching in this human world. "Good people! Thank you for coming here tonight to hear the truth!" she proclaimed, her voice carrying over the murmurs of the crowd. "I know it is a great risk for any of you to be here, but you must know that a reformation is coming! And what happened in Bestla only proves it!" At those words, both Maxwell and Dorian felt a cold pit form in their stomachs. "How does she know about Bestla?" Dorian whispered to Maxwell, who stroked his chin thoughtfully. "Who wouldn't know about it?" he replied quietly.

The pair watched as the elf continued to speak, her words striking a chord with them. "My dear people, the church has been lying to you for far too long! They have deceived you into believing that there is only one God, but I tell you now that there is also a Goddess who loves you just as much!" Her voice resonated with conviction as she spoke of a mother's love for her children. Both Maxwell and Dorian felt like they had been hit in the face with a rock, realizing that she spoke the truth. The elf looked out at the crowd, tears forming in her eyes as she continued, "The church wants to silence me, to stop me from sharing this truth! Magic is real, and it is not a sin to embrace it! Those born with magic are not cursed but blessed! And in this knowledge, there are two gods who love you all – not just one!" Her words were met with gasps and murmurs from the crowd. "There is no shame in seeking equality for all people - women fighting for their rights, love being allowed to flourish between any two individuals, regardless of gender. No more worrying about following strict rules to gain access to paradise in the afterlife!" As she spoke these words, it was as if a weight had been lifted off Maxwell and Dorian's shoulders. They could not believe they had never thought of these things before. The elf's voice grew stronger as she proclaimed, "You should also know that a child is coming – a child who will bridge our worlds and unite them in love and hope!"

The woman's urgent words hung in the air. The pair stood frozen, their ears straining to catch every word. Suddenly, Maxwell sensed a flicker of fire in his periphery and whipped his head around just in time to see a swarm of tiny flames dotting the forest. They were approaching at a breakneck pace.

Without hesitation, Maxwell signaled for Dorian to follow his gaze, and they pushed their way through the panicked crowd, desperate to reach the source of the danger. "The Order!" Maxwell cried out urgently, pushing through the crowd with Dorian close behind him. "Make way! Excuse us!" Dorian shouted, trying to clear a path.

Soon enough, they could hear the thundering hooves of dozens of horses and the sound of people screaming as they ran for their lives. The sight of torches blazing and soldiers on horseback struck terror into their hearts – they knew what would happen if they were caught.

But Maxwell and Dorian were determined to reach the woman who had just finished speaking. Maxwell quickly lifted her off the barrels she was standing on while Dorian grabbed hold of his scepter. "Evanescere!" he cried, and in an instant, all three of them disappeared from sight.

Meanwhile, chaos erupted as soldiers rode through the town, trampling anyone unfortunate enough to be in their path. Knights cut down anyone trying to flee while ropes flew through the air, ensnaring those who could not escape fast enough. The screams of terror echoed through the night as dozens were arrested and dragged away.

Maxwell and Dorian watched it all unfold from their hiding spot behind a massive oak tree several hundred feet away. The woman was with them, breathing heavily as she bore witness to the devastation. "Those poor people," the woman whispered in horror.

"Don't worry about them," Maxwell reassured her with a hardened expression. "They'll be interrogated and released once The Order realizes they have the wrong people."

As they waited for things to calm down, Dorian noticed the woman's striking features – her deep emerald green eyes, full pouty lips, and a labradorite necklace identical to the ones worn by Thamyris and Tiatria. "So that's how you've managed to keep your elven heritage hidden," Dorian remarked, leaving the woman stunned.

"You can see that I'm..." she started to say but trailed off in shock.

"An elf!" Dorian finished for her, his own eyes widening in realization.

"But how? No human has ever seen an elf. Not since..." The woman's words trailed off as she thought of the final battle between their two people.

"We've seen the forest and the Queen," Maxwell added with folded arms. A heavy silence fell over them as they all processed this newfound knowledge.

The elf's eyes widened in surprise as she looked at the men before her, "My name is Veronna," she said softly, her voice carrying a sense of wisdom and ancient knowledge. "I was left here the day the forest came and all the people who wished to follow the old ways." Her hand instinctively went to the pendant around her neck, gently clasping it between her thumb and index finger. "This pendant was given to me to hide among the people here. I'm here to spread the whispers, spread the truth, and remind the people that there was once harmony and equality in this world. That there are two, not just one, who love them for who they are, what they are. That there isn't a list of strict rules to follow in order to gain favor or a place in the afterlife. To hide myself further and bring my word to the people, I adopted the name Eve."

"How long have you been doing this?" Maxwell asked.

"Ever since the forest closed," Veronna replied solemnly.

"For that long?" Dorian exclaimed in shock. "And you've never been caught?"

Suddenly, a group of men wearing cloaks and hoods appeared, running towards them with angry shouts and wielding clubs. "Release the prophet!" they demanded.

"The prophet?" Dorian questioned with a hint of amusement in his tone. "My my, quite a change from being called a heretic."

One of the men approached with a thick stick held tightly in both hands. "Let her go!" he commanded, prompting Maxwell to step forward and hold out his right hand in a calming gesture. "We're not here to hurt her!"

"Well then, what are you here for?" another man asked, lowering his club but still gripping his stick tightly. Dorian had no intention of playing games with anyone who could potentially bash their brains in. "We were sent here by the Order to find any potential heretics and either arrest or kill them on sight."

Maxwell rubbed his eyes wearily with his left hand as he let out a frustrated sigh. He was now convinced that these men were determined to attack them. Although he knew they would not stand a chance against him and Dorian, there was no need to provoke them unnecessarily. Veronna held out her hand, gesturing for her people to stay where they were. "If you truly saw me as a threat, you would have already killed me," she said calmly. "What do you want?"

Maxwell and Dorian exchanged glances, both thinking the same thing. Veronna looked at them with hopeful eyes. "We want you to leave," Maxwell told her gently. "We can see that you are not lying about your world, and therefore you pose no threat to us." Tears welled up in Veronna's eyes as she could not believe what she was hearing.

The air was thick with tension, each breath feeling like it could be her last. "One more question," he demanded, his eyes piercing into hers. Veronna's eyes flicked between Dorian and Maxwell, her heart racing as she tried to hide her fear. She knew their questions were only meant to further incriminate her, but she could not bear the thought of losing her friends. With a weak smile, she turned to leave, but Dorian's sharp words stopped her in her tracks. "How is it that you've managed to avoid capture by the order all this time? Are you willing to sacrifice your friends for your cause?"

Veronna felt tears welling up in her eyes, but she refused to let them fall. Her mind raced as she searched for an answer, unable to meet their intense gazes. Her friends stood behind her, their faces etched with worry. Finally, she spoke, barely above a whisper. "The others...were these men," she said, gesturing towards her loyal companions.

Dorian and Maxwell narrowed their eyes at the small group of men before them. "Your friends?" Dorian scoffed. "Do you enjoy sacrificing your friends for your beliefs?"

Maxwell's shock was evident on his face, and he opened his mouth to speak out against Dorian's cruel words. But one of the men stepped forward, his expression firm and unyielding. "She didn't sacrifice us," he said firmly, meeting Dorian's gaze head-on. "We go willingly to spread the true word and embrace death if necessary."

Dorian had no argument against such unwavering devotion. Maxwell looked at Veronna curiously, "You talked about another message, a child. What were you talking about?" he questioned. But before Veronna could answer and continue their conversation, the ground beneath them began to tremble.

Nimriar's roar echoed through the air, as it shook the earth as fire erupted from his maw, engulfing everything in its path. The winds picked up, causing the trees to creak and bend as fire engulfed the treetops.

Amidst the chaos and screams of terror, Maxwell and the others watched helplessly as every soul caught in the flames perished. Veronna's heart constricted with grief and guilt as she saw the horror of the scene. The Order gathered their captives while the fire consumed everything in its path. People screamed and ran as the chaos ensued.

Veronna felt Maxwell jump on top of her, shielding her from the flames with his body. Despite knowing he did not have Cullen's protective cloak, he was willing to risk it all for her. The heat was unbearable as Dorian raised his scepter, casting a protective shield around their small group.

Dorian held up his scepter above his head, "SCUTUM!" he cried out, a shield cast around them just in time for the dragon's fire to pass over them as they watched Nimriar fly off.

They watched in horror as the dragon flew off towards Westevia, leaving behind a trail of death and destruction. Maxwell helped Veronna to her feet, checking if she was alright. "Thank you," she whispered shakily, tears streaming down her face. She nodded before turning to see the devastation left behind. Dorian hugged Maxwell tightly, grateful to have escaped the dragon's wrath once again.

The soldiers lay dead on the ground, their bodies burned beyond recognition. Veronna could barely make out their faces through the melted metal surrounding them like a broken egg. Tears streamed down her face as she mourned the loss of life. "The child of two worlds is a child that the Goddess prophesied would one day come." Dorian looked towards their horses and saw that they, too, had fallen victim to the dragon's fire. He let out a frustrated snort, realizing they would have to make the journey back on foot.

"A child born of two worlds," Veronna said with tears in her eyes as she looked at the devastation and death. Maxwell and Dorian turned around as they listened to the elf's words. "That is what the Goddess' promised, a child born of the human and magical worlds, a parent from each, to bring peace and unity once more." Veronna closed her eyes as tears dripped down her eyes. "That is what was promised." Dorian and Maxwell looked at each other, uncertain as to say or even do from such powerful words.

Veronna felt a hand on her shoulder and turned to see her friends standing behind her. Maxwell joined them soon after. "Go now," they urged her. "Be careful and continue spreading the word." As Veronna walked towards the bodies of her fallen comrades, Dorian heard footsteps behind him. He turned to see Veronna's friends standing there, Maxwell beside them. With a heavy heart, Veronna gave them a nod and walked away, her mind filled with prayers for a quick resolution to the violence and bloodshed plaguing their world.

She turned to face the two men, her eyes scanning their faces before speaking. "One more thing," she said quietly, her voice barely audible over the bustling sounds of the marketplace. The two men turned to her, their expressions filled with curiosity and concern. "I heard elven words in the air," Veronna continued, her voice growing stronger. Maxwell furrowed his brow in confusion while the other man's eyes widened with interest. "What did they say?" Maxwell questioned, eager for answers. Veronna looked at them both earnestly before answering. "They were commanding the dragon to find them," she stated, her gaze shifting between the two men. With a final nod, she turned away from them and made her way through the clearing and into the forest, leaving them to process this new information on their own. As she walked, Veronna could not help but wonder what this could mean for their journey ahead.

They made their way back to their fallen horses. Maxwell reached for Dorian's hand, intertwining their fingers in a show of affection. Dorian smiled at the gesture and returned the squeeze. In a bold move, Maxwell raised Dorian's hand to his lips and kissed it passionately, sending shivers down the Acolyte's spine.

"If someone is asking it to find them, we can assume that Amalia is talking to it. And she's still being held captive," said Dorian, voice laced with concern. Maxwell nodded in agreement, knowing that no one else could have such control over the mighty beast.

"It seems they have yet to find each other," he remarked sadly, "We're going to have to tell the others when we get back." He could not help but feel sympathy for Thamyris, as this news would surely devastate him. Not only was his sister still missing, but the dragon was killing everything in its path in order to find her. Maxwell could not imagine how much this would crush Thamyris' already burdened heart. As they continued their journey, the weight of this realization hung heavy in the air between them.

As they walked to their horses, Maxwell reached for the saddlebags and handed them to Dorian without a word. But instead of taking them, Dorian dropped his own bag and grabbed Maxwell, slamming him against a nearby tree in a fit of passion. Their lips crashed together in a desperate embrace, hands roaming and grasping at each other's bodies. Maxwell eagerly wrapped his arms around Dorian's neck, his right hand tangling in his lover's hair as he pulled him closer.

Feeling the heat between them rising, Dorian's left hand boldly cupped Maxwell's groin, eliciting a low moan from the man whose half-flaccid cock was quickly growing under his touch. In that moment, they both could not help but be grateful for surviving yet another encounter with the dragon's wrath.

Their cheeks flushed with desire and their breaths coming in ragged pants, they succumbed to their primal urges. Maxwell pressed his body against Dorian's hard form, relishing the feeling of their skin against each other. And while normally Dorian was not as aggressive, neither could fault him on this occasion; their passion burned hot like the fire of a dragon's breath.

As their bodies pressed against each other, Dorian's left hand deftly unlaced the threads of his lover's pants. Maxwell shook his head in disbelief, grabbing Dorian's hand with his right. "What are you doing?" he questioned, trying to emerge from his lust-filled haze. Dorian looked at Maxwell with a mix of curiosity and desire, "Don't play coy, Amant. You know exactly what I'm doing." Maxwell pushed himself off the tree they were leaning against, planting a deep kiss on Dorian's lips before pulling back. "We can't; we have to be back before dawn," he reminded Dorian, trying to resist the urge to give in to their desires. But Dorian just shook his head, looking slightly put off. "But you're already hard," he pouted, indicating that he was ready and willing for more intimate activities. Maxwell sighed deeply, knowing that there was no nearby lake or river where they could cool off and clear their heads. The heat between them was palpable and tempting, but they had to resist for now.

Dorian's hands tightened around Maxwell's chest, his grip almost bruising as he forcefully pushed him against the rough bark of a nearby tree. Dorian slowly sank to his knees, his dark, intense eyes looking up at Maxwell through a veil of thick, dark lashes. Maxwell's left hand lazily cradled Dorian's head as he took deep, shuddering breaths. His tongue darted out, teasingly licking at the tip of Maxwell's cock before engulfing it completely in his mouth.

Maxwell felt himself get lost in the sensation of Dorian's mouth engulfing his cock. Each movement of Dorian's head sent waves of pleasure coursing through Maxwell's body, causing his head to loll back and his eyes to roll into the back of his head. A sly smile curved on Dorian's lips as he set a steady, rhythmic pace with his skilled mouth. Maxwell could not believe how long it had been since he was last with Dorian, and the feeling of his warm mouth and moist tongue swirling around the girth of his cock made him ache with desperation.

Dorian knew all of Maxwell's weak points when it came to this, having been together for so long. As they moved together in perfect harmony, Maxwell's warm breath could be seen in the cool and crisp air. His fingers tangled in Dorian's hair, holding onto the back of his head as he surrendered completely to the overwhelming pleasure. With expert hands, Dorian hollowed out his cheeks and increased the intensity of his movements, causing Maxwell's cock to throb and lurch forward as he cried out in ecstasy. And in that moment, nothing else mattered except for the two of them entwined in each other's embrace.

With a firm grip, Dorian slowly pulled down Maxwell's pants, baring his flushed skin to the cool air. The sensation sent shivers of anticipation through Maxwell's body. As Dorian's nails dug into his thigh, Maxwell felt himself grow even more eager for what was to come. His hips moved instinctively, driven by the growing fire within him. He tightened his hold on Dorian's hair, urging him on as his hips moved instinctively. Dorian's movements were deliberate and sensual as he trailed his hand up Maxwell's thigh. And then, without warning, his finger found its way to Maxwell's entrance and pushed in with a forceful determination. This sent Maxwell over the edge, his body trembling as he released himself into Dorian's awaiting mouth.

Satisfied with the result, Dorian stood up and passionately kissed Maxwell, who was still coming down from his high. With one hand cradling the back of Dorian's head, Maxwell rolled over and pressed the Acolyte's body against a nearby tree. A sly smile graced his lips as he gave Dorian a suggestive look. "Come on," he said breathlessly. "We need to get back." With a playful wink, he passionately kissed Dorian. After a long moment, they grabbed their saddlebags and began their journey back home, both satisfied and content with their fiery encounter in the woods.

Chapter 11

eavy footsteps echoed off the cold, stone walls of the castle at a hurried pace. A soft light peeked from under the grand oak wood doors as they were pushed open by the Cardinal, who rushed to the King's bed. "Your Majesty! Your Majesty!" he cried out, shaking Arthur's left side until he stirred from his deep sleep. "For God's sake, Reede, what is it?" Arthur questioned groggily as he sat up and rubbed his eyes. "Your Grace, I've received a letter by pigeon! Bestla has been attacked by a dragon!" The Cardinal's voice was filled with urgency and fear. His hands shook as he spoke, "Bestla's docks have been destroyed, ships burned, homes and lives lost!" Arthur swung his legs over the bed and had a grave expression on his face. He turned to his groomsmen and ordered, "Dress me!" He then turned to the Cardinal and commanded, "Call a gathering of the council!" As his groomsmen quickly helped him put on a luxurious velvet robe with wolf neck fur collar and slippers, Arthur's mind raced with thoughts of the devastation in Bestla - *how many were dead, how extensive was the damage to the docks and town itself?* He realized that his groomsmen were not moving fast enough for his liking and bellowed, "Hurry for God's sake!" causing them to scramble even faster. "Sorry, your Majesty!" they squeaked as they rushed to finish dressing him.

The Duke entered the castle at a brisk pace, swinging open the door that led to the King's council room. He was the first to arrive. "What's going on, your Majesty? I came as soon as my footman woke me." Arthur stood by a window overlooking the horizon where dawn was just breaking and birds were starting to chirp. The Duke knew his friend well enough to recognize from his posture alone that the news was grave. "Bestla is destroyed, by a dragon no less,"

Arthur answered in a somber tone. The Duke's shock was evident as he sat down in a chair. "Any word on the death count?" Just then, other members of the council began to arrive.

"Not yet," the King replied. "But I have learned that a cohort of the order has also been killed in Cesileon forest, along with others." The Duke leaned over the table, his arms supporting him as he studied a map of the continent, marked with symbols representing different kingdoms. He grabbed a marker coin made of black onyx and placed it over Bestla before grabbing another and placing it over the forest. "Any sign of the dragon heading towards us? What about my son?" he asked urgently. The Cardinal entered with a solemn look on his face. "No news on either, I'm afraid."

The King shook his head in frustration, furrowing his brow as he sat up in bed. The darkness of the night surrounded him, but his mind was racing with thoughts and worry. The Cardinal groaned as he stood from a nearby chair and began to pace the room, his footsteps echoing off the stone walls.

"I'm sorry, your Majesty," he said, "I shouldn't have woken you without all of the details, but I felt you needed to know...to prepare for what lies ahead of us in the morning."

Arthur let out a heavy sigh, knowing that the Cardinal was right. If he had not been informed until the morning, he would have been even angrier. As soon as his tunic, pants, robes, and shoes were on, he turned around to face the Cardinal with determination.

"I want supplies and aid to be sent to Bestla immediately," he declared.

"Yes, your grace," the Cardinal answered, bowing respectfully. "I will also send our priests to travel there and assess any damage to the church."

Satisfied with this plan, King Arthur continued. "And we must also gather information about the town itself. How severe is the damage? We'll need to focus our resources there – clearing rubble, burying the dead, and rebuilding the town and docks."

As the king spoke, he walked over to a small dresser in the corner of the room. He filled a bowl with water from a pitcher and splashed it on his face, trying to wash away some of his exhaustion and worries. He then placed both hands on either side of the dresser, steeling himself for the tasks ahead.

"We have a lot of work ahead of us," he said firmly to the Cardinal.

"Yes, your grace," replied the Cardinal, knowing that they had a daunting task ahead of them. Together, they would rebuild and restore Bestla to its former glory.

)o(

The sweet melodies of birds filled the air, coaxing Tiatria from her slumber. She slowly opened her eyes to find Cullen's cloak draped over her body, providing warmth and comfort. As she sat up, her gaze fell upon Thamyris sitting about six feet away, tending to a small fire with a stick. His head turned towards her as he greeted her, "Good morning. That young knight asked me to watch over you while he went to the church for morning prayers." Tiatria noticed the other survivors scattered around the campsite, some gathering scraps of food while others tended to the remains of their fires. In the distance, she could see Dorian and Maxwell speaking with a few monks about how to best care for the injured survivors once they left. Despite their efforts, they looked dirtier and more exhausted than when she had last seen them.

"Why are they not inside their church?" Tiatria inquired, gesturing towards Dorian and Maxwell.

Thamyris gave her a sly smile before responding, "You tell me." Tiatria's eyes could tell him who was better than he could. Tiatira noticed there were more bodies discovered in the morning light, their lifeless forms wrapped in blankets or sheets and gently moved to be taken to the church cemetery. Tears streamed down Tiatria's cheeks as she realized that no matter how hard she fought, she could not save them all.

"Do you finally feel something for these humans now?" Thamyris taunted, his keen ears picking up on her attempts to hide her tears.

With a heavy heart, Tiatria admitted, "Perhaps I do. I have never encountered humans before this journey. I never expected them to be so... fragile."

Thamyris simply nodded in understanding as they both watched the ongoing chaos of survival unfold before them.

Thamyris let out a heavy sigh, resting his elbows on his lap and clasping his hands together. "More death will come before this is over, Tiatria. That is inevitable," he said somberly. "We must find Amalia quickly if we want to minimize the destruction wrought by the dragon." His words weighed heavily on Tiatria as she rose to her feet, holding Cullen's cape on her right forearm while brushing off dirt from her clothing.

Maxwell was busy helping set up what little food and water they had left. Dorian stood beside a massive soup pot, stirring the ladle around its contents. "Is this all that's left?" he asked incredulously. "I distinctly remember having more than half of the pot and three loaves of bread just yesterday!" Maxwell placed the dishes he had collected from people last night onto a nearby table, knowing they would need them again soon. Dorian gave him a disapproving look. "I suspect some people have been sneaking extra portions," Maxwell replied, noting the hint of disappointment in Dorian's voice.

He began to stack plates one by one when Dorian interjected with disapproval. "People are hungry, Dorian," Maxwell stated matter-of-factly. "Can you blame them for sneaking an extra ladle or slice of bread?" Dorian's disapproving expression did not waver. "I can when it means there won't be enough food for these people," he retorted. Maxwell turned to his right and saw a line forming already. He sighed, realizing there may not be enough to go around. "God help us," he muttered under his breath.

Dorian shook his head and placed his hand on his hip, looking exasperated. "And the Mother too!" he added with a hint of desperation in his voice. He raised his right hand in front of him. "Alright everyone, you will each receive either a bowl of soup or a piece of bread. There simply is not enough for both," he announced to the crowd, who began to grumble and protest. Dorian furrowed his brow and gave a stern glare. "None of that!" he shouted over the noise, brandishing the ladle in his hand. "If people hadn't been selfish and taken extra food during the night, we wouldn't have this problem!" He pointed the ladle at the crowd. "Now line up!" The villagers quickly fell into line without a word.

Maxwell could not help but be impressed by how smoothly Dorian was handling the situation. He had expected some resistance, but no one wanted to argue with the acolyte at the moment. Dorian turned to Maxwell with a cross expression. "Don't just stand there, Amant! Start handing out either bread or soup bowls," he barked. Maxwell quickly snapped to attention and began distributing the meager rations among the hungry and exhausted crowd.

Cullen knelt in the quiet hush of the church; his body bowed before one of the meticulously carved pews. The smooth, polished wood of the pew was made from white oak and gleamed under the soft light filtering through stained glass windows. Cullen's hands were clasped together on the back of the pew, a set of rosary beads woven between his fingers. His lips moved silently as he whispered prayers in Latin, his voice barely audible in the stillness:

"Páter nóster qui es in cáelis,sanctificétur

nomen túum.Advéniat régnum túum.

Fíat vóluntas tua,sicút in Cáelo et in térra.

Pánem nóstrum quotidiánum da nóbis hodie,

et dimítte nóbis débita nóstrasícut et nos dimíttimus debitoŕibus nóstris.

Et ne nós indúcas in tentátionem,sed líbera nos a málo.

Amén."

The words echoed off the smooth stone walls, creating an ethereal atmosphere within the church. Cullen's hands rested on the back of the pew, his whole body consumed by the weight of his faith. Cullen's eyes were closed, his mind focused solely on his prayers and his connection to a higher power. The scent of burning candles and incense filled his nostrils, reminding him of all the times he had sought solace and guidance within these very walls.

Rays of sunlight streamed through stained glass windows, casting colorful patterns across the floor and illuminating his bowed figure. The air was heavy with incense and reverence, creating a sense of sacredness in the small church. As Cullen finished his prayer, he sat back on his heels and closed his eyes, feeling at peace within the holy sanctuary.

The sun had barely risen when Cullen began his meditations, murmuring the same words over and over with fervent determination. As he prayed, Cullen felt a comforting presence surrounding him, reassuring him that he was not alone. Yet, despite this reassurance, he could not help but feel a desperate need for understanding. Why had God sent them on this path? To witness such destruction and death? The weight of it all hung heavy on his heart.

By mid-morning, Maxwell joined him by leaning against the door of the small church. Maxwell could see the weight of their mission crushing down on him, and he was desperate for guidance. "Cullen!" Maxwell called out softly, hesitant to disturb anyone's prayers, but they needed to leave. Cullen made the sign of the cross with his right hand before rising to his feet and joining Maxwell at the door. "Dorian and I need to talk to you and the others," Max said solemnly, knowing that a lot had happened in just a short amount of time. "But I want you to know that you're doing well, don't let anyone say otherwise." Cullen nodded, grateful for Maxwell's words of encouragement.

Cullen noticed a monk walking him to enter the church, "Excuse me," said Cullen. The monk stopped to look at Cullen, "Yes sir?" he answered. Cullen pulled out the letter that he wrote to Edith. "Can you send this to the castle?" The monk took the letter, bowed his head, and walked back into the church. Cullen turned back to look at Maxwell, who motioned for them to walk on.

As they walked down the hill together, Dorian appeared and joined them. He had a grave expression on his face as he led them to what was left of the stables. To their surprise, all the horses were still there, including the majestic unicorns. Dorian had assumed they would have either run away from the dragon's attack or been taken or consumed by the beast. But unicorns were wise enough not to flee from any magical creature; it would only draw their attention and put them in danger. No unicorn wanted to become a dragon's meal.

Upon their return to the group, Maxwell and Dorian managed to secure two horses that were left in the stables. Luckily, The Order always kept extra horses in case of emergency. Tiatria noticed Cullen and the others walking towards her, carrying Cullen's cloak carefully draped over her right forearm. With a bright smile, she handed it back to him as he approached.

"Thank you," Cullen said gratefully, taking the cloak from her. "I'm glad you were kept warm last night."

Tiatria smiled sweetly at him as she noticed his rosary. "They are very beautiful."

Cullen tucked the rosary back into the leather pouch on his belt. "Thank you. They belong to my mother."

Tiatria's eyes met his, and she spoke softly, "I'm glad to see that they bring you great comfort." With a nod, she walked over to her unicorn and gently stroked its cheek as she took the reins from Dorian.

Cullen could not help but notice the playful fairies swirling around Tiatria, drawn by her pure and kind spirit. Even now, it was hard for him to quiet his thoughts and ignore the improper desires that threatened to surface. He knew she could hear them, which is why he struggled to keep his mind focused on more virtuous matters. Tiatria looked back at him with a radiant smile, her eyes seeming to sparkle just like the fairies dancing around her.

Dorian handed Maxwell his horse's reins before mounting onto his own steed. Cullen watched as Maxwell briefly held Dorian's hand while taking the reins. A blush crept up Cullen's cheeks as he observed the subtle exchange between the two men. He quickly pushed any impure thoughts out of his mind; homosexuality was a sin and strictly forbidden by the church. The consequences of such actions were severe, and Cullen did not want to think about what would happen if their relationship was discovered.

"Shall we continue?" Dorian asked, snapping Cullen out of his thoughts. Flustered, Cullen nodded and mounted his horse, eager to focus on their mission ahead.

)o(

Princess Edith awoke with the ethereal glow of the rising sun creeping in through her cathedral windows on the east side of her bedchambers. The richly embroidered silk curtains draped gracefully around the massive windows, framing a breathtaking view of the rolling hills and crystal blue waters beyond. As she rose from her bed, a team of chambermaids were already bustling about, assisting her into a soft silk robe and a pair of embroidered slippers. In her mind, Edith envisioned her life with her beloved husband Cullen once again – they had two sons who were both future heirs to the throne. Cullen was a wise and powerful king, and she was his devoted queen. She dreamed of them sipping tea on the balcony while their children played with wooden swords and toy horses. They had even discussed their plans for another child, hoping for a little girl this time.

Edith hummed contentedly as her maid carefully combed through her long locks, gently arranging them into a partially swept-up ponytail twisted into an elegant bun. For today's ensemble, the princess chose a delicate silver circlet adorned with three shimmering moonstones arranged in a triangle formation, with a teardrop-shaped diamond dangling from its tip. She also selected a dainty silver chain necklace and sparkling diamond earrings to complete her regal look.

Gracefully, she slipped into a powder blue dress that hugged her curves and flared out in long bell sleeves. The off-the-shoulder cut revealed just enough skin to be alluring yet still left room for the imagination. Her hips were adorned with a delicate silver chain belt, adding a touch of elegance and charm to the ensemble. As she twirled in front of the mirror, the fabric swished around her, creating a soft rustling sound like leaves in a gentle breeze. She could not help but feel like a princess in this dress, ready to conquer any event or occasion.

As she sat down for breakfast, she could not help but notice the absence of her father's usual seat at the table. She turned to one of the footmen standing nearby and asked, "Where is Papa?" The footman replied with a slight bow of his head, "He is at the council, your grace. An urgent matter called for his attention during the night." As another footman placed a plate of delicious food in front of her, Edith's eyes fell upon the elaborate silver hood cover that adorned it. With a graceful hand, she lifted the cover off to reveal a perfectly arranged breakfast. Picking up her utensils, she delicately cut into a piece of ham, savoring every bite as she spoke again, "I do hope it is nothing too serious. I miss my father dearly when he must attend to matters during our morning meal. It's one of the few opportunities we have to spend time together throughout the day." Her heart ached at the thought of not seeing him until later in the evening.

Edith sat gracefully on the windowsill of her parlor room, a serene smile on her lips as she hummed a soft tune while working on her embroidery. The sunlight streamed in through the large windows, casting a warm glow upon her delicate features. With nimble fingers, she sewed intricate tulips and orchids onto a pure white handkerchief, adding other embellishments with care and precision.

But as she sewed, her mind wandered to Cullen, and she could not help but feel a twinge of sadness, knowing he was not stationed somewhere where he could receive letters from her. So, instead, she poured all her love and longing into every delicate thread that passed through her fingers.

She knew him to be shy and kind, but she also saw in him the potential to be a great leader with his quiet strength and unwavering courage. His courage to stand up against those who were wrong was admirable, and she had witnessed it firsthand during his occasional arguments with his father.

Suddenly, the whispers of Edith's maids broke through her concentration. They huddled on the floor next to her, their voices hushed as they gossiped about another member of their social circle.

Frowning in disapproval, she set down her work and turned to them. "What is it that you are discussing so eagerly?" she asked, trying not to let her annoyance show.

The maids shifted nervously, clearly caught gossiping. "Did you hear about Bestla?" one whispered, unable to contain the juicy news any longer. Edith's heart sank at the mention of the name – Bestla was where Cullen was sent to deal with matters for the order.

"No," Edith answered with a cold pit in her stomach, "I heard that your beau was sent there before the dragon attack." Edith's eyes widened in shock and concern for the unknown man who had captured her heart.

"What!" she exclaimed sharply, causing all the maids to jump in fear. "Enough with this vicious gossip!" she snapped, "Mind your duties instead of spreading rumors." she scolded sharply, disturbed by their vicious and intrusive gossip. The young maid immediately bowed her head in apology. "Forgive me, your Grace! We thought you were already aware."

Edith flicked her fingers as she laid her hands on her lap, signaling for them to leave. The maids bowed their heads and left. The moment they left, Edith gripped onto her kerchief in desperation. Her heart raced and tears welled. Her imagination started to run away with itself as she thought of where Cullen was and if he was all right.

Back in Amalthea, Princess Edith's heart raced as she sprinted towards the council room. She knew that as a woman, she was forbidden from entering, but the urgent news she had heard from the women at court as they whispered while working their needlework drove her to push past any rules. As soon as she arrived, still breathless from her run, she burst into the room just as the council was in session. The king's piercing gaze fell upon his daughter, and he immediately noticed the tears glistening in her eyes.

"Edith?" he questioned, concern etched on his face.

The members of the council stood at attention as the princess ran into her father's open arms. "Say it isn't true!" she sobbed, burying her face in his chest. "Please tell me that Cullen is not dead! Everyone is saying he perished in Bestla from dragon fire!"

No one in the council had any further information to offer Edith, leaving them at a loss for words.

The Duke's hand slammed down on the table in rage, causing everyone to jump. "Curse those who spread such vicious rumors! We should have their tongues cut out for spreading such falsehoods!" His anger rose even more when he saw the heartbroken state of Princess Edith. For a moment, he considered carrying out such a punishment – after all, he held enough power to decree it.

But then he heard his daughter's cries and watched as his friend, King Arthur, comforted and consoled her. He could not help but feel sympathy for their sorrowful display – especially since it came from a princess.

As he stood up from his seat, the Duke rested his hand on the pommel of his sword. "I suggest we send another pigeon and possibly a messenger to Bestla," he suggested calmly. "They will surely update us on the extent of the damage and let us know if my son or any other members of our order have survived.

As the members of the council filed out, their heavy footsteps echoed on the marble floors. The Duke's sharp eyes caught sight of something white glinting on the ground. Curiosity piqued, he strode over and bent down to pick up the object, his fingers brushing against delicate embroidery. It was a handkerchief, pure white and intricately decorated with swirling designs and shimmering threads. Its intricate stitching betrayed the skill and care put into its creation. Suddenly, a realization struck him — this was no ordinary handkerchief but a wedding gift for his son from the Princess. The Duke's heart clenched as he realized whose it must be — the Princess's. And judging by the unfinished state of the handkerchief, she had been working on it before her disappearance.

A pang of worry prickled in the Duke's chest as he thought about his son, still missing and possibly in grave danger. He could not help but wonder where the dragon had come from and where it would strike next. How were they supposed to defend themselves against such a formidable creature? With a heavy sigh, the Duke placed the handkerchief back on the table and turned to leave.

As he walked out of the council chamber, his mind was already racing with plans and strategies for dealing with this new threat. He knew that harder choices lay ahead and that discussions with the King would need to be had. But for now, all he could do was wait and hope for his son's safe return.

Finally getting a moment alone with his daughter, King Arthur gently held her tear-stained face in his hands. "My dear, we have your best interests and the safety of our Order at heart," he assured her before placing a loving kiss on her forehead.

)o(

As the group made their way down the road, Maxwell led them southwest from Bestla and towards another small town called Westevia. Tiatria's gaze was constantly wandering, taking in the sights and sounds of this new world. The trees towered above them, their branches swaying in the gentle breeze. Birds sang out sweet melodies, filling the air with a symphony of different notes.

Curiosity got the better of Tiatria as she turned to Maxwell and asked, "What kind of town are we heading to?"

"It is a poor one," Dorian answered before Maxwell could reply. Tiatria raised an eyebrow at the acolyte's response. "Westevia is a small town with less than five hundred inhabitants. It mainly serves as a resting place for travelers on their journey from Amalthea to Carpo. The town's economy relies on the gold earned from these travelers."

Confusion crossed Tiatria's features as she questioned, "But if there are inns and markets, why is it considered poor?"

Dorian sighed deeply, his expression serious as he explained, "Bandits... They plague the road between Westevia and Carpo. As Carpo is known for its riches in minerals and jewels, many couriers travel through this route with minimal protection. These bandits also hold control over Westevia, draining any potential income the town may have from visitors."

Tiatria scrunched her nose in disapproval. "We should offer aid to the town while we're passing through!"

"Tiatria," Thamyris' voice was stern as he reprimanded her for even considering meddling in human affairs.

"But it's not right for innocent people to suffer under the rule of bandits!" Tiatria argued back, determined to make a difference.

"I agree with you," Cullen added, turning away from Tiatria to face Maxwell. "Is it not the Order's duty to protect and help those in need?"

Maxwell nodded in understanding, but his expression grew grave as he spoke, "I understand your sentiments, both of you. But we also must consider the safety of the people who reside there. If these bandits catch wind of representatives from the Order in their town, who do you think will suffer the consequences?" He leaned forward on his saddle, emphasizing the gravity of the situation.

Tiatria paused to ponder this, chewing on her lower lip as she looked up at Maxwell. "What if there was a way for us to gather information about the bandits on how to make them leave? Without any of them knowing?"

Thamyris' eyes widened with disapproval as he snapped back in elvish, "Absolutely not!" He placed his hand firmly on his thigh and leaned forward. Thamyris knew exactly what Tiatria was suggesting – using Kethinar's abilities to spy on the town.

Feeling frustrated, Tiatria turned away from Thamyris to face Maxwell once again. "How else are we supposed to gather intel without putting anyone at risk?" she muttered under her breath in elvish.

"What's going on?" Maxwell questioned, growing tired of the bickering in a language he couldn't understand. Tiatria huffed and looked away sullenly while Thamyris responded sharply that it was none of their business.

Realizing that they were missing something important, Dorian shook his head and turned to Maxwell. "Clearly, there is more to this argument than meets the eye," he remarked.

With a defeated sigh, Thamyris closed his eyes and relented, "Fine, do as you wish." He signaled for his unicorn to continue walking as Tiatria turned back towards Maxwell with a determined look in her eyes. "I have an idea," she said eagerly, waiting for Maxwell's approval.

Chapter 12

As the sun began to set behind the towering mountains, casting a warm golden light over the small town of Westevia was draped in the golden light of late afternoon. The sun, sinking behind the majestic mountains in the distance, cast long shadows over the small and run-down town. Many of the buildings showed signs of neglect and disrepair, their facades bearing cracks and peeling paint. As a finch flew over an empty market, a stray dog meandered through the streets in search of scraps. It paused to sniff at discarded food and then continued on its way, eventually landing on a windowsill to preen its feathers.

Suddenly, a burly man strode into the local bar. His skin was pale, and his hair was thinning atop his head. His face wore a hardened expression, and his eyes glinted with a mean edge. He leaned against the rough-hewn bar, casting a fleeting glance at a few other men loitering nearby. "Hey bartender!" he barked gruffly. "Another ale, now!"

The bartender, who appeared worn and tired in comparison to the other patrons in better condition, looked at the man wearily. "Haven't you had enough?" he asked, gesturing to the man's unsteady stance. "I can barely stand as it is."

Enraged by this response, the man slammed his fist on the counter and demanded again, "I said bring me another!" In one swift motion, he grabbed hold of the bartender's shirt and pulled him close. "You heard me!" he growled, his breath heavy with traces of vomit.

Struggling to break free from the man's grasp and avoid passing out from the stench, the bartender slid a mug towards him.

The man released his grip on the poor bartender and snatched up the mug eagerly, muttering, "That's more like it."

He then sauntered over to a table about ten feet away from the bar where another man was seated. This man, slightly overweight and middle-aged, went by the name Hector. As he leaned in towards the burly man with a sly grin, he asked, "Did you hear about that despicable scoundrel, Naromu?"

Setting down his ale, the other man responded with a snort. "Naromu? You mean that fat bastard of a merchant who hires thugs to pillage and plunder, then turns around and profits from their stolen goods?"

The large man let out a deep chuckle, the sound echoing through the dimly lit tavern. "I heard he stumbled upon some rare wine, so rare, it might actually be priceless!" he said to his companion, leaning in with interest.

"Impossible," the other man responded, equally intrigued. "Everything has a price. Is he bringing it here?"

Hector shook his head, "No, I heard he managed to catch the last ship before Bestla burned down."

"What?!" The other man leaned forward, eager for more information.

"Yeah," Hector continued, "Half of the city was destroyed and most of its people were killed by some kind of fire-breathing creature."

"What kind of creature can possibly do that?" The man's eyes widened in fear, "Is it coming here? Do you know?"

Hector shrugged solemnly. "I don't, but I heard it disappeared into the clouds. No one knows where it went."

The drunkard took a long swig from his mug and sat back in his chair. "Where is this Naromu now?"

Hector tapped his fingers nervously on the table, leaning in closer to his friend. "He's headed to Malania for a wine auction," he whispered conspiratorially. "Only the wealthiest and most prestigious families reside there, so you can imagine the value of this wine he was after."

Glancing around to make sure no one was eavesdropping, Hector continued. "I heard from some men who escaped Bestla that they saw them paraded about by Naromu. They described the wine as having a peculiar body and a fragrant aroma. And the cap on the bottle was unlike anything they had ever seen before."

The drunkard let out a loud belch and leaned in eagerly. "We should head there ourselves and see this bottle of wine ourselves."

"I doubt we could afford such a prize, judging by the deep pockets of the vacationers." Hector said gravely. "Especially since we have our own wine to sell."

"Do you think we can sell our wine for half as much?"

"Are you daft?" Hector mocked, rolling his eyes. Then he leaned in even closer, a mischievous glint in his eye. "No one can outsell that bastard. He's clever and does whatever it takes to get the best price for it."

As if on cue, a finch with vibrant feathers flew past Thamyris, perched on a nearby tree to keep watch for any intruders. With Kethinar's enhanced sight, he could see for miles around and nothing could approach the camp without him noticing. Meanwhile, Cullen had set up the tents nearby, but his thoughts were consumed by Tiatria. She had been gone for hours now, and no one knew when she would return.

Suddenly, a finch flew towards camp, chirping excitedly. Thamyris whistled back in response, signaling for Cullen to come towards the center of camp. The finch landed gracefully on a log and suddenly, a bright white light burst forth from it. The light swirled and took shape, revealing Tiatria standing before them.

Dorian dropped the wood he was carrying in surprise. "Welcome back! Our friend has returned," he exclaimed with relief. Maxwell had finished collecting wood and put some into a pit surrounded by stones. He had put pieces of birch bark in between the logs. The bark kept blood-sucking bugs away with the smoke, which, when you're out in the open, was a blessing. Maxwell held out his right hand, causing fire to shoot out and ignite the birch.

Tiatria looked at Maxwell, "They talked about a cargo of wine traveling to Malania." Tiatria folded her arms, "They said something about an auction being held there. I only wish I could've found out more."

Dorian stroked his chin thoughtfully, his mind racing with possibilities. "Malania is a secluded island, several days away by boat. It is known as a popular vacation spot for the wealthy. I find it odd that a wine auction would be held there at all."

Thamyris stood with his arms crossed, listening intently to Tiatria's words. There was a particular detail that caught his attention. "Why would bandits be concerned about wine?" he asked, feeling a cold pit form in his stomach.

Cullen hadn't given it much thought until Thamyris brought it up. "That is rather strange," he agreed. "Why would they be?"

Maxwell pondered for a moment, hands on his hips as he looked down at the ground. When he finally looked up, concern creased his features. "Because they weren't talking about wine," he said gravely.

"What do you mean?" Cullen inquired.

"A person. The 'wine' they were referring to was actually a slave." Maxwell turned to Thamyris with honesty in his eyes. "Your sister, to be specific. And by the sounds of it a high-end slave auction in Malania."

Dorian noticed Maxwell rubbing the back of his neck nervously, something he only did when highly anxious or worried. This sparked suspicion in Dorian's mind, and he knew they would need to have a talk about it later. "With all the wealthy nobles vacationing in Malania, there's bound to be plenty of money involved," Dorian mused aloud.

Tension hung thick in the air as everyone waited for Thamyris' reaction. The elf prince seemed frozen, unsure how to respond. Suddenly, he let out a roar of anger and punched a nearby tree with all his might. The sound echoed through the woods as Thamyris took deep, ragged breaths. "My sister is to be sold," he growled through gritted teeth. "She is to be sold like cattle, a high priestess of Danu, sold to whoever has the most coin!" With clenched fists, Thamyris stormed off into the darkness without another word.

Tiatria's eyes locked onto Cullen, who was visibly unsure and at a loss for words. "It's because he's the high priest of Cernunnos," she finally explained.

Cullen's eyebrows furrowed in confusion. "What does that mean?"

"Being a high priest goes beyond just guiding others spiritually. It means being the mortal vessel for the gods on this plane. He is so deeply connected to Cernunnos that he feels everything God does. Right now, our God is crying out for his Goddess, and our high priest is feeling it all."

Dorian shifted his weight, his hand resting casually on his hip. "So, this erratic behavior is just a God pining for his lover?"

"Yes," Tiatria confirmed with a nod.

"That would explain the unnatural obsession with his sister," Dorian mused.

"But not all of it can be attributed to the god. Some of it is truly Thamyris himself," Maxwell interjected before hurrying after Thamyris, calling out "Your Highness!" as he jogged to catch up. Every step of Maxwell's could be heard by Thamyris, who was quickly calculating how close he was getting. Without warning, Thamyris turned and threw a powerful punch at Maxwell's nose, the sickening sound of cartilage breaking echoed through the air. But Maxwell was quick to react, sweeping Thamyris' legs out from under him and causing him to fall hard on his right shoulder.

"Son of a - " Maxwell cursed, rolling onto his left side as blood gushed from his nose. "We will find her before that happens!"

Thamyris snarled as he propped himself up, seething with rage. "You knew my sister..." he trailed off, unable to finish his sentence. In his fall, he had dislocated his shoulder, aggravating the pain even more.

Maxwell nodded, "Yes, I knew! The moment Tiatria said it, I knew." he told the prince with a knot in his throat. Maxwell made a swift motion with his right hand. With a sickening crunch, Maxwell reset his nose, which caused him to groan in pain. "If we find her before we get to her be...."

"Shut up!" Thamyris snapped as he got onto his feet, his left hand holding his arm that seemed to be just dangling. Maxwell caught the glimmer of tears in Thamyris' eyes, the moon's light. He looked at a tree not far from the elf. "There is a tree five feet from you."

"Left or right?" Thamyris questioned.

"Straight ahead," Maxwell answered. He watched as the elf had a good pace walking forward and then rammed his shoulder against the tree. The elf cried out from the pain as he fell back onto the ground. He took huge breaths as he fought tears, feeling as if now that his sister was utterly lost. Maxwell got up and slowly walked up to the Prince. He could hear Maxwell's footsteps approaching, which led him to use his left hand, trying to swipe him away.

The sound of screams pierced the air, causing everyone to come running after the two figures in the distance. Maxwell caught sight of his friends and quickly raised his left arm, signaling for them to stop and stay where they were. Thamyris stood on all fours, his nails digging into the soft grass beneath him as he clenched his fists tightly. Tears streamed down his face as he let out a gut-wrenching scream, his pain and anguish pouring out of him in waves. In a fit of anger, he began ripping up handfuls of grass and punching the ground.

As the chaos unfolded, Tiatria slowly approached Thamyris, who seemed unable to stop crying and screaming. She knelt next to him and placed her hands around his shoulders in an attempt to comfort him.

Meanwhile, Dorian's attention was drawn to Maxwell's broken nose, which he had sustained during the altercation with the elf. "You let him break your nose, didn't you?" he questioned sternly. Maxwell simply watched the scene before him as Dorian used his healing abilities to mend his nose. But Maxwell knew that physical pain could not compare to the emotional turmoil he was feeling inside. "It doesn't even compare, Dorian. Having your heart broken and your soul ripped apart," he said somberly.

Dorian could not help but feel irritated at the fact that Maxwell had allowed himself to be hurt by the elf. He knew that Maxwell was skilled enough to avoid such a strike without question.

Thamyris' chest heaved as he struggled to catch his breath amidst his cries. Tiatria held her prince close as he wept, and Thamyris could feel every emotion she was experiencing. Through her eyes, he could see the sorrow and loss reflected in the faces of their friends around them. The sound of his anguished cries echoed through the forest, filling the space with a haunting sorrow. Tears streamed down his face, each one a testament to the depth of his pain. He screamed until his voice was hoarse, feeling utterly alone in the vastness of his emotions. He doubled over in pain, tears streaming down his face like a waterfall. The weight of his solitude pressed down on him, suffocating him as he struggled to contain his overwhelming despair.

"I'M ALL ALONE!" he screamed, his voice echoing as if another force was behind it. Maxwell's tear-filled eyes glistened as he gazed at Dorian, his voice quivering with raw emotion. "I cannot fathom a life without you, Dorian," he whispered.

Tiatria's delicate fingers gently brushed back Thamyris' sweat-soaked hair as she placed a comforting hand on his forehead. Her words were filled with both comfort and sorrow, urging him to allow himself to mourn before facing the challenges ahead.

The trees surrounding them seemed to lean in closer, their branches entwined like old friends, creating a cocoon of protection and solace. Maxwell, Dorian, and Cullen stood together in the moonlit forest - each lost in their own thoughts and fears. The weight of their duty pressed down upon their shoulders, but their bond as friends shone bright like a guiding light amid the darkness.

Maxwell's gaze lingered on Cullen before returning to Tiatria and Thamyris. He let out a heavy sigh before speaking, "Tiatria, why don't you go back to the camp with Cullen? Dorian and I need to have a talk with Thamyris." Dorian's head whipped around at the mention of talking to the "grumpy elf."

"What do you mean? We need to -" Dorian intervened.

Maxwell turned to face him, his gaze firm. "Yes, Dorian, we do. There is something important you need to understand."

Tiatria rose from her spot on the ground, placing a comforting hand on Thamyris' shoulder before walking away with Cullen. Both could see in Maxwell's eyes that something needed to happen, and they did not need to be party to it.

Dorian watched them leave before turning his attention back to Maxwell. "What exactly do we need to talk to him about?" he asked, feeling apprehensive. Without a word, Maxwell took Dorian's hand and led him over to where Thamyris was sitting. This simple act caught Dorian by surprise - they never held hands in front of others. As they approached Thamyris, he could smell Maxwell's unique scent of old leather and musk mixed with the faint trace of Dorian's exotic perfume and spices.

Maxwell knelt in front of Thamyris, capturing his attention unable to see his tender gaze. "You're not alone; we're going to find her," he said softly, causing Dorian's eyes to narrow in confusion. It was clear that Dorian knew what Thamyris' Sister meant to him, and Maxwell wanted him to know that he had support.

Dorian's eyes narrowed as he folded his arms, still unsure of what was happening. "What are you doing?" Dorian asked warily. Ignoring him, Maxwell gently held Thamyris' face in his hands. The elf stiffened at first but then slowly relaxed as he saw everything that Maxwell wanted him to see.

Tears threatened to spill from Maxwell's eyes as he struggled to keep his emotions in check. "You're not alone," he repeated, his voice barely above a whisper. Dorian saw a rush of emotions pass between them - everything that Maxwell wanted Thamyris to understand. As he held his breath, realization dawned on Dorian - Maxwell was telling Thamyris that he was not alone because he was just like them. Thamyris' body began to tremble as the weight of this revelation settled in. Without hesitation, he threw himself into Maxwell's embrace. Dorian watched in surprise as Maxwell's expression shifted from shock to pure love and acceptance. Slowly, his own hands reached out and gently touched Thamyris' back as he joined in on the embrace.

Dorian let out a contented sigh as he realized that they were taking in a new member of their family - a prodigy, as it were.

Back at camp, the fire crackled and snapped as Dorian finished healing Thamyris' wounds. Maxwell glared at him, still angry about the punch he had received earlier. Cullen, Tiatria, and Thamyris sat around the fire, anxiously waiting for an explanation from Maxwell.

"Last night, Dorian and I went to find the heretic," Maxwell began, catching everyone by surprise. "Without me?" Cullen exclaimed in shock. "Why? It's the whole reason I was sent?" He looked hurt and betrayed; his brows furrowed in confusion. Maxwell and Dorian exchanged a glance before Dorian spoke up.

"We wanted to see for ourselves before making any rash decisions," Dorian chimed in, trying to justify their actions. "We wanted to spare you more bloodshed," said Maxwell.

"You mean you thought I was too green to be of any help." Cullen pouted, feeling left out and useless.

"If you want to know, yes," Dorian confirmed.

Maxwell's hand abruptly landed on Dorian's chest with a loud smack, causing the acolyte to flinch in pain. "Dorian!" Maxwell scolded him before turning back to Cullen. "Cullen, I made the call.

It was not because you were too inexperienced," he explained, giving Dorian a disapproving look. "We needed to deal with the heretic first before going after the Princess. And after everything that happened yesterday, we didn't want to put you through more danger."

Cullen's expression softened at this revelation, but he still could not help but feel hurt by their decision to leave him behind.

"We found her and discovered a few things," Maxwell continued, shifting the focus of the conversation away from Cullen's hurt feelings.

"Like what?" Cullen asked eagerly.

"She's an elf," Dorian answered nonchalantly.

"An elf? How is that possible?" Tiatria interjected, her eyebrows furrowed in confusion. She had always believed that all the elves had fled into the forest.

Thamyris sighed and pulled his knees closer to his chest. "She must have stayed on my Mother's orders in hopes of preserving our world here."

"Precisely," Dorian confirmed. "While we were listening, the Order rode in and started arresting people."

"Did they catch her?" Tiatria asked with concern etched on her face.

Dorian shook his head. "God no, we managed to get to her first. I used my superior magical skills to hide us and escape with her. As we were leaving, a dragon attacked everyone there."

Tiatria's eyes widened in fear at the mention of a dragon. She could not even imagine the horrors that took place during the attack.

"Did they all die?" Cullen asked hesitantly, already anticipating the answer.

"Most of them," Dorian answered with a heavy heart. "Only the so-called 'heretic' and her friends survived."

Tears welled up in Tiatria's eyes as she struggled to ask the next question. "What did you do to her?"

Maxwell shifted uncomfortably; he looked down at the ground, his foot aimlessly kicking at the dirt beneath him. "We let her go," he said quietly.

Thamyris let out a heavy sigh. "It doesn't matter now since she was telling the truth."

Maxwell nodded in agreement. "That's what we thought too. We watched her leave with her people and then made our way back here. Unfortunately, we had to walk since that damn dragon killed our horses."

Cullen furrowed his brow, suddenly realizing why they were dirtier than when they had left and why they needed new horses. The gravity of their situation weighed heavily on all of them as they sat around the fire, trying to process everything that had happened.

Cullen paused for a moment, considering his next question carefully. An uneasy feeling settled in the pit of his stomach, and he knew that the subject of conversation needed to change.

Cullen took a deep breath, hesitating before finally mustering the courage to ask his burning question. He turned to Maxwell, his eyes locking onto the older man's gaze.

"Can I ask you something?" Cullen asked, his voice wavering slightly with unease.

Maxwell met his gaze, understanding the weight behind the question the young knight was about to ask. "Of course," he replied calmly, giving Cullen his full attention.

"You seemed to know about the terms that Tiatria used when she reported back on what she'd heard in Westevia. Did you learn this information during your travels?" Cullen pressed, watching as Maxwell shifted uncomfortably and avoided eye contact by staring at the ground. His hands clasped over each other as they hung over his knees. He did not want to talk about it, not now. Dorian observed the exchange from his spot leaning against a nearby tree, arms crossed and legs casually crossed.

Dorian could see the situation was delicate, and they needed to handle it carefully. Perhaps it would be best to discuss it with King Richard upon their return to Almathea. "We could go back to Almathea and report everything to the King," Dorian suggested, breaking the tense silence. "I'm sure he would provide aid and support for our cause."

Maxwell let out a heavy sigh and began to pace back and forth, clearly conflicted. He knew that speaking to King Richard could potentially lead to aid, but it also meant revealing damning evidence against the heretic and possibly putting Tiatria's life in danger. They would have to tread carefully if they were to navigate this delicate situation successfully.

Thamyris sat perched on a nearby tree branch, gently petting his hawk's head as he absentmindedly rubbed off the wax from its pin feathers, listening to the conversation. "What about the innocent people in that town? We cannot just leave them at the mercy of those bandits," said Tiatria, voicing her concerns.

"They are not our concern," Thamyris replied bluntly, jumping down from his perch with silent grace. "We have more pressing matters to attend to."

Dorian let out a resigned sigh. "As much as I hate to admit it, Thamyris is right. If we were to march into that town as we are, it would only provoke the bandits and potentially put innocent lives at risk. It's best to retreat for now and come back with a better plan."

Cullen, who had been quietly listening this whole time, suddenly spoke up with a sly smile on his face. "Actually, I have an idea," he announced. Dorian could not help but chuckle at the irony of Cullen having a clever idea.

"And what might that be?" Dorian asked, raising an eyebrow in amusement in a slightly condescending tone.

"You'll see," Cullen responded cryptically, a mischievous glint in his eye.

Cullen's face twisted into a deep scowl as he glared at the mage, his eyes flicking to each person in turn. "We need to find a way inside and take back the town."

"How do you propose we do that?" Dorian spoke up, uncrossing his arms and raising an eyebrow.

Dorian raised his right hand from its place folded against his chest, and his eyes narrowed with curiosity. Maxwell growled, indicating that he had an idea brewing in his mind. "What's your plan?"

Maxwell turned to face Dorian, determination etched on his features. "I'll have to dust off an old skill of mine." Dorian was taken aback - Maxwell never mentioned having any other profession besides being a servant of the order. But he knew there were things Maxwell kept hidden, secrets that haunted him in the dead of night. Perhaps now was the time for him to reveal them and potentially save not just one life but many.

With his hands on his hips, Maxwell fell silent, the weight of his words hanging heavily in the air. The crackling fire was the only sound in the stillness that followed. Dorian nodded, waiting patiently for Maxwell to speak. "What is it, Amant? Tell us."

All eyes were on Maxwell as he lowered his head, hesitating before continuing. He shifted his right hand from his hip and looked directly at Dorian with sincerity shining in his eyes. "This was before we became partners, Dorian. You have to understand that," he glanced at the rest of the group, "You all have to understand that." Cullen gave a nod of understanding while wrapping his left arm around Tiatria, unsure of what he would soon learn.

Dorian's curiosity peaked; his eyebrows raised in question. "What kind of old profession could possibly lead one to equate a wine auction with a slave auction?" Maxwell let out an exasperated sigh as he met Dorian's gaze. "I know because I've been involved in it," he admitted gravely. Dorian's expression turned quizzical as he struggled to comprehend Maxwell's words. "What role did you exactly play in these wine auctions?" he prodded, emphasizing the words 'wine auction' with a gesture of his fingers as if they were foreign to him.

Maxwell grew increasingly agitated, his right hand dropping from his chin as he paced back and forth in frustration. "I was a slaver, Dorian! I sold slaves!" he blurted out, bracing himself for the reactions of those around him...but there was not any. Everyone simply stared at Maxwell in shock. The only response came from Cullen, who spoke up with a flushed face, "That explains how you knew about the slave auction in Bestla." Dorian could not help but feel uncomfortable as all eyes turned to him. Normally, he would have lashed out at such a thoughtless statement from Cullen, but his attention was fixed on Maxwell.

"So, you were a slaver," Dorian stated, drawing Maxwell's focus back to him. His eyes narrowed as he became more intrigued by this revelation. "Tell me more."

"Yes, I was...once," he confessed. He folded his arms across his chest and shifted uncomfortably from foot to foot. "It was before I met you, Dorian. I had just completed a mission for the order when I ran into some former associates."

Dorian shrugged nonchalantly as Maxwell paused for a moment. "And then what? You decided to go into business together? Break the law for profit?"

Maxwell shifted his weight onto his left leg, avoiding Dorian's gaze. "Essentially, yes. We didn't make much money in the order, and I needed more. My role was to guard the cargo and maintain order during auctions."

Dorian gave a dry chuckle. "Ah yes, your elemental powers must have come in handy for that."

Maxwell knew he had to continue his story, no matter how uncomfortable it made him. So he continued, "On one particular run, my companions and I were betrayed by rival sellers. We were arrested by the Order and my friends were executed on the spot while the slaves were set free...and I..." he continued, his voice trailing off as he recalled the memory. Dorian nodded in understanding as he deduced what happened next. "And you were punished severely. It's surprising they didn't execute you on the spot, to be honest." It was at this moment that Tiatria was able to access Maxwell's thoughts for the first time. His mind had always been tightly guarded, as if he was afraid to let her read him in any way. Cullen noticed her expression change, and he leaned in to whisper, "Are you okay?" Tiatria shook her head slightly, unable to tear herself away from Maxwell's story.

"My punishment was...different," Maxwell revealed with a pained expression.

Cullen's mind recalled the grave marks littering Maxwell's back, his stomach twisted into knots. Dorian's foot tapped anxiously as he stood with arms crossed, the air heavy and tense with anticipation. "What did they do to you? Knowing their merciless ways, I can only imagine the horrors you endured." The punishment for such a crime was known to be severe, and Dorian could feel the weight of it pressing down upon them all. Maxwell nodded solemnly, meeting Dorian's gaze before turning to Tiatria. "I have a plan to infiltrate the town and help drive them out. But I will need your help, Tiatria," he said, motioning towards her.

Thamyris shook his head vehemently, "Absolutely not!" He was not going to let one of his own kin be put at risk for a reckless, half-baked scheme. Thamyris glanced at Tiatria, knowing it was his duty to protect her at all costs. She was an innocent in this dangerous world, unaware of the depths of cruelty that existed among these mortals.

"What are you proposing?" Dorian asked, curious yet cautious. He knew that Maxwell would never endanger Tiatria without absolute certainty of success.

Maxwell turned to Tiatria once again, "I'm going to sell you--"

"No!" Thamyris cried out, stepping forward aggressively. His anger was palpable, veins pulsing in his neck as he took a step forward. "That is not an option! If anyone should go, it will be me." Dorian gave the elf a skeptical look from the corner of his eye. "No offense, but no one would buy a blind slave. Most would pay to see you executed on sight," he stated bluntly. Thamyris glared at Dorian with disdain as he brushed past him, resisting the urge to lash out physically. Maxwell could not deny Dorian's logic - selling Tiatria would not be a viable option. But he could have been more diplomatic about it.

Maxwell approached Tiatria, his expression grave. "I need you for your unique ability," he explained softly.

"I suspected as much," she replied calmly. Maxwell nodded in understanding before turning to Tiatria. He approached Tiatria with a serious expression, "I need you because of your gift."

"I had a feeling that was the case," Tiatria replied gently, understanding Maxwell's need for her abilities. He nodded in agreement before adding, "I would never actually sell you, of course." Dorian stepped forward, declaring, "I'll come with you as well."

Maxwell's voice was firm yet eerily calm as he spoke. "No," interjected Maxwell, "People are well aware that you work for the order, and I need them to believe that I have gone rogue." He turned to look at Cullen, his brown eyes piercing through the dim light of the night. "You'll be coming with me."

"Why him?" Dorian's tone dripped with disappointment. He hated being left out of anything, especially when it came to important missions like this one. Maxwell placed a hand on his hip as he regarded Dorian with an honest look. "Cullen is new, and no one knows he's part of the Order yet. Also, he shares a bond with Tiatria, and they can communicate telepathically. If she picks up on anything, she can relay information to him quickly and discreetly."

Cullen looked at Tiatria, his Amber eyes filled with curiosity. "Could we do that?" Tiatria smiled warmly, her sapphire blue eyes shining with confidence. "Probably. It wouldn't be difficult for you to learn." Dorian begrudgingly admitted that Maxwell had a point, though he would never admit it aloud.

Tiatria nodded in agreement with Maxwell's plan. "Alright, I'll do it," she said firmly. Maxwell appreciated her unwavering trust in him. "Two things," he added sternly, "First, you need to take off your necklace and reveal your elven heritage."

"What? Why?" Cullen's skin prickled with cold dread at the thought of removing her pendant.

"Because it will help us deceive our enemies. They will become greedy and ignorant of their surroundings once they see an elf in their midst," explained Maxwell calmly. Cullen couldn't help but worry about the potential dangers that awaited them in Westevia. His biggest fear was someone trying to harm him or Maxwell in order to get to Tiatria.

"What's the second thing?" Cullen asked, his voice filled with trepidation.

Maxwell looked at both of them with a serious expression. "You must trust me completely. I will be acting differently, speaking differently, and there may be times when you question my actions and words." He locked eyes with Tiatria, his gaze intense. "Your instincts may tell you to run or fight against me, but it's all part of the act. Do you understand?"

Tiatria nodded firmly, her determination unwavering. She had read Maxwell's thoughts and knew that this was their best chance at infiltrating Westevia and helping its people without causing any unnecessary damage.

Chapter 13

as the Moon rose over Westevia, a lone guardsman stood at his post outside of town. He leaned against his spear, fighting to keep his eyes open after a long day of guarding. The sound of hooves on the road jolted him awake and he stumbled to stand at attention as two riders approached, with someone walking alongside them. As they drew closer, he could see that the person walking was cloaked and hooded, their hands tied and being towed by one of the horses.

It was Maxwell on the lead horse; his tunic and any identifiable items of the Order were removed. He sat in just his leather armor, a piece of long grass hanging from his mouth as he casually addressed the guard. "We're looking for a place to spend the night," he said, nodding to his companion. "We're transporting some cargo."

The guard narrowed his eyes skeptically. "I've never seen you here before."

Maxwell leaned forward, placing a hand on his thigh. "It's almost dark," he growled. "I'm not risking such an exotic beauty to be mauled in these woods." He nudged his captive with his foot, prompting them forward.

The guard was unsure what exactly was going on but sensed that something was off about this situation. When Maxwell pulled back his hood, revealing a delicate and ethereal elven woman, the guard's eyes widened in awe. It took him a moment to notice her pointed ears, marking her as an elf. The man looked at the two men, turned and walked away.

"What is he doing?" Cullen questioned. Maxwell leaned forward with his right forearm on the horn of the saddle. He chewed on the long piece of grass in his mouth. "Asking someone more senior, I'd expect." Maxwell's eyes drifted to Tiatria, "Remember what we discussed. Everything I do or say is only an act." Tiatria looked back at Maxwell and nodded.

After a few minutes, another man appeared alongside the guard. Tiatria's elven eyesight allowed her to see in the darkness just as well as she could during the day. She recognized him as the tough-looking man she had seen earlier that day. The man looked up at Maxwell and spoke in a gruff tone: "So you're the one who wants passage into our quaint little town?"

Maxwell dismounted his horse and approached the man. "I wouldn't call it quaint, more like a shithole," he replied nonchalantly. Tiatria watched as the two men locked eyes, tension thick in the air. "What did you say?" the man growled.

Maxwell took a step forward, undeterred. "I said it's a shithole." Suddenly, both men burst into laughter, their animosity diffused.

They clasped each other's forearms in a show of camaraderie. "Maxwell, where have you been?" the man asked. "I thought you gave up the slaving business."

Maxwell shook his head with a small smile. "It's good to see you, Edger," he replied. "And I haven't given up the business, just laying low after that incident in Bestla a few years back."

Edger gazed at the other man seated astride a horse, his curiosity piqued. "Who did you bring with you?" As his companion threw back his hood, Maxwell turned to reveal a new recruit – Cullen. A smirk danced across his lips as he introduced him, "I acquired a new member for our cause." he replied casually.

The man scoffed and let out a hearty laugh, eyeing Cullen with disdain. "Where did you pick this one up? Not many are eager to join us in our line of work." Maxwell chuckled and clapped the man on the shoulder, his left hand resting heavily on the leather-clad arm. "A disgraced noble's son found him wandering the streets. Perfect for our needs."

Cullen observed as Edger's gaze shifted to Tiatria. She shrank back under the human's leering stare. "Well, well, well," he drawled, his thumb and index finger grasping her chin and tilting her head up for inspection like a piece of merchandise. Maxwell chimed in, "She is a beauty, my friend. Pure perfection. And such beauty deserves to be seen in a much better light."

Edger led the group to a nearby tavern, not far from the bustling center of the city. Tiatria walked slightly ahead of her captors, her eyes downcast and her body tense.

Cullen maintained a neutral expression but kept a close eye on the elf. (Are you alright?) he silently communicated with her.

(Yes, I'm fine.) Tiatria responded in their mental link.

(I will not let anyone harm you, I swear it.) Cullen vowed.

(I trust you, do not worry.) Tiatria reassured him.

As Edger swung open the heavy wooden door of the tavern, all conversation ceased, and every patron turned to stare at the ethereal beauty before them. Maxwell exuded confidence as he strode in, chest puffed out and feet propped up on a nearby table.

Cullen watched as Maxwell stood next to him, observing Edger as he circled Tiatria like a predator eyeing its prey. "Where on earth did you find this one?"

Maxwell let out a disgruntled groan as he shook his head and crossed his arms over his stomach. "Same place Naromu found his."

Edger could not help but admire the elf's flawless, pure, milky-white skin, begging to be touched. He gingerly lifted her chin with his fingers, only to have them quickly snatched away by Cullen. "She is not for your amusement," Cullen growled, his amber eyes blazing like hot coals.

Edger gave a sly smile, feeling a shiver run down his spine at the display of protectiveness. "No touching until after purchase, I presume?" He glanced over at Maxwell. "You have a smart one here."

Maxwell eased himself into his seat, the wooden chair creaking under his weight. His body was weary from the day's endeavors. The aroma of ale still lingered in the air as he picked up a mug and took a sip. "He's had to learn the hard way, but I think he's finally starting to grasp it," he commented in an attempt to redirect the conversation. Edger chuckled with a sly grin on his lips. "I can only imagine. I bet you have had to bend him over the table a time or two," he jested, causing Maxwell to shoot him a sharp glare before taking a long sip from his mug.

Cullen, who had been observing the exchange between Maxwell and Edger, furrowed his brow in confusion at their words. Tiatria, standing beside him, remained stoic and motionless.

(You do not want to know), she warned Cullen through telepathy, her eyes darting around to ensure she did not give away her ability.

Maxwell slammed down his empty mug with some force, no longer in the mood for Edger's jokes. "Now that you've had a look at our merchandise, do you think I could add her to the wine auction? Word on the street is that Naromu is hosting one in Malania."

Edger raised an eyebrow, impressed by Maxwell's continued involvement in the slave trade despite working for the Order. "Looks like you've been keeping tabs on things," Edger observed as he strolled away from the elven woman. "It's good to see you haven't completely abandoned your old trade."

Maxwell let out a tired sigh as he lowered his mug from his lips. Cullen watched as Maxwell put his feet on the table and crossed them. "Working for the Order doesn't pay well, so it's always nice to have a side hustle." Edger chuckled and leaned back in his chair. "That's what I like to hear. One can never have too many irons in the fire, am I right?" He then turned to Cullen, who maintained a stern expression on his face. "So, what exactly are you hoping to accomplish at this auction?"

A mischievous grin spread across Maxwell's face as he leaned forward. "I want to outbid Naromu." Edger burst into laughter, slamming his hands on the table. "You're still sore about him, aren't you?" he asked with a hearty cackle. Maxwell took his feet off the table, set his mug down, and leaned forward. "That bastard is the reason I spent five years in Carpo's mining prison camp! It's time for payback, and I'm going to take the one thing he values most...his money."

Edger leaned back in his chair, deep in thought for a moment, before pulling out a rolled-up piece of paper from his pocket. He unrolled it to reveal a map. "If you want my help with this little revenge scheme, it will cost you," he said with a smirk.

Cullen's hand instinctively went to his sword hilt as the men around them grew restless and eager to get a closer look at the elven woman. "Stay back!" he barked, causing them to retreat slightly.

Tiatria's pointed ears twitched as she watched the men leering at her, every inch of her body poised and ready to defend herself if necessary. She was an expert in a thousand ways to kill any who dared touch her, but she felt comfort in knowing that Cullen was willing to fight for her.

Feeling Cullen's left hand gently nudging her backward, Tiatria reluctantly tore her eyes away from the group of men and turned to face Maxwell. She kept her head and gaze low, showing proper respect. "Master," she addressed him demurely. Both Maxwell and Edger looked at her curiously, along with Cullen who had turned his head towards them as well. "May I sing for your friends? They seem eager for my entertainment." Maxwell seemed taken aback by her request while Edger turned his chair around to sit facing them. His fingers flicked in a signal for the elven woman to proceed.

Cullen scanned the crowd; his sword held firmly in front of him as he forcefully pushed back anyone who tried to get too close to Tiatria. "Stay back, and do not touch her!" His voice was stern and commanding. Edger sat back in his seat, a smirk playing on his lips. "Your boy seems quite eager to protect your precious cargo," he chuckled. Maxwell rose from his seat and sauntered over to the table, sitting down next to Edger. "Perhaps he thinks he can have her before you even receive payment?" Edger shook his head, glancing at Maxwell with a skeptical look. "What is she anyway?"

Maxwell folded his arms across his chest as he watched Tiatria step into the center of the room. Her lips parted, and she began to sing an otherworldly, elvish tune that filled the room with an air of magic – listening to her was like listening to the voice of an angel. Cullen and others were entranced by her singing, but Maxwell remained focused, using his left hand to feel around the back of the table until his fingers found Edger's hidden map.

"She's an elf," Maxwell answered quietly.

Suddenly, a man in the crowd called out, "I'll give you a hundred coins for her!"

"Make it one-fifty!" shouted another.

As more bids were called out for Tiatria, she stopped singing and looked around at all the men vying for her ownership.

Maxwell had enough and slammed his right fist onto the table, letting out a deep roar that silenced the room. All eyes turned towards him, feeling the icy chill in his gaze. He stepped in front of Tiatria and drew his sword. She looked at him with shock and fear in her eyes as he grabbed her by the rope that tied her hands together, pulling her close. "You want her?" Maxwell's face twisted in anger, sending shivers down Tiatria's spine. "Then you'll have to bid for her like everyone else, in MALANIA!" Tiatria began to panic, unable to read Maxwell's thoughts and feeling trapped in his grasp. With a racing heart, she struggled to break free from his hold, but her bindings were too strong.

Cullen's body tensed as he could sense the tension in the room, evident in the stiff postures and wary glances of those around him. He wanted to believe that Maxwell was there to protect Tiatria, but he could not be sure. Still, he would do everything in his power to keep her safe, even from Maxwell himself.

(What is he doing?) Triatria asked Cullen as she tried to look at him.

Cullen shook his head slightly (I do not know, hopefully protecting you.) he answered back.

Edger raised his hands slowly, a look of resignation on his face. "Alright, alright! No need for violence," he said, trying to defuse the situation. His men followed suit and backed off, knowing full well the reputation of Maxwell and what he was capable of. Cullen and

Tiatria were unaware of this, but he made a mental note to inform Dorian about it later.

Maxwell's stance was defensive and protective. Cullen prayed that Maxwell was truly protecting Tiatria, but he roughly grabbed Tiatria and shoved her behind him as he declared, "We're leaving." She stumbled back, keeping her eyes lowered as she followed him out of the tavern. But one man sitting at a back table had other plans. He did not like the way Maxwell was speaking to them and had every intention of taking the girl for himself. He pulled out his dagger and stepped towards Maxwell's back.

Just as he was about to strike, Maxwell spun around with lightning speed and plunged his sword into the man's stomach. Blood spurted from the wound as the man fell to his knees and then collapsed onto the floor with a sickening thud. The room fell silent except for the slow drip of blood onto the floor.

Maxwell withdrew his sword, leaving the man to bleed out on the floor. His eyes burned with anger as he turned to face the rest of the patrons. "Get out. Get out of this tavern. Get out of this town and never come back! THIS TOWN IS MINE!" he bellowed; his voice filled with fury.

Everyone scrambled to leave, not daring to cross paths with an enraged Maxwell. Cullen kept his hand on his sword as he gave the remaining men a stern look, warning them to stay away. Maxwell then turned to his companions and roughly grabbed Tiatria's restraints, leading her outside.

The group mounted their horses, with Tiatria sandwiched between Maxwell and Cullen. Kethinar flew overhead, keeping watch for any potential enemies as they rode through the town. Thamyris was also informed of their movements in case they were being followed by anyone else.

Cullen's heart raced as he quickly dismounted his horse and frantically untied Tiatria's bonds, his hands trembling with urgency. He pulled her close, holding her tightly in his arms as she sobbed into his chest. "You're safe now," he whispered, desperation lacing his words. Thamyris strode over, his hawk landing on his shoulder, "What happened?" he demanded in a cold tone.

Dorian watched as Maxwell dismounted his horse and stormed past him without a word. Something inside Dorian snapped, and he could not let Maxwell shut him out. He had never seen Maxwell in such a state of emotional turmoil before. "Amant!" he called out, but Maxwell kept walking, tears streaming down his face. "Slap me," he suddenly demanded, turning to Dorian with a fierce look in his eyes. Confusion and concern flooded through Dorian as he did what Maxwell asked; the sound of their skin meeting echoed through the silence. Maxwell dropped to his knees and Dorian quickly followed suit, wrapping him in an attempt to soothe his friend. "You're alright now," he murmured soothingly.

Meanwhile, Cullen found himself wiping away Tiatria's tears with gentle thumbs before an overwhelming urge took hold of him and without hesitation, he pressed his lips to hers in a soft kiss. Thamyris could only scoff at the display of affection while he watched from the side. He instead watched Dorian and Maxwell, "Is he okay?" he questioned as he folded his arms.

Maxwell stumbled several times as he tried to get up. He was in such a state he was terrified of the damage he had done. "Is she, is she, is she...okay?" he questioned frantically. Thamyris stepped aside, showing the two Cullen and Tiatria kissing.

Dorian was not surprised by this development at all. "Finally!" he declared as Maxwell regained his footing, still visibly shaken. He rushed over and grabbed Tiatria by the arm, startling her. But before he could say anything else, she pushed him back with an invisible force that sent him tumbling onto the ground. Maxwell sat there on the grass, overwhelmed with shame and remorse. "I'm sorry," he whispered, feeling the weight of his actions.

Dorian followed Maxwell into a nearby clearing, demanding to get some answers from him. Tears flowed freely down Maxwell's cheeks as he stared up at the moon and stars overhead. Dorian could sense the weight of his friend's guilt and pain, and without a word, he knelt in front of him. Gently, he took Maxwell's hand in both of his, offering silent comfort and support. He then reached up to caress Maxwell's cheek with his left hand, his own tears threatening to spill over.

Dorian's eyes did not even glance towards anyone else as he kneeled next to Maxwell, his warm hand brushing away the stray locks of hair that had fallen over Maxwell's closed eyes. "You're alright, Amant," Dorian said softly, his voice full of concern and reassurance. "You just need to come back from wherever you've gone." He reached out to take Maxwell's hand in his own, his fingers intertwining with Maxwell's.

Cullen walked slowly beside Tiatria, his arm protectively wrapped around her shoulders. They both looked on with concern at the scene unfolding before them. "Did I hurt him?" Tiatria asked quietly, breaking the tense silence, worry etched in her voice.

Dorian gave a weak smile as he shook his head. "No, this sometimes happens. It's just a side effect of his past traumas resurfacing." He explained gently. "Maxwell's past can be a haunting presence at times." He glanced over at Tiatria, meeting her worried gaze with a sideways look from his left eye. "Maxwell's mind can be a tricky thing to navigate at times. I suspect in his desperation to play his part and deceive those cretins, he may have pushed himself too far."

Tiatria stepped away from Cullen and approached Maxwell carefully, her heart heavy with worry for her friend. She took his left hand in hers, holding it gently as she tried to reach out to him, offering silent comfort. But all she felt was a deafening silence in Maxwell's mind, almost like a long pause before a storm. She was then suddenly overwhelmed by a flood of images; memories began flooding into her mind at an alarming speed. There were so many of them that Tiatria's head started spinning, and she fell to the ground, convulsing.

Dorian quickly pulled her away as Cullen ran over and scooped her up into his arms. "TIA? TIA, WAKE UP!" He cried out desperately. After a few moments, Tiatria's eyes slowly fluttered open. She looked up at Cullen with fear in his eyes, she looked around in confusion. "I saw...so many things!" she exclaimed, holding a hand to her forehead and trying to shake the traumatic visions from her mind. "It was horrible!"

"I suspect it was," Dorian said with a heavy sigh. "In all the years I've known Maxwell, he has never been one to talk about his past freely, and what little I have been able to glean from him...well, it's not for everyone's ears." He looked at Cullen and Tiatria with a pained expression, knowing that they were now privy to a part of Maxwell's history that he had kept hidden for so long.

There was a somber pause before Dorian gestured for the others to leave them alone for a while. As the others slowly walked away, leaving Dorian alone with Maxwell, Cullen could not shake off the feeling of a knot in his stomach. He looked over at Tiatria and gave her a reassuring smile. "Go on ahead, I'll be joining you shortly," he told her. Tiatria nodded understandingly and left Cullen by himself as she headed back to camp.

Cullen aimlessly walked for a few minutes before stopping in front of a nearby tree. Something compelled him to reach out and place his hand against the rough bark, almost as if he needed to seek solace from the sturdy trunk. He could not fully comprehend what had just happened with Maxwell, but he could not help but wonder if this was what had happened to his own Father as well - broken by the weight of his duty until his mind and soul were no longer whole.

Meanwhile, Dorian sat beside Maxwell with tears glistening in his eyes. He gently took both of Maxwell's hands into his own and brought them up to their chests, holding them close as his thumbs caressed Maxwell's knuckles. "It's alright, Amant," he murmured softly, his voice full of love and understanding. "It's alright."

Watching from a distance, Cullen could not believe what he was seeing. He had always thought of Dorian as a sarcastic and detached person, but now he saw a side of him that he never knew existed - one full of tenderness and deep emotions. He blushed and quickly looked away, not wanting to intrude on this intimate moment between the two lovers.

As Dorian's hands moved to gently stroke the side of Maxwell's face, Cullen could not help but feel a pang of jealousy. He had always known that there was more to their relationship than just being partners and friends, but now he finally understood the depth of their connection. They loved each other in a way that went beyond simple physical attraction or friendship. And it was evident in every touch and every look they shared.

Feeling like he was intruding on a private moment, Cullen slowly backed away and left the couple alone. They deserved this time together after everything they had been through. As he walked back to camp, Cullen saw Tiatria leaning against a tree, waiting for him. She smiled warmly at him and held out her hand, which he took gratefully. As they made their way back to camp, Cullen kissed her forehead affectionately, feeling grateful for her understanding and support.

Dorian remained at Maxwell's side, tears glistening in his eyes as he gently held both of Maxwell's hands in his own. Bringing their hands up to rest on Maxwell's chest, Dorian caressed Maxwell's knuckles with his thumbs. "It's alright, Amant," he whispered softly. As if drawn by a magnet, Dorian leaned in and placed the gentlest kiss on Maxwell's lips, his right hand stroking the side of Maxwell's face with utmost care.

As he wrote, Cullen thought about why Dorian and Maxwell's relationship seemed more than just that of partners and friends - they shared a deep love and understanding that went beyond words. And perhaps it was that love that allowed them to argue and tease each other with such passion while keeping their pasts shrouded in secrecy. With newfound understanding, Thamyris watched the couple with a newfound respect and a tad bit of envy.

The rest of the evening passed quietly as everyone gave Maxwell and Dorian space to be alone with each other. And as the stars twinkled above them, Cullen started writing in his journal. As he did so, he could not help but think about love and all its complexities - how it could bring people together in unexpected ways, but also how it could break them apart if not handled carefully. By looking at Tiatria beside him and thinking of Maxwell and Dorian's love for each other, Cullen could not help but believe that it was worth all the risks and challenges that came with it.

Dorian's heart swelled as his gaze lingered on Maxwell, taking in the intense emotion reflected in his lover's eyes. Dorian watched as Maxwell slowly came around. He noticed that the acolyte's eyes were filled with so much emotion that it was almost overwhelming. He could not help but feel a surge of happiness at seeing him return.

A small smile threatened to break through Dorian's cool facade, but he quickly twitched his nose to hide it.

In response, Maxwell pulled him in for a deep and passionate kiss, their lips meeting with a fiery intensity. As they slowly stood up, the cool of the night's air caressed their skin while the damp grass beneath their feet added a refreshing touch to their moment together. Dorian realized they were dancing a slow waltz. In its glow, each feature of the other seemed to be highlighted and magnified, creating an ethereal aura around them. Each step they took seemed to bring out the best in one another, as if they were made for this very moment.

Meanwhile, back at camp, Thamyris leaped up into a nearby tree with Kethinar perched on his shoulder. He wanted to keep watch for any potential danger, so he climbed higher and scanned the area for any signs of approaching villagers or bandits. Lost in thought, he absentmindedly walked along the tree line until he stumbled upon Dorian and Maxwell dancing in the moonlight, and he stopped in awe.

Intrigued, he settled onto a thick branch and watched them with hawk-like focus. His right arm rested on his knee while his left leg dangled off the edge of the branch. Despite his duty to keep watch over the camp, Thamyris could not resist the urge to observe this rare and beautiful moment between two men in love.

Maxwell averted his gaze, feeling the weight of guilt settling heavily upon him. "I am sorry, Dorian. I should have -" he began, only to be silenced by Dorian's gentle but firm interruption. "Shhh," Dorian murmured, his attention fully focused on counting each step they took together. His blue eyes sparkled mischievously as he continued walking, leading them deeper into the forest. Despite Maxwell's inner turmoil, Dorian refused to let the moment be tainted by his friend's remorse.

As their eyes met once again, Maxwell could not help but feel overwhelmed by the depth of emotion in Dorian's gaze. As they danced, Dorian caught Maxwell's gaze again, seeing the raw emotion in his eyes. In that moment, Maxwell realized just how much Dorian meant to him. A deep blush spread across his cheeks, and he could feel his heart racing as if it were on fire.

Unable to resist any longer, Maxwell closed the distance between them and kissed Dorian with such intensity that it almost knocked the two of them off their feet. Fortunately, Dorian's back collided with a nearby tree instead, eliciting a soft groan as he instinctively grasped onto Maxwell's jawline. In the same instant, Thamyris, who was perched on the branch above them, held onto the trunk of the tree for support.

With Thamyris' keen elven senses, he had allowed him to witness every intimate detail of their embrace. Kethinar, perched high above in a nearby tree, silently flew off to survey their surroundings. With his hand pressed against the rough bark of the tree, Thamyris could almost feel the pulse of nature around him as he observed his two friends lost in their passionate moment.

Their bodies ignited with an uncontrollable fire, their hearts pounding so hard that it felt like they might burst out of their chests, every nerve ignited with desire. Dorian could feel the hot, insistent pressure of Maxwell's erection against his thigh, setting his own desires ablaze with need. Their lips were locked in a fierce battle with each other as hungry kisses were trying to consume one another completely. As Maxwell's lips broke away from his, Dorian gasped for air, his skin tingling where his lover's tongue and lips had just traced over. He grabbed onto the back of Maxwell's neck, threading his fingers through the soft black strands of hair while Maxwell's hand roamed over Dorian's body, exploring every inch with expert precision, sending shudders of pleasure through Dorian's core.

Thamyris could not believe what he was witnessing, unable to tear himself away from the two men kissing with such raw passion that it bordered on violence. His cheeks flushed with embarrassment and arousal as unfamiliar sensations coursed through his body, making him feel off-balance and desperate for release. He fought the urge to touch himself, feeling like he was about to boil over with heat and desire. It was futile as his body betrayed him, responding to the intense sensation coursing through him.

With reckless abandon, the two men tore at each other's pants, practically ripping them off in their desperate haste to free themselves from their clothing. Dorian's pants finally fell to his ankles. He moaned loudly as Maxwell took a firm grip on his cock almost assaulting it with the force of his strokes, causing his cock to harden in excitement. Dorian struggled to hold on, his hand gripping tightly onto Maxwell's wrist as waves of pleasure pulsed through him. With each thrust of Maxwell's hips, their cocks rubbed together and throbbed with desire. Dorian was on the verge of losing control when Maxwell's thumb leisurely teased the sensitive head of his cock, drawing out an elicited moan that escaped from Dorian's pouty lips. Overwhelmed by sensation, Dorian buried his face into Maxwell's shoulder as he panted and moaned.

Maxwell was fueled by the sight and sound of Dorian's pleasure, feeling his own body reaching its boiling point. He bit down into Dorian's neck, relishing in the sharp cry of pain that turned into a moan as he sucked hard enough to leave a mark. The possessive gesture sent a thrill through both men, reminding them of the forbidden love and passion they shared in a world where they were not allowed to openly claim each other. In this moment, all laws and expectations were forgotten as they gave themselves fully to the exhilarating pleasure and intensity they shared together.

Maxwell's blood boiled with primal desire as he watched Dorian rut against his hand and hips. In a sudden burst of intense need, Maxwell turned Dorian around and pressed him firmly against the tree. Dorian's chest and abdomen writhed against the rough bark of the tree as Maxwell's hand and hips continued to work him into a frenzied state. The blood in Maxwell's veins burned with a primal desire, pushing him to take control. He gripped his pulsing cock with one hand while lining it up against Dorian's slick entrance. Dorian gasped as he felt himself dripping with want, ready for whatever Maxwell had in store.

With a forceful thrust, Maxwell entered Dorian, eliciting a groan of pleasure mixed with a hint of pain. Dorian clung to the tree for support as he pushed his butt back against Maxwell, taking him deeper inside. Turning his head to the side, Dorian met Maxwell's gaze with a look of pure lust and need. Their bodies moved in perfect harmony, each of his powerful thrusts pulsing inside him. His own moans mingled with Maxwell's as their desire reached heights.

But Maxwell couldn't hold back any longer. His passion turned into raw desperation as he moved faster and harder, almost punishing in his rhythm. Dorian let out loud cries of ecstasy as Maxwell's thrusts left marks on the tree, where his nails dug in with every movement.

Thamyris's cheeks flushed with embarrassment at being caught up in such intense desire, but he could not help himself wanting to be part of it. With deep breaths and silent moans, Dorian and Maxwell remained in a symphony of passion and pleasure.

Dorian's body trembled with pleasure as Maxwell's powerful thrusts rocked him against the tree. Dorian's arms burned with exhaustion, but he pushed through the pain, desperate to keep up with Maxwell's relentless pace never wavered, each movement causing the tree to creak and groan under their combined weight.

Dorian did not notice any of that. All he could focus on was the intense pleasure building inside him, fueled by Maxwell's skilled movements and the way they pressed against a spot inside him that made pain and pleasure meld into one. Maxwell pressed himself against Dorian's back, his hot breath tickling the nape of his neck. Their hands intertwined as Maxwell's cock reached deeper and deeper inside Dorian, hitting a spot that sent bolts of pain and ecstasy through his body. Dorian could not hold back any longer. He cried out in ecstasy, his voice echoing through the woods as Maxwell claimed him fully.

The sound caught Tiatria and Cullen's attention, who were lying nearby. But Tiatria silenced Cullen's concern with a look. She could hear how enraptured Dorian and Maxwell were in their passion. She gently stopped Cullen from interrupting them by leaning over and giving him a gentle but passionate kiss. Cullen's left hand cradled the elf's cheek; his right arm pulled her in close to his chest. Cullen's left hand threaded through Tiatria's raven-black hair. The scent that came from it was intoxicating. Tiatria loved the warmth of Cullen's hands; they may have been calloused, but they were always gentle, which always made her feel safe within them. With Cullen now firmly distracted, Tiatria smiled as she had him all to herself, and he no longer had the desire to disturb their friends.

The intensity of their lovemaking was too much for Dorian to handle, but Maxwell could not stop even if he wanted to. His body was on fire, fueled by his insatiable lust and energy. Dorian felt waves of sensation crashing over him as his head rested on his forearms, which rubbed against the rough bark. But even as he felt himself cum, Maxwell's unrelenting thrusts kept him hard and wanting more. He could feel the heat of Maxwell's forehead and chest onto his own back, sweat dripping down onto his skin, the heat only adding to their intense connection. And when he couldn't take it any longer, Dorian grasped onto the back of Maxwell's head and pulled him into a passionate kiss as they approached their collective climax. Thamyris listened as the two men continued to be lost in ecstasy, feeling a mix of shame and arousal flood through him.

Maxwell finally came with a guttural cry, his forehead resting on Dorian's shoulder as he desperately tried to catch his breath. After a few moments, Dorian gently pulled away, still trembling from the force of their lovemaking. As they kissed and held each other, Thamyris came down from his own high, feeling a mix of longing and guilt for witnessing such an intimate moment between two lovers.

Nestled in the lush grass of a small clearing, Dorian and Maxwell lay side by side, gazing up at the endless expanse of stars above them. The cool blades of grass tickled Maxwell's bare back as he breathed in the crisp night air. His right hand cradled his head while his left rested on his stomach. Dorian's mind was filled with thoughts, but he could not shake off his curiosity. With a gentle shift onto his left side, he propped himself up with one arm and turned to face Maxwell.

"Amant?" Dorian spoke softly, breaking the comfortable silence between them.

"Hmm?" Maxwell responded, his voice carrying a hint of sleepiness.

"Are your nightmares from when you were arrested by the Order?" Dorian asked with a serious tone, causing Maxwell's heart to skip a beat. He knew this question would come up eventually, but he was surprised that Dorian chose now to ask it. Slowly sitting up,

Maxwell caught Dorian's gaze as he looked over his shoulder. With crossed legs, Dorian waited for an answer while Thamyris listened intently from his spot against a nearby tree.

Thamyris' ears perked up as he heard the conversation between the two men. He had always wondered why Maxwell would wake up screaming in the dead of night while staying at his Mother's castle. As he leaned against the tree, his right arm resting on his knee and his left leg dangling from a branch above him, he recalled hearing those same screams echoed throughout the castle - screams of pure terror.

"Partially," Maxwell answered quietly, causing Dorian to sit up with him and rest one arm on his knee while using the other to support himself. "I was disciplined," Maxwell continued, flicking his fingers to emphasize his words before bringing up his knees and resting both arms on top of them. Glancing at Dorian out of the corner of his eye, Maxwell added, "That's what the Order would say. In reality, I was tortured for days." The memory of that fateful night flooded back to him - the cold stone walls, the chains and shackles hanging from every surface, the burning hot pokers and branding irons heating in the fireplace, and the various instruments of torture laid out on wooden tables. He could still smell the metallic scent of blood mixed with feces and death that hung heavy in the air.

"I remember being beaten with a thin metal rod that had been heated in a fire," Maxwell continued, tracing his fingers over the scars on his back. Dorian wrapped his arms around his knees as he listened intently.

Dorian turned away for a moment, seemingly lost in thought before looking back at Maxwell with a curious expression. His right hand absently scratched at his head before he spoke again. "Were you forced to lie over a large plank of wood, your hands tied behind your head and lifted up to prevent you from moving?" Maxwell's eyes widened in surprise as he narrowed them at Dorian. "How do you know that?" he asked, puzzled by Dorian's knowledge.

Dorian shook his head before resting it on his knees. Suddenly, he looked up at Maxwell with a look of realization on his face. "I was there," he said quietly. Maxwell could not believe what he was hearing - how could Dorian have been there?

"I was waiting in a cell constructed into the eastern wall of that wretched room," Dorian explained, a hint of pain evident in his voice. "With two others in the same cage, we were forced to sit, and because of that, we couldn't stretch our legs and would get terrible cramps." He remembered feeling close to tears from the excruciating pain in his calves and thighs.

Maxwell remembered feeling helpless in that same cell, pushed to the brink of tears as his muscles screamed in protest. "Why were you even there?" he asked, confused.

Dorian's hand trembled as it ran through his disheveled hair, a gesture of distress and discomfort. His eyes flickered with pain and regret as he spoke, "I was being *disciplined* as well." Maxwell's eyebrows shot up in surprise and confusion, "Wha-what for? What could you have possibly done? You're half my age and cannot have done--" Dorian cut him off, his voice low and filled with shame, "I slept with a man and got caught."

Maxwell knew what that meant; it explained a lot about Dorian. Maxwell had noticed since the first time they'd slept together that Dorian's testicles were gone. He'd never asked questions about it as that would've been an enormously sensitive subject. He waited for Dorian to tell him, just like Dorian waited for him. To talk about each other's past when the other was ready.

Maxwell's eyes widened in shock as he struggled to process this information. Maxwell shook his head in disbelief, his fingers digging into his forehead. "I watched as they whipped you," Dorian muttered, recalling the image vividly in his mind. "With your arms restrained as they were, you couldn't put up any sort of struggle, even when they took your fingernails." A pained expression crossed his face as he remembered the scene. "I remember you disappeared the next day."

Maxwell nodded silently, not wanting to relive those memories. "Yeah," he finally spoke up again, "I was sent to one of Carpo's brutal prisoner mining camps for five years." He turned away from Dorian as he felt a shudder running through him at the mere mention of Carpo.

Maxwell explained that the horrors he had faced there nearly broke him. "The first night I was there, I was beaten and raped by the guards." Dorian could see the pain etched all over Maxwell's face as he attempted to harden his face, trying to stop any flow of tears. "Five of them, they bent me over a table. Two held out my arms so they could break my arms in three places with clubs. After they each took their turn with me, I can't remember all that happened. My mind must have blocked them out, except when I dream."

Dorian snatched Maxwell's hand, holding onto it quite possessively, "I don't need to hear anymore."

Maxwell turned and looked at Dorian, "I thought you wanted to know?"

Dorian gave a stubborn look, "Not when it tortures you. I know enough anyway. It explains the nightmares. That's all I needed to know."

Maxwell gently pulled his hand away from Dorian's hold and took hold of it again himself. "What about you?" he questioned, "What happened to you?"

Dorian sighed as he gave a clever smile, "I assume you mean *why* certain things are missing?"

Maxwell gave a nod, "Yes, but you don't have to say anything. You haven't in all these years."

Dorian gave a small side smirk, "I don't mind really, I was just waiting for you to ask." Maxwell saw Dorian lean backward with his arms propping him up, "The day you left was when the captain of the guard came and grabbed me. He had two others hold me down against the same table you were on. The bastard took one of the heated knives out of the fire and took them." Maxwell felt the air leave his lungs as Dorian seemed to talk about it so smoothly like it was the most natural thing to talk about. No shame, no remorse, nothing that showed any pain.

"I watched as they threw them into the fire and left me bleeding on the floor." Dorian looked away for a moment before looking back at Maxwell. "I healed myself the moment I heard the door shut." Maxwell felt his skin crawl as he could imagine enduring such horrors.

However, Dorian seemed unaffected by it, which seemed odd, honestly. If this happened to him, Maxwell knew he'd be destroyed in every respect and probably would never recover. However, Dorian was different and his next words to Maxwell proved it. Dorian's eyes became sharp, "I refuse to give those bastards an inch of satisfaction. If they even think that they destroyed the one thing that makes me whole. They can think again! I refuse to apologize for anything I've done or for who I am or who I love." Maxwell snapped at the moment as his hands snatched Dorian's face and brought him in for a passionate kiss.

It was at that moment both understood why they became reassigned to the missions that kept them away from others of the Order and received jobs through messengers to avoid any potential risks or temptations. A convicted slaver who shamed the Order and a man who was now described as the 'Flower of the Order.' Little did the Order know in punishing them; they rewarded them in the best possible way.

Chapter 14

The first few rays of dawn painted the sky subtle shades of pink and orange as Cullen sat atop his horse, surveying the distant town. He had been keeping a watchful eye on the town since witnessing Maxwell and Dorian's intimate moments together, feeling remorse for his own outburst. His gaze scanned the town, making sure no bandits dared to return, especially Edger who always seemed to find a way back in where he didn't belong. Cullen had completed a full perimeter check of the village and now pondered how best to assist its people. He had a few ideas but would need to send a message to the King for help.

Clicking his tongue, Cullen urged his horse forward through the streets. Villagers were already up and about, cleaning up debris and rubble left behind by the bandits. As they caught sight of Cullen, their faces lit up with smiles and tears. He stopped at the tavern, still in disarray from the previous day's events. Tables and chairs were overturned, remnants of a chaotic scene that was now slowly being cleaned up. Cullen dismounted from his horse and stepped inside.

The body of the man Maxwell had killed lay untouched on the floor, a silent reminder of the violence that occurred. No one dared to touch it. Cullen grabbed a tablecloth from a nearby table and draped it over the body, obscuring it from view. He then picked up a nearby chair and set it upright, turning to see a bartender standing nearby.

In an act of gratitude, the bartender held out his hand to Cullen, who accepted it with tears in his eyes. "Thank you," he said softly, taken aback by the gesture. Looking around with uncertainty, Cullen struggled to find words before finally saying, "I...uh...I'm sorry for what happened here."

The bartender smiled as he gave a quick pat on the shoulder. "What you and your friends did here young man is more than we could ever repay. Don't worry, what happened needed to happen."

Cullen could see in the man's eyes the truth and gave a nod as they both grabbed the ends of a table and put it back onto its feet. Cullen noticed Tiatria, Maxwell, and Dorian walking in; they helped clean up the tavern.

Thamyris stood at the edge of the camp, his faithful hawk perched on his shoulder as he scanned the surrounding area for any signs of danger. The sun was setting, casting a warm orange glow over the landscape. He could feel the tension in his muscles ease slowly as he took in the peacefulness of the moment.

As he kept watch, his thoughts drifted to Maxwell and Dorian, his new companions. They had something that Thamyris had only dreamt of - a deep, loving bond with each other. He could not help but feel a pang of envy at their relationship.

Growing up in his Mother's kingdom, Thamyris had always been an outcast among his fellow elves. They were all eager to mate with females, while Thamyris found himself drawn to males. As far as he knew, he was the only one with this preference. But now, traveling with humans, he was starting to see that there were others like him.

Despite his initial distrust and dislike for humans, Thamyris couldn't deny that they were slowly redeeming themselves in his eyes. However, he wasn't ready to admit it just yet - not until he knew for sure that they could be trusted. For now, he would keep his guard up and continue to observe from the outskirts of the camp.

As they worked together to clean up the mess, Cullen couldn't shake off the uneasy feeling that lingered in the air. The bartender's words echoed in his mind, "What happened needed to happen."

The atmosphere in the tavern was one of shared relief and silent gratitude. Cullen stole a glance at his friends as they worked together to repair the damages caused by the bandits; a quiet understanding passed between them all. Each member of their group had played a role in defending the town, and now they were bound by a camaraderie forged in battle.

Once the tables and chairs were back in place, the bartender poured them each a drink on the house. Cullen raised his glass, and the others followed suit, toasting to their victory and newfound friendships.

They sat around the table, sharing stories and laughter, but Cullen felt a sense of belonging he hadn't experienced in a long time. These were not just his companions in arms; they were his family now, forged through fire and steel. And as the night wore on, with the warmth of good company filling the room, Cullen knew deep in his heart that no matter what challenges lay ahead, he would face them with unwavering devotion.

)o(

The setting sun cast a warm, golden-orange glow over the castle as it bathed its light on Edith. She stood in her balcony, anxiously awaiting any word from her beloved Cullen. Her eyes scanned the sky for any messenger pigeons from Bestla, hoping to receive news of his whereabouts and safety. As she waited impatiently, she continued the delicate embroidery on a handkerchief that she planned to give him upon his return.

As the hours and now days had passed, Edith had come attuned to recognize the sound of their wing beats and knew the specific times they would arrive. She continued her embroidery on the handkerchief for Cullen, and before it was even time for the pigeons to arrive, she heard a rapid flapping of wings coming from a different direction than usual. Her heart leaped with hope as she ran to the edge of the balcony, peering towards the south-west, where the bird seemed to be coming from.

To her surprise, it was coming from the south-west instead of the expected south-east. Filled with urgency and excitement, Edith made her way down to the aviary where the birds were kept. Breathless and exhilarated, Edith burst through the doors of the aviary and approached the cleric who tended to the pigeons. He was in the middle of reading a note sent by the bird when she snatched it from him and eagerly read its contents herself. A wide smile threatened to split her face in half as she raced back down the stairs, barely able to contain her excitement as she called out for her father.

Meanwhile, in another part of the castle, King Arthur was in deep conversation with his trusted friend and Duke of Summerset while sipping on afternoon tea. They often used this time to catch up on any important matters and discuss new business. With a sigh, Arthur picked up his cup and glanced over at his friend, who was delicately buttering a scone with one hand while holding it with the other.

Taking a sip of his tea, the Duke casually asked about any updates on his son's movements. The Duke shook his head, "Not yet. Although the Bishop did send a letter that mentioned seeing Keynes and Abreo accompanied by a knight he didn't recognize. We can assume it was your son. They were also seen with a young girl who seemed unaware of God and his teachings. It seemed to bother him greatly." The Duke raised an eyebrow in surprise, "And no one thought to take her into custody?" The King shrugged,

"Really Cavan? I don't see how a young lady's ignorance of God's teachings poses a threat. I suppose they didn't see a young lady as much of a threat either if they didn't take her."

The Duke leaned back into his ornately carved chair, its arms adorned with intricate patterns and symbols of the kingdom. He rested his strong arms on the smooth wooden arms of the chair, leaning in towards the King who sat across from him. "Does Edith know about this sighting?" he asked, his voice laced with concern. "She's eager to learn about Cullen's fate, as is his Mother." The King gave a slit smirk as he held up a letter with Cullen's seal on it. "I was planning on giving her this at dinner. I'm looking forward on seeing her face when she sees a message from Cullen himself, confirming his safety."

"PAPA!" Both men turned their attention to the doorway where Edith had burst through. Her face was flushed with excitement and tears streamed down her cheeks. "Edith? What's wrong?" Her father questioned, worry etched on his features. Edith bounced up and down on her heels as she waved a crumpled piece of paper in front of her father's face. "CULLEN'S ALIVE!" she cried out joyfully. The Duke reached out and took the paper from the princess's trembling hands, stepping away to read it for himself. The King stood up and strode towards his daughter, wrapping an arm around her shoulders and pulling her into a warm embrace. "That is such wonderful news, sweetheart! He looked at his friend, who was now reading the letter with an intense expression. "What does it say Cavan?"

"It says that Cullen and the others have successfully freed Westevia from those bothersome bandits."

Arthur narrowed his eyes as he broke into a wide smile. "That's incredible! We've been trying to drive them out for months with no success. Who would have thought that sending Cullen out into the world was the best decision we could have ever made." He placed a hand on his daughter's shoulder, beaming with pride. "He is an honorable knight, truly favored by God. What about the heretic? Any news on his whereabouts?"

The Duke shook his head and turned to face his friend, "No, but he requests a small garrison to protect the town and resources, as well as enough workers to aid in the town's rebuilding efforts." Arthur nodded thoughtfully before turning to Edith. "My dear, we have much to celebrate!" He gestured for her to join him on the rug in front of the fireplace, where they began dancing and twirling together in joyous celebration. Edith then bowed before her father, who revealed the other letter he'd received from Cullen.

Edith jumped in joy as she snatched it, kissed it and hugged her Father. The King then turned to the Duke and his smile only grew wider as he clapped his hands together in excitement. "Excellent! Send word to the Knight Commander at once. Tell him it is by order of the King to send a garrison and enough workers to assist the people of Westevia." The Duke bowed in reverence before leaving to carry out his King's bidding.

)o(

Tears streamed down Amalia's cheeks as her cries echoed through the confined space, her voice muffled by the slats of the wooden crate she was forced to sit in. She frantically tried to peek through the narrow slats of the wooden crate She was forced to sit in. She had been forced to curl herself into a tight ball; knees pushed up against her chest and arms wrapped tightly around her legs as she sobbed uncontrollably. The cramped quarters offered little room to move, and the rough wood of the crate dug into her skin, leaving behind angry red marks.

But it was not just the discomfort that made Amalia cry. It was the fear and uncertainty that plagued her mind. Where was this ship taking her? What fate awaited her at the end of this journey? And most hauntingly, she could not shake the image of Tahl'rail's face from her mind. His eyes, once filled with love and life, now haunted her with their emptiness as he slowly faded away in front of her.

As she cried, Amalia could hear the sound of the sea all around her. The gentle lapping of waves against the ship's hull, the cry of seagulls flying above. But she refused to listen to anything else - not the men talking nearby, not even Naromu's heavy footsteps that she had become familiar with during her journey on this cursed ship.

Suddenly, there was a loud creaking noise and the box opened before Amalia could comprehend what was happening. She screamed in terror as fat fingers grabbed onto her and pulled her out of the crate. Her wrist burned from being yanked around by Naromu, causing her to stumble over her own feet.

"LET ME GO!" Amalia shrieked, struggling against his grip with all her might. But Naromu just growled and looked upon what remained of the once ethereal beauty before him. Her cheeks were dirty and tear-streaked, her lower lip swollen and bleeding from where she had been hit. Her nose was still broken and her eyes were now black and bruised, but Naromu had plans for those. Once they reached their destination, he would have access to leeches that could suck out the blood and bring back her "normal" coloring.

"Come on now!" he barked, "We're going to get you all cleaned up and looking nice!" Amalia struggled to understand his words as she was roughly pushed towards a wooden door that Naromu kicked open with a strong foot. Inside was a small closet filled with mops and buckets, which had conveniently been moved out of the way. Before she could even process what was happening, buckets of freezing cold water were dumped over her head, drenching her hair and clothes. She screamed in shock and pain as more water was thrown at her, causing her nails to dig into the wooden floor beneath her.

"Why are you doing this?" Amalia cried out in horror and confusion.

Naromu just laughed as another man tried to rip off what remained of her clothing, replacing it with a simple dress that had been prepared for her. She desperately fought against him, trying to hold onto any shred of dignity and protection left.

"We have to get you looking nice for prospective buyers!" Naromu exclaimed with glee. And then it hit her - these men were planning to sell her. A high priestess of Danu, reduced to nothing more than a piece of meat on display at the market. As she thought about all that had happened - what had been done to her, what had been done to Tahl'rail, everything they had worked so hard to escape from in their forest home - anger coursed through Amalia's veins like fire. This was not how it was supposed to be. They were meant to build a new life together, have children, and grow old together. But now all those dreams seemed impossible as she was trapped in this nightmare.

In a fury of anger, Amalia's nails dug into the wooden floor, splintering it with her strength. She gathered the broken pieces in her fists as she spoke, her voice crackling with fire and rage. "You did all this to sell me?" Her words echoed with a burning intensity. "You killed the man who meant everything to me just for your greed?" As she looked up at them, her eyes transformed into cat-like slits. The men stepped back in fear as they watched her bones contort and shift beneath her skin, and flames began to engulf her body. "I summon the ancient magick," she chanted, her words carried on the wind to reach her servant and soon-to-be avenger.

Naromu stumbled backwards, his eyes wide with terror as Amalia stood before him, ablaze with fire. With arms outstretched like a majestic phoenix rising from the ashes, she took a step forward and everything around her seemed to catch fire. The flames danced and licked at her body, but she remained unscathed by their heat. Even her tears disappeared in a sizzle as they fell from her eyes, evaporating into thin air. Speaking in an ancient elvish tongue, Amalia's body began to transform - spikes sprouted from her back and shoulders, glinting dangerously in the fiery light. Her clothing burned away in mere seconds, revealing a powerful figure underneath. Her once-human features twisted and contorted as her canines elongated into sharp points and her skin became covered in intricate patterns resembling flames. The swirling inferno of red and black fabric swirled around her, creating a mesmerizing display of color and movement. And amidst it all, what was revealed was a breathtaking sight - Amalia adorned in a blood-red strapless petal and heart corset, hugging her figure and emphasizing her ample amount of cleavage. She truly looked like a creature born from fire, unstoppable and awe-inspiring.

The woman's hourglass figure was accentuated by a sleek black leather underbust corset, cropped to just the right length. The edgy piece added a sense of daring to her ensemble, commanding attention with each purposeful step. But it was the intricate silver mithril accents that truly set the outfit apart, shimmering and catching the light as they traced delicate patterns along the edges of each piece. Against the dark leather, they seemed to glow like stars in a moonless sky. It was a striking and alluring sight, drawing curious gazes from onlookers.

As she spun, a billowing red and black skirt materialized, revealing daring slits on each side that exposed hints of her smooth skin. The bottom layer was a deep, rich black that seemed to absorb all light, while the top layer matched the fiery hue of her corset, creating an alluring contrast. The back of the skirt fanned out like a peacock's tail feathers into a stunning train that trailed behind her as she moved, swishing with every step. The front cascaded gracefully, revealing her slender legs and showing off the intricate patterns of the fabric. Three delicate pieces of mithril connected the sides of the skirt, adding weight and structure to the garment while also adding an edgy touch to the overall ensemble. The skirt hung low on her hips, helping bridge a six-inch gap between them and enhancing her hourglass figure. Every movement she made seemed to be accompanied by a mesmerizing dance of fabric and metal, making her appear both elegant and fierce at the same time.

At the very top, a glimmering mithril accent curled gracefully outward from where the metallic pieces met. A delicate, foot-long chain dangled from its center like a pendulum, catching and reflecting the light in mesmerizing patterns. Her footwear was a perfect match; sleek and supple black leather thigh-high boots that hugged her already statuesque frame, elongating her legs and adding an air of elegance to her appearance. Gleaming mithril armbands adorned her arms, the intricate embellishments glinting in the sunlight. The upper arms were wrapped in delicate silver designs, while the bracers on her wrists extended up to her elbows in a display of strength and beauty. A dazzling blood ruby pendant hung from a delicate mithril chain around her neck, catching the light and casting a crimson glow upon her skin. And atop her head, a regal mithril circlet encrusted with sparkling rubies sat majestically, commanding attention and respect. She was a vision of power and elegance, an embodiment of grace and finesse.

A chorus of horrified cries filled the air as the humidity rose and crackled with energy. "He comes," Amalia hissed in a voice of fire, directing her words towards the fat man who had taken everything from her. "I will make your world suffer for your crimes, mortal! You have taken everything from me, now I will do the same to you." In an instant, Naromu was consumed by flames, his screams echoing across the water.

In a flash, the man's sanity shattered as the searing pain consumed him. With a bloodcurdling scream, he threw himself into the icy, choppy waters of the sea, desperate to quell the burning flames that engulfed his body. But even as he sank deeper, the fire refused to be extinguished, crackling and sizzling against his skin like a raging inferno. The stench of scorched flesh filled the air, mingling with the salty smell of the sea. It was a battle between agony and survival, and it was unclear who would emerge victorious. It was a sight that would haunt anyone who witnessed it for years to come.

But Amalia wasn't finished with him yet - with a flick of her hand, she extinguished the flames and pulled his body from the water. Her eyes glinted with cruelty as she made sure his heart continued to beat and his mind remained conscious.

As she relished in his pain, Amalia's attention turned to the boat around them, now engulfed in flames and smoke billowing into the sky. But amidst the chaos, her eyes remained fixed on her ultimate goal - to bring down the one responsible for all her suffering. Suddenly, Nimriar emerged from the clouds, revealing himself with shimmering scales and piercing eyes. Without hesitation, Amalia clenched her fist, causing Naromu's body to explode into ash that scattered into the water below. Climbing onto Nimriar's back, Amalia held onto his mighty scales as he carried them both away from the burning wreckage. The taste of revenge was bittersweet on her tongue, but she knew that justice had been served.

With graceful, fluid movements and a voice filled with ancient elvish words that seemed to dance on her lips, flames erupted from his breath, engulfing everything in its path - the water, the earth, and even the heavens above. The flames danced and licked at their surroundings, leaving trails of destruction in their wake. From her perch on top of the dragon's powerful back, Amalia surveyed the landscape with a sense of triumph. Amalia's keen eyes spotted a grand castle in the distance, its turrets reaching towards the heavens. She spoke in a commanding tone, using the powerful language of her ancestors, "Head towards that castle. We will bring death and devastation and death to all who stand in our way!" The dragon released a vicious roar, eager to fulfill Amalia's desires as they soared through the air towards their next destination of devastation. The wind whipped around them, carrying the scent of smoke and fear as they left a trail of destruction in their wake.

)o(

Cullen sat atop a grassy knoll, the lush green blades tickling his ankles as he peered out over the town below. Beside him sat Tiatria, her loose hair cascading around her face as she took in the view with him, her presence bringing a sense of calm to his mind. Tiatria leaned comfortably against Cullen's strong, muscular arm, her head resting gently on his broad shoulder. The warmth and weight of her presence brought Cullen a sense of belonging and home that he had never experienced before. The sweet scent of Tiatria's hair, a delicate blend of lavender and jasmine, filled his senses and always seemed to have a calming effect on him, enveloping him in peace and contentment. It was as if she had the power to soothe him with just her presence. He closed his eyes and breathed deeply, savoring the moment of contentment with the woman he loved. As she nuzzled closer, the soft strands of her hair tickled his cheek, adding to the feeling of being home in her embrace.

Cullen turned his head to admire her delicate features, wishing to etch every inch of her into his memory. But then he saw it - the sadness that crept into her expression and the tears that welled up in her eyes. He didn't need to read her mind to know what was troubling her. "I'm not going to marry her," he said, his voice trembling with emotion. A gentle smile graced her lips as she gazed at Cullen. "You have a duty."

"Screw duty," Cullen retorted, his irritation evident as he clasped onto Tiatria's hand with fierce determination. "I love you Tia. I don't love her." He declared his love for Tiatria with a passion and determination; he knew he wasn't going to love anyone else. She could see the sincerity shining in his eyes. "My heart knows what it wants...and it isn't her, and it never will be." Even as Tiatria smiled, Cullen held tightly onto her hand, knowing that these feelings had developed much faster than anyone could have expected. But they were there, strong and unwavering.

Though their feelings had developed quickly, they were undeniably strong and unwavering. But Tiatria also knew that Cullen's people would never accept her for who she truly was - a forest-dwelling elf. She refused to hide or change herself to appease them. She belonged in the woods, and she was determined to return there.

Cullen watched the tears slide down her cheeks as she fought to maintain a smile. "Your people will still need you, Cullen," she whispered, her voice filled with sorrow. "Even if we find Amalia and put the dragon back into its slumber, your people will need you to lead them." Cullen snorted in frustration and shook his head, feeling tired of being told what to do and who to be his entire life. But then Tia's hand touched his face, her touch gentle yet reassuring.

"I'm going to make a choice for myself for once," he declared with determination. "I choose you, Tia, and I will always choose you."

The ground trembled beneath their feet, causing Dorian and Maxwell to instinctively hold onto each other for support.

A sudden gust of wind roared through the air, picking up strength and velocity as it circled around Westevia's tavern. It tore at the roof with a ferocious force, ripping it off and sending it spinning into the sky. The powerful current lifted them both off their feet and flung them several feet away, crashing into a nearby wall with a resounding thud. As they struggled to regain their bearings, they gazed up at the now-exposed sky where the roof had been and saw Nimriar, the dragon, flying over the town in all its majestic glory. The fierce gust of wind caught Cullen and Tiatria off guard, sending them tumbling several yards across the field of tall grass; blades of the grass whipped past them like tiny soldiers. He could feel the heat of the dragon against his skin and ringing in his ears as it roared, but all he cared about was keeping her safe in his arms. Cullen's grip on Tiatria tightened as he refused to let go of her, determined not to be separated from her in this chaotic moment. As the grass continued to whip around them, filling their nostrils with its sweet, earthy scent, they clung to each other; bodies pressed together as the wind forced them to roll against a tree. It was a wild and exhilarating ride, but Cullen knew he would hold onto Tiatria no matter what obstacles came their way.

Thamyris had climbed up an oak tree with Kethinar close behind him, his wings beating furiously against the strong winds. From this vantage point, Thamyris could see the dragon's impressive size as it soared over the village and into the forest beyond. But what caught his attention most was the figure riding on the dragon's back.

Thamyris felt bile rise in his throat as he recognized the rider - Amalia, in her new form as a dragon rider. Tears streamed down his face as he watched her fly past, her form becoming smaller and smaller until she disappeared into the horizon. Kethinar, sensing Thamyris' distress, broke off his pursuit of Nimriar and circled back to his friend's side. He could feel Thamyris' unspoken plea to not witness any more of this heartbreaking sight.

Chapter 15

amalia's eyes blazed with a twisted euphoria as she rode on the back of Nimriar, their bodies soaring over the town of Amalthea. With a commanding voice, she goaded the dragon to unleash its wrath upon those below. Nimriar opened its massive jaws and, with a deafening roar, unleashed a scorching inferno that consumed the town in seconds.

The air filled with piercing screams and the sickening scent of burning flesh as Amalia laughed at the chaos she had wrought. Nimriar swooped down from above, its razor-sharp claws slicing through buildings like they were made of paper. The once pristine streets were now littered with broken bodies and smoldering debris. The priests of the town's church screamed for God to save them as two of them grabbed large, thick ropes with their hands and used their bodies to ring the bells to tell the people to run and seek shelter.

As if possessed by a primal urge for destruction, Nimriar tore through homes and businesses with ferocious abandon. The town's inhabitants ran for their lives, but there was no escape from the dragon's relentless pursuit. With every sweep of its colossal wings, more buildings crumbled and collapsed into rubble. As the beast flew through the city, Nimriar's claws took hold of the church's steeple with claws of his back feet and crushed it, causing the bells to fly and crash into other buildings. The sounds of destruction were deafening - the agonized screams of the dying, the crashing of collapsing structures, and the triumphant roars of Nimriar as it laid waste to everything in its path. Amalia looked down at the shattered remains of Amalthea and couldn't help but revel in the power and terror she had unleashed upon this peaceful community.

The Dragon soared over the castle, its massive wings casting a shadow that engulfed the entire fortress. Its massive tail whipped into the walls, shattering stone and sending debris raining down upon the panic-stricken soldiers below. Every fiery breath of the dragon left a trail of destruction, incinerating anything in its path. Helpless soldiers were snatched up from their posts on the ramparts; their screams were drowned out by the roar of the beast as it dropped them from dizzying heights to their doom.

)o(

Duke took down the grand staircase. With each step, the air seemed to sizzle and crackle like the flames of hell. A scorching wind whipped through his hair, tugging at his clothes as if trying to pull him back. When he finally reached the bottom, he could feel the ground tremble beneath his feet and hear faint whispers swirling around him.

The guards nearby inched away, their hands shaking as they clutched onto their spears for dear life. "GET BACK TO YOUR POSTS!" the Duke's voice boomed through the chaos, commanding authority even as terror gripped his heart.

As he made his way through the palace corridors, the screams and roars grew louder and more chaotic. The stench of burning flesh filled his nostrils, overwhelming any other scent around. Finally, when he reached the balcony, he was met with a horrifying sight - a massive red dragon reigning terror over the city below. Its fiery breath scorched everything in its path, devouring buildings and people without mercy. And this was no mere beast - it was twenty-two feet of pure destruction with a wingspan that could blot out the sun.

The Duke stumbled back in shock, throwing his arms out to rally his soldiers into action. "GO! Protect the King and sound the alarm bells! NOW!" he roared, desperation creeping into his voice as he knew they had little time left. But even as he spoke, Nimriar swooped lower with deadly precision.

The terrified cries of innocent victims echoed through the air, pleading for salvation from this hellish nightmare that had descended upon them. Fire rained from above like an inferno, leaving nothing but destruction and death in its wake. As Nimriar continued its rampage, the Duke only watched helplessly while the city burned beneath him.

King Arthur's grip on his daughter's hand was like a vise as the ground violently shook beneath them. Edith's terrified and panicked cries were drowned out by the sounds of crumbling stones and roaring flames. With her arm wrapped tightly around his, Arthur led her towards the nearest exit and down a flight of stairs, dodging falling debris and ignoring the searing heat that enveloped the city brushed against their skin. As they ran into the courtyard, Arthur caught sight of the dragon ravaging the city in the distance. Arthur pushed Edith to continue to run for safety, but Amalia commanded Nimriar to fly towards the castle. Once Arthur saw the dragon break through the castle's gates, he screamed at Edith to continue running towards safety.

The once majestic castle was now a chaotic battlefield, with soldiers fighting for their lives and buildings collapsing all around them. The Duke, who had been keeping watch from afar, spotted Edith and immediately rushed to her side. "Where is your father?" he demanded, searching frantically for King Arthur amidst the chaos. Edith could only shake her head in confusion, "He was behind me, telling me to run!" The Duke took her hand and guided her towards the chapel, knowing it was their best chance at survival against the fiery beast. "Get to the chapel and stay there!" he ordered.

Finally, he spotted Arthur sprinting towards the barracks in an attempt to protect his kingdom from further harm. With adrenaline surging through his veins, the Duke ran towards him, determined to stand by his side until the very end. As they faced the fiery wrath of the dragon together, their bond as friends and warriors grew stronger than ever before.

Cullen and his companions urged their mounts to run as fast as they could through the dense forest, branches whipping against their faces and the wind howling in their ears. Tiatria's mount slowed slightly, allowing Cullen's horse Seraphim to catch up. As she reached out to touch the beast's powerful neck, a surge of energy seemed to pass between them and Seraphim took off with renewed speed, almost seeming to fly. Tiatria did the same for Dorian and Maxwell's horses, using her mysterious powers to help them keep pace with hers and Thamyris'. The group rode on, knowing in their hearts where they were heading as their blood ran cold with fear.

Cullen couldn't take his mind off of his mother and sisters as he rode on, determination fueling him forward. Kethinar soared overhead, keeping watch over them as they raced towards their destination. Kethinar soared overhead, keeping watch as Thamyris could still see the destruction that had already been unleashed upon Amalthea by the monstrous creature that had invaded their town. Thamyris, filled with a burning desire to end this cycle of death once and for all, rode at the front of the group. His sister's actions had caused too much pain and suffering, and it was time for it to come to an end. With every beat of his horse's hooves against the hard ground, he pushed forward with unyielding determination.

)o(

The King and the Duke burst through the doors of the barracks, their footsteps echoing off the stone walls. They frenzied to the armory, their hearts racing with adrenaline. Grasping swords and shields, preparing for battle. As they hastily donned their armor, the king's mind raced with worry for his kingdom and his people. "Where is Edith?" he asked urgently, steeling himself for what was to come.

The Duke checked the weight balance of his shield as he replied, "I sent her to the chapel. It should be a safe place for her."

"That will have to do for now," the King responded grimly.

"The chapel is strategically placed within the castle, supported by several load-bearing points. Even if the structures collapse, it should remain standing."

"May God protect her and all who seek shelter there," the king murmured. He looked at his friend. "It has been an honor to serve you, my Lord," said the Duke with a respectful bow.

"And it has been a privilege to call you my friend and advisor," replied the king with a nod of gratitude. Taking a deep breath, he bolted out of the barracks.

Meanwhile, Edith burst through the doors of the chapel, gasping for breath. The Cardinal and his priests were huddled together, praying fervently. A few servants and Edith's ladies-in-waiting were also present, their eyes wide with fear. With debris falling from above and bits of stone crashing to the ground, the girls frantically motioned for Edith to seek shelter with them. She wasted no time in obeying their urgent pleas as they all fled deeper into the chapel for safety.

The red-robed cardinal knelt reverently before the altar, his hands stretched upward in a fervent plea for divine grace. The stained glass windows bathed the ornate cathedral in a kaleidoscope of colors, casting an otherworldly glow on the holy man's humble form. His voice echoed through the hallowed space, carrying his prayers up to the heavens above. As he closed his eyes and bowed his head, his heart overflowed with faith and devotion to his Maker.

"I shall walk through dark valleys. I fear no harm for you are at my side. Your rod and staff shall give me courage. No evil shall befall me, No weakness in my stride. God wills not my foot to slip Or my guardian sleep, He guides me from all evil, The Lord is my guardian; The Lord the shade I keep, By day the sun cannot harm me Or the moon by night. For the Lord said, "Do not let your hearts be troubled. Have faith in God and also in me. In my Father's house, There are many dwelling places. If there were not, Would I have told you That I am going to prepare A place for you? And if I go And prepare a place for you, I will come back again And take you to myself, So that where I am You also may be." If the Lord is with us, Who can be against us?"

The Cardinal and his men murmured this prayer repeatedly, their voices trembling as they sought protection from the chaos unfolding around them. Edith cautiously peered out from behind a fallen pew, her eyes widening at the sight of the ceiling crumbling and showering debris onto the floor. The once serene space was now filled with screams and dust as everyone scrambled to find shelter. But even as they cowered, the dragon's roars grew louder and more fierce, causing the chapel's walls to shake and tremble in response. The beautiful stained glass windows shattered into a million pieces, sending shards of colored light cascading down upon the terrified crowd.

Just outside, the King and Duke emerged from the barracks. They were met with a wall of searing flames. The heat was so intense it felt like standing too close to a furnace. The two held up their shields, feeling them grow hot to the touch as they absorbed the heat. Even a brief touch could leave them scarred for life. Fire raged all around them, threatening to consume everything in its path.

As the flames died down, the two cautiously emerged from behind their shields. What they saw before them left them frozen in fear - face to face with a massive dragon, its scales shimmering in the sun's light. Its powerful wings spread overhead. The creature bared its razor-sharp teeth and let out a guttural growl that echoed through their ears. Its glowing eyes bore into them as its massive claws dug deep into the rocky ground, leaving deep gouges in their wake. The heat radiating from its body was suffocating as if standing too close to a raging inferno. They knew they were no match for this formidable beast.

Amalia's lips curled into a wicked smile as her eyes scanned the two figures standing before her. Though she didn't know their names, their elaborate attire spoke volumes about their importance.

)o(

As Cullen and his companions rode through the towering gates of the castle, their horses' hooves echoed off the stone walls. All eyes were on the magnificent dragon that perched in the upper courtyard, its scales glinting in the sunlight. Cullen, familiar with the layout of the castle, knew that anyone trapped up there would have no chance of escape, with the dragon blocking the only exit.

Tiatria transformed into a bird and soared up to where the dragon's attention was fixed. "TIA, NO!" Cullen's cry rang out, his heart racing as he watched her ascend towards danger.

In a blur of motion, Tiatria transformed back into her original form and darted between the dragon and the two frightened men. Her arms rose as she shielded them with her outstretched arms.

"Amalia, princess, please stop!"

Her voice rang out with a mixture of urgency and authority. The two men shared a bewildered look - who was this brave woman risking her life for strangers? Tiatria stood her ground, facing down the fearsome dragon. The wind carried the scent of burning embers and fear, but she refused to falter in her mission to protect innocents.

Amalia's eyes were unyielding stone, devoid of any emotion. She had come here with one purpose and nothing could stop her now, not even her own kind. "Don't do this," Tiatria pleaded desperately. But Amalia's dragon showed no mercy as its jaws parted slightly, flames flickering dangerously in the depths of its throat. Tiatria could feel the burning pain and seething hatred that consumed her Princess's mind. She heard Tahl'rail's screams as he fought to free and protect his beloved, and she felt the love that bound Amalia and Tahl'rail together, now torn apart. Tiatria wept as she shared in their agony, determined to feel every bit of suffering that her princess endured.

With a steely glint in her eye, Amalia extended her right hand and declared, "Humanity had its chance." A shrill whistling pierced the air as an arrow charged with divine light struck Nimriar's left eye, causing the beast to recoil violently and almost throw Amalia from its back. It was Thamyris who had made such an incredible shot, having jumped off his unicorn while it bucked wildly beneath him. Through Kethinar's eyes, he aimed for the perfect mark. Amalia turned in fury to face her attacker, eager to unleash her wrath upon whoever dared wound her dragon.

Meanwhile, Dorian, Maxwell, and Cullen took advantage of the distraction to sneak into a section of the castle that led up to the upper courtyard. They knew time was running out, and they had to reach Tiatria before it was too late. Amalia and Thamyris finally saw each other eye to eye. Kethinar's eyes showed Thamyris his sister, and how much she had changed. He landed on Nimriar's back and ran towards his sister, "Lia stop! Come home!" he cried out as he charged at her. Amalia held out her right hand and made a flick motion to the right, which caused Thamyris to fall into one of the stone turrets.

Thamyris gasped for air as he felt the wind knocked out of him, plummeting towards the ground, his body falling limp and lifeless. Kethinar desperately flew around him, trying to grab onto his friend's long black hair and slow their descent. But Amalia, consumed by rage and madness, no longer recognized anyone but her enemies. She snarled as she watched the hawk attempting to save Thamyris, pulling out an arrow from her dragon's eye and launching it with deadly accuracy at the bird. With a surge of magic, she propelled the arrow towards its target at breakneck speed, watching with satisfaction as it struck the hawk in the breast. The bird screeched in agony as both the bird and Thamyris crashed to the earth below.

Maxwell and the others finally reached the top of the tower, gasping for air as they burst into the upper courtyard. Amalia's eyes burned with determination as she turned to face Tiatria and her companions. The dragon's massive jaws creaked open, releasing a thick plume of smoke that curled and billowed into the air. Sparks of red fire flickered within the depths of its throat, hinting at the flames that were ready to burst forth. Dorian felt his heart race as he watched in horror, realizing that stubborn Tiatria was willing to risk being burned alive in a desperate attempt to wake her fallen Priestess and beloved Princess. The intense heat radiating from the dragon's breath felt like they were standing at the edge of an inferno, with no escape in sight. Suddenly, Dorian shoved Tiatria aside with a powerful force, sending her sliding several feet across the ground.

In a flash of brilliance, Dorian raised his scepter and summoned a powerful shield over himself and two men behind him. "Apologies for our tardiness, Your Majesty," he said, his voice dripping with arrogance.

Cullen quickly grabbed his cloak and held onto it with his left hand in the hope of minimizing any burns from dragon fire. He held up his shield in one hand and drew his sword with the other, ready to defend against any attack. The Duke looked on in shock as he saw his son standing between them and the ferocious beast, his young face resolute with unyielding courage.

With a roar that shook the very ground beneath them, without hesitation, Maxwell ran towards the beast with both swords raised high, the blades gleaming with a deadly icy enchantment. With all his might, he leaped into the air and plunged both swords deep into the massive creature's neck. The beast let out an ear-splitting roar of agony as blood gushed from the deep cut into its flesh, with Maxwell's body weight forcing the blades to slice through even deeper, staining Maxwell's clothes crimson. The beast thrashed wildly, its roars echoing through the air as it tried to shake off the piercing pain. But before Maxwell could even land himself on the ground, Amalia's fury erupted like a volcano. With a fierce blast of magic, she sent Maxwell flying as he clung to his bloody swords off Nimriar's neck, crashing onto the ground below. The giant beast thrashed about wildly, its roars echoing throughout the courtyard as it tried to shake off the excruciating pain caused by Maxwell's attack.

But just as quickly as her rage had flared up, Amalia's calm demeanor returned as she gracefully mounted Nimriar's neck. Placing her left hand on his wounded neck, she spoke ancient, elvish words that glowed brightly in the air. And with a burst of powerful healing magic, Nimriar's wounds began to close, and the blood stopped. In a burst of magical energy, the wounds were healed, and the beast seemed stronger than ever, its eyes glowing with an otherworldly light. The battle was far from over.

The Duke watched in awe as Amalia controlled the beast with such ease, her power and mastery over magic undeniable. For a moment, he could not help but wonder if perhaps she was not just an ordinary human after all. But before he could dwell on that thought any further, Cullen charged forward, his sword raised high as he joined Maxwell in attacking the mighty Nimriar. With a swift and calculated movement, his left arm raised his shield to smash it against the dragon's gaping maw. The sound of metal on scales echoed through the air as he thrust his sword forward with all his might, piercing the beast's flesh and drawing a spray of hot blood.

The adrenaline rush was almost overwhelming as he battled for his life against the fierce creature. Sweat dripped down his face, mingling with the spray of blood and creating a salty tang on his lips. The weight of his shield and the heat of the sun bearing down on him only added to the intensity of the moment, but he remained focused, determined to defeat the dragon and protect his King, Father and friends.

Nimriar had finally reached his breaking point. With a single furious swipe, he sent Cullen flying through the air, only to collide into Tiatria, who was struggling to get up from a previous attack. After they crashed into the ground into a heap, she quickly rose and started to assess Cullen's injuries. Nimriar, on the other hand, unleashed a blast of scorching fire toward Dorian and the others. Dorian gritted his teeth and held his scepter high, desperately trying to shield themselves from the dragon's full rage. He braced himself against the intense, searing heat. The flames licked at his skin, threatening to consume him, but he refused to cower. Sweat dripped down his face, mingling with the ash and soot that covered him from head to toe. His muscles strained under the weight of his determination as he defied the fiery inferno before him. With each passing moment, the heat grew more unbearable, but Dorian stood strong and determined, refusing to back down in the face of danger.

Amidst the chaos and confusion, Maxwell's attention was abruptly drawn to Thamyris. The once proud and fierce warrior now stood helpless, blinded without his hawk by his side. His hands frantically searched the ground for answers, grasping at nothing but air. Desperation was etched across his face. He struggled to understand why his vision had been taken from him. In a moment of despair, he unknowingly clutched onto Kethinar's feathers, still warm from the life that was now gone. A gut-wrenching cry of anguish escaped his lips as he held onto the dead bird, its beautiful plumage marred by the arrow that had ended its life.

Without hesitation, Cullen sprang into action, throwing his cloak over Tiatria to shield her from any harm. He knew he could not reach Dorian or the king with the dragon's fiery breath unleashed upon them, so instead, he charged toward Maxwell and Thamyris, determined to protect them both with all his might. Adrenaline surged through Maxwell as he reached for his swords, his mind honed and focused on the impending battle. With every sense heightened, he stood ready to defend against any further attacks that may come their way.

With a determined look in his eye, Maxwell rose to his feet and surveyed the scene before him. Dorian, once strong and sure-footed, now faltered as he struggled to maintain control of his scepter. Maxwell could see the beads of sweat forming on Dorian's forehead and knew that time was running out for their friend.

Cullen's mind raced as he grasped the impossible task before them. The weight of their mission pressed down on him like a heavy cloak, threatening to suffocate him. There seemed to be no conceivable way to reach Dorian, let alone save him and the others trapped with him, including his own father. He frantically reached into his pouch of magic dust given to him by the Queen. The iridescent blue powder glittered in the sunlight as he tossed it to Tiatria, who caught it with trembling hands. She murmured ancient elvish words under her breath as she hurled the dust into the air, creating a dazzling cascade of colors and light that surrounded them.

Maxwell could feel the potent swirl of magic engulfing them as the portal began to crack open. Despite the allure of escaping this dangerous realm, he couldn't tear his eyes away from Dorian. The thought of leaving him behind, alone to face the beast, filled Maxwell with fierce determination. He longed to rush to Dorian's side, to fight off the creature and make their escape together. But as the heat of the Dragon's fire intensified, Maxwell knew it was an impossible task. Cullen noticed the tight grip on Maxwell's swords, a telltale sign of his inner struggle. It was clear that Maxwell was considering risking everything to reach Dorian, even if it meant certain death. Perhaps, in his heart, Maxwell wanted nothing more than to die alongside the man he loved rather than live without him.

The portal burst open before them in a swirl of shimmering blue and purple energy, beckoning them forward. Tiatria's grip on Thamyris tightened as she fiercely pulled him through with all her might, ignoring his desperate cries for his beloved bird. Thamyris' body was paralyzed, fear coursing through his veins like electricity. He could hear the sounds of movement around him, but he couldn't see anything. His mind raced with questions - who was moving him? Where were they going? Panic threatened to consume him as he remained frozen in place. Tiatria touched his hands gently, "You need to let me help you! We have to leave!" she told him gently. She could hear all the fearful thoughts that consumed Thamyris' mind but she knew now was the time to focus and to get him to trust her enough to move.

Meanwhile, Maxwell's gaze remained locked onto Dorian, his eyes blazing with determination and fury. Cullen's hand shot out and grabbed Maxwell's arm, pulling him towards the portal with a sense of urgency. They needed to escape before Nimriar's fiery wrath would fall upon them. The air crackled and sizzled with energy as the flames rained down upon them, their heat searing against Thamyris' skin. "Please, my Prince!" Tiatria begged, her hands gently touching Thamyris's, who seemed to startle from not knowing who touched him. Tiatria watched as he protectively held Kethinar's body. She knelt down and gently held his face. Thamyris saw flashes of Tiatria's mind as he did any he touched. Tiatria focused her thoughts and helped Thamyris see what he needed to see. Dorian struggled to keep up his shield to protect himself, the King and the Duke. Cullen tried to get Maxwell to move as the portal formed behind them. "We need to leave if we have any hope of survival." Thamyris felt Tiatria's fingers tighten against his face. "Please trust me enough to help you."

Tiatria put her hands on Thamyris to help cradle Kethinar's body in his arms. As Tiatria helped Thamyris stand, he stumbled forward, blindly following her towards safety. But even as they fled through the portal, Thamyris couldn't shake off the feeling that they were leaving something important behind. His heart pounded in his chest, his mind consumed by fear and uncertainty. What awaited them on the other side? Only time will tell. Thamyris could smell that the air was thick with the acrid smell of sulfur and smoke, and the ground beneath his feet shook from the force of Nimriar's anger. With each step they took towards the portal, it seemed to grow larger and farther from the people they loved.

Dorian's eyes were filled with tears, not just from the intense heat and strain of maintaining a protective shield but also from the overwhelming fear that he would fail his King. Beads of sweat dripped down his face, mingling with the tears as he fought to hold up his shield against the scorching flames of the dragon's breath. His body trembled with exertion, muscles straining against the immense power emanating from the dragon. Maxwell stood by helplessly, watching as Dorian's shield shook and wavered, knowing that it wouldn't hold for much longer. The air around them was thick with smoke and the stench of burning flesh. Every second felt like an eternity as they waited for either their shields to break or for reinforcements to arrive. But in this moment, it was just Dorian and his unwavering determination to protect those he had sworn himself to.

Desperately, Cullen tried to drag Maxwell towards the portal. But Maxwell refused to budge, fighting off Cullen's efforts with all his might. Dorian's gaze flickered between them, frustration and fear evident on his face. "What are you waiting for, Amant? Go!" he pleaded with them, even as he himself dropped to one knee, struggling to maintain his protective shield. Maxwell's heart ached as he watched Dorian with tears streaming down his face. He longed to embrace him, to tell him how much he loved him. At that moment, Dorian gave him a weak smile and whispered hoarsely, "I love you."

But before they could say anything else, the dragon unleashed its full fury upon them. The flames grew hotter and more intense, consuming everything in their path. Dorian cried out in pain and desperation as the fire finally broke through the shield and consumed him, along with the King and the Duke. With a final burst of strength, Cullen managed to grab hold of Maxwell and push him through the portal just as it began to close. He followed quickly behind, narrowly escaping the dragon's wrath as it turned its head around to incinerate them.

Chapter 16

as they emerged into the Enchanted Forest, Maxwell collapsed onto the ground, his body wracked with sobs and screams. He grasped handfuls of dirt and threw them about in a frenzy, letting out guttural cries as he went insane from the gravity of what had just happened. Tears streamed down his face, mixing with sweat and dirt as he mourned for Dorian, who had selflessly sacrificed everything for their cause. In that moment, all that remained was a scorched and barren landscape where they had once stood together in battle, surrounded by the remnants of their fierce love and bravery.

Cullen lay on his back, breathing heavily as sweat trickled down his forehead and neck. He hadn't even noticed that his arms were outstretched, instinctively reaching for something or someone to hold onto. Tiatria slowly sat up, checking on Thamyris, who continued to sob while cradling Kethinar's lifeless body. Her heart broke for her Prince as she had never seen him so vulnerable before. Gently, she helped him sit up and comforted him, feeling the tightness of his grip on his beloved hawk's body. "It's alright," she whispered softly, "Let me help you stand, your majesty." Tiatria carefully placed one arm around Thamyris' shoulders while using her other hand to support Kethinar's body. Slowly but steadily, she guided Thamyris to his feet, allowing him to lean on her for support.

Meanwhile, Cullen sat up and shook with adrenaline as he looked at Maxwell still on all fours, head bowed as he wept uncontrollably. His hands still clenched dirt inside them spoke volumes of his anguish. Cullen turned to Tiatria, both knowing that they needed to get the rest of their group back to the safety of the Elven castle. With compassion and understanding, Cullen helped

Maxwell to his feet. "On your feet, soldier," he said gently, knowing that there were no words that could ease the pain and grief Maxwell was feeling. After all the years they had spent together, the bond, love, and companionship between them, for Maxwell to lose Dorian in such a manner was a huge and profound loss. Cullen took a quick inventory of his belongings, finding that he had lost his sword in the fight with the dragon. His shield was also nowhere to be found, most likely still lying on the ground where they had battled the fierce creature. In its place, he picked up Maxwell's swords and held onto them tightly. With Maxwell's current state of mind, Cullen knew it was best to keep the weapons close at hand.

As he turned to survey the others, Cullen could see the pain etched on their face, especially Tiatria, who looked overcome with grief and fear. The pain and sorrow emanating from Thamyris and Maxwell almost overwhelmed her. But he knew there was no time for consoling her just yet - their safety came first. Tiatria wiped away tears and looked around at the forest surrounding them. Her voice was shaky as she spoke, "I know this part of the forest. We're not too far from home."

"How far?" Cullen asked, trying to focus on their next steps.

"Only a few miles," Tiatria replied. "But we must proceed with caution. There may be guards watching the borders, but with Prince, Maxwell and myself present, we should be able to make it safely."

The sunlight peeked through the dense canopy, casting a warm golden glow over the forest floor. The trees were painted with shades of yellow and orange, creating a serene scene despite the dangers that lurked within the shadows. The setting sun painted the sky a beautiful blend of pinks, purples, and oranges, casting a warm glow over the trees and their surroundings. The thick canopy above allowed small speckles of golden light to filter through, creating a mesmerizing dance of shadows on the forest floor. The sun's rays shone through the dense foliage, casting a golden glow over the forest floor. Trees stretched upwards, their leaves creating a canopy of vibrant greens and yellows, dappling the ground with shifting shadows.

Cullen couldn't help but notice how the light created a warm and inviting atmosphere despite the dense foliage that surrounded them. As they made their way deeper into the woods, he noticed that the brush was thicker in this particular location compared to where they had first entered. Tiatria had explained that certain areas were purposely left overgrown as a means of concealment for hidden entrances. In other areas, she kept the brush carefully trimmed and maintained to avoid any unnecessary attention. Senses on high alert, Cullen took note of every detail in their surroundings, knowing that danger could be lurking just beyond the lush greenery.

Thamyris' highly skilled ears pricked up at the faint sound of snapping twigs, causing his face to tense with focus. Tiatria's eyes mirrored his alertness as they scanned the surrounding trees for any signs of movement. The gentle rustling of leaves accompanied the distant snapping of twigs, growing louder and more urgent as something made its way through the brush. Thamyris' eyes narrowed in concentration as he tried to pinpoint the source of the noise, his brow furrowed in concern. Tiatria could see his tensed body language and grew anxious herself. The silence was suddenly broken by the closer rustling of leaves and the sound of something large moving through the foliage. Cullen's eyes widened in alarm. He quickly scanned their surroundings, ready for danger, just like his companions.

"It's coming from our left," Thamyris announced, his voice tight with determination. The sounds grew closer and more urgent, causing Maxwell to welcome whatever form of death was coming their way while Cullen tightened his grip on Maxwell's swords. Suddenly, with a few snorts and the twitching of branches, a massive grizzly bear appeared before them. It was unlike anything Cullen had ever seen before and he instinctively stood in front of his friends, holding out both swords defensively.

But before anyone could react, the bear exploded with a bright light that caused Cullen to take a step back in surprise. After a few moments, the light dimmed and revealed a humanoid shape standing before them. Tiatria let out a sigh of relief when she realized it was Ásbjǫrn, "Thank the gods!" she praised. The large elf gave a gentle smile and chuckled as he opened his arms wide as if to give everyone a huge bear hug.

However, upon getting a good look at everyone's faces, Ásbjǫrn's usual cheerful demeanor changed. It filled with sadness and worry. "Friends, you've returned," he said with concern before embracing each of them in turn.

His breath caught in his throat, his eyes widened, and he felt a sharp pang in his chest when he saw Thamyris - the fierce warrior known for his strength and stoic demeanor, was cradling Kethinar, the sharp-eyed hawk with whom he shared an unbreakable bond. A gentle breeze blew through the clearing, causing Thamyris' dark hair to sway slightly and carrying with it the sweet scent of wildflowers. In this moment, Ásbjǫrn's heart clenched as he gazed into his Prince's eyes, filled with the weight of death and tragedy that they had just escaped from. The others in their group shared a similar expression, all in desperate need of comfort and solace after the harrowing events they had endured. The scent of smoke and fear lingered in the air, mixed with the metallic tang of blood. Ásbjǫrn could feel the tension radiating off of his companions, their bodies stiff and weary from the fight for survival. He knew they needed to find a safe haven soon, to heal and regroup before facing any more danger on their journey.

Thamyris' ears twitched as the forest came alive with the sound of Ásbjǫrn's steps, each one echoing through the trees in a steady beat. The rustling of leaves underfoot added a gentle percussion to the symphony of nature that surrounded them. The soft thud of each footfall was like a drum, guiding Ásbjǫrn towards Thamyris with purpose and determination. The peaceful sounds of the forest only intensified the weight of the moment as Thamyris cradled Kethinar in his arms and Ásbjǫrn approached with a heavy heart. It was as if the forest itself recognized the significance of this moment and joined in with its own melancholy music. As he approached, Thamyris' nose picked up the scent of pine, sharp and refreshing, like a burst of clean air after a rainstorm. The crisp of air carried a hint of freshness, reminiscent of freshly cut grass and blooming flowers. The scent lingered on Åsbjǫrn's clothes, bringing a sense of familiarity and comfort to him as he approached his beloved Prince. It was a reminder of his home in the woodlands, with its earthy aromas and natural beauty combined. The scents were both invigorating and soothing, creating a harmonious balance that reflected the bond between Åsbjǫrn and Thamyris as elves.

Ásbjǫrn's rich, amber, honey-brown eyes met Thamyris' sightless milky eyes with a deep sense of empathy and understanding. A gentle smile, like a warm breeze on a cool day, played on Ásbjǫrn's lips, radiating comfort and reassurance. He wanted to convey his friendly intentions through his expression alone, knowing that words were not always necessary when it comes to comforting someone in need. As he stepped closer to Thamyris' side, Ásbjǫrn placed a hand as soft as a feather on his friend's shoulder, letting him know that he was not alone in this dark and unfamiliar place. The touch felt like a lifeline in the midst of chaos and despair, offering a glimmer of hope and companionship in the void.

Thamyris could feel the roughness of Ásbjǫrn's calloused fingers against his own, with visible calluses from years of tending to the land. The touch was firm but not forceful, conveying a sense of strength and reliability. It both comforted and reminded Thamyris of the danger and uncertainty he faced. His grip on Kethinar tightened as he felt at peace amid chaos. It was a reminder of Ásbjǫrn's strength and resilience, a physical representation of his unwavering support and protection through the years.

As he felt the tug of someone trying to steal Kethinar from his grasp, a low growl bubbled in Thamyris's throat - a primal response to protect his friend. But he also sensed a genuine empathy and kindness in Ásbjǫrn's touch as he couldn't see the pleading expression in his eyes. With all the years he'd known him, Ásbjǫrn understood better than anyone else the very nature of Thamyris and Kethinar's bond and was asking for permission before intervening. "May I have the privilege?" he asked softly, sending shivers down Thamyris' spine..

Thamyris inhaled deeply, trying to steady his racing heart. He felt Ásbjǫrn's touch like a jolt of electricity, sending shivers down his spine. As their energies intertwined, Thamyris' vision blurred, and he was overwhelmed with a flood of images and sensations. In an instant, he was transported into Ásbjǫrn's memories, experiencing them as if they were his own. The wildness and freedom of living in nature pulsed through his veins, the scent of pine and earth filling his nostrils. He could feel the warmth of the sun on his skin, hear the rustle of leaves underfoot, and taste the sweetness of wild berries on his tongue.

But it wasn't just the physical sensations that consumed him. Flashes of intimate moments danced before his eyes - passionate lovemaking with both men and women, all genders coming together in lustful abandon. Thamyris had never known this side of Ásbjǫrn or that he'd experienced such raw intimacy before. It left him breathless as he then got a flash of what he assumed was a fantasy about the two of them. Thamyris blushed as he saw the intimate nature of it, and to be honest, it left him wanting to know more.

As he came out of Ásbjǫrn's mind, Thamyris could not help but feel a twinge of envy for Ásbjǫrn's uninhibited spirit. To live so freely, unafraid to indulge in one's desires - it was exhilarating and intimidating all at once. And yet, here he was, sharing this intimate connection with another man who shared those same desires without hesitation or shame. It was a feeling unlike any other, and Thamyris reveled in it with every fiber of his being.

With a heavy heart, Thamyris gently lowered Kethinar's lifeless body into the capable hands of Ásbjǫrn. The large elf turned to the others and spoke in a somber tone, his voice carrying the weight of their loss. "I will lead you back home. Much has changed, and our Prince is sorely needed." A cold pit settled in Thamyris' stomach as he absorbed the gravity of these words. He turned to Tiatria, finding comfort in her supportive presence, before following behind Ásbjǫrn as they slowly made their way back to the castle.

The path was littered with debris and the air was thick with a sense of devastation. As they arrived at the massive set of intricately carved doors nestled within one of the largest trees, Thamyris couldn't help but remember every inch of his home's layout. His right hand grazed against the wooden wall as he stood taller, taking in his surroundings. But as his fingers brushed against the smooth surface, vivid memories flooded his mind. He saw the castle trembling and debris crashing down as Nimriar awakened from his slumber. His mother's frantic pacing in the throne room caught his attention before the ground began to shake violently. As she caught sight of the dragon emerging from the earth and taking flight, the room itself started to crumble.

Guards rushed to her side, creating a protective shield around her as chaos erupted around them. All eyes fell upon Thamyris as his expression twisted in alarm. "She's...gone," he whispered, his voice filled with grief and disbelief. Tears welled up in his eyes as he saw the destruction that had taken place within these walls, and he felt a sense of overwhelming grief and disbelief at the loss of his mother and what that meant for the kingdom. The once grand hall now lay in ruins, the ornate columns and intricate tapestries destroyed by the dragon's wrath. The smell of smoke and ash lingered in the air, a haunting reminder of the tragedy that had occurred.

Tears poured down Thamyris' face as it turned pale; with his fingertips still touching the wood. He watched as the guards fiercely tried to get the shield up from his Mother but were crushed by the ceiling, which in turn also crushed her. Tiatria read her Prince's mind as she desperately wanted to help him. Maxwell said nothing, did nothing; he just walked away and made his way toward the library. Cullen wasn't sure what to do or say at the moment; should he attend to Maxwell or help the elven Prince? He lost his Father, Sister and now his Mother.

Thamyris' fingers walked away from all who were watching him, Cullen was about to follow him, but Tiatria's left hand took hold of his right. "Let him be," she whispered softly. "He goes to the gods for solace."

In the chapel of the gods, Thamyris stood in front of the statue of Cernunnos; the God's majestic antler seemed to hold the rays of the sun in between them. He'd sat there for over an hour as he contemplated what the Gods wanted from him. His parents were gone, his beloved hawk Kethinar was dead, murdered by his own sister, who was now consumed by madness and thirst for revenge. This was a crushing blow for Thamyris, who had always tried to be a devout servant of nature and its deities. The more he thought about it, the more Thamyris wondered if this was a punishment for not being as faithful as he could have been.

As High Priest, Thamyris knew that nature could be beautiful and bountiful but also cruel and unforgiving. He had learned this harsh truth since birth as a servant of the gods. And now, with Kethinar's death, Thamyris felt truly helpless and hindered by his blindness. He couldn't imagine how he would continue to serve the gods without his faithful companion by his side. In taking his sight, maybe this would force him to find where his faith truly lay.

Thamyris' hands touched the hands of the Horned God's statue, his fingers tracing the intricate carvings and feeling the coolness of the stone. He dropped to his knees as he wept, his grief and despair overwhelming him. "How am I supposed to serve you now?" he questioned aloud, his voice filled with sorrow and confusion. The once powerful and confident High Priest now felt lost and alone, uncertain of what the future held for him and his kingdom.

In the grand library, Maxwell's eyes roamed over row after row of towering shelves, each one filled to the brim with books of knowledge and untold stories. He couldn't help but recall the last time he had been here...with Dorian. The memory of his lover poring over the pages with an avid gleam in his eye still lingered in Maxwell's mind. Dorian had always been hungry for new information, eager to uncover tantalizing mysteries and explore the unknown depths of the world.

Maxwell's heart clenched in pain as he stepped into the familiar room, filled with the lingering scent of leather and old paper. Memories of his love for Dorian flooded his mind, stirring up a lifetime of emotions - from passionate love to fiery arguments and teasing banter. But now, with Dorian gone, the emptiness of his absence weighed heavily on Maxwell, crushing his chest and causing tears to well up in his eyes. The walls echoed with the hollow ache of his heart and soul, a wound that could never be healed or forgotten.

Cullen held Tiatria tightly in his arms as if he were afraid that she might be taken away from him at any moment. His right hand gently caressed her cheek before he grasped it. "I love you," he whispered. Tiatria snuggled into his embrace, tears slipping down her sapphire blue eyes. She could sense Cullen's fear and relief that she had survived the dragon's flames thanks to Dorian's sacrifice.

"I'm sorry about your father," she said softly.

Cullen let out a sigh, "I may not have known my Father very well or gotten along with him for that matter, but I never wanted him to die in such a horrific way."

Tiatria met Cullen's amber eyes with her deep blue ones, lost in their honey-like depths. They kissed, grateful to still be together by the grace of their Gods. When they pulled apart, Tiatria placed her hand on Cullen's wrist. "I need to go to the temple and see what our next steps should be." Cullen nodded understandingly and kissed her forehead and plump lips before watching her walk away.

As Cullen looked around, wondering where Maxwell had gone off to, he eventually found him in a place that reminded him of Dorian. Maxwell sat with his head in his hands, elbows resting on his thighs. Cullen didn't know what to say or do to help his friend in pain. The room was dimly lit by a gentle purple and pale blue glow, softening the edges of the furniture and casting soothing shadows along the walls. Hints of warm orange and yellow added a touch of brightness to the calm atmosphere, like rays of sunlight filtering through stained glass windows. The colors swirled together, creating a serene and ethereal ambiance that was both calming and comforting.

"Go away," Maxwell growled through clenched teeth, his tone dripping with bitterness and frustration. Cullen started to turn away, but a flicker of concern made him pause. He turned back towards the brooding battle mage. "Dorian would scold you for sulking and creating deep furrows on your once smooth brow," he said, his voice gentle but firm.

Maxwell's eyes flashed with annoyance, but he couldn't deny the truth in Cullen's words. Dorian was always quick to remind him of the importance of maintaining one's appearance, especially as a respected battle mage of the Order. But more than that, Dorian would also point out Maxwell's unique ability to wield powerful magic effortlessly, something that even the most skilled mage would have struggled with.

"He would also remind you that no one else could have held off that ferocious beast with such grace and skill," Cullen continued, gesturing towards the wound on Maxwell's arm where he had defended them all from the creature. "He would have given you credit as well. He would have showered you with praise. Not everyone could have protected us like you did." Maxwell's expression softened slightly at Cullen's words, and he nodded in acknowledgement. Despite his gruff demeanor, he couldn't help but feel grateful for his companions' unwavering support and belief in his abilities.

Maxwell's shoulders slumped as he leaned his head back onto a tall mahogany bookcase, the scent of aged leather and ink filling his nostrils. "I don't know what to do now," he said in a low, solemn voice. His eyes flicked to Cullen, who stood with folded arms and a furrowed brow against the same bookcase. "Without Dorian... I feel lost." The words carried weight, like an anchor dragging him down into the depths of uncertainty. "I'm pretty sure you're not the only one who feels that way," Cullen replied, his tone sympathetic yet tinged with his own sense of loss. The quiet of the library seemed heavier, as if it could no longer contain the weight of their shared sorrow.

Thamyris' fingers ran along the smooth, polished wooden walls of what he now knew to be his palace. As he stepped out into the lush courtyard, a sense of familiarity washed over him, and he made his way toward the majestic Temple of Cernunnos. The scent of earth and the symphony of nature's sounds surrounded him, bringing a sense of peace and comfort to his troubled mind. Even without his beloved Kethinar by his side, Thamyris felt confident in knowing where he was going. He could hear the gentle rush of a nearby waterfall, a familiar sound that always indicated he was close to the temple. But as he walked, his foot caught on an uneven stone protruding from the ground, causing him to stumble. Just before he hit the ground, two large, powerful hands caught him and steadied him. With the familiar scents of earth, flowers, and leather filling his senses, Thamyris knew immediately that it was Ásbjǫrn who had saved him.

"Are you alright?" Ásbjǫrn's deep voice held a surprising gentleness as he looked down at Thamyris with concern in his warm amber eyes.

Feeling a bit disoriented and confused, he could see, actually see if Kethinar was still alive, which was impossible, but still, there it was. Feeling emboldened by Ásbjǫrn's warmth and kindness, Thamyris reached out to take the elf's hand once again - wanting to confirm if what he had experienced earlier was real or just a fluke. Their hands intertwined, Thamyris couldn't help but notice the softness and warmth in Ásbjǫrn's touch, a stark contrast to his own rough exterior.

Thamyris's heart skipped a beat as he gazed up at Ásbjǫrn's handsome face before stepping away from his grasp. But he couldn't help himself - he reached out to take Ásbjǫrn's hand again, needing confirmation that what he had just experienced was not simply a figment of his imagination.

Ásbjǫrn arched an eyebrow curiously but allowed Thamyris to hold onto his hand as they stood facing each other. Honestly, Ásbjǫrn didn't mind; he knew that look on Thamyris' face, which told him that he was working something out. He didn't know what that was but it was clearly something. In this moment, Thamyris could not help but admire the elf's shoulder-length auburn hair which caught streaks of sunlight as it fell in gentle waves around his strong jawline. Had he never noticed these things with him before? A hawk's vision was quite different than an elf's. He actually liked what would have been considered normal vision for him. Thamyris noticed Ásbjǫrn's soft amber-brown eyes held a warmth and kindness that contradicted his rough exterior and the leather bands around his biceps that seemed to only add to his rugged charm. He didn't know he wore anything like that and became curious as to what else he didn't notice. As Thamyris' gaze traveled down, he couldn't help but notice Ásbjǫrn's leather corset, intricately carved with designs, hugging his broad and perfectly toned chest. A slight pink hue spread across Thamyris' cheeks as he realized he had been staring a little too long.

"Are you alright?" Ásbjǫrn asked again, curiously as he narrowed his eyes as he observed Thamyris closely.

Embarrassed by his lingering hold, Thamyris quickly let go of Ásbjǫrn's hand and lowered his eyes in embarrassment. "Yes, I'm sorry."

But Ásbjǫrn deep rumbling chuckle cut through the air, "No need to apologize." Ásbjǫrn gently held Thamyris' chin with his thumb and index finger; he gently pulled him in. His amber-brown eyes bore into him. "Clearly, you saw something you liked," he teased playfully.

Thamyris blushed deeper at the implication before mumbling, "I don't know how since Kethinar is dead."

Ásbjǫrn's eyes, pools of honey, filled with compassion and understanding as he stepped away from the altar to let Thamyris pass, his hand reaching out in a gesture of support. His head was low in a show of deference, his movements graceful and controlled. "I have placed him on the altar for you," Ásbjǫrn's voice was soft yet steady, "do not hesitate to ask if you need anything." his words were solemn and filled with respect.

Thamyris nodded in gratitude before Ásbjǫrn seemed to hand him something; before taking a step forward, his fingers had lightly brushed against a smooth piece of wood. Curiosity sparked within him, and he grasped it tightly, causing Ásbjǫrn to let go of it and let Thamyris marvel at its cool touch and solid weight in his hand. Its surface was smooth and comforting against his fingertips, and as he ran them over the intricate carvings and designs etched into the wood, he could sense a delicate aroma of sweet roses emanating from it. It was as if the very essence of the flower had been enchanted into the staff, alluring yet calming at the same time. He felt drawn to it as if it held secrets and powers waiting to be unlocked.

"Rosewood," Ásbjǫrn's voice told him gently, breaking him out of his reverie, "so that you may always carry love wherever you go." Before Thamyris could respond, the Ásbjǫrn had already turned and walked away.

But something within Thamyris stirred, and he called out, "Wait,"

Ásbjǫrn stopped and turned around, his expression one of unwavering obedience and loyalty. "As you wish, my King." The title hit Thamyris with unexpected force, a heavy mantle that came with both honor and duty.

As they made their way towards the entrance of the Temple, Thamyris suddenly felt a weight settle upon his shoulders, one that came with great responsibility. He paused before the altar and gently rested his staff against the cold stone surface. His trembling fingertips reached out, searching until they found what they were looking for - feathers. They belonged to Kethinar, now gone forever. Tears welled up in Thamyris' eyes as he stroked the soft feathers, struggling to come to terms with his new reality - being alone, blind, and burdened with the immense duty of becoming King. But amidst all the turmoil, there was a fierce determination burning within Thamyris as he silently vowed to do whatever it takes to fulfill his new role.

Thamyris' fingers recoiled in horror as he felt the shaft of the arrow, his arrow, piercing through Kethinar's chest. The arrowhead had torn through flesh and bone, causing Thamyris to scream in anguish, "He wouldn't have suffered," Ásbjǫrn reassured him with a calm and steady voice, but it fell on deaf ears as Thamyris' eyes overflowed with tears. With shaking hands, Thamyris grasped the shaft of the arrow and pushed it through until its head emerged from the other side. Blood gushed out like a river, staining his hands crimson red. With a sharp snap, he pulled the arrow out and flung it aside, the sound of wood and rock hitting the stone floor echoing through the wood. "Bring me fresh linen and a bowl of honey," he commanded, his voice filled with grief and determination.

Ásbjǫrn swiftly retrieved the requested items and approached his King. Thamyris could hear his footsteps approaching, heavy with sorrow. He held two stone bowls with the requested items in them. Ásbjǫrn carefully put the bowls down on the altar before taking up the linen and gently placing it in Thamyris's blood-stained hand. The High Priest of Cernunnos delicately felt for the top of Kethinar's head; once he found it, he began to wrap his friend's body in the linen, his fingers occasionally brushing against the sticky, sweet honey that he speared onto the bandages to ensure they would stick and would not fall away. As he worked, Thamyris wept openly, his heart heavy with regret for not being able to protect Kethinar as he gave his life to protect him.

As a priest himself, it was Ásbjǫrn's duty to attend to the dead. But this time, as High Priest, Thamyris insisted on tending to Kethinar's body himself. With each passing moment, it became harder for him to let go of his beloved friend. Ásbjǫrn watched as the last of the linen and honey were applied to Kethinar before Thamyris put both his hands on the body and lowered his head.

"From the dawn of your birth,

To the sunset of your death,

I honor you.

From the missions you completed,

To your duties left undone,

I honor you.

From the seasons of your being,

Through the cycle of your life,

I honor you.

From your time beyond the veil,

Lie your entrance back again,

May the spirits support you,

May my healing love reach you,

From this moment until the end of time,

So, mote it be."

Thamryis felt a knot well up in his throat as he fought back tears. "I want his body placed in an urn and put at the foot of the statue of Cernunnos; he will lay in honor." Ásbjǫrn nodded, "I will see it done."

As Thamyris made his way out of the room, Ásbjǫrn couldn't help but glance back at Thamyris, watching as the King tenderly touched Kethinar's body one last time before letting go. And in that moment, Ásbjǫrn couldn't ignore the intense desire that burned within him as he smelled the honey that was coated on his king's hand.

In a moment of longing and desire, he reached for Thamyris' left hand, causing Thamyris to look at him with surprise. Ásbjǫrn's gaze was filled with a predatory hunger and desire as he slowly brought each finger to his lips and gently sucked them clean, tasting the sweet honey mixed with Kethinar's blood. This caused Thamyris to take a deep breath as he felt Ásbjǫrn's tongue swirl sensually around his skin, sending delicious chills down his spine.

As the last finger left his eager lips, Ásbjǫrn whispered in a husky voice, "I love the taste of honey, but I will not let it draw any unwanted attention to you from it." His gaze was filled with pure desire for Thamyris, igniting a spark of passion within him despite the heaviness of grief weighing on his heart.

)o(

The grand Temple of Danu loomed before Tiatria, its walls adorned with intricate carvings and paintings that depicted scenes from their ancient mythology. As she stepped inside, the air was heavy with the scent of incense, and the sound of chanting echoed throughout the halls. As a priestess of the Goddess herself, Tiatria felt a sense of reverence and awe wash over her. She gazed up at the towering statue of Danu, marveling at its beauty and power. But her heart was heavy with grief and guilt, for so much had been lost in this war - innocent lives, royalty on both sides, Dorian and her Prince's faithful hawk, Kethinar. And worst of all, Amalia, once a kind and gentle soul, now consumed by darkness as she commanded Nimriar.

Tears streamed down her face as she approached the statue, overcome with emotion. Bowing before it, she begged for forgiveness from her Goddess. "I have failed you, my Goddess. I have failed them all."

In that moment, a blinding burst of pure white light engulfed Tiatria's body. It radiated from within her, shining outwards from her very eyes, lips, and fingertips. She was filled with an overwhelming sense of power and purpose as she realized that her goddess had not abandoned her - she had been chosen to carry out a greater destiny. The light surrounded her like a protective shield, empowering her with newfound strength and determination to fulfill her divine duty.

Chapter 17

As Tiatria slowly opened her eyes, she found herself engulfed in a thick white mist. Slowly, the mist lifted and revealed a forest unlike any she had ever seen before. The light was different here, casting a vibrant hue over everything it touched. Colors seemed to radiate from every tree and flower, making the forest appear more lavish and magical than anything she had ever imagined. She watched in awe as deer grazed on the lush grass and fairies flitted about, their wings sparkling with pure magic.

But then, Tiatria noticed a figure walking towards her. It was a being made of pure light, shining so brightly that it was almost blinding. As the deer caught sight of the light, they raised their heads and followed it as if they were being called.

A soothing feminine voice echoed through the air, "Be at ease, my Daughter." And there, standing before Tiatria, was a resplendent woman dressed in forest green. Her off-the-shoulder dress flowed elegantly around her, with long draping bell sleeves and a simple gold chain adorning her hips. She wore a long forest-green cloak with a hood that hinted at her long strawberry-blonde hair underneath. And atop her head sat a simple yet regal gold circlet.

Tiatria couldn't believe what she was seeing. She dropped to her knees, tears falling from her eyes at the sight of her goddess. "Am I dead?" she questioned, looking up at Danu, who showed a quiet smile.

"No, my daughter," Danu replied gently. "I have brought you here for a purpose."

Tiatria's heart swelled with both fear and excitement as she waited for the goddess to continue. "My high priestess has forsaken the Gods, forsaken me," Danu explained solemnly. "And so I am in need of a new high priestess to be my voice, my representative on the mortal plain."

Tiatria could not believe what she was hearing. "You're going to make me a high priestess of Danu?" she asked in disbelief.

Danu's expression turned remorseful. "I cannot have two high priestesses in the name of Danu," she explained. Tiatria furrowed her brow in confusion.

"Then I don't understand," she said.

Closing her eyes, Danu's face became somber. "I have loved all my children, but especially your people as the Goddess Danu," she began. "However, as you know, I am known by many names, and it is time for me to take on a new name. And with that name, I will need a new High Priestess...you." Tiatria's heart skipped a beat at the thought of being chosen by her goddess. It was a great honor and responsibility, one that she hoped she could fulfill and bring hope and peace to her people.

As Tiatria watched in awe, the Goddess transformed into pure light again, changing her form completely. She now had long blonde hair, which was adorned with a crown of antlers and wisteria flowers draping from where her hair met the antlers. She wore a sheer white dress that was almost transparent, with a deep V neckline that revealed her ethereal beauty. At her waist, a belt made of branches hugged her like gnarled fingers while a gold necklace dripped with a cluster of emeralds that cascaded down her chest. And draped over her arms was a rich sapphire blue shawl.

The newly transformed Goddess Elen smiled at Tiatria with grace and power radiating from her very being. "I am Elen, Goddess of the forest, the sacred spring, and many paths," she declared proudly. Then, extending her right hand towards Tiatria, she pointed her index finger at her new servant. "And I call upon you to be my high priestess!"

With a graceful flick of her slender finger, Tiatria's old clothes disintegrated into shimmering threads, only to be replaced by an exquisite new ensemble that seemed to emerge from the very fabric of magic. She donned an emerald green strapless petal and heart corset shaped to hug her skin, outlined in delicate gold filigree that glimmered under the light and accentuated her generous cleavage. Beneath it lay a dark brown leather under-bust corset that added a touch of structure and elegance.

Her attire flowed into a striking fishtail skirt, cleverly tailored so that the front was daringly short, revealing her toned thighs, while the back cascaded into a long, fluid train that swayed with each step she took. Long emerald sleeves draped elegantly from her arms, floating free without attaching to her bodice, enhancing the ethereal quality of her look. Delicate gold wire bracers adorned her forearms, their shimmering surfaces catching the light as she moved. Above them rested elegant gold arm bands, each one adding a regal touch to her warrior appearance. On her right shoulder sat a three-layered pauldron of polished gold that glimmered like sunlight on water.

Around her neck hung a beautiful necklace featuring a five-inch opal-shaped emerald at its center, radiating an aura of mystique and power. Two sturdy brown belts were draped loosely around her hips; one supported a leather quiver brimming with arrows, ready for whatever challenges lay ahead. Atop her head crowned a golden circlet embedded with a triangular emerald that gleamed like a star in the night sky. In her left hand, she cradled a magnificent wooden bow crafted with precision and care, its surface smooth and polished as if it had been carved from the heart of an ancient tree.

As she stood poised in this regal attire, Tiatria could not help but marvel at the surge of power coursing through her veins—a potent energy that made her feel unstoppable and alive.

Elen's radiant smile beamed down upon her newly anointed priestess, her ethereal form shimmering with divine light. "Bring honor to my name," the goddess intoned, her melodious voice reverberating through the sacred space, "and may the powers I bestow upon you be used in all manners of good." Her words carried the weight of celestial authority, each syllable resonating with otherworldly power. Tiatria knelt reverently before her goddess, her heart swelling with devotion and purpose. "I will strive to be worthy," she pledged solemnly, her voice trembling slightly with the magnitude of the moment. As the last word left her lips, Tiatria closed her eyes, basking in the divine presence.

When she opened them again, Tiatria gasped in astonishment. She found herself back in the familiar confines of the temple, the transition so sudden and seamless it left her momentarily disoriented. Looking down, she marveled at the ornate robes that now adorned her body - tangible proof of her ascension to her new role. Her gaze drifted to where Elen had stood moments before, and Tiatria's eyes widened in awe. The ancient statue of Danu that had graced the temple for generations was gone, replaced by a magnificent new effigy of Elen. The statue seemed to glow with an inner light, its features capturing the goddess's benevolence and power with uncanny accuracy.

Overwhelmed by the gravity of her new position and the honor bestowed upon her, Tiatria bowed deeply once more, her forehead touching the cool stone floor. Rising gracefully, she took a deep breath, squared her shoulders to leave the temple and assumed her new role as High Priestess. The weight of responsibility settled upon her like a mantle, but Tiatria felt ready to face the challenges ahead, fortified by Elen's divine blessing.

)o(

Thamyris walked slowly and purposefully to the courtyard, his footsteps slow and deliberate. As he reached the center of the open space, he paused and turned his head to the left, feeling a powerful energy shift emanating from the nearby Temple of Danu. A tingling sensation ran down his spine as he sensed something approaching him - something new yet familiar, ancient yet fresh.

The sound of soft footsteps broke through the silence, causing Thamyris to turn around and face the source. He caught a whiff of a delicate scent, like that of wisteria blossoms in full bloom. Tiatria, his High Priestess and consort on this plane, smiled softly, gently as she drew closer. Her hand gently brushed against Thamyris' cheek as she spoke, "My love." Realization dawned on Thamyris as he beheld her voice - she was now not just his lover but also his High Priestess.

Both of them understood what this meant - they were now bound by duty and tradition to be married and rule together as High Priest and Priestess, King and Queen. As Thamyris cupped Tiatria's cheek in his hand, he could envision her being approached by Danu herself, their conversation leading to the Goddess' transformation into her new aspect of Elen - the Goddess of the wood and paths. "How intriguing," Thamyris mused with a sigh.

Tiatria gave a quiet smile and spoke softly, "Beltane approaches in two nights."

Thamyris nodded in agreement as he leaned against his staff. "I know," he said ruefully. "I cannot say I look forward to marrying you or making you, my Queen. You deserve someone who can give you children and love you fully."

Before Tiatria could respond, she noticed Cullen watching them with a pained expression on his face. Had he really been so blind to their love being one-sided? She called out to him and chased after him when he started walking away. "Cullen, wait!" she called out as she caught up to him and stood in front of him, blocking his path. She took hold of his hands and looked into his eyes. "Cullen, you don't understand," she pleaded. "I don't love Thamyris. It is my duty to be with him, marry him. With the Queen gone, he must take her place as King. And as the High Priest of Cernunnos, it is expected for him to marry the High Priestess and make her his Queen."

Cullen's expression turned to one of anger and disgust as he pulled his hands away from Tiatria's grasp. "So, he was meant to marry his own sister?" he questioned, recalling Dorian's suspicions about Thamyris' unnatural obsession with Amalia.

Tiatria gazed at Cullen with determination, determined to make him understand. "The Queen knew her son's nature," she explained gently. "That is why she arranged for Thamyris to marry his sister - only in name and without children. They would still share a sibling's love for each other." As understanding dawned, Cullen's face softened as he realized that Thamyris was no different from Maxwell and Dorian - all three craving the company of men. Tiatria leaned in and kissed his lips softly. "I will only be his wife in name," she reassured him.

Tiatria sealed their conversation with a kiss, reassuring Cullen that she would always be his. And as they walked together hand-in-hand, Tiatria couldn't help but feel grateful for having such a caring and understanding partner by her side.

Overwhelmed with emotion, Cullen embraced Tiatria tightly and held her close. She led him by the hand, and they walked together, their bond stronger than ever before.

)o(

Maxwell's footsteps echoed through the dark, quiet halls of the library as he made his way to the courtyard. As he passed by Thamyris, who was sitting peacefully under a tree, Maxwell resisted the urge to stop and speak to him. Instead, he continued towards the grand staircase with heavy steps and a troubled expression.

Reaching the top of the stairs, Maxwell pushed open the door to a familiar room that held memories from his first visit. His eyes immediately fell upon the bed, and he found himself drawn towards it. Sitting down heavily, he leaned forward with his arms resting on his thighs. Fingers threaded through his hair before intertwining at the back of his head in frustration.

Suddenly, Thamyris' voice interrupted his thoughts. "The last time you were here," he said calmly, "It was just before Imbolc." Maxwell looked up to see Thamyris standing in the doorway. He rubbed the back of his neck, trying to recall how long ago that had been. "And how long ago was that?" he asked as Thamyris made his way into the room.

"In this realm," Thamyris explained, leaning against his staff, "We measure time differently. While only a few days have passed in your realm, it has been nearly four months here." Maxwell sat up straighter in surprise. "But...that's impossible," he protested.

"Time is relative," Thamyris replied with a small smile. He used his staff to navigate around the room, tapping it against furniture and walls to guide him. The base of the staff hit the side of the bed, causing Thamyris to stumble before he caught himself and sat down next to Maxwell. "Just like how my staff helps me navigate this unknown world," he said wisely, "Time also has its own way of guiding us."

Maxwell's expression shifted to one of surprise as he noticed the elf's hand intertwined with his own. He turned to see Thamyris, the elf who had been their guide and protector on their journey, looking up at him with a faint blush coloring his cheeks. "I know what you sacrificed in order to bring us back here," Thamyris spoke softly, turning his gaze back to the ground. "And for that, you are most welcome to stay here." Maxwell was clearly confused, giving a slight shake of his head. "What do you mean?" he questioned, pulling away from the elf's grasp.

Thamyris let out a heavy sigh as he hung his head, his hand slipping off his knee and onto the bed beside him. "I must admit, I held hatred towards your people after all they had done to mine," he admitted, his voice laced with bitterness. Then turned to face Maxwell again, his expression softening, "But I cannot deny your actions or those of your friends in trying to find and save my sister. You did everything in your power to stop the dragon's wanton destruction."

Maxwell met Thamyris' gaze, seeing ancient wisdom and pain etched into the elf's features. "What does that mean?" he asked, unsure of what the elf was trying to convey.

As Thamyris emerged from Maxwell's room, Ásbjǫrn stood waiting for his King. His tall frame leaned casually against the stone wall, muscles flexing under his fitted leather corset and pants. The scent of earth and leather drifted towards Thamyris, mixing with the faint aroma of smoke from a torch he was holding. Thamyris turned to face Ásbjǫrn, their eyes meeting in a silent understanding. "We only have two days until Beltane," Thamyris said, breaking the silence. "Will that be enough time for preparations?" Ásbjǫrn straightened up, his posture proud and confident as he bowed before his King. "I will see it done," he replied with a hint of determination in his voice. Thamyris could not help but feel grateful for such a loyal and capable friend and servant by his side.

)o(

Cullen and Tiatria strolled hand in hand through the palace's sprawling gardens, filled with an array of vibrant flowers that released a heady fragrance as they passed. The gentle sound of running water could be heard from small streams that wound their way through the lush greenery. Tiatria's arm was wrapped around Cullen's, offering him comfort as they walked. "What does this marriage to Thamyris entail?" Cullen asked nervously, his heart beating faster at the thought.

Tiatria gave him a warm smile, her sapphire eyes sparkling. "We will be married in the grand throne room, surrounded by priests and priestesses from the temples. Our hands will be bound together with a sacred ribbon or cloth in a ceremony known as handfasting. Prayers and blessings will be bestowed upon us, and then we will be wed."

Cullen's stomach churned at the thought of Tiatria being tied down to someone she didn't love. "And what about consummating the marriage?" he asked, beads of sweat forming on his brow. Tiatria let out a sigh, knowing exactly what he was thinking. "Normally, yes, that would happen. But not in our case." Cullen couldn't hide his relief, even though it meant not being able to fully express his love for Tiatria. "So what will happen instead?" he pressed.

Stopping by a stream, Tiatria gazed into its gently moving waters, her reflection staring back at her. "Beltane is in two days," she said softly, "it is a day when the God and Goddess consummate their love, and all are free to do so as well, without any repercussions or judgment." A shiver ran down Cullen's spine at the thought of finally being able to make love to Tiatria without fear or restrictions.

As they continued their walk, Cullen could not help but notice the enchanting glow of fireflies dancing around them, lighting up Tiatria's face and making her look almost ethereal. But amidst all the beauty and love, Cullen's mind was still filled with doubts and questions. He had been raised to believe in certain traditions and customs, but being with Tiatria made him question everything. His forced betrothal to someone he didn't love, his role as a knight that never felt right to him, and the ways of their society that seemed to force people into situations they didn't want.

As he looked at Tiatria, with her captivating blue eyes and loving heart, Cullen realized that he didn't need any of those things. His heart told him he belonged with her, no matter what others may say or think. But before they could truly be together, there were many obstacles to overcome. They both longed for a shared life and children, but it seemed impossible under the reign of a king who couldn't provide these things for himself. "I believe the King will see reason," Tiatria said confidently, as if reading his thoughts, "and allow us to have the life we desire."

Cullen clung to her words like a lifeline, praying that they would come true. As they walked, Tiatria suddenly stopped in her tracks and turned to face two female elves watching them from a distance. "I must go and prepare for Beltane," she said with a mischievous glint in her eye, "I can't wait to celebrate it with you."

Immersed by the sacred temple of the goddess' walls, Tiatria enveloped herself in a pool of shimmering water. This revered pool was known for its purifying properties, cleansing not only the physical body but also the soul of any spiritual impurities before significant rituals. The water seemed to glimmer with an otherworldly radiance emanating from the open roof of the temple, where stars twinkled in the velvety night sky. As she bathed, Tiatria gently traced her fingers along her left arm, feeling a powerful connection to the divine energy that permeated every inch of the temple. The tranquil atmosphere and gentle lapping of the water against her skin brought a sense of peace and serenity to her mind and spirit.

The pond was a silent and tranquil oasis, with moon lilies lazily floating on the glassy surface. Their delicate, milky-white petals shimmered against the soft and gentle light of the moon, creating a dreamy and ethereal atmosphere. On all four sides of Tiatria, priestesses stood in a circle with their hands raised to the sky, their voices lifting in prayer and chanting to their goddess. They beseeched for blessings upon their High Priestess for the upcoming Beltane celebration - blessings for love, fertility, bountiful crops, and self-discovery. The air was thick with the sweet scent of incense and flowers, adding to the mystical ambiance of the scene as if the very spirit of their deity had descended upon them. Tiatria felt her heart swell with gratitude and reverence as she closed her eyes and absorbed the energy around her.

Meanwhile, outside in the courtyard, Ásbjǫrn and his priests were preparing for the festivities. Small bonfires, built with precision and care, were being assembled around a larger one in the center where they would celebrate nature at its most primal and glorious. The crackling sounds of burning wood and the dancing flames cast warm, flickering light on the faces of those gathered. For Ásbjǫrn, this was the most anticipated holiday of the year - a time for passionate love and embracing one another to keep warm. He could feel the electricity in the air, buzzing with excitement and anticipation. He savored every moment, relishing in the primal energy that pulsed through him. With each step, he felt closer to nature and all its raw beauty, ready to indulge in every pleasure offered by this sacred celebration.

In the grand throne room, Thamyris sat on his ornate throne, surrounded by a bustling group of servants. The head cook stood before him, a notepad and quill in hand, discussing the menu for the upcoming celebration. Thamyris had never experienced such a festivity before, and he listened intently, his brow furrowed in concentration. With a compassionate smile and understanding look, the cook suggested an array of delicious dishes - vibrant berry and honey cakes that would melt in one's mouth, warm milk infused with fragrant spices, honeyed wine, and raw honey spread on top of freshly baked oat bread. Thamyris nodded wearily, feeling overwhelmed by the choices, but ultimately agreed to these simple yet pleasing options. He rubbed his temples with his left hand, trying to ease the growing tension in his head. As he closed his eyes, he could almost taste the sweet treats that awaited him at the celebration. The head housemaid, her blond hair pulled back into a half ponytail, bustled around the King with an air of purpose and pride. She assured him that every detail of the castle's decorations and tidiness would be perfect for the eagerly anticipated night.

Maxwell watched from the window as the castle servants scurried about, decorating the halls with ribbons of dark green and red and draping garlands over everything in sight. The halls were transformed into a festive wonderland, with vibrant bouquets of yellow and white flowers - primrose, hawthorn, and gorse - placed in windows and doorways to invoke the warmth of the sun. Thamyris noticed Maxwell's restless pacing, his wandering steps betraying his inner turmoil as he struggled to come to terms with his grief. Thamyris could feel the weight of Maxwell's heartache; it was almost palpable in the air.

Maxwell's steps were listless as he wandered through the grand library, his heart heavy with grief and longing. The shelves of books loomed over him, their tall spines reaching towards the ornate ceiling. Each volume held a certain weight, not just physically but emotionally. They were a reminder of the time spent with Dorian, the one he loved so deeply. His fingers traced the titles, feeling the rough edges and crevices of each cover. As it was anywhere, they went, it was books that brought Dorian such immense joy, now serving as a bittersweet memory of their time together. As Maxwell continued to walk among the rows of dusty tomes, he remembered the nights spent in this very library, with Dorian eagerly devouring every word, fueled by his insatiable thirst for knowledge. The smell of old pages and ink filled his nostrils. Maxwell closed his eyes; he was transported back to a night when he held Dorian in his arms, breathing in his intoxicating perfume. He could almost feel the weight of Dorian's head on his chest as they stayed up late into the night, discussing literature and philosophy.

But now, as he stood alone in this vast space, Maxwell's heart ached with sorrow at the thought of never sharing these moments with Dorian again. Yet, despite his grief, he couldn't help but smile at the memories they had created within these walls. For that brief moment, surrounded by books and memories, it felt like Dorian was right there next to him once more. "I can hear you moping about, you know," came Thamyris' voice from behind him. Maxwell turned to see Thamyris standing in the doorway, his staff in hand, the expression on his face was that of concern. "You refuse to settle, continually walking about. And according to what the servants tell me, you haven't eaten anything."

Maxwell ran his fingers through his raven black hair, tears welling in his eyes. "My brain won't process it. It refuses to," he said tearfully. Thamyris approached slowly and gently reached out to touch the left side of Maxwell's face, which Maxwell helped him do with his hand. In a flash, images flooded Maxwell's mind - moments shared with Dorian, hundreds of them. Some showed Dorian teasing Maxwell playfully; others showed him offering comfort and support. There were also memories of passion and intimacy and of the two of them working together as an unstoppable team, unafraid to help anyone who needed it. They had been loyal servants to their king and country, united in love until the very end.

Chapter 18

Beltane had finally come. The sky painted a bright orange and pink as the sun descended towards the horizon. The temple of Cernunnos was bathed in warm, inviting light, its walls adorned with intricate carvings and symbols. The air was filled with the scent of flowers and incense, creating an enchanting atmosphere. Surrounding the temple were fields of blooming wildflowers, adding splashes of vibrant colors to the landscape. In the distance, birds sang, and insects hummed as nature prepared for the ritual to come. As the sun continued to set, the golden glow intensified, casting long shadows across the temple grounds. The air filled with anticipation and energy as people gathered in preparation for the sacred ceremony. Inside the temple, Ásbjǫrn carefully attended to Thamyris as the preparations for the Beltane ceremony continued. With a steady hand, the elf dipped a fine brush into a small pot of crimson paint and began to trace intricate pagan designs onto Thamyris' exposed skin. The symbols swirled and danced on his chest, arms, and face, connecting him to the spirits of nature and ancient traditions. Each stroke was precise and purposeful as Ásbjǫrn imbued Thamyris with the power of their ancestors. The air in the tent hummed with energy and reverence as they completed this age-old ritual of transformation.

As Ásbjǫrn leaned back to admire his work, Thamyris could not help but feel the hungry look in his eyes. He wondered if it was simply admiration or something more. But there were other things on his mind as well - things he could not explain. How he could see through touching Ásbjǫrn, something that he had only ever experienced with Kethinar? How was any of this possible?

Thamyris' mind swirled with thoughts and confusion as Ásbjǫrn's hands enveloped his own. The elf's hands were surprisingly large and powerful, reminiscent of bear paws. As their fingers intertwined, Thamyris felt a soothing sense of balance and harmony wash over him. But as he gazed into the elf's intense eyes, Thamyris could not help but notice a subtle narrowing in his own. It was as if Ásbjǫrn could see right through him, unraveling all his inner turmoil with just one look.

After a long moment of peaceful silence between them, he finally mustered the courage to ask the question that had been burning in his mind. "How is this possible?"

Ásbjǫrn's features remained impassive as he offered a simple shrug in response. "Perhaps nature, or the gods themselves, felt a need for balance," he suggested with a hint of uncertainty in his voice. The sun began to dip below the horizon, casting a warm glow over their surroundings and painting the sky with hues of pink and orange. The distant sound of gentle water flowing through a creek bed could be heard in the distance, adding to the serene atmosphere. Despite the beauty around them, there was a sense of unease in the air as they pondered the mysterious forces at work. Was it simply chance or something more?

As Thamyris moved his hands with intention and care over Ásbjǫrn's face, he couldn't ignore the burning desire he felt coming from the elf. And when Ásbjǫrn gently bit down on his thumb muscle, Thamyris felt a flicker of excitement mixed with confusion. "Why did you do that?" he questioned cautiously. Again, Ásbjǫrn shrugged nonchalantly. "I don't know...because I felt like it?" His voice was filled with desire, and Thamyris could not ignore the heat of his breath against his skin.

In that moment, Thamyris realized that he had never been sought after by anyone other than female elves. He and Ásbjǫrn had known each other for years, but they never paid each other much attention beyond polite acknowledgement. Thamyris was always busy guarding the forest's borders, while Ásbjǫrn spent most of his time exploring the wilds or helping at the temple.

They were acquaintances, yet also strangers. But in that moment, as their eyes locked and their bodies gravitated towards each other, they both realized there was more to discover about each other - and themselves - than they ever imagined.

Tiatria stood among her priestesses, preparing for what was to come after sunset. She had been adorned in a dress that replicated that of the goddess herself - a simple white fabric cascading down her body. With delicate paintbrushes in hand, her priestesses carefully decorated her skin with shimmering silver symbols representing the phases of the moon. The triple moon symbol, a mark of divine femininity, was painted proudly on her chest. Despite knowing her role and duties as a priestess, Tiatria couldn't help but feel her stomach twist into knots. She was marrying a good man, but he was not the one she yearned for with every fiber of her being. Doubts and fears crept into her mind, causing inner turmoil amidst the sacred preparations for the ceremony ahead.

Cullen paced back and forth in his room like a caged animal desperate for freedom. The sun was setting outside, casting soft orange hues into the room. He had been given elven clothes to wear, a stark contrast to the heavy armor he usually donned. He silently thanked the servant who had presented him with the clothes, only to be informed that it was at the King's request. Maxwell entered the room, wearing new attire as well. Cullen stopped in his tracks at the sight of his friend. Despite his youthful appearance, Maxwell's eyes held an unmistakable pain, and he seemed much older than his years.

"Are you going to the ceremony?" Maxwell sighed, folding his arms and avoiding eye contact as he dug his feet into the floor.

Cullen understood that this celebration was meant to revolve around love and sex, something that weighed heavily on both of their hearts after losing Dorian. "I'll attend out of respect for Tiatria and Thamyris," Maxwell continued, "but I won't be participating in any of the festivities afterwards. It's just not something I can handle." Cullen sympathized with his friend's sentiments. While he also wanted to show support for the newlyweds, but being surrounded by joy and love without Dorian by his side would be too painful.

Cullen's expression softened as he walked over and placed a hand on Maxwell's shoulder. "Come on," he said gently, "Dorian would want us to enjoy the night. Let's honor him by celebrating with our friends."

Maxwell gave a small nod, grateful for Cullen's understanding and support. Together, they left the room to join the rest of the crowd gathered for the ceremony and celebration ahead. As they walked through the corridors of the palace, Cullen felt a mix of emotions - sadness for Dorian's absence but also joy for his friends' happiness and the memories they would create on this special night.

Each step down the grand staircase filled their senses with the sweet scent of flowers and incense, carried by servants who roamed about with trays of delectable canapes. Their garments were refined and tasteful, adorned with intricate patterns of silver and gold thread. Hair was expertly styled and pinned back, braids woven through as a symbol of the divine bond between God and Goddess, earth and sky. Flower crowns rested upon their heads, fragrant blooms of primrose, hawthorn, and gorse representing the Goddess, while leaves embodied the essence of the God. Not just servants but every attendee wore these crowns, including the two elves who placed them upon the heads of our protagonists at the bottom of the stairs.

The crowd led them into a throne room adorned with elaborate floral arrangements and ivy archways framing the thrones. Beneath one arch stood a priestess from the temple of the Goddess, and beneath the other stood Ásbjǫrn, high priest of the God.

The priestess glided into the room, her off-the-shoulder dress cascading down her figure in soft, elegant, smooth layers. The sweetheart neckline revealed just enough skin to be alluring, and the fabric flowed like liquid silver against her skin, accentuating every curve of her body. A delicate silver chain belt rested on her hips, embellished with intricate charms and symbols, adding a touch of elegance to her ensemble. Her accessories were equally stunning - her neck was adorned with a dainty chain necklace, while a silver circlet sat atop her head, enhancing her natural beauty. In contrast, Ásbjǫrn's outfit exuded power and regality. On his head, he wore a majestic antler headdress, representing his connection to the divine. A leather corset hugged his torso, intricately carved with symbols and designs that spoke of his strength and prowess. His leather pants were adorned with elegant embroidery accentuating the waistline and sides, adding a touch of luxury to his attire. He stood tall and proud, displaying a sense of authority and command as he prepared for the sacred ceremony ahead.

The gentle plucking of a harp and flute floated a delicate melody through the air, reminiscent of a soft spring breeze rustling through a field of flowers. The light, airy notes flew seamlessly, creating a soothing and calming atmosphere in the room. As Thamyris entered, the music crescendos, wrapping him in its ethereal embrace and adding to his regal presence. The sound of flutes joined in, adding a warm and joyful tone to the overall composition. The combination of these instruments created a harmonious and enchanting ambiance, setting the stage for the sacred ceremony that was about to take place.

Thamyris wore a richly embroidered robe with gold and silver threads; the fabric draped elegantly over his broad shoulders. The antler headdress glinted in the light, its intricate carvings and intricate details showcasing his status and power. Tiatria followed behind, her flowing white gown shimmering with delicate embroidery and intricate beadwork. A silver circlet rested atop her head, perfectly complementing her natural beauty and adding to her ethereal presence. As she walked, her goddess-like aura radiated from her every step. Cullen's heart fluttered as he saw her; his breath caught in his throat. He imagined her walking towards him at the altar.

Maxwell stood tall at the edge of the room, his dark regalia contrasting with the bright colors of Thamyris and Tiatria's attire. He watched with a stoic expression as the priestess approached with a glimmering silver chalice and Ásbjǫrn stepped forward with a sharp dagger in hand.

The chalice was crafted from pure silver, with intricate designs carved into its smooth surface. Tiatria's delicate fingers hovered over the cool metal before gently wrapping around it, feeling the weight of its significance in her palms. As she waited for Thamyris to take his turn, she could feel the coolness of the chalice seeping through her skin. Thamyris' fingers carefully wrapped around hers, his touch sending a surge of warmth and energy through her body, as if passing on some kind of sacred power. As she said, "May you never know thirst and may your cup always be full." her voice was firm yet gentle, igniting a sense of solemnity and reverence within Cullen as he felt those words were for him and no one else. The chalice seemed to glow under Thamyris' touch and as he raised it to his lips, "So mote it be." Tiatria could feel a sense of connection between them through the vessel. With each sip, she could feel the energy flowing from Thamyris into her, filling her with vitality and strength for the journey ahead. He slowly handed it before passing it back to the priestess. Ásbjǫrn then took Thamyris' right hand, granting him the power of sight.

Thamyris' eyes were drawn to the blade in Ásbjǫrn's hand, a sharp gleaming silver that seemed to catch the light and reflect it back in dazzling patterns. As he met Cullen's gaze, there was a silent understanding between them, a mutual trust and respect. But then Thamyris turned his attention back to Tiatria, his expression softening as he reached out with the dagger, its edges glinting dangerously in the candlelight. The handle was intricately carved, with intricate designs etched into the metal. And as Tiatria accepted it, their hands touched briefly, sparking a sense of connection and protection between them. At that moment, the dagger seemed to take on a life of its own, promising to defend and keep her safe on their journey together. Cullen's eyes were fixated on the scene before him, watching Ásbjǫrn taking back the glimmering dagger while the priestess presented a braided ribbon. Dark colors - green, red, and brown, were intricately woven together, symbolizing something of immense importance. The ribbon was about eighteen inches in length, long enough to wrap around both Thamyris and Tiatria's hands as Ásbjǫrn joined them together. Cullen could see the loose knot being tied by the priestess, sealing their fates together.

The moment was both beautiful and nerve-wracking, filled with uncertainty and hope for what their future would hold as they embarked on their journey together. Cullen's heart clenched with a heavy weight, his fists tightening in frustration as he watched the woman he loved being forced into marriage with another. His gaze was fixed on her, unable to look away as she stood stoically beside her soon-to-be husband. Every fiber of his being wanted to scream and shout, to declare his undying love for her and beg for her hand. Imagining himself standing before her, presenting her with a dagger as a symbol of his promise to protect and guard her with his life, even until the end of their mortal days. But he knew that this was not just about love - it was a political game for the security of their people and stability for the realm. A sense of helplessness rushed as he realized there was nothing he could do to stop it from happening. His mind swirled with anger and despair, but on the outside, he remained composed, hiding the turmoil within him behind a stoic facade. The air around them seemed to thicken with tension, the unspoken words between them almost tangible in the air. As the ceremony ended with the phrase "So mote it be," Cullen could almost feel the weight of the bond between Thamyris and Tiatria, knowing that it would forever tie them together.

The voices of the crowd burst forth in perfect unison, their words echoing through the air like a resounding chorus of thunder. "So mote it be!" they declared with jubilant smiles as they watched the newly joined couple exchange tender kisses on each other's cheeks. The sound of their collective joy was almost tangible, vibrating through the atmosphere and filling every heart with warmth and love. The sun shone down upon them as if blessing this union with its radiant rays. It was a moment of pure bliss and celebration, one that would be remembered for years to come by all who bore witness to it.

Thamyris held his bride's hand up to the sky and said, "Your new queen!" The crowd once again cheered and clapped in unison. The sound of their claps echoed through the courtyard, mixed with the soft melody of a flute in the background. Thamyris stood tall, his staff grasped firmly in his hand, as he led Tiatria out into the open space. Ásbjǫrn stepped forward and presented Tiatria with a torch, its flames dancing and flickering in the evening breeze. Thamyris could feel the heat emanating from the torch as he reached out to take it from her, their hands briefly touching in the exchange.

Together, they threw the torch onto the pile of wood at their feet, igniting a roaring bonfire that seemed to light up the entire forest. Thamyris couldn't help but smile as he looked around at the revelers surrounding them. "Let the festivities of Beltane begin!" he cried out, raising his arms in triumph. The cheers and applause that followed were almost deafening, but Thamyris reveled in it.

In the midst of the boisterous celebration, Thamyris felt a twinge of envy as he felt Tiatria slip away from his side. The music blared and bodies swayed around them, but all he could focus on was disappearing into the crowd. Her long hair flowed behind her like raven black ribbons, catching the light and casting it back into his eyes. He squeezed her fingers, which were still intertwined with his, and she turned to look at him with a gentle smile on her face. "Go to him," he told her softly, trying to push aside the jealousy that gnawed at his heart.

Deep down, Thamyris knew that he could not give his new bride everything she deserved - someone who could fulfill all of her deepest desires. This was a night for indulgence and Tiaria should have the person who could truly give her that satisfaction. And as much as it pained him to see her in someone else's arms, he wanted nothing more than for her to be happy on this special night of celebration. So, with a heavy yet loving heart, he released her hand, allowing her to melt into the night and into the arms of another person; their bodies would move together in perfect harmony to the pulsing beat of the music. It was a bittersweet moment for Thamyris, but one that he knew was necessary for both their happiness in this wild and fleeting night of revelry.

As Maxwell disappeared into the throngs of people, Cullen emerged from inside the palace. The grand structure loomed behind him, its marble pillars and ornate balconies bathed in golden light. He turned his head at the sound of approaching footsteps and saw Tiatria running towards him, her long hair flying behind her like a ribbon caught in a breeze. Without hesitation, he swept her up into his arms, and their lips met in a fiery kiss. Every sense was engulfed by the softness of her lips, the taste of her strawberry-scented breath, and the warmth of her body pressed against his.

For a moment, they were lost in each other's embrace - until Tiatria interrupted Cullen's thoughts, "It's fine. He told me to go to you." she said with tender reassurance. Their lips found each other again, their hands entwined as if magnetically drawn to each other. Cullen's hand caressed the side of her face as they kissed, their bodies pressed together in a longing embrace under the moonlit sky. It was as if time had stopped just for them - the world fading away into the background as they savored this intimate moment together.

Emerging from the passionate embrace, Tiatria intertwined her fingers with Cullen's and led him away from the bustling courtyard and into the depths of the forest. The moon's soft glow filtered through the leafy canopy, creating playful shadows on their path. Tiatria had a secret spot in mind, a secluded oasis where they could indulge in their desires under the cloak of darkness. With a mischievous glint in her eye, she knew that this Beltane night would be etched in their memories forever. As they ventured deeper into the woods, the air became heavy with the scent of earth and wildflowers, adding to the intoxicating atmosphere.

Maxwell entered his room, the door creaking softly behind him, exhausted from the long day. He let himself fall onto his bed with a heavy thud, his mind weighed down by sorrow. As he lay there staring up at the ornate ceiling, the sounds of joyous celebrations outside his balcony reached his ears. Tears escaped from his eyes as he remembered how Dorian had always been so passionate about learning about this particular festivity. He could almost hear his lover's voice demanding to partake in every aspect of the event, eager to try every type of delight - whether it be food, drink, or physical pleasure. It would have been an unforgettable night for both of them.

But now, Maxwell was alone and lost in his memories. "Missing out on the festivities, I hear," came a familiar voice from beside him. Thamyris leaned casually against the wall of his room. He had shed all his regalia and was now only wearing a pair of pants adorned with crimson red paint - drawn on by Ásbjǫrn. Despite himself, Maxwell couldn't deny that the new King looked exquisite in the low light of the room. With his hair down instead of tied back in its traditional ponytail, Thamyris looked ethereal.

Using his staff for guidance, Thamyris made his way over to Maxwell's bedside and sat down gracefully next to him. Maxwell moved over slightly to give him room. As Thamyris' hand brushed against the cool fabric of the bedding, he turned to face Maxwell. He could hear the human's breaths coming quicker, and he couldn't help but turn towards him as well.

Maxwell refused to meet Thamyris' gaze, feeling himself blush under the elf's intense stare. "No, your majesty," he replied softly. "I don't care to participate in the festival...seeing as I..." His voice trailed off for a moment before he continued with a heavy heart, "Since I lost Dorian." Thamyris let out a sympathetic sigh, understanding the pain of celebrating Beltane without the one you cared for. The two sat in silence for several minutes before Maxwell felt Thamyris' hand on his. He blushed even more as he felt the warmth of it. "Dorian would have wanted you to find happiness, even in his absence," Thamyris said gently. As much as those words stung, Maxwell knew they were true. Dorian had always hated seeing him pout and wallow in sadness.

"I...I have to thank you," Thamyris finally spoke up, his eyes looking towards Maxwell. "For helping me see that I wasn't alone...that I wasn't the only one who felt the same way." He was surprised at how difficult it was to say these words out loud.

The firelight dancing across Thamyris' skin illuminated his sharp features and cast deep shadows that only enhanced his beauty. The soft glow of the candles added warmth to the intimate atmosphere. Thamyris' touch was gentle and loving as he moved his left hand lifting Maxwell's chin, his fingers delicately brushing against the rough hairs of his beard. The sensation was both familiar and new, making Maxwell's heart race with anticipation.

As Thamyris cupped his cheek, the warmth and softness of his palm sent a shiver down Maxwell's spine. He couldn't help but lean into the touch, feeling the tenderness and affection radiating from the elf's hand. It was a simple gesture, yet it held so much meaning and emotion behind it. His beard rustled against Thamyris' hand, adding another layer of texture to the sensation. He could not resist the urge to close his eyes and savor the moment as he felt Thamyris' fingers brush against his cheek and linger there, causing his heart to beat faster. The elf's face softened beneath his touch, almost as if he was overcome with emotion. Maxwell couldn't help but wonder if Thamyris was about to kiss him, the anticipation building in his chest as their lips drew closer.

Suddenly, Maxwell's body tensed, and he pulled away from Thamyris' touch, standing up quickly and making his way towards the door. Thamyris could sense the hesitation in his movements and didn't want to push him into anything he wasn't ready for. He respected Maxwell too much for that. As he walked away, Thamyris could hear the conflict in his breathing - a longing for connection but also a fear of vulnerability. He knew it was best to give him some space to process everything, hoping that maybe later in the night, they could share this special festival together - only if Maxwell wanted it too. The room fell silent with all the collective tension as both men were lost in their own thoughts, and the sounds of laughter and music drifted in from outside. Thamyris watched as Maxwell disappeared through the door, uncertain of what would happen next but determined to let things unfold naturally between them.

Chapter 19

iatria led Cullen to a secret spot she often visited, deep in the heart of the mystical forest. The air was filled with thick scents of a variety of flowers that led to its source of a secluded grove of wildflowers that exuded a heady fragrance, surrounded by weeping willows. As they entered the clearing, the sound of the weeping willows rustled in a gentle breeze. Cullen's face was caressed by the branches of the trees, leaving behind small cuts and scratches that he did not even feel in the midst of his excitement. Underneath their feet, the grass and flowers swayed in a gentle dance, beckoning them closer to the tranquil heart of the grove, towards one of the trees, anticipation building between them.

Cullen noticed the field surrounding the grove was alive with fireflies, their luminous glow casting an otherworldly light over everything. Tiatria led Cullen towards one of the grand willow trees, its massive trunk stretching towards the sky. He watched in awe as she placed her left hand on the rough bark of the large tree, and her features lit up with an ethereal light as if she were absorbing energy from it. Her connection with nature was truly enchanting. Before he could process this fully, Tiatria turned to him with a seductive smile and placed her hand on his chest, drawing him closer. Lost in the moment of tranquility, Tiatria's left hand slipped into Cullen's and he could not resist pulling her closer to him.

His right hand caressed her cheek with gentle strokes as their lips met in a tender kiss. With a sense of urgency, their bodies melted into one another as years of pent-up desire erupted like a volcano. Cullen lifted Tiatria up and pressed her against the tree behind them, deepening their embrace. The warmth and passion grew as Cullen's hands roamed hungrily over Tiatria's body, her dress hung loosely on her shoulders as he gently pushed it down until it pooled at her forearms, revealing her bare breasts. Cullen's breath caught in his throat at the sight before him. He blushed at the sight of her exposed form, her beauty almost overwhelming him. Cullen felt himself harden as he began stripping her of her clothes until she was exposed before him. He couldn't help but blush further at the sight of her perfect curves and felt his heart race with anticipation.

Tiatria gazed up at him with her sapphire blue eyes, lit up by the glowing fireflies, met his own gaze filled with desire. She ran her fingers through his hair and down his chest, feeling his muscles tense under her touch. Her right hand cupped his cheek as they shared another intense kiss. Feeling his arousal against her, Tiatria's breath hitched, and her right hand traveled lower until it cupped his groin, eliciting a gasp from Cullen as he hardened against her hand.

Feeling his embarrassment and his resolve wavering, Cullen quickly removed her hand as he almost became embarrassed by his own uncontrolled reaction. "I'm sorry I -" he said as he took deep breaths in an attempt to cool his blood. Tiatria silenced him with a kiss and then surprised him by boldly palming his groin, causing him to harden even more. She used her body to push Cullen backwards onto the ground. With a wanton look in her eye, she straddled him and leaned forward to claim his lips once more.

Cullen's hands gripped her hips firmly as they ground against each other, their bodies moving in a primal rhythm. With trembling fingers, Tiatria unlaced the threads that bound Cullen's pants, causing them to slacken and revealing his arousal. In that moment, he confessed to her with shame in his eyes, "I've never been with another," But instead of judgement, Tiatria looked at him with love and compassion. "It's alright, neither have I." In that moment, they both laughed, and all pretenses were forgotten as they gave into their desire for each other.

With a predatory look in his eyes, Cullen used his body to roll Tiatria back, her legs eagerly parting for him. As their lips met once more, Cullen ground his hips against hers in a delicious friction that sent shivers down their spines. As the fireflies danced around them, they became lost in a passionate frenzy, their cries echoing through the grove as they explored new heights of pleasure together. And in that sacred place among the willows and wildflowers, their love blossomed like no other before it.

Cullen's breath grew ragged as he eagerly pressed the tip of his cock against Tiatria's slick entrance, teasing her with every brush and rub against her folds. The elf moaned softly as Cullen's lips trailed a path of fiery kisses down Tiatria's neck, his tongue leaving a trail of heat in its wake. Her whole body flushed with desire as his right hand kneaded and squeezed her breast while his lips and tongue lavished attention on her hardened nipple with his teeth. With his left hand steadied on the ground, Cullen leaned in closer to Tiatria, feeling her arching back in response to his touch. As Cullen's cock brushed against her entrance, Tiatria felt a surge of anticipation and desire wash over her body. As she felt Cullen's body and especially his tongue, move downward, Tiatria's skin flushed hot and her fingers tangled in Cullen's hair as he continued to worship her with his mouth settled between her legs.

After a few moments of tending to her, Cullen used his right hand to steady himself, and he slowly pushed into Tiatria, savoring the feeling of her wetness enveloping his shaft. But just as the mere sensation was enough to almost make Cullen give into his primal urges, Tiatria's gasps of shock and pain jolted him back to reality. His concern for her well-being suddenly outweighed his own desires. Quickly shifting his focus, Cullen cradled Tiatria's neck in his right hand and peppered her face with reassuring kisses. "I'm sorry, did I hurt you?" he asked, genuine concern etched on his features. Tiatria met his gaze and saw nothing but love and worry reflected back at her. She knew that any pain she felt would only be temporary, a small price to pay for a night of passion with the man she loved.

With a nod and a smile, she reassured him, "I'm alright, I promise," before gently pulling him out of her. Cullen noticed a small trickle of blood on the grass and immediately felt guilty for causing Tiatria any discomfort. But as she held his face in both of her hands and smiled warmly at him, he could feel her fingers slowly thread themselves through his hair. Both knew that their love was strong enough to weather any storm, even one as small as this. And for now, they could simply bask in each other's embrace and revel in the passion between them.

)o(

Thamyris stepped out from the courtyard, leaving behind Maxwell's chambers and unsure of where the battle mage had gone. The sounds of celebration surrounded him, voices rising and falling in laughter and conversation. He could feel the air move as people danced around the bonfire, its flames burning bright and radiating heat that warmed Thamyris' skin. As he walked, a cool breeze brushed against his face, beckoning him to follow. He followed the breeze, each step bringing him further away from the noise and closer to a peaceful stillness. As the noise ended, Thamyris felt himself cooling down from the intense heat of the bonfire. Using his staff as a guide, he carefully made his way through the darkness until he reached a tree. Thamyris could feel the rough texture of the tree bark against his back as he leaned against it, his staff resting against his chest.

The gentle rustling of leaves in the wind, accompanied by the soft clicking of insects and distant calls of nocturnal animals. The elf's keen ears picked up on every subtle sound, creating a symphony of nature that brought a sense of tranquility to his being. The hoots of owls resounded like soothing lullabies, lulling him into a state of calm. The chirping of crickets added a comforting rhythm to the peaceful night, completing the harmonious chorus around him. Overall, the elf could sense the peacefulness and harmony of the natural world, and it filled him with a deep sense of contentment.

The coolness of the bark provided a stark contrast to the warmth of the bonfire nearby. He could also feel the dewy grass under his bare feet, a refreshing sensation that seemed to ground him and bring him peace. With his staff resting against his chest, Thamyris paused for a moment and did what he loved most on nights like this - listen. As he listened to the rustling of the leaves from the trees overhead, the chirping of crickets swirled together with the soft hoots of the owls, creating a soothing symphony that cradled Thamyris in its peaceful embrace. Memories flooded Thamyris' mind - his father's death, his sister captured and her lover mercilessly slain. Finding humans in the heart of the woods was unexpected, yet it led him to Maxwell. Despite his people being responsible for driving many others into hiding to save their own lives, Maxwell had shown Thamyris kindness and understanding when there was no reason to do so. It made him question his belief that all humans were greedy, proud, and self-serving creatures, often causing more harm than good. But through meeting Maxwell and experiencing genuine friendship and connection with a human, Thamyris learned not to judge an entire race based on the actions of some individuals.

In that kindness, Maxwell had also shown him that he wasn't alone in his feelings for their same sex. For Thamyris, it was a liberating realization. He had hoped to share the Beltane festival with Maxwell and honor him by making him his first. Over time, Thamyris had grown to care for the human deeply and desire him just as passionately, especially after witnessing the intense lovemaking between Maxwell and Dorian one night.

The memory of their bodies intimately entwined made Thamyris ache with longing. Without hesitation, he loosened the laces of his pants and let them fall around his waist, his trembling hand finding its way to his aching and hardened cock. As he began to stroke himself, he could feel every sensation magnified by his heightened arousal. He leaned back against the sturdy trunk of a tree, fully embracing the pleasure coursing through every nerve in his body.

Abruptly, Thamyris's ears caught the distinct sound of heavy footsteps approaching - each step growing louder as they drew closer. Gripping his staff tightly, he turned sharply towards the direction of the sound, ready to defend himself if necessary. His heart raced as he waited, every muscle in his body tense with anticipation. And then suddenly, without warning, he felt someone's hot breath against the back of his neck which caused the hairs on the back of it to rise. He then felt strong arms wrapped around him from behind, trapping him in a tight embrace. The scent of pine and leather filled his nostrils, reminding him of the forest where he had spent so much time training and honing his skills. He remained still, trying to discern who or what was behind him before deciding on a course of action.

"Do you know how long I've been waiting for this?" The low, seductive voice of Ásbjǫrn sent shivers down Thamyris' spine. He felt the elf's strong body pressing against him, barely leaving any room for air to pass between them. As he turned around, Thamyris' hands gently, slowly roamed over the hard muscles of Ásbjǫrn's bare chest. He realized for the first time just how powerful and alluring the elf truly was. Again, by merely touching Ásbjǫrn, Thamyris was able to see again. And what he could see was beautiful; with his right forearm resting against a nearby tree, Ásbjǫrn let out a deep sigh as he felt his king's fingers tracing patterns over his warm skin. Thamyris' touch traveled up to Ásbjǫrn's broad shoulders, eliciting a moan from the elf, who eagerly reciprocated by holding onto Thamyris' hand and kissing the tops of his knuckles.

The blush that spread across Thamyris' cheeks only intensified as he moved his hand lower until it came into contact with something that had grown to an unexpected and massive size. His eyes widened in surprise as he measured the girth of Ásbjǫrn's throbbing cock in his hand. The elf's eyes burned with desire as he encouraged Thamyris to continue stroking him before claiming his lips in a passionate kiss. Now being able to see clearly, Thamyris could not help but feel overwhelmed by the predatory look in Ásbjǫrn's eyes, they seemed to take on an amber glow. "I want to devour every inch of you," the elf declared with raw hunger in his voice. Thamyris could sense Ásbjǫrn's hesitation, knowing that giving in to their deepest desires could lead to insatiable cravings for each other. But the temptation was too great and both men knew they would not be able to resist consuming every last drop of pleasure from one another.

Thamyris' heart raced as he gazed into Ásbjǫrn's intense eyes, realizing what was about to happen - something he had been yearning for centuries. But in that moment of realization, a wave of panic crashed over him, knowing he was hopelessly inexperienced and unprepared for what was to come. However, Ásbjǫrn's smile sent shivers down his spine, his eagerness to show Thamyris every sensation of pleasure evident in the way he moved closer, their bodies almost touching. "I'll be gentle," Ásbjǫrn whispered, causing Thamyris' skin to tingle with anticipation. Just then, Ásbjǫrn's fingers left his chin, and their lips met in a gentle kiss, igniting a fire within Thamyris that burned hotter with each passing second.

As they continued to kiss passionately, Thamyris felt Ásbjǫrn's fingertips trace a trail down his chest and stomach until they reached his hardened cock - taking hold of it with a firm but gentle touch. "At least I'll try," Ásbjǫrn murmured against Thamyris' lips, sending a jolt of excitement through his body. And as Ásbjǫrn knelt before him, using his skilled tongue to worship every inch of Thamyris' body, the king couldn't help but let out a gasp of pleasure. With each touch and caress from Ásbjǫrn's lips and hands, Thamyris felt himself surrendering completely to the intense pleasure coursing through him. The moonlight illuminated their entwined forms. Ásbjǫrn gently held Thamyris' face with both large hands, "You are so beautiful," he praised, his hot breath tickling his skin between kisses and licks, making him feel desired and cherished. As they both fell deeper into the throes of passion, Thamyris knew he had never felt more alive. Ásbjǫrn looked up at him as he slowly fell to his knees. "Just as nature intended," his eyes full of adoration and lust, Thamyris could not help but surrender completely to be consumed by desire under Ásbjǫrn's skilled touch, lost in the intense and primal connection between them under the moonlight.

Thamyris gasped as Ásbjǫrn's hands gripped his hips with a bruising force, pulling him closer until his throbbing cock was enveloped by Ásbjǫrn's hot mouth. As pleasure shot through his body, Thamyris threw his head back and moaned with a mixture of shock and ecstasy. Ásbjǫrn's grip on his hair tightened as he devoured him, expertly using his tongue to swirl around the sensitive head and shaft of his cock. Thamyris could feel himself getting lost in the overwhelming sensations, his head dropping to his chest as Ásbjǫrn's cheeks hollowed with each powerful suction. His eyes rolled back in his head as he approached a mind-bending climax, but before he could reach it, Ásbjǫrn stood up abruptly and captured Thamyris' lips in a fierce kiss.

As they broke apart, panting heavily, Ásbjǫrn led Thamyris to a secluded clearing among the trees. A grin spread across the elf's face as he pulled Thamyris into his arms, growling in a low, predatory tone for him to come closer. With one hand on Ásbjǫrn's chest and the other on his cheek, Thamyris eagerly responded to the passionate kisses and felt the heat radiating from Ásbjǫrn's body merge with his own. As their erections pressed against each other, Ásbjǫrn took hold of Thamyris' hand and guided it to stroke both their cocks together. With a blush creeping up his cheeks, Thamyris let himself be guided by Ásbjǫrn until they stumbled and fell onto the cool grass. They laughed together, their voices echoing through the forest before being drowned out by the booming sound of Ásbjǫrn's voice. In an instant, Thamyris' lips were claimed once again by the large elf, who settled between his legs. As Ásbjǫrn's cock teased his entrance, they kissed with a raw intensity and held onto each other desperately.

With a feral growl, Ásbjǫrn grabbed Thamyris' wrists and pinned them above his head as he positioned himself at his lover's entrance. Both men took deep breaths, their hearts racing as Ásbjǫrn's lips trailed down to the sensitive skin behind Thamyris' ear while his middle finger teased at his entrance. Thamyris could feel himself teetering on the edge of pleasure and pain as he surrendered completely to the intense passion between them.

Ásbjǫrn right middle finger found its way inside Thamyris, causing the elf to gasp. It felt like nothing he'd ever felt, something indescribable. A second finger went in a moment, a warm sensation that caused Thamyris' muscles to relax. Ásbjǫrn's hand took on a golden glow that seemed to cause his lover to relax as a warm sensation washed over him. It caused his left hand to grab onto

Ásbjǫrn's wrist as he moaned from all the pleasurable sensations that seemed to swallow him from the inside out.

Thamyris felt Ásbjǫrn's strong left hand grab hold of his right leg, exposing his vulnerable body to the elf's insatiable desires. The elf's lips and tongue ravaged Thamyris' tender skin with a possessive hunger while his nose and tongue explored every inch of his trembling form. Ásbjǫrn gave a gentle look, "Relax, it'll help. Remember, I will be as gentle as I can be." Ásbjǫrn would be true to his word - he would be gentle with his beloved king. Yet even in his gentleness, Thamyris couldn't help but scream as he felt the first thrust of Ásbjǫrn's member penetrating him deeply. Ásbjǫrn continued to push himself inside, causing Thamyris to let out a primal scream that echoed through the forest. The pain was intense, almost unbearable, and Thamyris' back arched in agony as he clutched at anything within reach as he tried to adjust to the unfamiliar sensation of being filled so completely.

As his leg was gently placed over Ásbjǫrn's shoulder, Thamyris' back arched in agony, unable to control the sensations racing through him. But even amidst the pain, he heard Ásbjǫrn's soothing voice and felt his hand gently squeeze his as an affirmation of love and concern, "Relax,"

With each slow and deliberate movement, Ásbjǫrn pushed himself further into Thamyris' tightness, causing a mixture of pleasure and pain to course through both of their bodies. Thamyris' hand desperately clawed at Ásbjǫrn's back, digging his fingers into his muscular back as he tried to come to terms with all of the overwhelming sensations. Ásbjǫrn sensed his lover's fear and agitation. He paused, giving them both a moment to adjust before continuing.

With Ásbjǫrn's soothing voice and caress on his left cheek, Thamyris felt a large bead of pre-cum dribble onto his stomach, causing Ásbjǫrn to gently take his hardened cock in hand, gently stroking him. Doing so caused Thamyris' body to relax enough for him to slide in further. This caused the large elf to kiss Thamyris passionately, "Good boy," he purred, his hot breath tickling Thamyris' neck. Thamyris started to get frustrated, "Just take me already!" Ásbjǫrn froze in place as Thamyris's right hand held his forearm. Ásbjǫrn's eyes hardened, "No," he said in a low growl, "Doing that would do more than hurt you." Thamyris could feel Ásbjǫrn's body become tense as he said those words.

Slowly, Thamyris felt Ásbjǫrn's hands gently hold his chin, "I will not do that. This is a night that you will remember forever and I want nothing but happiness and joy when you reflect upon this night." Thamyris felt the air leave his lungs. To know Ásbjǫrn was determined to make sure he wasn't injured in any way and wanted this to be an experience thought of with joy. Ásbjǫrn watched as Thamyris' cheeks burned bright red, and his whole body blushed, causing his eyes to soften as he captured Thamyris' lips once more.

Just then, Asbjorn had an idea. With precise movements, he lowered Thamyris' leg and wrapped both of Thamyris' legs around his waist in a tight embrace. This new angle caused Thamyris to cry out. Ásbjǫrn had inadvertently pushed past the tight resistance until he was fully buried inside. Thamyris tightly wrapped his arms around Ásbjǫrn, who slowly leaned back on his knees before standing and carrying Thamyris to the nearest tree. Every step sent waves of pleasure and pain through Thamyris' body as Ásbjǫrn remained deep inside him, pushing them both to their limit.

)o(

Cullen's body moved with a gentle but passionate rhythm, his hips pressing into Tiatria's as their bodies melted together in a sea of sweat and desire. Her fingers dug into his firm muscles, her nails leaving trails of red marks across his back as she clung to him for dear life. With each stroke, Cullen felt his love's legs wrap tighter around his waist, pulling him deeper into their shared pleasure. As they moved together, their bodies seemed to merge into one, the heat and intensity between them growing with each passing moment. Suddenly, Tiatria lifted her head from Cullen's shoulder, capturing his lips with hers in an urgent and hungry kiss. Their tongues danced together in a passionate tango as they lost themselves in the moment. In a burst of passion, Tiatria's body took control as she turned him onto his back so that she could feel every inch of him inside of her. A questioning look crossed Cullen's face, but Tiatria nodded reassuringly, letting him know everything was okay.

As he sat up, Cullen's hand cradled her cheek tenderly as their lips met once again in a gentle yet passionate embrace. Tiatria started to move her hips with a new vigor, guided by the steady grip of Cullen's left hand on her hip. The two lovers intertwined their arms around each other. Their fingers threaded through one another's hair as their bodies moved together in perfect harmony. Their foreheads touched as they gazed into each other's eyes, lost in the moment and consumed by the fiery passion between them. Despite their mutual desire to make this moment last forever, both Cullen and Tiatria were struggling to resist the intense pleasure building within them. This was not just physical intimacy but a deep connection between two souls entwined in the throes of ecstasy. And they would savor every second of it together until they could not hold back any longer.

As they moved in perfect harmony, Cullen's mind was a battleground, torn between thoughts of his beloved Tiatria and the life he could have been trapped in with Edith. He forced himself to focus on Tiatria, but the memories of Edith kept creeping in. He did not want to think about her, especially not now when he was finally with the one he genuinely loved. Yet, his mind could not help but wonder what would have happened if things had gone differently between him and Edith.

Tiatria paused, causing Cullen to furrow his brow in confusion. But as her gentle gaze met his, her delicate fingers traced the contours of his face, soothing him with their touch. In the warmth of her touch and the sweet scent of flowers that seemed to emanate from her skin enveloped him, transporting him to a place of peace and contentment. He closed his eyes and let himself be fully present with Tiatria, grateful for her words and her presence in his life. In that moment, all thoughts of what could have been and his past love faded away. He was fully present with Tiatria, feeling her warmth and affection enveloping him.

"Don't dwell on the past or on her," she whispered softly. "Just be here with me now; be fully present with me in this moment," she whispered tenderly, her voice like a soothing balm for his troubled thoughts. Every word she spoke was infused with sincerity and affection, enveloping him in a warm embrace that he never wanted to let go of.

Cullen's body was on fire as Tiatria's hands roamed over his skin, igniting every nerve with a burning desire. He couldn't resist pressing his face into her chest, inhaling her sweet scent as she wrapped her arms around him. Their bodies molded together perfectly, like two pieces of a puzzle finally fitting into place. But just as he felt completely at peace and content in her embrace, Tiatria's movements stirred a primal urge within him. With each motion of her hips, Cullen was reminded of their intense lovemaking and the insatiable hunger that burned between them.

Unable to hold back any longer, Cullen groaned deeply and bucked his hips upwards as Tiatria sank onto him with a gasp. The sensation of her tight walls gripping onto him sent waves of pleasure coursing through his entire being.

"Oh god..." Cullen moaned, unable to contain the overwhelming sensations that consumed him.

"Cullen, please," Tiatria whimpered urgently, rolling her hips against his and whining as he filled her completely. "I need you."

Her words only fueled Cullen's desire as he eagerly complied with her request to lay back. His hands gripped her hips tightly as she began to move above him, setting off fireworks of pleasure with every stroke.

Their bodies moved in perfect sync, reaching new heights of ecstasy as they worked together to fulfill each other's desires. Tiatria could feel Cullen's muscles tensing beneath her touch and knew that he needed more.

Driven by an all-consuming need for each other, Cullen put his right arm around his love's waist and flipped her onto her back. He kissed her passionately as he reveled in the new angle, able to control their movements even more now. Tiatria moaned and clung to him desperately, losing herself in the sea of sensation. Their bodies moved in a feverish rhythm, reaching peak after peak of pleasure until they were both breathless and spent. And in that moment, they were completely lost in each other, consumed by their insatiable love and desire.

Cullen's eyes burned with unrestrained desire as he gazed at his love, her body writhing beneath him. "I will never stop loving you!" He growled; the intensity of his words matched only by the ferocity of his thrusts. "You are my heart, my soul, my everything!" With each movement, Cullen's left hand held onto hers tightly, their knuckles digging into the grass beneath them.

Tiatria surrendered herself to the overwhelming heat and pleasure coursing through her body, begging for more as Cullen hit all the right spots inside her. She was lost in a sea of pleasure, gasping and moaning as Cullen brought her closer and closer to the edge. As they both reached their peak, Tiatria clawed at the ground and cried out Cullen's name, unable to form coherent words.

"Make me see the stars," she pleaded, pulling herself up to kiss him as he moved faster and harder, pushing himself to the brink. "Come see the stars with me, Cullen. My love." she whispered in his ear, driving him wild with need. And with one final thrust, they both tumbled over the edge together in a blur of ecstasy and passion. Cullen let out a primal roar as he released himself inside Tiatria, collapsing on top of her with trembling limbs and a heart full of love. They lay entwined for what felt like eternity, both catching their breaths after such an intense release.

With significant effort, Cullen slowly opened his eyes. The bright moonlight filtering through the trees momentarily blinded him before he focused on the sight of Tiatria, the female elf he loved. She was lying next to him, her hair loose and tousled around her face as she gazed over at him with tenderness and exhaustion evident in her flushed skin and damp tendrils of hair. Her mouth was slightly agape as she panted for air, her blue eyes hazy but brimming with happiness.

When she noticed Cullen looking at her, a warm and affectionate smile spread across her lips. "Cullen," she breathed, reaching up to gently cup his cheek in her hand, "I love you." Her touch was gentle and loving, sending shivers down his spine.

"I love you," Cullen echoed back, his voice filled with exhausted yet passionate emotion. Leaning in, he kissed her deeply, pouring all of his love into the kiss as he ran his fingers through her silky locks. They tasted the salt of their sweat mixed with the sweetness of their love.

Finally settling back against the soft grass with a content sigh, Cullen pulled Tiatria closer to him, feeling grateful and overwhelmed by their intense connection. At this moment, nothing else in the world mattered except for their love for each other.

)o(

Thamyris' back collided with a tree. His body pushed against the rough bark as Ásbjǫrn gently lowered his right leg to the ground. The king felt a jolt of anticipation shoot through him as Ásbjǫrn's strong left arm cradled his leg in its crook. A fierce heat burned in Ásbjǫrn's eyes as he examined Thamyris, his hand tenderly caressing the king's cheek. "Does it still feel tight?" Ásbjǫrn asked, his voice dripping with desire. Thamyris could feel a difference, and he shook his head eagerly, his breath hitching at the thought of what was to come. Without hesitation, Ásbjǫrn pressed his lips to Thamyris', a passionate kiss that made the king weak in the knees. Using all of his weight, he pinned Thamyris firmly against the tree, their bodies melding together in a frenzy of movement. With each thrust of his hips, Ásbjǫrn sent shivers of pleasure down Thamyris' spine, the fireflies around them providing an ethereal glow to their passionate encounter.

As they continued to move in unison, Thamyris gazed into Ásbjǫrn's amber brown eyes, both of their cheeks flushed with arousal and groans escaping their lips. Every touch and sensation felt amplified in the moonlit forest, adding to the intensity between them. Thamyris could not help but gasp as he felt Ásbjǫrn's cock brush against a spot inside him that sent waves of ecstasy through his body. Sensing Thamyris' muscles finally relax, Ásbjǫrn seized the opportunity to claim his king's lips once again, pressing their bodies even closer together. Thamyris wrapped his arms tightly around Ásbjǫrn's neck, their lips locked in a heated battle for dominance as they took brief moments to catch their breath.

After what felt like an eternity, Ásbjǫrn released Thamyris' leg and pulled him even closer, his fingers firmly gripping the king's flesh as he lifted him up. Thamyris eagerly wrapped his legs around Ásbjǫrn's waist, allowing himself to be completely consumed by the other man. With each slow and deliberate movement of his hips, Ásbjǫrn sent Thamyris spiraling into a state of pure pleasure, the king unable to control the cries that escaped his lips as he rested his forehead on Ásbjǫrn's damp shoulder. "Rest on me if you need it," he whispered, the fingers of his right hand threaded through his lover's raven-black hair as he cradled the back of Thamyris' head. Ásbjǫrn could feel the fingers of Thamyris' right hand digging into the back of his shoulder as tears trickled down it. Slowly, gently, their bodies moved in perfect harmony, lost in a world of passion and desire under the soft light of the moon. And as they continued to reach their climax together, it was as if time stood still, and all that mattered was reaching this moment between them.

The sound of skin slapping against skin echoed through the forest as Ásbjǫrn's hips thrust at a frenzied pace. Thamyris clung to his lover's back, nails digging into the rippling muscles underneath his slick skin. Sweat dripped down their bodies, making it difficult to maintain their grip, but they pushed on, driven by an insatiable desire for more pleasure. As they neared their climax, Thamyris couldn't help but offer grateful prayers to the God and Goddess for allowing him to experience such intense ecstasy with Ásbjǫrn.

Suddenly, Ásbjǫrn shifted his weight, forcing him to look into Thamyris' milky-blue eyes. Despite the cloudy film covering what would have been alluring blue eyes, Ásbjǫrn found them to be the most beautiful thing he had ever seen. He sealed their lips together in a searing kiss, never breaking the rhythm of his thrusts. Thamyris moaned as he felt his cock pulse and throb under Ásbjǫrn's expert touch, matching the intensity of his lover's assault. Without warning, Ásbjǫrn lowered Thamyris onto both of his feet and turned him around, guiding his own throbbing member back inside him with his right hand. The sensation caused Thamyris to cry out in pure bliss before feeling Ásbjǫrn's hand wrap around his aching cock. He could feel Ásbjǫrn's hot breath on his back as he began to move once again.

Thamyris threw his head back against the rough bark of the nearby tree, his breath coming in ragged gasps as Ásbjǫrn pounded into him with a relentless fervor. Every thrust sent waves of pleasure rippling through Thamyris' body, making him feel like he was on fire. He braced himself against the tree, gripping it so tightly that his knuckles turned white while Ásbjǫrn's left hand tangled in his raven-black hair, pulling and guiding him. Thamyris' mind was consumed by the intense sensations coursing through him, unable to think about anything else but the throbbing ache between his legs and the powerful man behind him who was bringing him to ecstasy.

As Ásbjǫrn's attention shifted from Thamyris' cock to him directly, as he felt Thamyris' knees start to buckle. But Ásbjǫrn was determined to keep him steady with a strong arm around his waist, each of their thrusts pushing them closer and closer to their climax. With one final deep thrust, Thamyris cried out as he spilled his seed against the tree, feeling like he was exploding from the inside out. He could feel Ásbjǫrn's sweat dripping onto his back, but they were not done yet. As Ásbjǫrn filled him with his seed, Thamyris felt a surge of pleasure unlike anything he had ever experienced before. It was as if his very soul was being opened up to new levels of ecstasy. And as Ásbjǫrn's voice erupted into that of a bear and his features transformed, fur erupted from his back; his canines elongated and grew to sharp claws. Thamyris couldn't help but be both terrified and aroused.

As they collapsed onto the grass, panting and covered in sweat, Thamyris realized that his world had been opened up to a whole new level of pleasure. And it was all thanks to Ásbjǫrn, whose voice now echoed with a primal growl and whose features were transformed into those of a bear - revealing a hidden side that only intensified Thamyris' desire for him. They lay there in blissful exhaustion, knowing that they had discovered something incredible together - something that they could now enjoy again and again.

Ásbjǫrn's body slowly shifted back to its normal form, his muscles trembling as he rose to all fours and took deep, ragged breaths. He refused to let the wild nature of his beast win over him. Thamyris, unable to see what was happening, could only hear the guttural growls of a beast mixed in with Ásbjǫrn's voice. As he rolled onto all fours, his fingers brushed against coarse bear fur that quickly retracted into smooth elven skin. Ásbjǫrn fought hard to regain control. His face contorted in a mix of agony and determination. Finally, he was able to steady himself and reach out to hold his king's face in both hands. "Forgive me, my King," he pleaded with genuine remorse. "My blood can run too hot at times, and it becomes a challenge for me to tame the beast within." Thamyris smiled understandingly, finally able to see the relief and concern expressed on Ásbjǫrn's face.

Chapter 20

as the sun's golden rays rose in the elven realm, birds sang sweetly and the fresh scent of morning filled the air. The castle lay still as most of its inhabitants slept peacefully, some nestled on beds of grass, others scattered around extinguished bonfires. Maxwell strolled through the halls, taking in the remnants of last night's festivities. The scent of flowers lingered, mixed with the sweet scent of wine and food. Servants bustled about, tidying up the remnants of last night's wild festivities. The floor was littered with colorful flowers, ribbons, and streamers that had been cast aside in excitement. Servants carefully collected any forgotten wine glasses or dishes with bits of food still clinging to them.

Inside the castle, people slumbered peacefully in various states of exhaustion on chairs and chaise lounges. Maxwell couldn't help but reminisce on past parties he had attended with Dorian, but this one seemed to surpass them all. It was unlike anything he had ever experienced. He had witnessed people passionately engaging in amorous activities all over the castle, even hearing passionate lovemaking against his bedroom door that had made it nearly impossible for him to sleep.

Instead, he found himself drawn to his balcony, where he could observe the remaining guests dancing around the glowing embers of the bonfires. The music continued to play as people sang and danced. Maxwell smiled as he saw strangers embracing each other in various forms of love. His gaze followed Thamyris as he disappeared into the night; Maxwell's heart ached to follow him. He knew Ásbjørn would soon join him for what he assumed would be a passionate tryst. Reflecting on everything he had witnessed and looking around at the scene before him, Maxwell finally understood what last night meant to these people and why they celebrated it with such fervor. To commune with their gods in such an open and with such loving devotion was a beautiful sight to behold. It was something he had never been taught to do but now wished he had been able to experience it before this moment. And in that moment, he couldn't help but wish he had been a part of it all.

)o(

Thamyris awoke to the warmth of the sun on his skin, its rays filtering through the leaves of the surrounding trees. Judging by the sweet sound of birdsong filled the air, accompanied by the gentle chirping of crickets. He could tell that it was past dawn as he stretched his limbs. He could feel the dew still clinging to the grass beneath him, evidence of the early hour. He reached out for Ásbjǫrn but only felt the cool smoothness of his staff. A jolt of pain shot-up his back. Thamyris growled as the pain forced him to curl up as he held himself. Thamyris couldn't help but feel a pang of disappointment fill him as he longed for his lover's embrace, especially now that he was suffering from the effects of last night's activities. He rose to his feet and listened to his surroundings - a peaceful meadow that gave off the scent of the wildflowers and bristling branches of tall oak trees. But Thamyris could not shake off the feeling that something was missing.

As he recalled falling asleep in Ásbjǫrn's large and protective arms, he couldn't help but wish that they were waking up together. For once, Thamyris had felt safe and truly loved. Sleeping on one of the large elf's pectoral muscles and being held in his arms gave him a sense of safety. With a heavy sigh, Thamyris reminded himself that Beltane was not just about the union of God and Goddess but also free and open love. Not everyone desired to wake up with their lover in the morning, but this time, Thamyris wished Ásbjǫrn had stayed with him.

But now that the festivities were over, he had to face his next big challenge - dealing with his sister and her dragon. Thamyris knew he would have to suppress any remaining feelings of love and compassion for her. She was no longer the kind, gentle elf he once knew. Now, she was consumed by evil, vengeance, and cruelty. She needed to be stopped and her dragon put back into eternal slumber. With Tiatria now holding the title of high priestess and wielding immense power, Thamyris hoped she would be able to stand up against Amalia's wrath. Thamyris knew it was a daunting task, but one that needed to be done for the safety of all.

)o(

Cullen's senses slowly came alive, the sweet scent of Tiatria's hair caressing his nostrils like a gentle breeze. The elf was still nestled in his arms, her delicate fingers tracing lazy patterns on his bare chest. As Cullen took in a deep breath, signaling his awakening, every inch of his body felt electrified by the warmth radiating from Tiatria's embrace. Her soft lips pressed against his skin, leaving a trail of fire in their wake.

Tiatria shifted against him and looked up with a soft smile, her sapphire eyes shining with love and contentment. She loved feeling his strong arms wrapped around her, protecting and cherishing her. The fingertips of Cullen's right hand gently trailed up and down her bare back, sending shivers of pleasure through her body. Her own left hand played with strands of his long golden hair, entwining them between her fingers as they reveled in each other's touch.

The two shared several moments of passionate kisses before reluctantly realizing that they would have to return to the castle soon. As their lips parted, Cullen felt his blood rush and something else started to awaken. His heart raced as he gazed into Tiatria's eyes, seeing the depth of their connection reflected back at him.

But before they could continue their playful banter, Tiatria suddenly arched her back and let out a gasp so loud it echoed through the air. Her body began to convulse violently as her eyes rolled back into her head.

Cullen immediately sat up, holding onto Tiatria's arms as he tried to restrain her from hurting herself. Fear laced his voice as he called out to her, trying to bring her back from whatever was causing this terrifying episode. "Tia? Tia?" he repeated desperately, willing her to come back to him and praying that she would be okay.

)o(

Tiatria found herself back in the thick, misty realm of Elen, surrounded by swirling clouds and an eerie fog. She peered through the haze, searching for her goddess, but saw nothing familiar. Instead, she felt the ground beneath her tremble with each step she took, if there was even a solid floor to be walking on. Suddenly, Tiatria stumbled as she lost her balance, as a deep growl filled the air, causing Tiatria to freeze as she felt shivers race down her spine. This caused her to scan her surroundings.

As she continued to look around, something finally caught her attention as it seemed to emerge from the mist. A massive green dragon, its shimmering scales reflecting every shade of green imaginable- from pale hues to deep, rich hues of emeralds, stood before her. Standing at least ten feet tall, it tucked its wings close to its body, revealing bits of moss and flora clinging to its iridescent scales. Tiatria estimated that the creature must have had an impressive eighty-foot wingspan.

Mesmerized by the majestic beast before her, Tiatria could only watch with awe as it spoke in a deep yet feminine voice. "Be calm my child. I will not hurt you," the dragon assured her. Her eyes sparkled like precious emerald gems and never had Tiatria seen such a magnificent creature.

Feeling a mixture of fear and curiosity, Tiatria dared to ask, "Who are you?" She spoke gently and carefully, not wanting to anger the powerful being before her. "My name is Myrae," the dragon boomed proudly. "I am the dragon of the north and keeper of the Earth and all that grows." As it spoke, tendrils of smoke curled from its nostrils and floated up into the misty air. "I have come to lend you, my aid. Nimriar has awoken prematurely and I know it is not time for him to do so. What has happened?" Myrae questioned with concern.

Tiatria took a moment to compose herself before explaining everything that had transpired in the mortal realm, leading up to Nimriar's unexpected awakening. She couldn't believe she was conversing with a dragon, let alone one so wise and powerful. As they spoke, Tiatria couldn't help but feel grateful for Myrae's presence and guidance. She knew that with the dragon's help, they stood a chance against Nimriar's wrath.

)o(

Maxwell strolled leisurely through the courtyard, the fallen leaves rustling beneath his feet with each step. The crisp morning air was filled with the gentle sound of Thamyris' approaching footsteps, a soft swish and crunch as he glided closer. As they drew near to each other, Maxwell could sense a slight unease emanating from the elf, his body tense along with a familiar telltale limp. The courtyard was quiet and still except for the occasional chirp of a bird or the wind causing the rustling of leaves.

"Did you have a pleasant evening, your majesty?" Maxwell inquired, his voice carrying through the stillness like a soothing song.

Thamyris felt a pang of guilt as he realized the astute human had sensed something amiss. Did he know of his night with Ásbjǫrn? "It was quite enjoyable, thank you," he replied smoothly, his pointed ears flicking ever so subtly. He flashed a clever smile, "How was yours?" he questioned with equal smoothness, turning the question back on Maxwell.

The human shook his head but then remembered that Thamyris could not see him and hastened to respond. "No, but I did hear quite a lively commotion of thumping against my chamber door," he chuckled. The two shared a knowing look and chuckled before Maxwell stepped aside to let Thamyris pass.

But just as they were about to continue their leisurely stroll, the peaceful atmosphere was shattered by a blood-curdling scream for help. It pierced through the serene air like a knife, causing both men to jolt with alarm. Their heads snapped in the direction of the cry and they saw Cullen coming into view, his face contorted with agony as he sprinted towards them, clad only in pants, sprinting towards them with a naked Tiatria cradled in his arms. Her pale skin gleamed in the sunlight as if illuminated by some ethereal light. "HELP! I NEED HELP!" Sweat poured down his face as he gasped for air between his panicked cries. Maxwell's heart raced as he took in the sight of his friend's distressed expression, his mind racing with possible scenarios that could have led to this moment. He felt a sense of urgency wash over him as he realized something terrible must have happened to cause such panic in Cullen.

With a sense of urgency and adrenaline pumping through their veins, without hesitation, they sprang into action to aid their frantic companion. They raced towards Cullen and Tiatria; the leaves crunched under their feet as they sprinted across the courtyard. The air was heavy with tension and fear, the birds silenced by the sudden chaos that had erupted. As they reached Cullen, Maxwell could see the sweat glistening on his skin, his eyes wild with desperation. Thamyris' elvish grace allowed him to move swiftly and gracefully despite the urgency, his long legs propelling him forward with ease.

The elf's voice trembled with concern as he asked, "What happened?" Cullen's face was wrought with worry as he shook his head. "I don't know. We woke up in a lush meadow this morning, but before we could even say or do anything, she started having violent convulsions. And now she won't wake up." Maxwell placed his hand on Cullen's shoulder, offering a reassuring touch. "It'll be alright. Let's get her inside," he said calmly.

Thamyris' hands gently cupped his wife's face as he tried to make sense of what was happening. As he did, images flashed through his mind - images of Myrae, the emerald dragon, talking to her about something important. He let out a heavy sigh, determination etched on his features. "We need to take her to the Temple of Cernunnos. It's our best chance at finding answers and waking her," he instructed the group, urgency lacing his words. Together, they turned as Thamyris began leading their way towards the temple, praying for a miracle along the way.

)o(

Myrae sat in rapt attention; her massive and majestic form lay sprawled before Tiatria. Her front claws crossed over each other as she listened intently to Tiatria's story. When Tiatria finished speaking, Myrae effortlessly rose to her feet, towering over the elf. With a heavy sigh, "If all you say is true, we are going to need more help," she said, her voice declared firmly.

Tiatria looked at the dragon curiously, wondering what she meant. "What do you mean? Surely you are strong enough to fight Nimriar as we -" she started to say before being interrupted by Myrae's resolute statement. "I am not!" declared the dragon, turning her head back towards Tiatria. "Nimriar is the largest and strongest of us, and I cannot tackle him alone."

Tiatria stood up and walked alongside Myrae, feeling a sense of urgency building within her. "What are you going to do?" she asked, anxious for a plan.

Without hesitation, Myrae looked ahead of them and raised her voice in a commanding tone. "Naga! You must awaken!" she cried out. As if in response to Myrae's call, deep and familiar tremors shook the ground beneath them once again. A deep growl reverberated through the air, sending chills down Tiatria's spine. The air suddenly turned icy cold, and she wrapped her arms around herself for warmth.

Through the mist emerged a large white dragon, its powerful presence almost palpable. Standing at an impressive sixteen feet with a seventy-two foot wingspan, it was clear that this dragon was a force to be reckoned with. Its scales shimmered with a faint blue hue, almost making it invisible against the misty surroundings. The creature's eyes were a piercing blue, reminiscent of the clearest river waters. Its sleek profile and triangular overlapping scales along its neck gave it an intimidating appearance. Tiatria couldn't help but notice the sharp beak on its upper lip, with menacing teeth protruding from its closed mouth.

The dragon's gaze shifted between Tiatria and Myrae, assessing them with a skeptical eye. "Why have you summoned me?" it asked in a deep, rumbling tone.

Tiatria's gaze followed Myrae's to rest upon the colossal dragon before her. "This is Naga, Lord of the West and ruler over all forms of water." Tiatria's eyes widened in awe as she gazed upon the majestic dragon before her. She kneeled before him, showing great respect. "My Lord," she spoke with reverence, "it seems you are needed once again." She turned her head to Myrae, who gestured with her head for the elf to continue.

"As High Priestess of the Goddess," Tiatria addressed Naga, "I ask for your help. I humbly ask for your assistance to stop Nimriar and his Priestess Amalia from bringing darkness upon our land."

Naga's piercing and calculating eyes shifted between Tiatria and Myrae. "I do not recognize you, little one," he spoke in a deep rumbling voice, "and yet, I can sense that you are new to your powers." He turned his attention to Myrae in front of him. "Can it be true?" He questioned; a hint of disbelief in his tone. "Has another High Priestess of the Goddess fallen into darkness?"

Myrae nodded solemnly, her massive head bowing slightly in confirmation. Naga took a step back, seemingly stunned by the news - or as taken aback as a dragon could be. His gaze returned to Tiatria, and he spoke with determination in his tone. "I will serve in this task, Priestess," he declared with authority. His powerful wings rustled as he prepared himself for battle and looked at Myrae for agreement. She gave a subtle nod of her head, wordlessly expressing her consent. "As will my companion," Naga added firmly, indicating Myrae at his side.

)o(

Thamyris led the two down a well-worn path that he had walked countless times before, the familiar scent of earth and moss filling his nostrils. He proudly escorted his companions to the Temple of Cernunnos, pointing out the rustic beauty of the surroundings as they approached. As they drew closer, Maxwell and Cullen couldn't help but marvel at the intricately carved stone walls and the soft glow emanating from within. Maxwell realized he'd only seen a small part of it from the view off of his balcony.

But Thamyris had one more surprise in store for them. He stopped in front of a section of wall covered in thick vines and gently touched them with his left hand. He paused for a moment, hesitant about what he was about to do. "This is sacred ground," he whispered, his voice filled with reverence. "Treat it as such." After a moment, he pulled back the vines to reveal a hidden doorway, beckoning for them to enter.

Stepping inside, they were greeted by an open space with an altar at its center and a towering statue of the god himself perched on a cliff above them. Maple trees, flowers, moss and vines were all around. It was nature in its truest form. But the peaceful moment was soon interrupted when Ásbjǫrn, emerged from a side chamber with a menacing growl.

"What are humans doing here?" he bellowed, his eyes blazing with fury. He stalked towards them as if ready to attack, but Thamyris quickly positioned himself in front of his guests with unwavering determination. The air between them crackled with tension as Ásbjǫrn dared to challenge his king's decision to bring outsiders into their sacred space. But Thamyris stood tall, stamping his staff on the ground for emphasis.

"Enough!" he declared, light bursting forth from the tip of his staff and casting an otherworldly glow around them. Even Ásbjǫrn seemed momentarily taken aback by this display of power.

"I brought them here!" Thamyris asserted, meeting the elf's fierce gaze with unwavering conviction. Ásbjǫrn pushed back, his voice rising in anger, "They do not follow our God or even the laws of nature!" Thamyris let out a derisive snort, understanding the elf's outrage but knowing that this was not the time for it. "As your king, it is my decision that they are here."

But then Ásbjǫrn's sharp gaze landed on Tiatria, cradled gently in Cullen's arms. His anger flared at the sight of her nakedness. Seeing his high priestess in such a vulnerable state was blasphemy, if nothing else. "What happened to her?" he demanded, his form shifting as brown fur sprouted from his skin and his nails transformed into deadly claws. "Did you rape her and now seek to feign ignorance before my lord could claim his right to consummate his marriage?" The accusation hung heavily in the air as Ásbjǫrn's rage began to consume him.

Without hesitation, he lunged towards Cullen, but Thamyris was quick to react, standing between them once again. The air crackled with tension as the two powerful beings faced off, their conflicting beliefs and allegiances threatening to erupt into violence.

Thamyris held out his right hand, fingers splayed and tingling with magic as the thick vines sprouted from the forest floor, snaking their way towards Ásbjǫrn's feet. The elf stumbled and fell to the ground, caught off guard by the sudden attack. Thamyris' staff, carved from a single piece of rosewood, tapped gently against Ásbjǫrn's temple before he could react.

"He did no such thing!" Thamyris declared in a firm tone. "The only rights he took were those that belonged to him." The vines released Ásbjǫrn. He slowly stood up and reverted back to his elven form. As he took in the fresh scent of the forest air mixed with Thamyris' powerful words, he realized he had spoken the truth. He then walked over to Cullen, whose eyes blazed with anger from such horrid accusations.

"If you ever accuse me again of hurting her," Cullen growled, his arms tensing as if ready for a fight, "I don't care what form you take. I will kill you." With a protective stance, Ásbjǫrn lifted Tiatria from Cullen's arms and refused to let her go. Cullen's expression told him to back off, but Ásbjǫrn knew he needed to supervise her.

"We need to put her on the altar," Ásbjǫrn said softly, still gazing at Tiatria's unconscious form. Nodding in agreement, Cullen gently laid her on the stone altar, careful not to jostle her too much.

Ásbjǫrn then removed his tunic and placed it over Tiatria's naked body, providing some warmth and modesty. Thamyris approached the altar with his staff and moved outward in front of him as a guide. The ancient runes etched into its surface glowed faintly as he reached the altar, and his staff tapped it against the stone.

The elf placed his staff off to the side and extended his fingertips towards Tiatria's head. He first felt her silky hair, following it until he reached her forehead. With a gentle touch, Thamyris placed his hand on her skin, feeling for any sign of life.

Maxwell's eyes widened as he took in the breathtaking sight before him. At the northern corner of the room stood a small stone altar, and then he noticed there were three more altars on each side of the room adorned with symbols for each of the four elements - earth, water, fire, and air. The intricate alchemy symbols were painted in their corresponding colors, creating a vibrant display against the dark walls of the chamber.

Ásbjǫrn approached the east symbol, painted in a calming shade of blue representing water. The altar here held a bowl of clear water and another pillar candle. Once again, Ásbjǫrn used his powers to light the candle and spoke his prayers in elvish.

Next he went to the south symbol called for fire, and it was painted in a fierce shade of red. Three pillar candles sat upon the altar here, and Ásbjǫrn lit them one by one with precise movements of his hands. Each time he muttered prayers in elvish that filled Maxwell with wonder.

Then, Ásbjǫrn came to the west symbol - air. The pale blue paint on this wall seemed to almost glow under the soft light of the candles.

Finally, he went to the symbol of the north; a crown of ivy seemed to wrap itself around his head. In front of the symbol was a small altar holding a bowl of rich soil and lush ivy. A tall pillar candle stood at its center; its flickering flame from his right index finger cast dancing shadows on the walls. Ásbjǫrn lit the candle, speaking words in elvish that Maxwell couldn't understand.

With confidence, Ásbjǫrn pulled out an athame from his belt - a ritual dagger used in magical ceremonies - and pointed its blade down towards the ground. As if cutting through thin air itself, he walked around the room in a circular motion while holding his left hand upwards. A shimmering white light followed the path of his blade, forming a perfect circle around the area. Ásbjǫrn completed the circle and stepped back with a satisfied smile, his task complete.

Maxwell couldn't help but feel a sense of awe at the elf's mastery of magic and the connection he had to the elements. He could only imagine what powerful forces were now present in the room, ready to assist them in their quest.

In all the years Ásbjǫrn had dwelled in the forest, he had never seen humans witness such sacred rites. Thamyris spoke words in a melodic elvish tongue, his voice carrying the weight of prayers as he sought to complete his task of retrieving his wife and Priestess. Through his mind, Thamyris could see Tiatria standing before two magnificent dragons, her regal form exuding power and grace. He couldn't hear anything the three were saying between them. Cullen, by her side, felt his stomach twist with worry and concern. He held her hand tightly in both of his, like a lifeline, while he prayed with all his heart. His mother's rosary was intertwined between his fingers as a source of comfort and strength, as he whispered fervent pleas to the one God, hoping for a miracle to heal his beloved.

As the moments passed, a sense of dread fueled Cullen's anxiety grew until it threatened to make him sick, as he saw no change in Tiatria's condition. Tears escaped his eyes and fell upon the sanctified floor of the Temple, a symbol of his desperation. And then, suddenly, a burst of piercing white light exploded through the temple, throwing everyone backward in shock and confusion. Cullen shielded his eyes with his right hand, still clutching the rosary with trembling fingers while still holding Tiatria's hand in the other. As the light faded, he could see that everyone else was struggling to make sense of what was happening and regain their vision as well. But what they saw next was beyond anything they could have imagined.

A man emerged from the fading light, flying gracefully above Tiatria's body with pure white wings spread wide behind him. He was breathtakingly beautiful - with long blonde hair cascading down his back, it shone like spun gold in the light, piercing blue eyes that seemed to hold an otherworldly power, and skin as pale as moonlight. Adorned in resplendent armor and carrying a set of keys on his leather belt, he emanated an aura of divinity.

In that moment, Cullen knew that this was no ordinary man - this was an angel who came to save them all. And as he continued to pray for Tiatria's healing, he felt a glimmer of hope in his heart.

Ásbjǫrn slowly crawled over to Thamyris, his movements shaky and hesitant. With a trembling hand, he reached out and took hold of the elf's right hand, his grip strong and determined. In that moment, Thamyris' vision changed as if a veil had been lifted from his eyes. He could now see what was happening before him, a being of ethereal beauty and power - a rare and unexpected encounter with a creature he had only ever heard tales about.

Thamyris recognized the being before them as a Peri, though its appearance was unlike anything he had seen or imagined. Its skin shimmered with an otherworldly glow, and its wings stretched tall and proud behind it. But there was something different about this Peri - a trace of darkness in its aura that set it apart from the ones Thamyris had been taught about.

As Cullen gasped at the sight before him, the Peri turned its gaze towards him. "You're an angel!" Cullen exclaimed, his voice filled with awe and wonder.

The ethereal being looked at Cullen with a mixture of curiosity and amusement. "Yes," it replied simply, "and no."

Confusion clouded Cullen's face at the cryptic answer. "Why have you come to us?" he asked hesitantly. Cullen's mind reeled at the contradiction.

The angel smiled kindly at them. "Never before has the words of the One God been uttered here in the Temple of the Pagan God," it explained. Cullen's heart dropped as he realized the gravity of his actions - speaking words of blasphemy in such a sacred place could spell disaster for him. But then the angel's words took an unexpected turn. "Take heart, young one," it said soothingly, "you have done something all would have deemed impossible."

Cullen's brow furrowed in confusion. "What have I done?" he asked.

The angel's smile grew wider, its eyes shining with a sense of hope and possibility. "A human of the One God has prayed for the restoration of one they love from the old Gods," it revealed. "It seems your world is not as selfish as we once thought."

Maxwell, who had been listening intently, finally rose to his feet. "What does that mean?" he asked, his voice laced with curiosity.

The angel turned to face him, its gaze warm and understanding. "It means that your world is not lost," it answered. "And old wounds can be healed." Cullen and Maxwell exchanged looks of disbelief and joy as they realized the significance of this message from a divine being.

The ethereal being gazed upon the young knight with a gentle smile, emanating warmth and kindness, their luminous form radiating an otherworldly aura. "It means I'm going to help you!" Its voice echoed like a chorus of bells, filled with untold wisdom and power. "In your world, I am known as the Archangel Michael, servant of the one God. But in this world, I am a Peri - a type of fairy that embodies harmony between two worlds."

With a graceful gesture, the Peri raised its hand high above its head and summoned forth a magnificent sword from thin air. It glinted in the sunlight and emitted an otherworldly glow, mesmerizing Cullen, who had never seen anything so beautiful before. "This is Ka'imil," the Peri announced, "the dragon's promise. With it, you can slay the dragon and its mistress."

Cullen watched in awe as the blade slowly drifted towards him without hesitation, his right hand instinctively reaching out to grasp its hilt as if it were meant to be there all along. "I give this to you, young knight," the Peri declared, "to vanquish the evil plaguing your world." Cullen bowed his head in gratitude, grateful for the powerful weapon bestowed upon him. He could not help but think about Tiatria - the woman he loved, "Thank you, but what of Tia? I prayed for her safety, not for a sword."

To everyone's surprise, including Maxwell, who was stunned by Cullen's boldness in addressing an archangel so casually, Cullen braced himself for any reprimand or divine punishment that may come his way. But instead of anger, the archangel simply smiled in response. "She will awaken soon," it assured them all. "She will awaken soon. She is communing with creatures of this old world to aid your cause. And when she sees this sword, she will know what you have done for her. And she will also tell you the price you must pay for this gift."

"Price?" Cullen questioned, still perplexed by these cryptic words. But before he could get any answers, the Peri vanished into thin air, leaving everyone awestruck by the otherworldly encounter. All were left speechless as they processed what had just happened.

Chapter 21

Tiatria's bright sapphire eyes lit up with hope and admiration as she gazed at the majestic dragons, Myrae and Naga. "When will you come? How?" she asked eagerly. Myrae chuckled; her green scales seemed to shimmer in the non-existent sunlight as she adored the elf's enthusiasm. The two dragons were lounging in front of her, their tails gently swaying back and forth as they basked in the warmth of the elf's admiration. "Simply call upon us when you have a need, and we will come," Myrae replied with a hint of amusement in her voice. Naga lifted his head, his piercing blue eyes scanning the surroundings. "You are being summoned back, Priestess, and you must go," he stated firmly, turning to look at Tiatria. "But before you do, there is something you should know."

Cullen leaned his sword against the ancient stone altar before placing a comforting hand on Tiatria's forehead. "Tia, Wake up," he pleaded in a hushed tone. Ásbjǫrn had found a nearby blanket and gently draped it over Tiatria's delicate and lithe frame with it. He then turned to Cullen with apologetic eyes. "I must apologize for my earlier actions. I judged you too quickly without knowing the full story," he said with remorse. Cullen looked at the towering elf, his honey-brown eyes filled with sincerity as he nodded in understanding.

As Cullen watched over her, his heart skipped a beat as he noticed the color returning to her cheeks. He couldn't hold back tears of relief and joy from welling up in his amber eyes.

Tiatria slowly started to stir; her eyelids slowly fluttered open as her gaze landed. "Cullen?" she whispered, her voice soft and weak. Overcome with emotion, Cullen could only nod before leaning down to kiss her hand. She quickly realized she was naked as she felt the cold stone of the altar against her skin, which made her feel vulnerable. "Why am I naked?" she questioned, confusion evident on her face. Cullen let out a half sob, half chuckle as he replied, "I'm sorry, I forgot to grab your clothes." He gently kissed her hand again.

Slowly, Cullen helped Tiatria sit up. She noticed others gathering around her. Her sight landed on Thamyris, who was looking at her with a small smile. "Welcome back," he said softly. Cullen reached under the blanket and pulled out Ásbjǫrn's shirt, helping Tiatria put it on herself. She then pushed the blanket away. Cullen used his body as a shield to protect her from revealing her bare body. Cullen quickly lifted her up and off the altar, avoiding any awkwardness. Tiatria noticed Cullen picking up his sword, and a look of concern crossed her face. "So this is Ka'imil?" she asked, her fingers brushing against Cullen's as she looked at him. "Yes," he confirmed with a nod.

A shadow of worry passed over Tiatria's face before she spoke again, grasping Cullen's hand tightly. "You mustn't use this sword," she warned urgently. Confusion and concern filled the faces of the others as they listened in on their conversation. "What do you mean? We have to use this sword to defeat Amalia and her dragon," Cullen reasoned.

Tiatria's face contorted with distress. "No, Cullen, you can't. You mustn't!" she protested.

"What do you mean? Cullen's right, we have to use it." Maxwell interjected, crossing his arms over his chest. He was curious to know what could possibly frighten Tiatria so much to take away their only hope of defeating a deranged priestess and her dragon. Still trying to grasp everything that had happened with the angel or peri

- whatever it was - Maxwell added, "The entity said there would be a price. I imagine you know what that is, don't you?"

Tiatria's resigned expression clearly showed on her face as she lowered her head, admitting reluctantly, "Yes."

Cullen's hand dropped from his chin as he fell deep into thought before turning back to his companions with determination in his eyes. "Whatever the price may be, I'll pay it, gladly. It's a small sacrifice for the safety of your world and mine," he declared firmly. With that, Tiatria left the temple with Ka'imil in hand, leaving behind a worried group of friends. Cullen followed after her, leaving the others behind. But by the time he reached the side entrance, she was nowhere to be seen. As an elf, she was agile and swift like a deer, disappearing into the forest without a trace.

Maxwell emerged from the temple, his long hair flowing behind him as he strode to a standstill behind Cullen. His dark eyes held a mixture of sadness and concern as he surveyed the scene before him.

Cullen's face mirrored his emotion as he gave a deep and long sigh. "She's gone," his voice thick with regret.

"Yes, she is," Maxwell replied, his voice in a solemn tone.

Thamyris started making his way towards Cullen and Maxwell. He reached down to pick up his staff from the altar, his tall frame casting an imposing figure in the dimly lit temple. "Don't ever question me again in front of outsiders," he scolded Ásbjǫrn,"I am your High Priest and your king. My judgement is never to be questioned, do you understand?" Thamyris' words were sharp and commanding as he awaited a response.

Ásbjǫrn bowed his head in submission, clearly understanding the gravity of his mistake. "Yes, my king," he said in a subdued tone.

Thamyris then turned to walk away but not before issuing a final warning, "And if you ever dare to take me as a lover again at Beltane, let me know beforehand if I am to wake up alone. I apologize if I didn't satisfy you enough to stay."

Without another word, Thamyris turned and began to walk away. But before he could take more than a few steps, Ásbjǫrn's face displayed shock and horror as his hand shot out instinctively and grabbed Thamyris' wrist. "That had nothing to do with it." There was a hint of embarrassment in his voice as he revealed the truth. Thamyris stopped in his tracks and turned to face Ásbjǫrn, curious as to what he meant. With Ásbjǫrn touching him, he could see the sincerity in Ásbjǫrn's eyes.

"I didn't leave because you didn't satisfy me," Ásbjǫrn continued, his expression now remorseful. "In fact, I found myself wanting for more."

Thamyris narrowed his eyes in confusion, still not understanding why Ásbjǫrn would have left then. The elf's next words caught Thamyris off guard, "You don't even see how extraordinary you are, do you?" the elf's deep voice sent shivers down Thamyris' spine. "And that's not why I left," Ásbjǫrn added softly, causing Thamyris' face to flush with embarrassment.

"Then I...I don't understand," he stammered. His heart raced as he felt overwhelmed by the elf's words and the intensity of his gaze.

Ásbjǫrn let out a soft, contented sigh as he pulled Thamyris close, his hot blood coursing through his veins as Thamyis felt what was a comforting caress touch his cheek. "Last night was a gift from nature, allowing us to act upon our desires," he whispered in Thamyris' ear. The warmth of Ásbjǫrn's body enveloped him, and the scent of pine and earth filled his senses.

Thamyris felt Ásbjǫrn's large hand cup his face, his touch gentle but possessive. "I have lived for many centuries, far longer than you," Ásbjǫrn spoke with a hint of sorrow in his voice. "In that time, I have taken many lovers to quell my burning desires. But never has my heart stirred for anyone as it does for you." Thamyris could feel the weight of Ásbjǫrn's words.

Thamyris couldn't help but take deep breaths as he looked into Ásbjǫrn's intense stare; they spoke volumes of truth. He could feel the walls he had built around himself slowly crumbling away. He had always been an outcast among his kind, rejected by both male and female companions. It was hard to believe that someone like Ásbjǫrn could want him now. But the way Ásbjǫrn gazed at him spoke volumes of truth.

"Last night was something I have yearned for, for a very long time," Ásbjǫrn confessed, his gaze intense and unwavering. "Why did you wait until Beltane, until I left the forest?" his curiosity overpowering his hesitations. "You had all this time to tell me."

Ásbjǫrn blushed and looked away for a moment before meeting Thamyris' eyes again. "Because every time I tried to speak with you, my stomach tied itself into knots and short of breath. I know you were never one for ceremonies and left such things to your Father. My nature calls me to the wilds, to be free in the simplicity of nature most of the time. And when you left, I feared that you may never return. That the outside world would claim your life or that you would choose to stay there forever." His words were hesitant but filled with sincerity. "But when you came back, unharmed and strong. You instantly, seamlessly stepped into your role as our King and High Priest, my heart swelled with joy. Seeing you come into your own awakened something in me." With each word, Thamyris could feel his heart opening to Ásbjǫrn's confession, and he realized that perhaps he had been blind to the love that was right in front of him all along.

Thamyris took a deep breath, his heart pounding with anticipation as he reached out to touch Ásbjǫrn's cheek. As their hands met, Thamyris could feel the warmth and strength radiating from Ásbjǫrn's touch. "Beltane was the perfect reason to claim my feelings for you, to see if there was something there." Thamyris trembled with emotion, "And is there?" he questioned, needing to hear the words from Ásbjǫrn's own lips. Without hesitation, Ásbjǫrn pulled Thamyris into a deep, passionate kiss, their lips meeting in perfect harmony. As they kissed, Ásbjǫrn felt himself losing control, his hands gripping onto the sides of Thamyris's face, causing him to drop his staff as his hands found their way to Ásbjǫrn's, holding onto them tightly as if they were the only thing keeping him grounded.

But all too soon, Ásbjǫrn tore himself away, fur rising from his skin and covering his back and arms, his nails elongating into sharp claws. Without Ásbjǫrn's touch, Thamyris' world once again went black. "Ásbjǫrn? What's happening?" he called out in confusion and fear. But then he felt Ásbjǫrn's large hands touching his trembling ones again and he looked up to see him in mid-transformation.

"This is why I left last night," he confessed, shame evident in his eyes. Thamyris watched as the fur slowly receded and the claws turned back into normal human fingers. "I didn't want to risk hurting you. Sometimes I wake up like this, as a bear, and if startled, things can get...violent." The sadness in Ásbjǫrn's voice broke Thamyris' heart. "But I promise you, I would tear my heart from my breast before ever consciously hurting you."

As Thamyris took a moment to reflect on the events of the previous night, he came to the realization that Ásbjǫrn had only left out of concern and deep care for his safety. What seemed like a one-time encounter was never meant to be just that. And in distancing himself from the others, including Thamyris, Ásbjǫrn was protecting him from all potential harm. Thamyris could not help but feel touched by his protective nature. It was a bittersweet way to live, and it made Thamyris appreciate the sacrifices that Ásbjǫrn had made for not only his well-being but for all the others even more. Thamyris could not help but feel a sense of loneliness that only he felt all this time, but now Ásbjǫrn as well - that they were destined to never find love from another. "After all this time, I thought I was alone in this world, doomed to never experience love." Ásbjǫrn stood tall and met Thamyris' gaze with determination. "If you choose to continue down this path with me. I must warn you of the dangers you are putting yourself in. There are times when I lose control and my primal instincts, and the bear within me takes over. If that happens, I ask that you remain calm and back away slowly, with confidence. Running will only incite me to give chase and succumb to my wild side. But rest assured, once I regain my senses, I can change back, and no harm will come to you." This warning came with a sense of protectiveness and honesty that touched Thamyris deeply. "And there is something else I want to make clear, something that I do not require of you." Thamyris was taken aback by these words; no one had ever told him they didn't need anything from him before. It was both surprising and refreshing. "I will not ask you to dedicate your heart to me, if you do not wish it. My heart roams as nature dictates, and as I have observed your interactions with the bearded human, I suspect yours does as well." Thamyris felt foolish for longing after Maxwell all this time, even though his feelings were never reciprocated. It was time to let go of this futile dream. But hearing those words from Ásbjǫrn gave him a feeling of acceptance he never had before. It filled him with hope.

Ásbjǫrn's fingers held Thamyris's chin as his eyes melted in honeyed sugar. "My only desire is to share in it." Ásbjǫrn's words brought tears to Thamyris' eyes as he smiled, "I wish to share in it and more, if you'll have me." In that moment, Ásbjǫrn leaned in and kissed him passionately but with a newfound restraint. They both knew that their connection was more than just physical desire, and they were ready to explore it further together.

)o(

Tiatria stood in the sacred temple of the Goddess, her hands gently resting on the altar as she gazed upon the Ka'imil she'd placed before her. A priestess approached with an ornate white scabbard, intricately detailed with mithril inlay, which she presented to Tiatria. With reverence, Tiatria accepted the scabbard and carefully slid the sword into its protective embrace. She then lifted her right hand over the blade, whispering ancient elven prayers that imbued it with powerful enchantments. Her touch caused the sword to emit an ethereal glow, growing brighter and more intense with each word spoken. This was no ordinary blessing - it was a spell that would seal the sword to its scabbard, ensuring that it was unremovable; only Tiatria's chosen could wield it. As the light faded and the seal affirmed its hold, she knew that Cullen would never wield this weapon either against her or without her permission.

"Tia?" Cullen's voice called out from outside the temple. He had been searching for her since her sudden disappearance, wandering aimlessly through the unfamiliar surroundings. Unbeknownst to him, Tiatria was just steps away.

"Tia?" he called out once more, his voice filled with worry and longing. Emerging gracefully from behind a cascading curtain of branches from a towering weeping willow, Tiatria answered his call in a calm and composed voice. "I'm here," she replied, her eyes steady and resolute.

Cullen spun around and locked eyes with her, his strides quickening as he closed the distance between them. A sense of urgency radiated from him as he rushed her for answers with determination in his eyes. "What have you done with the sword?" His expression was a mix of fear, confusion, and desperation.

Tiatria remained composed, her face betraying no emotion. "I have sealed it. It can no longer be used," she stated matter-of-factly.

Cullen's eyes widened in shock, disbelief written all over his face. "What?!" he exclaimed, litely shaking his head in denial. "Why would you do that? How could you do that? That sword is our only hope to defeat that dragon bastard!" His grip on her arms tightened, fingers digging into her skin. "Do you even realize what you've done?"

Tiatria remained unfazed by his outburst. "Do you even understand the true meaning of that blade? Do you know what using it entails?" Tiatria's voice was firm and unyielding as she held his gaze.

Cullen took a step back, suddenly aware of the change in her demeanor. For the first time, her eyes burned with a dangerous fire. Normally, her eyes were calm and soothing. However now, they were filled with determination and anger. He let out a sigh and ran a hand through his hair, trying to comprehend the situation.

"Then tell me," He pleaded, putting a hand on his hip and rubbing the back of his neck with the other. "I need to understand."

But Tiatria shook her head adamantly, her arms waving dismissively. "No!" she snapped, causing Cullen to snort in frustration. "Why not?" he retorted, noticing the tears forming in her eyes. "Because you don't understand the true cost of wielding that sword," she replied sharply.

Cullen dropped his hand from his face, feeling defeated. "If you won't tell me, then it seems we're at an impasse." he said sadly, "And it also seems that you don't trust me enough to share this burden," he said with hurt evident in his tone. Without another word and a heavy heart, he turned and walked away, determined to find another solution because there had to be one.

)o(

Thamyris and Ásbjǫrn had made their way back to the grand, towering castle that was built from the insides of a tree. As they entered, servants bowed and greeted them, leading them down long corridors lined with tapestries and paintings. They finally reached Thamyris' throne room, where Ásbjǫrn helped him settle into his ornate, high-backed chair. The sensation of sitting on velvet cushions on the throne was still foreign to Thamyris, who was still adjusting to his role as King.

As he settled in and reclined into the chair, Maxwell and Cullen burst through the large ornate doors, clearly agitated. "We have a problem," Maxwell announced in a rushed voice. Thamyris tightened his grip on Ásbjǫrn's arm so he could see his friends and learn what they had to say.

"What? What happened?" he questioned, his brows furrowed in concern. Cullen let out a heavy sigh as he paced back and forth in front of the throne, his hands on his hips.

"Tia has sealed the sword," he said with frustration evident in his voice. "I can't use it to kill Nimriar or Amalia." Hearing that someone wanted to harm his sister still pained Thamyris deeply. Even though she had crossed a line that could never be forgiven, the thought of losing her still hurt.

"What? Why?" Thamyis questioned, searching for answers.

Cullen gave the king an honest look. "I don't know. I wish I could understand it myself." Cullen admitted as he stopped pacing and looked at Thamyris. He gave a slight shake of the head. "She won't tell me what using the sword entails or what consequences it may bring. We're at a stalemate for now."

Ásbjǫrn looked at Thamyris with an idea. "Perhaps you can reason with your wife," he suggested. "She may be more willing to open up to you about her decision."

Thamyris turned his head to face Ásbjǫrn, a hint of bitterness in his tone. "She's no more my wife than yours. If she truly was anyone's wife, she would be Cullen's. But if she won't share her thoughts with him, then there's little hope of me getting through to her."

Maxwell spoke up, his eyes fixed on Thamyris. "Maybe she'll tell me," he said cautiously, weighing his words carefully. He then looked at Cullen and then back at the king who both seemed equally puzzled. "What makes you think she would be amenable to talking to you?" Thamyris questioned skeptically.

Maxwell turned and began walking away. Over his shoulder, he replied, "Because she owes me." And with that, he left without another word. The castle fell into a heavy silence; each man lost in their own thoughts and worries of the future.

)o(

Tiatria knelt before the grand temple of the Goddess Elen, her slender fingers clasped tightly together as she poured out fervent prayers seeking clarity and comfort. The air around her was still and heavy with the sweet and heady scent of incense and fresh-cut flowers - a familiar fragrance that always comforted her troubled mind. As she poured out her heart to her goddess, an otherworldly light came from a moon pool in the center of the temple, which was behind her. As night was always in this part of the forest, the pool glowed with the light of the moon and all its many blessings. It had a rainbow moonstone inlay around the pool, lily pads and their flowers floated around the pool. A gentle breeze swept through the sanctuary, rustling the leaves of oak trees, vines and delicate tapestries hanging from the walls, carrying with it the sweet essence of spring.

Elen's melodic voice echoed through Tiatria's mind, filling her with a sense of peace and reverence. "Why do you seek my guidance, my child?" Her words were like a soothing melody, wrapping around Tiatria's soul.

Tears fell from Tiatria's eyes as she lifted her tear-stained face from the altar to gaze at the towering statue of her goddess. "Because I cannot bear to lose him," she whispered, her voice trembling with emotion. "He is my everything."

Elen's voice grew stern but remained full of love. "Even if it means sacrificing your people and causing the deaths of thousands of innocents?"

Tiatria turned away, overcome with agitation at her goddess' words. They pierced through her heart like a swarm of bees, stinging her very soul. "But he is my everything," she pleaded, asking for Elen to understand as tears streamed down her cheeks.

The goddess spoke again, her words carrying a weight beyond measure. "As my priestess, you are bound to follow my will and word. You cannot play favorites. All must walk the paths that have been laid before them, no matter the pain or sacrifice."

Tiatria's heart ached at Elen's words, knowing deep down that they were true. But the thought of losing him was unbearable. Tears spilled from her eyes as she struggled to find the answer to her own conflicting desires.

Elen's voice trailed off into a heavy silence, the weight of her words hanging in the air. "I must ask you," she finally spoke again, her tone somber and pensive, "Is it truly worth all the death and suffering to keep him safe? To share in his brief mortal life as it slowly dwindles away with each passing moment? Even if it means those remaining years are filled with an overwhelming sense of sorrow and loss?" The gravity of her question hung on every word as if daring Tiatria to answer truthfully. Her heart clenched at the thought of such a bittersweet existence, torn between love and pain, joy and despair.

Tiatria snapped her head up to stare at the statue, but no more words came. She was left with her own thoughts and a heavy decision to make, knowing that whatever path she chose would have consequences for both herself and those she loved.

She emerged from the grand entrance of the temple, carefully pushing the thick vines of the massive weeping willow. She was met by Maxwell, who stood waiting for her with his arms crossed against his chest. Moonlight filtered through the branches, casting dappled shadows on the ground. "How do you know where the temple is?" Tiatria asked curiously, noticing the exhaustion in his eyes. Maxwell shifted off the nearby tree and approached her slowly. "I haven't slept much since being here. I wander through the night, trying to tire myself out. It's my way of coping, I suppose." His words were laced with sadness. Tiatria's eyes softened; her heart ached for him, knowing he was still struggling to come to terms with Dorian's death.

Maxwell's attention then shifted to Ka'imil, resting in its scabbard as it was being held in Tiatria's hands. "Care to tell me why you're so afraid of Cullen using that sword? Your concern seems almost desperate." Tiatria studied the sword for a moment before meeting Maxwell's gaze again. She tried to keep her expression neutral, not wanting to reveal too much. "It's not meant for mortal hands," she replied cryptically. But Maxwell wasn't convinced. His narrowed eyes showed his suspicion. "If that were true, it wouldn't have been given to us by an angel of all things. Care to try again?" Tiatria felt a flash of annoyance at his persistence but kept her cool. "It was a Peri, and I don't have to explain myself to you." she retorted.

Maxwell's body bristled with tension and anger. His muscles coiled like a snake, ready to strike. He took an assertive step forward until his face was mere inches away from Tiatria's, his eyes burning with unbridled rage. "Yes, you do! If anyone deserves an explanation about that sword, it's me!" he spat, each word laced with venom." Cullen prayed for divine intervention to help you, to save you from whatever had caused you to have convulsions and you refused to wake up! And the sword was the answer he received!" His desperation and urgency were palpable as he continued, "It's the only thing that can kill them, don't you see?" His voice cracked with emotion as he added, "Amalia and her dragon must die before they annihilate everything in their path for blood!" Maxwell's face twisted with anger and grief as he spoke. His next words hit even harder, each one feeling like a stab in Tiatria's heart. "They would've killed you if Dorian hadn't pushed you out of the way! My King died, Cullen's father died because of that dragon, and so did Dorian!" His voice trembled with grief and determination. "Don't let their deaths be in vain," he pleaded with her, his voice softening slightly.

Maxwell's intense gaze fell upon the sword, its metallic gleam taunting and hypnotizing him. In a sudden burst of desperation, he snatched it from the elf's grasp, determined to break whatever hold it had over her. He pulled with all his might, but the sword remained resolute as if it was fused to the scabbard by her very being. As he turned to confront Tiatria, Maxwell couldn't help but notice the tears streaming down her cheeks. It was then that he realized the true reason behind her desperate attempt to seal the sword away. "This sword has a special connection between you and Cullen," he stated, his voice laced with accusations. "That's why you're so afraid of this weapon."

A pained expression crossed Tiatria's face as she nodded, confirming his suspicions. Maxwell let out a heavy sigh, his frustration melting into empathy for the tortured elf in front of him. "Please," he urged gently. "Tell me what this sword does."

For a moment, Tiatria simply wiped at her tears before meeting his gaze once more. She could see the sorrow and anguish etched on his features, and she knew she couldn't keep this burden from him any longer. "If I tell you," she began hesitantly. "it's up to you whether you want to tell Cullen or not." Maxwell shook his head, determination flashing in his eyes. "No," he interjected firmly. "No matter what you tell me, I'll leave that decision to you." Despite his words, it was clear that no matter what secrets were revealed about this cursed weapon, Maxwell would do whatever it took to protect both Tiatria and Cullen from its destructive power.

Chapter 22

Cullen took a leisurely stroll through the ornate halls of the castle, eventually stumbling upon what he had originally thought was the elven temple dedicated to their multitude of Gods. The grandiose space was filled with larger-than-life statues that Cullen recognized from his previous visits. As he passed by each one, he paused to admire their intricate details and craftsmanship, his eyes finally resting on the statue of Danu. Memories flooded back as he remembered this was where he and Tiatria had their first conversation.

He turned to leave when he heard a soft voice behind him. "Thought I'd find you here," Tiatria said, her gaze fixed on him. Maxell stood nearby, holding onto Ka'imil. With a gentle nudge from Maxell, Tiatria stepped towards Cullen and they embraced lovingly. As they gazed into each other's eyes, Cullen couldn't resist stealing a kiss, which only deepened their embrace. Maxwell then walked away to give the two their privacy. When they finally pulled away, Cullen noticed Maxwell holding a sword in his hand. His curiosity piqued, Cullen gently asked, "Did I see Maxwell holding the sword?" Tiatria's expression changed, her eyes filled with sadness as she stepped away from him. But before she could move too far, Cullen took hold of her hands in his own.

With a heavy heart, she looked up at him and whispered softly, "Yes."

Confusion crossed Cullen's face as he probed further, "What changed? You were so adamant before." Tears welled up in Tiatria's eyes as she struggled to find the words to explain herself. Seeing her distress, Cullen brushed a gentle hand against her cheek, wiping away her tears. "Why does the sword frighten you so much?" His simple question caused Tiatria to break down into sobs. Cullen's hands were rough yet gentle, calloused from years of handling a sword. He pulled her into his embrace once more, one hand cradling the back of her head as he kissed the top of it. "It's alright," he whispered, wrapping his other arm around her.

Tiatria continued to cry and struggle for words. Finally, she managed to choke out, "If you...if you use the sword, you'll die." The color drained from Cullen's face as he processed her words. Holding her even closer, he closed his eyes and said softly, "It's not true." As the tears fell Tiatria could hear Cullen's heart, the sound soothed.

But Tiatria couldn't be consoled. She feared losing him, the only man she had ever loved, especially if it was because of the cursed sword that she wanted to seal away forever. Cullen could feel the fear in her heart, and it pained him deeply. He had finally found his soulmate, and now there was a chance that they would be torn apart forever.

Cullen swayed back and forth in a gentle rhythm, cradling Tiatria in his arms as if she were a precious treasure. The warmth of her body seeped into his own, melting away any tension or worries. His voice was soft and soothing as he sang a lullaby, feeling her muscles gradually relax under his touch. A small smile curved on Tiatria's lips, basking in the comfort and safety of Cullen's embrace. His thumb brushed against her cheek with tender care, sending shivers down her spine. She wished and prayed for this moment to last forever, to be forever lost in his loving arms.

Tiatria's eyes followed Cullen's gaze towards the doorway, where Maxwell had left the sword leaning against it. During their journey back to the palace, Tiatria mentioned a ritual that needed to be performed in order for the sword to be removed from its scabbard. She hadn't divulged any further information, but Maxwell trusted her enough not to question it.

Tiatria shivered, wrapping her arms around herself as Cullen approached the weapon. Tiatria couldn't help but feel overwhelmed by the gravity of the situation, she watched as His fingers grazed over its hilt, a look of longing and determination in his eyes. His gentle but determined expression pleaded with her. "Please Tia," he murmured softly.

Tiatria stepped closer to Cullen as he lifted the blade in both hands. With reverence, she took it from him and walked towards the statue of Danu. As she reached the statue, she placed the sword carefully on either side of the rim of the bowl which was held in both of its hands. Turning back to Cullen, she retrieved her athame from her belt, a small ceremonial knife, and took his left hand in hers, turning it palm up. Using the sharp blade of her athame, she made a small cut on his palm. Then, holding his hand over the bowl, Cullen squeezed his hand and watched as the drops of his blood dripped into the water.

Feeling tears prick at her eyes, Tiatria then took her own athame and made a similar cut on her own palm. She held her hand over Danu's bowl, watching as her blood mingled with Cullen's in the water below. The two stood in awe as they watched a soft light emanating from the hilt and scabbard of the sword, peeking out from within its sheath. Suddenly, the entire room began to tremble and shake as if responding to Danu's will. The light within the scabbard danced and flickered until it burst forth in a blinding flash of pure white light that filled every corner of the room.

Cullen and Tiatria shielded their eyes as they felt a surge of energy wash over them, their bodies vibrating with power. And when they opened their eyes, they saw that the sword was now glowing with a radiant aura, pulsating with strength and purpose.

They knew then that it had been imbued with the blessing of Danu, ready to serve as her sacred weapon to stop her Priestess. Gently, Tiatria took the sword off of Danu's bowl. Cullen took it from her hands and used his right hand to pull the sword's hilt; it easily glided out of the scabbard. Unsheathed, Cullen looked at the sword; his eyes seemed to show his enchantment with the blade as it was beautifully forged.

Tiatria turned away as she closed her eyes. Tears fell from them as she wrapped her arms around herself again. She knew what would happen; she knew she spoke the words of his doom. Cullen looked at Tiatria and noticed her shoulders trembling, which prompted him to lower and re-sheath the sword before he walked over to her. Tiatria could feel Cullen's calloused hands wrap themselves around her.

As she turned within his arms, Tiatria looked up at him. She saw the love shining in his eyes like a beacon guiding them through the night. He continued to rock her gently, their bodies swaying in perfect harmony. "We'll have to return to your world tomorrow," Tiatria said in a solemn tone. Cullen's hands cupped her head, tilting it up to meet his gaze. "Then let us savor this moment and make it one to remember," he whispered in a low, passionate voice. The night belonged to them, and they held onto each other until morning came to steal them away from their sweet escape. Every second felt like an eternity of perfection as they reveled in each other's presence, lost in a world that only existed for the two of them.

Cullen's lips were a fire on Tiatria's, their passion searing through every touch and caress. His strong arms wrapped around her waist, lifting her effortlessly into his embrace. As she instinctively wrapped her legs around him, she could feel the heat and hardness of his body against hers. His body pressed firmly against hers as their tongues danced in a fiery frenzy. The flush in their cheeks mirrored the heat coursing through them as they lost themselves in each other. But as Cullen pulled away briefly, he could feel the warmth of Tiatria's breath on his neck, igniting a deeper desire within him. "We shouldn't be doing this here," he whispered to Tiatria, but before he could protest further, he found himself unable to resist her lips once more. "It's alright," she reassured him, her hands tangled in his hair, "Such an act of love is blessed when being witnessed by the gods."

Cullen couldn't help but feel a twinge of guilt for their public display of affection in such a sacred space. However in that moment, Cullen stopped worrying about the consequences of their actions and let himself be consumed by the passion between them. Cullen's skin felt like it was on fire from the inside out as he pressed Tiatria against a nearby wall. With one arm supporting her, he used his free hand to untie his pants. As his cock was released, he was shocked to find that Tiatria wasn't wearing any undergarments at all. With eager anticipation, Tiatria guided Cullen inside of her, letting out a moan as she felt him fill her completely. Feeling the heat and wetness of her desire surrounded him, causing his cock to throb with need.

Tiatria's mouth opened in a gasp as she felt Cullen filling her completely. Her fingers gripped his shoulders tightly as he began to move his hips in a steady rhythm, each thrust bringing them both closer to ecstasy. With one arm braced against the wall for support, Cullen used his free hand to hold Tiatria close to him. The sensation of their bodies pressed together, skin on skin, sent waves of pleasure through Tiatria's body. As they moved together in perfect rhythm, Tiatria's head fell back, and her breathing became ragged with pleasure. Cullen's hot breath on her neck only added fuel to the fire burning within her. As their bodies ground against each other, she could feel the sensations building in her core, making her nails dig into Cullen's skin.

As they moved together in perfect harmony, Tiatria's need for more friction became almost unbearable. Sensing this, Cullen lowered her back onto her feet and turned her around so she was facing away from him. Tiatria pulled him in close, guiding his hand between her legs and gasping as he discovered a bundle of nerves that sent electric shocks through her body. With one hand exploring her most sensitive areas, Cullen used his other hand to guide himself back inside of her.

As they continued to move together in a passionate dance, their bodies glistening with sweat, Tiatria felt Cullen's forehead press against her shoulder, his hot breath on the back of her neck. In that moment, she knew that this was where she belonged - in his arms, lost in the throes of passion.

)o(

As Thamyris strode down the hallway, his feet sunk into the plush carpet, feeling its velvety texture beneath his toes. His fingers traced along the walls, taking in the intricate designs of the hand-carved statues and feeling the smoothness of the gilded tapestries. Despite his blindness, he navigated with ease, relying on touch to guide him with precision and grace. The servants knew to stay out of his way, recognizing the powerful aura that surrounded him and understanding that he needed no assistance as he made his way through the opulent surroundings.

The silky fabric of the curtains brushed against Thamyris' hand as he carefully counted his steps. The warm aroma of roasted meats and sweet spices enveloped him, tempting his senses. He reached out and felt the smooth surface of a silk tablecloth, then gently trailed his fingers along the edges until they rested upon a large and ornate chair. As he moved to his right, he could feel the ornate carvings on the back of the chair - a symbol of his family's power. With each step, Thamyris relied on touch to guide him through the lavish dining room, determined to claim his rightful place at the head of the table.

Thamyris's fingers danced gracefully over the tablecloth, feeling its softness and intricate designs. As he reached for the utensils, his touch was met with the cool metal of the utensils, each one carefully placed in front of him. He heard the sound of wine being poured on his left and instinctively reached out, his fingers finding the base of the glass and bringing it to his lips. The smooth surface of the glass felt cool against his skin as he savored the rich taste of the vintage. Turning his head towards the source of noise, he could feel the warmth radiating from the person pouring his wine, their movements careful and precise.

"Are you just going to stand there?" he asked, a hint of amusement in his voice.

Maxwell leaned casually against the smooth wooden wall, his muscular arms folded confidently across his chest. He was holding one of his swords, the gleaming silver blade rested against his right arm, held in place by his strong grip on the hilt. As he straightened up in response to Thamyris' question, the weight of the sword provided a reassuring anchor for Maxwell's thoughts. The subtle sound of metal brushing against leather filled the air as he shifted his stance, exuding strength and control with every movement. A quiet intensity emanated from Maxwell as he spoke, his voice steady and assured. "I was seeking a peaceful moment to clear my mind," he responded with poise and purpose in his words.

Thamyris' laughter was a warm and rich sensation, like velvety smooth chocolate melting on the tongue. His hand held the delicate stem of the wine glass, fingers tracing over the intricate designs etched into the crystal. As he took a sip, the cool liquid flooded his mouth with flavors of dark berries and oak. "And you thought the dining room was the best place for that? Join me then." Maxwell's movement away from the wall was graceful but purposeful, sending a ripple of strength through the air as he settled into the chair. The elven servant's hands were soft and dexterous as they poured the wine, their presence almost ethereal as they quickly disappeared into the background once again.

Maxwell let out a deep sigh, his fingers tracing the delicate rim of his crystal wine glass as he gazed at Thamyris. The amber liquid swirled within, reflecting the soft candlelight and casting shadows across his face. "I can feel the power of the sword emanating from you. How did you persuade her to give it to you?"

Maxwell's gaze shifted to the swirling liquid in his glass, momentarily lost in thought before answering. "Well, for one, this blade is one of the two your Mother gave me." Thamyris' face grew solemn as he thought about his mother for a moment. "To answer your second question," Thamyris immediately snapped to attention, "I didn't have to do much, really. When I found her, she was leaving her temple and had the sword in hand. By the look of her, I think something must have happened that made her see the bigger picture." He took a slow sip of his rich red wine, savoring the bold flavors before continuing, "She said we'll have to return tomorrow and make our last stand. So I left the sword with her once we found Cullen." Thamyris nodded solemnly, knowing they would have to face Nimriar and Amalia once again. The weight of responsibility hung heavy on their shoulders as they prepared for what would be the final battle. The thought of having to kill his own sister, someone he loved so deeply, made Thamyris' heart twist in pain. He couldn't shake off the heaviness in his chest as he thought about the sacrifices they had all made in order to end this bloody war and bring peace back to their kingdom.

Thamyris' pointed ears twitched as he heard the heavy, deliberate footsteps of Ásbjǫrn enter the room. The sound reverberated off the walls, filling the room with a sense of weight and power. Ásbjǫrn settled into an ornate chair next to Thamyris, his muscular frame barely fitting comfortably in the seat. A sense of relief washed over him as he finally found his companions. After Maxwell had left their company in the throne room, Ásbjǫrn decided to take a walk outside of the castle, craving the fresh air and solitude away from his refined elven kin. He transformed himself into his bear form and roamed through the forest, luxuriating in the freedom and strength of his animal body. But when he spotted Maxwell and Tiatria with the sword, Ásbjǫrn's curiosity was piqued, and he followed them back to the castle. As he made his way back to the throne room, he wondered what their next move would be.

However, upon entering the lavish throne room, Ásbjǫrn realized that they were not there, and before he knew it, while searching for them, he became completely lost within the labyrinthine corridors of the castle. He had only ever visited the throne room and the courtyard on major holidays like Beltane, Samhain or Yule. The rest of the castle was a foreign territory to him. It took multiple twists and turns before he stumbled upon them in the dining room.

As wine was being poured for him, Ásbjǫrn settled deeper into his chair and looked around at his companions. "What are you discussing?" he asked casually, taking a sip of his drink. "Anything interesting?"

The atmosphere in the room was serious and tense, reflected in Thamyris' furrowed brow and Maxwell's clenched jaw. As he savored his wine, Ásbjǫrn couldn't help but think that he preferred to eat his own food and drink his homemade mead out of a deer hide skin around a crackling campfire rather than in this opulent setting. He was drawn to the simplicity and wildness of life, unlike his refined elven kin, who seemed more at home in these grand halls.

Maxwell leaned back in his chair, his fingers drumming against the wooden armrest. "Tiatria has agreed to release the sword from its scabbard," he announced to Ásbjǫrn and Thamyris, his voice low and serious. "We'll be returning to Cullen and my world to stop Amalia." Ásbjǫrn's brows furrowed as he mulled over the implications of Maxwell's words. He turned to look at Thamyris, who sat across him at the grand oak table. Without hesitation, Ásbjǫrn spoke up. "I'll go with you in the King's stead." Thamyris' posture stiffened instantly, his jaw clenching in disbelief. "Are you insane? I am the king -"

"That is precisely why you cannot go," Ásbjǫrn interrupted. "You have no heir. If you were to die, our kingdom would be left without a leader." Thamyris' face flushed red with anger as he slammed his hands on the table. "Amalia is my sister! It is my duty to stop her!" But Maxwell interjected calmly, "He is right. And without Kenithar by your side, you are a cripple." The two watched as Thamyris' nails dug into the table, leaving deep scratches in the wood as they curled into his palm. This was an insult that cut deeply for the elven king, especially coming from a mere human. "I am not a cripple," Thamyris growled through gritted teeth.

In a swift motion, Maxwell reached for a bread roll from a basket on the table and threw it casually at Thamyris, hitting him lightly on the cheek. The room fell silent as they all watched in shock, even the servants frozen in their tasks. Ásbjǫrn's eyes widened as fur began to stand on end as he stood up from his chair, his fingers curling into claws. "THAT'S ENOUGH!" he roared, his voice echoing a bear. "There was no need for that!"

Maxwell remained composed, sitting back in his chair as he casually took a sip from his wine glass. "I just proved your point," he stated calmly, "I'm not unjust or unkind but I *refuse* to see another person, blind or otherwise, struck down by those two." He then left without another word. Leaving Ásbjǫrn and Thamyris alone in the dining room, Ásbjǫrn turned his head as Thamyris' face was contorted in anger and pain. Ásbjǫrn was about to put his right hand on Thamyris' left shoulder. "I don't need comfort!" he snapped as he pushed himself off the table with his knuckles. He walked away without another word.

)o(

Cullen buried his face into Tiatria's shoulder, the heat from their bodies igniting a fiery passion between them. Their hips slammed together in a fierce and primal rhythm, each thrust driving them closer to the brink of ecstasy. Tiatria's left arm gripped the back of his head, pulling him closer as she gasped and moaned with each thrust. The air was thick with the heady scent of their sweat and desire, fueling their primal urges. The scent of sex and sweat filled the air around them, intensifying their already overwhelming desire. With every movement, their skin brushed against each other like flames, scorching their senses and fueling their lust. Their faces were flushed and glistening with sweat, their bodies trembling with need. Cullen's hands gripped her hips with a primal possessiveness, guiding her movements as they moved in perfect synchronization. Each thrust sent jolts of pleasure coursing through them, building towards an inevitable climax.

Cullen's left hand tangled into Tiatria's hair, pulling her head back as he plunged deeper into her. "I love you," he growled, lost in the intensity of their connection. As their movements grew more urgent, their legs shook beneath them. His hand cupped her breast possessively, eliciting a breathless cry from Tiatria. Every nerve was on fire as they built towards an explosive release. Her breaths came in ragged gasps as she felt herself reaching the edge. "I need you!" she moaned, her voice raw with desire. With a final, powerful thrust, they reached their climax together, screaming out each other's names in ecstasy. They collapsed onto the floor, limbs tangled and hearts racing as they rode out the aftershocks of pleasure.

"I love you," Cullen murmured as he kissed Tiatria's forehead tenderly, sending waves of adoration through her entire being. They lay there entwined, savoring the intensity of their love and passion for one another.

)o(

Thamyris stormed through the grand hall of the temple, his chest heaving with anger and tears streaming down his face. He cursed himself for forgetting his staff in the throne room, now forced to rely on his memory and hope that nothing would block his path. As he stumbled towards the side entrance, his hands grasped the raspberry vines hanging down the temple's side entrance for support. The sharp thorns pierced his skin, adding to the pain already coursing through him.

Finally, he reached the cool interior of the temple and made his way towards the altar, desperation driving him forward. But in his haste, he tripped over the base of the altar, only barely catching himself with outstretched arms before crashing onto the cold, hard stone surface. His fingernails dug into the rough stone, splitting and cracking under the force of his grip.

With a primal scream, Thamyris released all of his pent-up anger and pain from this humiliating moment. Deep inside, he knew that Maxwell was right, and deeper inside, even he knew it too. But for now, all he could feel was the overwhelming weight of shame and frustration consuming him, threatening to drown him in its depths. The dim light filtering through the canopy of tree leaves left an eerie glow on his contorted features as he let out another guttural cry of anguish and defeat.

Thamyris' heart nearly stopped as a large hand gently descended upon his left shoulder. The familiar scent of leather and earth filled his senses, bringing a sense of comfort and grounding; it was Ásbjǫrn.

Overwhelmed with frustration and helplessness, Thamyris couldn't hold back the tears any longer. He didn't care about the kingdom's expectations for him to produce an heir or the fact that he was blind. All he wanted was to end Amalia's cruel reign and bring peace to both the forest and the human world.

Thamyris felt the warmth in Ásbjǫrn's large, calloused hand which held his right cheek. Thamyris pulled his face away from the warmth of Ásbjǫrn's touch. "Go away!" he snapped. He refused to let anyone see him as weak. He turned his head, refusing to show his face; Ásbjǫrn's heart ached for the one he loved. "I can't go away," he told him gently, his hands attempting to force him to turn around. Thamyris refused to show Ásbjǫrn any form of weakness. "I can't leave you," said Ásbjǫrn as he moved to face Thamyris, his hands gently holding Thamyris' face. Ásbjǫrn's warm hands caused Thamyris to see the pain in Ásbjǫrn's eyes. "I can't leave you, not now. Not when you are in need of comfort."

Hearing those words coming from Ásbjǫrn's low and sultry voice gave Thamyris a sensation of comfort. He felt his face grow warm first; then it washed over his whole body. It was a warm, comforting feeling, as if he'd been wrapped in the softest blanket.

Thamyris closed his eyes as he felt Ásbjǫrn's lips press against his forehead. "I wish there was more I could do to help you," Ásbjǫrn spoke, his voice full of empathy. Ásbjǫrn's arms then wrapped themselves around Thamyris, his right hand holding the back of his love's head. "If only our bond extended beyond physical touch...if only I knew the ritual." Thamyris couldn't believe he'd say such a thing for someone who prized their freedom beyond anything else in the world. To be bound to him in such a way was a huge sacrifice. Thamyris' fingers held onto Ásbjǫrn's strong arms. "For someone who claims they don't want to be bound to anyone," Thamyris choked out, "you seem willing to bind yourself to me."

With a gentle gesture, Ásbjǫrn's left hand turned Thamyris' face back to him. He then seamlessly intertwined with his right hand, offering him both strength and comfort. "To give you back your sight and restore your independence? Without hesitation," he replied sincerely. His unwavering determination and sincerity shone in his gaze as he looked into Thamyris' teary eyes.

Feeling the warmth and strength of Ásbjǫrn's touch, tears threatened to spill from Thamyris' eyes once again. "You make it hard for me to keep an open mind about loving anyone else," he teased back with a small smile, grateful for Ásbjǫrn's unfailing support and friendship. The two stood there for a moment, the sound of nature surrounding them as they shared a silent understanding and bond. Thamyris knew he was lucky to have someone like Ásbjǫrn in his life. To know he was willing to give up even an inch of his freedom to help him showed the truest nature of Ásbjǫrn's heart. And in knowledge, he couldn't imagine facing his struggles without him by his side.

Ásbjǫrn's hand, roughened by years of roaming the wilds but still gentle, lifted Thamyris' chin with a touch as soft as a feather. Their lips met in a slow, passionate dance, each movement conveying the depth of their desire for one another. As their hands intertwined, exploring and learning every contour and crevice, Thamyris' fingers threaded through Ásbjǫrn's auburn locks, pulling him closer until there was no space left between them. The heat from their bodies mingled and intensified as they molded together, losing themselves in the moment. With expert fingers, Ásbjǫrn deftly unlaced the king's pants, his own desire growing with each passing second.

A low, animalistic growl rumbled from Ásbjǫrn's throat as his fingers slowly, gently tugged at the laces of Thamyris' trousers which dropped to the ground, baring his hardened cock. With a primal hunger in his eyes, with a swift motion, Ásbjǫrn hoisted the elf onto the altar. Thamyris broke their heated kiss, gasping for air while feeling the heat of Ásbjǫrn's lips trail down his neck.

"We shouldn't do this on the altar," Thamyris weakly protested.

But Ásbjǫrn only smirked, his hands exploring Thamyris' body as he whispered into his ear. "What could be more natural or fitting than to worship Cernunnos here, on this sacred altar?" And with that, he penetrated Thamyris with one finger, causing a moan to escape from the king's lips.

"I should have done this when we first slept together," Ásbjǫrn murmured as he added a second finger, skillfully finding a pleasurable spot inside Thamyris that made stars explode behind his closed eyelids. His left hand clutched at Ásbjǫrn's neck for support as he leaned back against the altar. With a mischievous grin, Ásbjǫrn watched as Thamyris writhed with pleasure, his fingers working their magic within him. "Do you like that, my king?" he whispered, savoring the flushed cheeks and passionate cries coming from Thamyris.

Ásbjǫrn's fingers traced the outline of Thamyris' trembling body, setting his skin ablaze with a searing heat that spread through every fiber of his being. With agonizing slowness, he pulled away from Thamyris' slick warmth and began toying with the laces of his pants. Every touch of his fingers felt like red-hot needles piercing into Thamyris' flesh, igniting a primal fire within him.

As Thamyris willingly opened himself wider, he braced for the onslaught of pleasure that was about to consume him. Ásbjǫrn's hands gripping his hips tighter, pulling him closer till their bodies pressed together, Thamyris legs hung over Ásbjǫrn's hips.

Ásbjǫrn's hand tangled in the dark locks of Thamyris' hair, gripping tightly as he guided his pulsing length to his lover's slick entrance. The anticipation and intensity between them were palpable, a heady mixture of past pain and insatiable longing coursing through their bodies.

"I promise you, it won't hurt like before. I've prepared you," Ásbjǫrn assured in a deep, husky voice laced with hunger and need. And then, with one powerful thrust, Ásbjǫrn was sheathed deep inside Thamyris. A sharp cry escaped Thamyris' lips as he tilted his head back, feeling a mix of pleasure and slight discomfort.

Ásbjǫrn paused, waiting for Thamyris to adjust to his length before beginning to move together in perfect rhythm. As they moved, their bodies became coated in a thin layer of sweat, the air heavy with the musk of their passion mingled with the scent of burning candles and incense. Their movements were fluid and urgent, igniting into a blazing inferno of desire and ecstasy.

Thamyris was overcome with intense pleasure, his body trembling and writhing under the skilled touch of Ásbjǫrn's expert hands as one stroked his cock and the other held onto and caressed his left hip. Each one of these strokes sent a burst of electrifying heat through his veins, igniting every nerve in his body and driving him closer to the edge.

In this moment, there was nothing else in the world for Thamyris except for the all-consuming desire and love that bound them on the sacred altar. As their bodies moved in perfect sync, lost in a frenzy of primal passion, it was as if they were two halves of a whole - incomplete without each other. The cold stone beneath them seemed to disappear as they collided in a flurry of desperate kisses and caresses.

Ásbjǫrn knew that this was where they truly belonged - in this sacred space, worshiping each other with every touch and moan. And as Thamyris cried out his name in pure ecstasy, their bodies entwined in a symphony of pleasure, it felt as though they were gods themselves, indulging in the divine bliss of their love. The flickering flames from the candles that had been placed in different areas of the space cast a warm glow over their entangled figures, adding to the ethereal atmosphere that surrounded them. Their sweat-slicked skin glistened in the light, a testament to the intensity of their bond and the fire within them.

Ásbjǫrn's body trembled with the effort of controlling the primal bear within him. His muscles flexed and strained as he fought to maintain the perfect temperature - just hot enough to keep his momentum but cool enough not to lose control. Thamyris' body arched beneath him, their hips moving in a wild, passionate dance as they both neared the brink of ecstasy. The scent of their mingled sweat filled the air, adding to the heady atmosphere of desire.

Beads of sweat dripped down Ásbjǫrn's brow as he thrust harder and deeper, lost in a haze of pleasure. He let out a feral growl, his head thrown back in pure abandon. Thamyris' fingers dug into his own scalp as he cried out in unbridled bliss.

Their bodies moved together in a beautiful frenzy, each thrust bringing them closer to that shared moment of release. Ásbjǫrn gritted his teeth and focused on holding on until Thamyris reached climax alongside him.

And then it happened - an intense burst of pleasure surged through them like a bolt of lightning, leaving them both trembling and breathless. Thamyris felt something shift within him, and when he looked at Ásbjǫrn, whose eyes were still squeezed shut in pleasure, he could see through him as if his vision was now connected to his lover's. A deep, ethereal voice filled their minds. "By my grace, two are made one. Such is my gift to thee for such a sacred act on my altar!"

They collapsed into each other's embrace, their bodies intertwined in a tangle of limbs and passion. Overwhelmed with the intensity of their love and desire, they clung to each other for long. Ásbjǫrn collapsed onto Thamyris, who lovingly ran his fingers through the elf's luscious, auburn hair. As Ásbjǫrn opened his eyes and gasped for breath, Thamyris sat up and helped him straighten up. They shared a tearful kiss, feeling the depth of their connection and the power of the divine gift they had received.

Wrapped in each other's arms, both men laughed in pure joy and hugged tightly, lowering their heads onto each other's shoulders as they basked in the afterglow of their sacred union. Their bodies still trembled with energy, but their hearts were filled with love and contentment.

Chapter 23

Asbjǫrn's large, calloused hands cradled Thamyris' tear-stained face as they both wept. The elf then pulled Thamyris into a tight embrace, his muscular arms offering comfort and support. "I can see!" Thamyris cried out in a muffled tone, his voice filled with disbelief and overwhelming joy. Through the deep connection of their bond, he could see through Ásbjǫrn's vivid amber-brown eyes just as easily as he could with Kenithar's. He gazed up at Ásbjǫrn, his gratefulness overflowing and evident in the tears streaming down his cheeks. "I can't thank you enough for giving this part of yourself," he said, his fingers gently tracing the curves of the other's broad chest. Ásbjǫrn remained silent, his hold on his king unwavering as he trembled with adrenaline and emotion. He was still trying to process what had just transpired; Cernunnos himself had answered their desperate prayers. "I believe this is a sign that we are meant to fight," Thamyris whispered, feeling a sense of determination ignite within him. Ásbjǫrn nodded in agreement as they held each other tightly, savoring the moment of unity and strength bestowed upon them by their god. The gentle wind rustled through the trees, carrying with it the sweet scent of blooming flowers as they prepared themselves for the war and reminded themselves of the challenges ahead. To know what they shared was sacred and it reaffirmed their unbreakable bond.

Thamyris gracefully descended from the altar, his steps echoing off the stone walls of the temple. Ásbjǫrn followed closely behind, his eyes scanning the unfamiliar surroundings. As they approached a seemingly indistinguishable wall, Thamyris deftly reached out and pulled back a tapestry that had been cleverly disguised as part of the structure. The tapestry itself was made of tanned animal hide, adorned with intricate red markings depicting the symbol of their god - a full moon in the center of the tapestry, with a delicate crescent moon resting atop, completing the sacred image. Ásbjǫrn stood in awe as he watched Thamyris reveal a magnificent birch wood bow. Its intricate and elegant carvings, expertly crafted by skilled hands, glistened under the sunlight. Silver and gold inlay adorned the bow, adding to its splendor and hinting at the immense power it held.

Ásbjǫrn's eyes widened in admiration and disbelief. "The legendary bow of Cernunnos...I never thought it would be real." Thamyris looked at the bow with a mix of pride and sorrow, his fingers gently caressing the smooth wood. "My father gave this to me when I became high priest. At first, I didn't feel worthy of its immense power," he paused, looking at Ásbjǫrn before continuing, "But now, I know I must use it to slay my sister...I wonder if my father knew this day would come?"

Ásbjǫrn's expression softened as he placed a comforting hand on Thamyris' shoulder. "Nature has a way of correcting its mistakes when necessary." Thamyris understood that Ásbjǫrn wasn't referring to his sister as a mistake but rather her choices that led her away from the forest. And the choices that lead her to hundreds, if not thousands, of lives. Now, from those choices, there would be a price to pay. Looking at Thamyris was like looking at someone who had aged a thousand years in just one day.

Ásbjǫrn reached out with his right hand and gently turned Thamyris' head to face him. "I will do everything in my power to help you bear this burden." Thamyris appreciated Ásbjǫrn's words and took them to heart. He walked back to the altar and carefully placed the bow upon it, pressing his hand against the sacred stone for support.

"I wonder...do you remember the world we once called home, before we allowed humans to take it over?" Thamyris asked, his voice filled with a hint of longing. Ásbjǫrn took a step forward, crossing his arms over his chest and tilting his head solemnly. "I do, and I don't regret leaving it for a moment. Humans are selfish, careless creatures without any thought for others or for nature." He scratched the back of his head and shook it in frustration. "Although I must admit, the humans you brought here seem to have a different mindset." His eyes glimmered with hope as he looked at Thamyris. Ásbjǫrn took a deep breath as he walked over to Thamyris, which the elf could clearly see. Elven's sight was a different adjustment than a hawk's. He felt Ásbjǫrn's hands snake around his waist as his lips kissed his skin. "I'll need to make a few arrangements before we leave." he said. Ásbjǫrn kissed his king's neck before withdrawing his hands from Thamyris' waist and without another word.

)o(

Maxwell trudged into his room, exhaustion weighing heavy on his shoulders after a long day. His gaze drifted to the balcony, where he was met with the beautiful sight of the setting sun painting the sky in hues of pink and orange. Faint rays of light filtered through the cracks in the closed curtains, casting a warm glow over the room. Carefully placing his two worn swords on the edge of the bed, Maxwell eased himself down onto the soft mattress with a heavy sigh. His body ached from the adrenaline and physical strain of the day's events. As he leaned forward and rubbed at his stiff neck and sore muscles, he couldn't help but feel guilty for humiliating Thamyris in front of everyone. However, he knew that it was necessary to protect his friend from being killed like Kethinar.

Maxwell had never thought of Thamyris as crippled since the moment they met, but now, with Kethinar dead, this was the first time anyone - including himself - viewed Thamyris in such a way. He knew that Dorian would have chastised him for his low and undignified behavior. And deep down, Maxwell knew that Dorian would have been right. But in the heat of the moment, protecting a friend was all that mattered.

Suddenly, Maxwell caught sight of Ásbjǫrn entering the room. The sun's rays caught his eyes and gave him a dangerous glint as he walked towards Maxwell. Without hesitation, Maxwell rose to his feet and held out his hands in defense. But before he could even speak, the elf had grabbed him by the throat and lifted him into the air.

Maxwell's hand clung onto Ásbjǫrn's wrist in an attempt to loosen his grip as he felt the elf's bear-like nails digging into his throat. Struggling for breath, he looked up at Ásbjǫrn, who had a menacing look in his eye. "What you did earlier was uncalled for and cruel," Ásbjǫrn growled in a deep voice, causing the hair on Maxwell's neck to stand up. "No one - *no one* - has ever dared to do what you have done!" Maxwell could feel the elf's grip on his throat tighten further. "If you ever do something like that again, I will take *your* eyes!" His words were filled with a deadly seriousness that sent a shiver down Maxwell's spine. "Do you understand?" he questioned in a bear growl.

Gasping for air, Maxwell could only manage a weak response. "Yes." he squeaked as his vision started to blur.

With one final warning, Ásbjǫrn dropped him onto the floor and began to walk away. But before leaving the room, he turned his head to look at Maxwell with his piercing right eye. "I don't know why he cares about you, but he does. I can see it in his eyes." Maxwell gasped for air while clutching his bruised throat.

Upon hearing this, tears welled up in Maxwell's eyes as he gazed at Ásbjǫrn, whose broad back was turned to him. "You can see a world in those eyes if you ever dared to truly look," Ásbjǫrn said, his voice laced with both sadness and disappointment. "But it seems you are the one who is too blind to see that." With those words, he left Maxwell alone in the room, his heart heavy and his mind racing.

Maxwell sighed deeply and stood there with his arms spread out like a defeated soldier on a battlefield. Despite the fear and turmoil he had just experienced, he couldn't help but feel grateful for still being alive. He closed his eyes and thanked whatever higher power may be listening for sparing him from the wrath of Ásbjǫrn. And in that moment, he made a silent vow to never underestimate the depth of Ásbjǫrn's power again.

)o(

Thamyris traced his fingers along the cool, smooth walls of the palace as he made his way towards the temple of the gods. The air was thick with tension, and he couldn't shake off the feeling that something momentous happened. As he turned a corner, he caught a glimpse through Ásbjǫrn eyes of him leaving Maxwell's room. His brow furrowed in confusion before he turned himself to walk past the grand library and to the grand staircase that went towards Maxwell's chambers.

"Are you alright?" Thamyris asked as he approached the open door, his sharp ears picking up on Maxwell's labored breathing. He could hear Maxwell's hands thudding against the floor as he struggled to sit up, using his arms for support.

Looking up at Thamyris, Maxwell's eyes widened in surprise, seeing the newly crowned King dressed in full battle gear. His leather armor was exquisite and intricately embroidered with gold accents and a magnificent wooden bow that slung over his shoulder. Thamyris' long hair was once again tied back into a ponytail, with a few braids adding to its elegant style. A simple golden circlet adorned his head filled with sparkling diamonds, a symbol of his royal status.

"You're going back then?" Maxwell asked, slowly getting to his feet.

Thamyris nodded solemnly. "Yes."

"But...," Maxwell trailed off, unsure of how to express what he wanted to say.

"Cernunnos granted me the restoration of my sight soon after you threw that roll at me," Thamyris revealed, gesturing towards his eyes that now held a glimmer of light once again.

Maxwell's face fell in shame and regret. "I'm sorry I....."

Cutting him off gently, Thamyris raised a hand. "No need to apologize. In the end, you were right. And I think Cernunnos saw that too." With those words, Thamyris turned to leave. But before he could take another step, Maxwell's voice stopped him. "So you have your sight back?"

"More or less," Thamyris answered. He looked over his shoulder, a small smile forming on his lips. "I see like before, but through another's eyes."

"And who might that be?" Maxwell questioned; his curiosity was piqued as he noticed Ásbjǫrn stepping from the shadows and back into the room. The large elf was also dressed for battle, his brown leather armor fitting perfectly over his muscular frame. His long hair was pulled back into a half ponytail. Maxwell couldn't help but notice that he carried Thamyris' rosewood staff on his back.

Ásbjǫrn answered with a proud smile. "Mine."

Maxwell nodded in understanding. "Alright then, we'll leave in the morning." He watched as Thamyris and Ásbjǫrn left the room, their confident strides echoing down the wooden hallway. Left alone once again, Maxwell couldn't help but feel a mix of emotions - pride and admiration for his friends' bravery, but also a sense of unease at what lay ahead for them in the upcoming battle.

Thamyris descended the steps of the staircase that led them down to the main hall with Ásbjǫrn. His hand gripped the polished wooden banister. The firefly lanterns lining the walls flickered as they made their way down. "We need to find Cullen and Tiatria," Thamyris said, his voice echoing off the stone walls. "The sword must be released from its scabbard."

"It has been," Cullen replied, his voice low and gravelly.

Thamyris spotted Cullen at the bottom of the stairs, fully clad in shining armor, his red cape draped over his right shoulder with the sword resting on his belt. Cullen pulled it partially out of its scabbard, the sharp metal glinting in the dim light. Thamyris glanced around, "Where's Tiatria?" he questioned.

Cullen gestured towards the courtyard, "She went back to the Temple of the Goddess. She said there were a few things she had to take care of before we leave in the morning."

Thamyris nodded in understanding, "She's right, I suspect." As they walked towards the dining hall, Thamyris placed a comforting hand on Cullen's shoulder. "Let's go to supper."

Cullen gave a grateful nod, his stomach rumbling with hunger after the day he had. Once seated at the grand dining table, Cullen turned to Thamyris. "When I first arrived here, I stumbled upon a room filled with statues…."

"You found the chamber of the gods," Thamyris interjected, taking a sip of wine as he leaned back in his chair. "It holds depictions of all the gods and goddesses. Anyone is welcome to visit since only priests and priestesses are allowed in their main temples."

Cullen looked over at Ásbjǫrn, who was sitting next to him, now understanding why the elf was so uneasy when he and Maxwell entered the temple of Cernunnos. Ásbjǫrn still looked uncomfortable in the fancy chair, trying to figure out how to use the unfamiliar utensils.

Cullen leaned over and whispered, "Start from the outside and work your way in."

Ásbjǫrn smiled gratefully, "Thank you, little human."

Cullen chuckled, adjusting himself in his seat. "Please, call me Cullen."

Ásbjǫrn gave a nod, "Of course, Cullen."

The elf then gently placed a reassuring hand on the young knight's shoulder before rising to his feet. "I'm going back to where I feel comfortable," he stated with a laugh, causing Cullen to clear his throat in shock. He was curious about Ásbjǫrn and wanted to get to know him better. "Where would that be?" Cullen asked, his voice slightly trembling. Thamyris grinned mischievously, his eyes sparkling with amusement as he responded, "Between my thighs." Cullen's face turned bright red at the suggestive remark, making Thamyris and Ásbjǫrn both chuckle. The tall warrior then patted Cullen's shoulder as he made his way towards the doorway. "He isn't wrong," Ásbjǫrn added with a smirk before walking after Thamyris. He paused at the doorway, turning to look back at Cullen. "Are you coming, little human?" he asked, gesturing for Cullen to follow them. Without hesitation, Cullen jumped up from his seat and hurried after them, eager to see where this unexpected path would lead him. Thamyris followed close behind, his own curiosity piqued.

Ásbjǫrn led them out past the grand palace and into the enchanted forest, where a massive oak tree stood tall and proud. Its gnarled roots spread out like fingers, adorned with colorful leaves and soft animal furs that created a cozy nook for the group to gather. A small fire blazed in the center, casting warm, flickering light onto their faces and casting shadows on the ancient bark of the tree. As Ásbjǫrn settled down next to the fire, Cullen couldn't help but notice the succulent aroma of roasting rabbit on a stick nearby. Thamyris smiled mischievously as Cullen's mouth watered at the sight of the perfectly cooked meat, its juices sizzling and hissing over the flames.

Through Ásbjǫrn's wise eyes, Thamyris could see Cullen eagerly eyeing the food and drink spread out before them - fresh fruits picked from the forest, savory meats cooked over an open flame, and rich mead poured from a large skin.

Cullen eagerly took a swig from a skin of mead, feeling its warmth spread through his body and his head started to spin. He tilted it back in an attempt to impress his new friends, only to cough and sputter as the strong drink burned his throat. Ásbjǫrn chuckled heartily at his reaction, patting him on the back and praising him for his bravery. Thamyris grinned from ear to ear as he watched his friend laugh and enjoy himself. This was what they had always dreamed of - to be surrounded by good company, feasting on delicious food and drink, and simply having a good time.

Tiatria watched from afar with tears in her eyes, overwhelmed with joy at seeing Cullen so happy among friends. She remembered when he had first stumbled upon their village, lost and alone. Now, she saw how far he had come, flourishing under their care and guidance. Ásbjǫrn noticed her watching and understood the unspoken message - to let Cullen savor this moment and be free from any worries or duties. With a gentle nod, Tiatria turned and disappeared into the night, leaving them to continue their merriment under the twinkling stars and the watchful eye of the wise oak tree.

Maxwell's heart swelled with pride as he observed Cullen and the others, watching them grow into their roles. He couldn't help but smile at the sight of Cullen becoming the noble knight he had always known him to be. His armor gleamed in the firelight, reflecting his inner strength and determination. And Thamyris, now a king in his own right, stood tall and regal, bearing the weight of his kingdom with grace and confidence.

But it was Tiatria who caught Maxwell's eye as she walked away from the group. Her movements were graceful and fluid, like a dancer carving her own path through the crowd. Her long, flowing robes swayed gently with each step she took. Curiosity piqued, Maxwell followed after her, wanting to ask her something that had been on his mind. He caught up to her just as she turned her head to look at him. Her piercing sapphire blue eyes met his, and for a moment, he was lost in their depths. His attention was quickly brought back to reality as he gestured towards the majestic sword that lay nearby, its hilt gleaming in the firelight.

"Can anyone wield that sword?" Maxwell asked, unable to contain his curiosity any longer. The sword leaned against the log Cullen was sitting on, gleaming in the firelight. The hilt was adorned with intricate designs and the blade glimmered like a river of liquid silver.

"Can anyone wield that sword?" he repeated, sensing there was more to it than just curiosity. Tiatria seemed taken aback by his question, her expression shifting to one of surprise before settling into contemplation. She gazed back at the fire before meeting his gaze once again.

"The dragons did not mention anything about Cullen being bound as its wielder," she mused. "Why do you ask?"

Maxwell could sense a hint of suspicion in her tone and knew he would have to explain himself carefully. Taking a deep breath, he began to tell her about his theory regarding the sword and its connection to Cullen and his destiny. As they talked, the fire crackled and popped behind them, adding an otherworldly soundtrack to their conversation.

The moment her gaze met Maxwell's, Tiatria felt a heavy weight settle in her chest. His eyes, once bright and full of life, now held a sorrow and resignation that struck her to the core. She wanted to protest and argue with him about the value of his life, but he simply shook his head. "He's too young to die," he told her, "and in retrospect, he has so much left to do." But as she looked at Maxwell, she could see that he had already given up on everything. "The only person, the only thing I cared about in this life, is gone," he told her in a grieved tone. The words hung heavy in the air, a final declaration of defeat. And as Tiatria looked into Maxwell's chocolate brown eyes, she couldn't help but feel a sense of emptiness and despair settling over them both. The moonlight shone weakly through the clouds above, casting a dull light on the barren landscape before them. This was the end for Maxwell - there was nothing left for him here anymore.

"What about Cullen?" Tiatria's voice echoed softly in the stillness of the night as she looked up at Maxwell, her fingers intertwined with his. "He sees you as a father figure, something he feels he's never had. And Thamyris...I can see how much he cares for you." She paused, searching his face for a response.

Maxwell lowered his head, his usually guarded expression softening for the first time since they had met. Tiatria could hear his thoughts racing, and she knew that the weight of their conversation was heavy on his mind. She also knew that it wasn't only her words that were causing this reaction - there was something else behind his sudden vulnerability.

As if sensing her unspoken question, Maxwell finally spoke. "It's because of Cullen," he admitted quietly. "What he thinks of me...it's why I wanted to do this." His voice trailed off, filled with emotion.

Tiatria's heart ached for him as she realized the true reason behind his actions. Despite his feelings for Thamyris and the desire to share a passionate moment with him, it all paled in comparison to his longing to be with Dorian again - just for one fleeting moment. To feel his touch, his lips, and his body against his own. She watched silently as Maxwell stepped back and turned away into the darkness of the night, leaving her alone with her thoughts. Tiatria couldn't predict what the next day would bring, but she knew without a doubt that it would be filled with heartache and turmoil. The events that were about to unfold were sure to be gut-wrenching for them all.

)o(

The sky was painted with a soft glow, pinks blending into purples and yellows as the sun rose over the horizon. Cullen stirred from his slumber, his body still tucked against a log with his arms crossed protectively over his chest. Slowly, he began to awaken and take in his surroundings. To his left, he noticed Ásbjǫrn and Thamyris curled up together on a bed of leaves and furs, their bodies entwined in peaceful slumber. Ásbjǫrn's left arm draped over Thamyris' shoulder while his right hand held onto Thamyris' smaller hands against his chest. The sight brought a small smile to Cullen's lips as he stretched out his own arms and let out a hearty yawn.

As if sensing his presence, the two elves' ears twitched and they opened their eyes in unison. With effortless grace, Ásbjǫrn sat up, propping himself up with one hand while rubbing the sleep from his left eye with the other. Thamyris followed suit, yawning and rubbing his eyes before getting up and retrieving their weapons.

The early morning air was crisp and invigorating. Cullen couldn't help but feel grateful for this moment of peace and camaraderie among friends.

Cullen crouched down, coaxing the fire back to life, eager to get breakfast cooking. But his efforts were interrupted by Ásbjǫrn, who knelt down next to him with a critical eye. It was clear the human wasn't doing it right. As Cullen's attention was pulled away from the fire, he noticed Tiatria and Maxwell approaching. A smile lit up his face as he warmly wrapped his arms around Tiatria and gave her a kiss. Meanwhile, Maxwell picked up Ka'imil and sheathed it on his belt in one smooth motion. Cullen couldn't help but notice the sharp look in Maxwell's eye as he did so. Sensing there was more going on, Cullen turned to Maxwell - his superior officer - with a quizzical expression. "We're not discussing this, Cullen," Maxwell stated firmly, placing a hand on Cullen's shoulder. "I'm your superior officer, it's my responsibility." Cullen furrowed his brow in confusion, wondering if this was about who would get credit for something or if there was something else at play. But before he could question further, Maxwell ushered him towards the cooking area with a gentle nudge. "Come on," he said kindly, "let's get some breakfast." The scent of sizzling meat and eggs filled the air as they made their way over to the campfire, the warm sun shining down upon them and birds chirping in the distance.

The fire crackled and popped as Ásbjǫrn cooked the last remaining pieces of deer meat. The smell of sizzling fat filled the air, causing everyone's stomachs to rumble with hunger. Ásbjǫrn wanted everyone to finish the roasted game and fresh eggs he'd collected from the forest. As they ate in almost total silence, each one was lost in their own thoughts.

Cullen's gaze drifted over to Tiatria, who sat across from him. "How are we getting back?" he asked quietly. His hand unconsciously reached for his satchel, where he usually kept the pouch the Queen had given him. But it wasn't there. Panic rose in his chest as he remembered dropping it somewhere in the forest during their escape.

Tiatria met his gaze, her expression calm and collected. "I still have it," she said, pulling out the leather pouch from her own bag. Cullen let out a sigh of relief, grateful that at least one thing had gone right during their chaotic journey.

But then a memory flashed through his mind - him handing the pouch to Tiatria after they had first received it from the Queen. He couldn't believe he had forgotten such an important detail amidst all the chaos and danger. In that moment, sitting by the fire with his companions, Cullen realized how much he relied on Tiatria's quick thinking and calm demeanor to keep them safe and on track. He made a mental note to thank her properly once they were back home safely.

As they finished their breakfast, everyone checked to make sure they had everything they would need for the journey ahead. Thamyris felt Ásbjǫrn's fingers gently tucking something into his hair. He peered through Ásbjǫrn's piercing blue eyes and saw that it was a hawk feather, intricately woven with a delicate piece of leather. The softness of the feather tickled his skin as he ran his fingers over its intricate patterns, marveling at its beauty and significance. A tender smile spread across Ásbjǫrn's face as he explained, "It's Kenithar's feather. I had noticed it had fallen from his tail when I found you. I thought you might like to keep it, to have a part of him with you on our journey." Thamyris' heart swelled with emotion as Ásbjǫrn took his right hand and pressed his lips to the back of it, a gesture of love and reassurance. The gentle breeze carried the faint scent of pine and wildflowers, creating a serene backdrop for this heartfelt exchange between the two lovers. The sun peeked through the trees, casting dappled shadows on their faces as they shared this intimate moment together. Thamyris couldn't imagine going on this journey without Ásbjǫrn by his side, and now, with Kethinar's feather close to his heart, he felt even more ready for whatever challenges lay ahead.

With a determined gaze, Tiatria held out the pouch for everyone to see. The weight of their mission and their destination rested heavily on her shoulders. "Ready?" she questioned, searching the eyes of each member of their small band. She could sense their mixture of determination and fear, knowing that they were all willing to do whatever it took to complete their quest. "I don't know where exactly this portal will take us," she warned, "It could put us in the castle, somewhere nearby but be prepared for anything." With trembling fingers, she opened the pouch and scooped out a handful of shimmering powder. The iridescent blue particles sparkled in the rays of the morning sun as she chanted ancient elven words and threw the dust into the air before them.

As soon as the powder started to form a circle in front of them, a powerful surge of magic surrounded them, swirling and pulsing with energy. The portal began to crack open, its edges glowing with a mesmerizing combination of blue and purple hues. It beckoned them forward, promising an adventure beyond their wildest imaginations.

One by one, Cullen watched as his friends stepped bravely into the portal, disappearing into its depths. He took a deep breath, steeling himself for whatever challenges and dangers lay ahead. With a final glance back at their world behind him, he walked resolutely into the portal, ready to face whatever fate awaited them on the other side.

Chapter 24

The sudden burst of light blinded Cullen as he stepped through the portal, momentarily disorienting him. As his vision cleared, a sight that sent shock and horror coursing through his body greeted him. The once majestic castle, with its towering ramparts and regal turrets, now lay in ruins before them. Crumbling walls and shattered stones littered the ground like broken bones.

A putrid stench hung heavy in the air, thick with the smell of death and destruction. It filled their nostrils with a pungent acridness that made them gag. Maxwell's keen eyes quickly scanned the area, taking in the charred marks left behind by the dragon's fiery breath along the walls. The very ground beneath their feet seemed to moan under the weight of devastation.

Debris and bodies lay scattered around them, evidence of a recent battle that had torn through this place. As the rest of their group emerged from the portal behind him, Cullen couldn't help but feel a sense of dread settle over him. His gaze fell upon his trusted horse, Seraphim, grazing with the unicorns nearby. A wave of relief washed over him as he realized that his faithful companion had survived the chaos that had taken place here. It seems he'd taken lessons from his unicorn friends about not running from magical beasts. But what about the other animals? The livestock or the remaining horses in the stables? Cullen wasn't sure if they had made it out alive. He tore his attention away from Seraphim and turned his focus back to the castle. The gates were only partially raised, just enough for them to squeeze underneath. Ásbjørn's once powerful gaze now appeared weak as he took in the devastation surrounding them. Trees were snapped like twigs and burned beyond recognition while the land lay in ruins before them.

Thamyris placed a gentle hand on Ásbjǫrn's back, allowing him to use his powers to see through his eyes. As he surveyed the destruction of both nature and man-made structures, sorrow and concern filled him. With this kind of force and devastation, it was clear they were severely outmatched, as this was done with anger and malice. Everyone started to wonder how they could possibly overcome it using their own powers.

The aftermath was a haunting scene of heart-wrenching devastation and death. The once grand courtyard lay in ruins, with horses sprawled dead on the ground and their riders crushed beneath them in twisted positions. The stench of burnt flesh made the air heavy, mixed with the lingering echoes of evil words and malice that seemed to permeate every wall.

Tiatria's heart sank as she surveyed the destruction, her eyes scanning for any sign of Amalia amidst the chaos. As they carefully made their way through the lower garden, Cullen led them past what was once a beautiful and peaceful sanctuary, now reduced to charred remains. The once brilliant white limestone was now blackened and cracked by dragon fire, and golden statues of angels had melted into unrecognizable shapes. Not even a bird dared to sing in this desolate place.

Maxwell tightly gripped the hilt of his sword, Ka'imil, ready to defend himself and his companions at a moment's notice as they cautiously approached the donjon. In eerie silence, they climbed a staircase that led up to the battlements. As they entered an open space, they beheld the innermost part of the castle that left them gasping with worry. There, curled up like a sleeping cat, was Nimriar, his powerful form surrounded by the grisly remains of animals he had consumed. Smoke billowed from under his nostrils as he snored, causing a reverberating feeling in their chests.

Ásbjǫrn placed a comforting hand on Thamyris' shoulder as they took in the sight before them. Thamyris nodded in silent understanding, having already seen this same scene through Ásbjǫrn's eyes when they emerged from the portal. Nearby, Cullen spotted an entrance to the main part of the castle's keep and motioned for everyone to follow him.

They hurriedly made their way towards the side entrance, carefully avoiding any noise that could alert Nimriar or Amalia to their presence. With a quick flick of his wrist, Cullen silently and cautiously opened the door and ushered everyone inside before entering himself. The sight that greeted them inside was one of utter chaos and carnage. Candelabras lay knocked over, their candles strewn across the floor. Dead servants, burned beyond recognition, littered the area where the main doorway had been shattered by dragon fire. Thick smoke and blood permeated the air, making it difficult to see and breathe. As they cautiously moved through the devastated halls, each step seemed to echo with the weight of their mission and the cost of their journey so far.

With a determined glint in his eye, Maxwell gazed at Cullen, his lips pursed in deep thought. He let out a soft whistle that echoed off the silent, lonely walls of the abandoned castle, causing everyone to turn and look at him. "I'm going to search for the blacksmith's shop," Maxwell whispered in a low voice, his eyes flickering with determination. "There may be tools or weapons that can aid us." Cullen furrowed his brow as he studied Maxwell closely, trying to decipher the reason behind his sudden decision. After a moment, he turned to the others with a questioning look. "What kind of things are you looking for?" he asked in a hushed tone. Maxwell's gaze swept over the group of elves before returning to Cullen with a determined fire in his eyes. "Well, iron is known to harm magical creatures, isn't it?" His words hung heavy in the air, reminding them all of the looming danger that awaited them outside the safety of the castle walls.

A flash of comprehension lit up Cullen's eyes as he grasped onto Maxwell's cunning scheme, a smile tugging at the corners of his lips. Cullen remembered the night Tiatria wore iron shackles, her delicate wrists blistering from the metal's touch, and surged through him once more.

The weight of guilt and regret settled heavily on his heart, realizing what Maxwell's plan now was. He sure was going to use every possible advantage to stop Amalia and her dragon. But in that moment, standing before Maxwell, seeing fire in his eyes and a determined set to his jaw, he knew he would do everything in his power to obtain redemption for letting Dorian, the King and Cullen's father, die. His fists clenched at his sides, ready to fight for justice and redemption for all those who suffered and continue to suffer under this new tyrant's reign.

"I'll find you all after I check it out and see if there is anything usable," Maxwell said before sprinting off as quickly and quietly as possible. Thamyris turned back to Cullen, his voice barely above a whisper, "I'm going to find my sister." Cullen nodded, taking Tiatria's hand in his own. "We'll go search for any survivors left in the castle," he said softly, determination shining in his eyes. The group split off into pairs without another word, each heading towards their designated locations.

Cullen made his way towards the stairs that led up to the upper garden, Tiatria following closely behind. As they ascended the steps, the air smelled of dragon fire. Cullen reached the open archway first, holding up his hand to signal for Tiatria to wait as he peeked outside. Pressing his back against the wall, he craned his neck to get a better look at their surroundings. It appeared clear, and he slowly stepped out.

Tiatria watched as Cullen carefully made his way towards the walkway, her gaze falling upon his shield, which lay discarded on the ground. To both Cullen and her amazement, it was still intact despite the chaos that had ensued. She walked out behind him as Cullen knelt down to retrieve it, her eyes scanning over the blackened and scorched ground surrounding them. The once pristine limestone now bore deep scorch marks in a twenty-foot diameter, a grim reminder of the devastation caused by the dragon's fiery breath.

As Tiatria approached the ancient stone structure, she could feel a sense of unease creeping over her. The fear emanating from the stone was palpable, causing her to take deep, calming breaths as she fought the urge to break down into tears. Cullen quickly jumped up from where he had knelt and grasped onto Tiatria's trembling arms, his own fear evident in his eyes. He knew they were vulnerable out in the open; any sound or movement could attract the dragon's attention. In an effort to soothe her, Cullen pulled Tiatria close and spoke in a soft, hushed voice, "Let's walk to the other side. There's a chapel we can take cover in." Gently wiping away the tears that streamed down her cheeks with his thumbs, Cullen took her left hand in his and led her across the shaky walkway towards safety. Even though they were surrounded by danger, Cullen's touch brought a sense of comfort and protection to Tiatria.

Cullen guided Tiatria across the limestone walkway, their footsteps echoing against the sturdy stone walls of the castle. As they descended the winding stairs, they entered a dimly lit hallway that stretched far into the depths of the inner keep. The sound of their boots against the cold, hard floor echoed in the stillness, creating an eerie atmosphere. The ornate tapestries and paintings that lined the walls depicted scenes of battles and heroes long gone, adding to the grandeur of their surroundings. Cullen's grip on her hand tightened as they made their way deeper into the heart of the fortress, a place filled with secrets and mysteries waiting to be unraveled.

)o(

Thamyris and Ásbjǫrn glided gracefully around the castle, their elven feet barely making a sound on the cold, unfeeling stone. Each step felt like a whisper, a gentle kiss against the rough surface of the ground. As they explored, Asbjorn couldn't help but feel a pang of sorrow at the lifeless castle that surrounded them, so different from the vibrant trees, warm sun, and soft grass of their beloved homeland. But duty called, and they continued on.

It was Thamyris who first noticed the set of overly large, intricately designed doors as he looked through Ásbjǫrn's eyes. They stood tall and grand, contrasting sharply with the drab walls of the castle. And yet, despite their impressive appearance, they were slightly ajar - just enough for an elf to slip through. Ásbjǫrn looked at Thamyris, knowing he was the one who would have to investigate. For him, even moving the door an inch could be dangerous.

With great care and caution, Ásbjǫrn slowly inched his way through the doors. The air inside was musty and stale, tinged with a hint of something sweet and sickly. As he cautiously navigated through the dimly lit room, he caught a glimpse of Amalia sitting on a grand throne. But this was no longer Thamyris' sister; she had been transformed into someone else entirely. Tears welled up in his eyes as he took in her altered appearance. No longer did she radiate warmth and light like she used to - she now exuded an ominous aura that sent shivers down his spine. His heart ached for what she had become.

The sound of a voice reverberated through the cold, dark halls of the palace, causing Ásbjǫrn's heart to race. It echoed off the polished marble walls and seemed to emanate from every direction at once, sending shivers down his spine. As Thamyris stood beside him, equally unsure of what was to come next, their footsteps echoed loudly in the empty corridors.

"Come in Brother," the voice called out again, chilling Ásbjǫrn to the bone. He turned to Thamyris for guidance, but all he received was a heavy sigh and a nod towards the throne room. With a deep breath, Ásbjǫrn followed Thamyris' lead, the weight of their impending confrontation weighing heavily on his mind.

As they entered the throne room, the air grew thick with tension and unease. The once grand and opulent halls were now marred by dead bodies, blood stains, and scorch marks, giving them an ominous and foreboding atmosphere.

They walked into the throne room, where Amalia sat on her newly acquired throne. Her arms rested on the armrests as she gave them a wicked smile. "There you are," she said in a cool tone, her eyes glinting with malice. "And it seems you brought a friend as well." Ásbjǫrn kept his gaze stoic as he glanced over at Thamyris, who let out another heavy sigh.

"So it has come to this Lia?" Thamyris questioned, using his sister's childhood nickname. Amalia's smile widened into a cruel grin. "I suppose it has," she responded, her voice dripping with venom. Her eyes locked onto Thamyris as if daring him to challenge her.

As her gaze fell upon Thamyris, she couldn't help but notice the golden crown adorning his brow. It seemed to reflect the light in a thousand different directions, casting a regal aura around him. "I see you have become King," she observed with a hint of detachment in her voice, not revealing any emotion towards his new title.

Thamyris took a hesitant step forward, his face etched with concern and sadness. "Please come home," he pleaded, but Amalia's expression turned cold and heartless. "Not until every despicable human is dead," she declared with hatred. Her fingers dug into the stone throne as she leaned forward, her eyes blazing with an intense fire. Thamyris stood with his arms crossed, shifting his weight to his left leg as he spoke. "You should know that Mother is dead. Your reckless summoning of the dragon killed her," he said, his voice laced with anger and grief.

Amalia's face contorted in pain at the news, but she quickly snapped back, cutting off her brother's words. She didn't want to hear it. But Thamyris wasn't going to let it go. "She was an innocent victim, just like all those you've killed with your dragon," he accused.

Amalia shot up from her seat, her eyes blazed with fury as she faced her brother. "You have no idea what they have done," she seethed, her voice trembling with a deep passionate rage. "I was also innocent! Not one of those beasts cared! I will make them pay. I will make them all pay for what they did and what they took from me." The fire in her eyes grew brighter as she vowed revenge against those who had wronged her.

Thamyris couldn't help but be taken aback by the ferocity in his sister's words. This was not the gentle, loving sibling he once knew but a figure consumed by vengeance and determined to seek retribution at any cost. The air inside the throne room felt suffocating, heavy with anger and sorrow as the two siblings stood on opposite sides, their bond shattered by a brutal war that should never have happened.

The thick, tense atmosphere seemed to press against Thamyris' skin as he pleaded with Amalia. But she walked down the steps with purpose, her steps echoing through the chamber. "You don't know everything," she growled, her voice dripping with bitterness. "But you'll know everything now." With one swift movement, she snatched the sides of her brother's face in her elegant fingers and forced him to see her memories.

In an instant, Thamyris was bombarded with a flood of images - Tahl'rail's death, Amalia being violated and beaten by countless men while they spat on her. His body went stiff, and he started to fall backwards, only to be caught by Ásbjǫrn, who rushed to his aid. Gasping for air, Thamyris struggled to make sense of what he had just witnessed. As he tried to regain his composure, Thamyris noticed Ásbjǫrn standing beside him, holding him in his large, thick arms, facing off against Amalia with an unyielding determination in his eyes. "And who are you?" she sneered at him.

"I am Ásbjǫrn," came the calm reply from the large elf who had saved Thamyris from collapsing. The tension between them crackled like electricity as they stood before each other, both willing to fight for what they believed in.

The she-elf's eyes narrowed as she looked up at Ásbjǫrn, her chin raised in a proud and haughty manner. Her left hand rested confidently on her hip while the other held onto Thamyris, who had just been helped to his feet by Ásbjǫrn. As she stared into his warm amber eyes, she could see something more behind them - a tenderness that caught her off guard for a split second before it vanished. "You are far more than just my brother's eyes," she said with a realization dawning in her own eyes. "Of course you are," she added bitterly, holding out her hand between them. A sudden burst of energy shot through the air, knocking both Ásbjǫrn and Thamyris back onto the ground in opposite directions.

Ásbjǫrn watched as Thamyris slammed into the wall while he himself slid across the ground. With a determined look in his eye, he slammed his massive hand onto the floor and his body began to partially transform, taking on bear-like features as he caused vines to erupt from the ground around Amalia's legs like slithering snakes. But Amalia was not one to be easily defeated; with a flick of her wrist, flames erupted from her fingertips, quickly setting the vines ablaze.

Undeterred, Ásbjǫrn continued to control the vines with his hand on the ground, trying to grab hold of Amalia's arms. But she was quick to retaliate, sending fire shooting out of her other hand with intense anger and determination burning in her eyes - emotions that Thamyris had never seen from her before. To human eyes, the two could have been invisible, considering the speed they were running, but to elven eyes, Thamyris could see everything through Ásbjǫrn's eyes. Amalia was quick as she sent flames through the air. Ásbjǫrn slammed his rosewood staff onto the floor, causing the floor to shake as sharp stakes of wood shot from the floor, making Amalia jump. The vines reached out to grab her once more with deadly speed. She dodged the vines and shot ice shards from her fingertips.

Ásbjǫrn used his staff to cause a wooden shield to come out of it, shattering the ice against it. He then moved the staff as he used his right hand to twist the vines to grow thorns as they moved again to ensnare her. Thamyris pulled back his bow, causing an arrow to be made of pure light. He let it loose but Amalia was able to gracefully dodge before grabbing onto them and setting them a flame, burning the whole of the vines to ash. Thamyris shot another arrow, trying to match his Sister's speed as he shot the arrows as fast as a heartbeat. With Amalia busy dodging Thamyris' arrows, Ásbjǫrn stumped the staff onto the floor, causing the spikes to break from the floor and fly at Amalia.

Just when it seemed like Ásbjǫrn might gain the upper hand, Amalia turned her head to glare at him with fierce intensity. In one swift motion, she moved towards Thamyris, which caused some kind of force to slam him into a wall, causing his bow to drop from his hands and rise into the air; then swiftly moved him in front of her and in front of the stakes flying towards her.

"Stop or I see my Brother skewered!" she threatened, each word dripping with venom.

Ásbjǫrn froze as he stood up, pleading to her. "Don't!" he cried out, then held out his right hand and clenched his fist to cause the stakes to shatter. "He's your brother, he's all you have left."

The crisp sound of a shrill whistle sliced through the air of the throne room, echoing off the walls and causing Amalia to cry out in pain. Her eyes widened in shock as she saw the sharp tip of an arrow embedded in her fleshy palm, blood trickling down her arm. She turned to face her brother, who was still floating in front of her, still able to hold onto the arrow of light even as he was forced to drop his bow. Thamyris turned his head, causing Amalia to see the determined expression on his face sent chills down her spine. He then used his right hand to summon his bow to his hand. He loaded another arrow and spun himself around as he took aim once again. His muscles tensed with precision as he prepared to unleash another deadly shot, his focus unbreakable despite his sister's cries.

)o(

Maxwell's frantic search for a solution led him to the unassuming blacksmith's shop, nestled in a secluded corner of the sprawling castle grounds. As he pushed open the heavy wooden door, a wave of searing heat washed over him from the roaring forge within. The deafening clamor of metal being hammered and shaped assaulted his ears, accompanied by an occasional grunt or curse from the burly blacksmith. His gaze darted around the dimly lit workshop, scanning the cluttered workbenches for anything that could aid them in this perilous quest. He saw an assortment of tools and weapons scattered about, but nothing seemed quite suitable for their needs. Just when he was losing hope, his sight landed on a set of sturdy shackles resting on a nearby table. Their weight and solid iron construction made them perfect for what he had in mind.

As he continued to scour the shop, Maxwell's attention was caught by something peculiar happening at the main forge. Intrigued, he cautiously made his way towards it. His eyes widened in amazement as he beheld what the skilled blacksmith was working on - a massive chain, its links thick as his thumb and long enough to stretch between two men lying head-to-toe. It was clearly intended for hauling heavy loads, possibly used in ore mining.

Maxwell was entranced by the smith's masterful techniques, his eyes following every movement as the blacksmith expertly wielded the ancient bloomery method to shape and mold a sturdy chain. Despite the intense heat radiating from the glowing coals, Maxwell couldn't tear his gaze away from the mesmerizing display of skill and craftsmanship. He finally addressed the blacksmith directly, "Are there any more of these chains available?" The blacksmith nodded, leading him over to a large table covered with a tarp. With practiced ease, he pulled back the tarp to reveal a mound of shiny metal iron-linked chains. Maxwell's eyes widened in awe and appreciation at the sight. This chain would undoubtedly be a valuable tool for what lay ahead in their fight. "Can you link them together?" he questioned, already envisioning how useful this creation would be for their current situation.

Chapter 25

Cullen cautiously peeked around the corner, his sharp, calculating eyes scanning every shadow and crevice for any signs of danger. Satisfied that the coast was clear, he motioned for Tiatria to join him, and they set off down the dimly lit hallway. The walls were adorned with faded tapestries, their once vibrant colors now muted by time. Each one depicted a different scene - epic battles and forgotten heroes etched into the fabric. As they approached a heavy wooden door at the end of the hallway, Cullen's hand flew up to signal Tiatria to stop. He placed a finger over his lips, his piercing gaze fixed on the door before slowly pushing it open, revealing what lay beyond.

The door stood tall and formidable, crafted from solid oak with intricate symbols etched into its surface. Two symbols were combined together - a long, thin shape with a loop on the right side and an 'x' in the center. Cullen grasped the heavy handle and pulled it open, the hinges creaking in protest. Beyond it lay a solemn chapel, bathed in flickering candlelight and shards of sunlight filtering through shattered stained glass windows. Tiatria's eyes scanned the room, looking at the rows of sturdy wooden pews that had once been polished to perfection but now bore scratches and scorch marks. The air was filled with a sense of reverence and mystery, drawing them further inside to explore its secrets.

But it was the altar that immediately caught her attention, its once pristine white cloth now marred with dark splatters of blood and charred remnants from an unknown ritual. The smell of burnt offerings lingered in the air, mingling with the metallic tang of fresh blood. A body lay slumped over the altar, dressed in tattered priestly robes that were now soaked in deep crimson. Cullen's sharp gaze swept over the scene, taking in every detail as he searched for clues amidst the chaos and devastation. The faint flicker of candlelight cast eerie shadows on the walls, highlighting the gruesome and macabre scene before him. It was as if a nightmare had taken hold of this sacred space, leaving behind a haunting atmosphere that seemed to seep into his very bones.

His sharp, observant gaze scanned the disordered pile of fabric scraps in the far corner of the room. With a graceful crouch, he stooped down to inspect them, noting the haphazard arrangement and varying textures. But one piece immediately stood out from the rest - a luxurious material with a glossy sheen and meticulously detailed stitching. However, it was not just the quality that caught his keen eye - nestled among the scraps was a dainty handkerchief, its fragile surface adorned with an exquisite display of tulips and orchids. Each petal seemed to bloom before his very eyes, crafted with delicate embroidery that spoke of patience and dedication. Without a doubt, this belonged to Edith - he could recognize her love for such intricate and feminine designs. As he held it delicately in his palm, her memories flooded his mind, each one carrying its own weight of bittersweet emotions.

Like a dark cloud creeping over the horizon, a sense of foreboding washed over him, seeping into his bones and filling him with dread. His hand clenched tightly around the soft, white handkerchief, his knuckles turning white as he stood up, ready to face whatever dangers lay ahead in this desecrated chapel. The walls were lined with crumbling bricks and stained-glass windows shattered on the floor, casting eerie shadows across the room. The air was musty, carrying the weight of centuries of neglect and evil deeds. He could feel the presence of something sinister lurking in the shadows, waiting for its next victim. But he was determined to face it head-on, his determination shining like a beacon in the darkness.

Tiatria could feel Cullen's mix of emotions, which caused her to turn around. She could see him smashing a piece of fabric in his hand. Cullen loosened his hand's hold on the handkerchief, and as he handed it to her, "It's Edith's," he told her before leaving the room. Tiatria turned her head as he passed her, "I have an idea about where they all are."

)o(

Thamyris pulled the string of his bow back further till the string creaked from being tot, "One thing you've forgotten, little sister, something you used to tell me all the time. I may be blind, but I'm not helpless." he told his sister as he ignited the tip of the light arrow on fire. In a flash, the arrow whistled through the air.

Amalia's screams of unbridled rage and fury reverberated through the air, sending shivers down the spines of all who heard it. Her voice cracked with raw emotion, each syllable dripping with venom and malice. With a primal growl, her right hand sent out a force of energy that shattered the arrow in mid-flight. She lunged forward and grabbed the arrow shaft with a fierce grip, yanking it out of her hand with such force that Thamyris fell to the ground in a heap of limbs and blood. The arrow of light disappeared into thin air. Ásbjǫrn's heart pounded wildly in his chest as he watched his companions collapse, his eyes widening in shock and fear at the sight before him. Time seemed to stand still as he witnessed the chaos unfolding, every detail etching itself into his memory. The scent of sweat and adrenaline filled the air, mixing with the metallic tang of blood and stench of dead bodies. Amalia's wild hair whipped around her face like a stormy halo, her eyes blazing with a ferocity that made Ásbjǫrn fear for Thamyris' safety as he wasn't seeing him attempting to get up. In that moment, she was a force of nature, unstoppable and untamed.

In a blink of an eye, Ásbjǫrn's elven form shifted into that of a mighty bear, his dark fur bristling and his teeth bared in a fierce growl. The tension in the air crackled like lightning as he charged towards Amalia, his massive paws pounding against the ground with shaking force. She could feel the power radiating off of him like a wild storm raging within. Amalia instinctively tried to use magic, but before she could even raise her hand, Thamyris' dagger flew through the air and narrowly missed her face. The sharp clang of metal clashing against stone echoed through the room as she quickly dodged out of its path. Meanwhile, Ásbjǫrn reared up on his hind legs, towering over Amalia with his sheer strength and size. His heavy breaths sounded like thunder as he let out a deafening roar, causing the ground to tremble beneath her feet. With a swift and powerful movement, he brought down his massive paw upon her, sending her flying backward with an impactful force that rattled her bones as she crashed against the wall.

Thamyris stumbled and fell to the ground, his head spinning from the initial drop. He quickly tried to regain his footing, but it was too late. With a fierce determination, Ásbjǫrn raised his massive paw once again, ready for another strike. With the amount of adrenaline and anger coursing through him, this would kill Amalia outright.

As Thamyris rose to his feet, he could only imagine the deadly glare in Ásbjǫrn's eyes and knew he had only seconds to act. Without a second thought, he lunged between the two, bracing himself for the impact of the impending attack. His heart raced with fear and adrenaline as he cried out "NO!" in a desperate attempt to stop the bear's rage.

In that moment, time seemed to stand still as Ásbjǫrn halted his advance just inches away from Thamyris' face. Despite remembering Ásbjǫrn's own warning about staying clear of the bear, Thamyris didn't care - this was his Sister and she was all he had left. The intensity of their gazes locked in a fierce battle of wills, each one refusing to back down. The air was thick with tension and the smell of sweat and fear as the two stood frozen in their positions. Thamyris could feel Ásbjǫrn's massive body radiating heat and hear the pounding of his own heart in his ears. He held his breath, waiting for what would come next - either victory or defeat in this fight for survival.

Moments felt like hours. The weight of anticipation felt heavy on his shoulders and caused his palms to sweat. Every second felt like an eternity as he held his breath, waiting for the massive bear to reveal its true nature. Finally, the musky scent of fur filled Thamyris's nostrils as Ásbjǫrn sniffed at the top of Thamyris' head before gracefully lowering himself onto his front paws. The ground trembled slightly beneath his immense weight, but Thamyris could only focus on the sensation of every inch of fur pressing against his skin till Ásbjǫrn reverted back to elven form.

Their bodies now molded together in a tight embrace, Thamyris could hear the thumping of their hearts synchronizing and feel the warmth emanating from Ásbjǫrn's body. A deep, rumbling sound resonated from within his chest, a remnant of his recent animal state, before he pulled away to look into Thamyris' milky blue eyes. Tears glistened in Ásbjǫrn's own eyes as he spoke, their previous anger now replaced with relief and gratitude. His grip tightened around Thamyris' face as he uttered words that were both a reprimand and a whisper of love, "I can't believe you risked yourself like that. I warned you about the danger of the bear." His words emphasized the gravity of Thamyris' impulsive actions and the potential consequences they could have brought upon them both. "You're lucky I regained my senses at the last moment."

After a moment, Ásbjǫrn stood motionless, his eyes widened in horror as he beheld the impossible: Amalia's left hand seemed to phase through her brother Thamyris' body as she rose to her feet, causing him to gasp and struggle for breath. Ásbjǫrn's fists clenched at his sides, his blood boiling with rage at the sight of Thamyris' suffering. But as he took in the scene before him, a sense of foreboding crept over him. The air crackled with an otherworldly power emanating from Amalia, her eyes blazing with an intensity that sent shivers down Ásbjǫrn's spine. He was both terrified and mesmerized by her unearthly aura, unable to tear his gaze away from her captivating stare.

With a low growl, Amalia spoke in a voice that dripped with malice and dark intent. "This ends now," she declared, her words ringing out like a death knell in the cavernous halls of the castle. Ásbjǫrn felt a chill run down his spine as he watched her grip on Thamyris' lung tighten, cutting off his air supply. He cried out in desperation and confusion, "What are you doing? He's your brother!" Still unable to comprehend why Amalia would do such a thing to her own brother, who had defended her life only moments before.

But there was no response from Amalia, only a cold and eerie silence that echoed around them, magnified by the vast emptiness of the castle. As Ásbjǫrn stared at her in disbelief, he knew that this was not the same woman that Thamyris had once loved and trusted. She was consumed by a dark force, one that threatened everything they all held dear. And in that moment, Thamyris knew that he would have to fight for what he loved most - even if it meant facing the very person he once called his own.

Amalia's right hand's slender fingers now curled into claws, her long nails glinting in the dim light as she slowly raised her right hand up to her shoulder. The air crackled with dark, malevolent magic, sending a chill down Ásbjǫrn's spine. He heard the faint clanking of metal and muffled thuds around the room, his heart pounding with fear as he frantically looked around to see the bodies of the dead soldiers starting to stir.

"What are you doing?" he gasped, his eyes wide with horror.

Amalia's face twisted into a wicked smile as she replied, "I'm just summoning some friends to join us." The room seemed to darken at her words as if the shadows themselves were drawn to her ominous power. "And don't worry about your companions," she added, her voice dripping with malice, "they'll be properly attended to." Ásbjǫrn's heart lurched as he realized that Amalia was aware of their friends who had accompanied them on their journey. "Oh yes, I know you and my brother brought your little friends along," she hissed with a wicked grin, "I sensed it the moment you all stepped back into this world." The sound of creaking armor filled the air as the lifeless bodies of the soldiers rose from their resting places, their vacant eyes fixed on Ásbjǫrn and Amalia with an eerie intensity.

Thamyris' chest constricted, panic and fear squeezing him like a vice as he struggled for air. His sister's body pressed against his, offering no comfort in this dire situation. She whispered in his ear, her warm breath tickling his skin, her voice dripping with venom. "I'm sorry, Brother," she said through a wicked smile, "but you have to die now." Her lips brushed against his cheek in a bittersweet kiss before she turned to face their attackers. The sun's light cast an eerie glow through the castle's windows, casting shadows that danced around them in a frenzied frenzy.

Ásbjǫrn caught between a rock and a hard place, transformed into a massive bear, its coarse fur bristling with anger and determination. Muscles rippled under its thick coat as it stood tall and imposing, ready to defend Thamyris from the undead at all costs. The air crackled with tension as the siblings prepared for the imminent battle ahead, their fates hanging in the balance, but Ásbjǫrn's courage was unshaken as he attacked all who got too close with reckless abandon. A sense of impending doom hung heavy in the air as they faced their enemies, their fate uncertain but their determination unwavering. The smell of sweat and blood lingered in the air as their opponents closed in, their weapons glinting in the sunlight. But Ásbjǫrn stood firm, determined to face whatever came his way for both their sakes. But there were too many of them - a dozen or more corpses trying to take down Ásbjǫrn with their swords and spears. His eyes glowed with determination as he fought.

The ground shook with the thundering charge of the undead soldiers, their decaying limbs flailing as they closed in on their targets. Ásbjǫrn, a powerful and fearsome creature with sharp fangs and piercing eyes, let out a primal roar that echoed through the air. With an explosive burst of strength, he reared up on his hind legs and swiped fiercely at the approaching enemies with his massive front paws. The impact of his blows was devastating, sending one soldier flying through the air and crashing into a nearby stone wall with bone-crushing force. The wall crumbled under the weight of the fallen soldier, releasing a cloud of dust and debris that filled the air. Among the rubble lay the severed arm of the now lifeless soldier, a grim reminder of the battle raging on.

The horde of at least a dozen lifeless bodies, their rotted flesh barely holding them together, lunged towards Ásbjǫrn with rusted swords and spears. The stench of death and decay filled the air as they closed in on him, their ragged breaths sounding like a chorus of hisses and moans. But Ásbjǫrn's eyes blazed with fierce determination as he swung his paws, unleashing a powerful magic that caused wild vines to sprout from the ground and entangle the attackers' limbs, slowing them down and giving him a brief moment of respite. With a primal roar, he charged forward, his muscles rippling beneath fur as he slashed and pounced on the relentless foes with incredible strength and agility. The sound of bones cracking and flesh tearing mixed with the heavy thuds of bodies hitting the ground as Ásbjǫrn fought for survival against the horde. But despite being outnumbered and outmatched, he refused to back down - his will fueled by the memory of his fallen comrades and the desire to protect what was left of his home.

Despite the countless undead soldiers he maimed and killed, they kept coming for Ásbjǫrn. Their rotting bodies either crawled closer or rose from the ground, their lifeless eyes fixed on him as they charged once again. The stench of decay hung heavy in the air as the endless cycle of battle and bloodshed continued. But Ásbjǫrn refused to back down, his muscles straining with every swing of his massive claws. He fought not just for his own life but for the safety and well-being of Thamyris, who was still immobilized by Amalia's grip and couldn't move. Thamyris could see through his love's eyes as he struck each foe. No matter how many times he did it, they kept getting back up, even after having their heads ripped off. Amalia watched with wicked delight as she watched the massive bear fight. Occasionally, a blade would nick or cut him. Thamyris knew that if this continued, Ásbjǫrn would exhaust himself and the consequences would turn fatal. Each strike was fueled by a fierce determination and Ásbjǫrn's primal instinct to survive against all odds. As the battle raged on, it seemed as though time itself had frozen in this never-ending struggle between life and death.

)o(

Cullen cautiously peeked around the corner, his heart pounding in his chest as he saw lifeless guards standing at attention down the dark and musty hallway that led to the dungeons. The flickering torches on the walls cast eerie shadows, making the scene even more unsettling. Some of the guards were missing limbs or had gaping wounds on their bodies, yet they stood rigid and still, their faces frozen in expressions of pain and terror. Cullen couldn't believe what he was seeing and quickly pulled back, his hand gripping Tiatria's arm for support as he locked his legs, preventing them from shaking beneath him.

"The guards...they're standing up," he stammered, his voice shaking with fear. "But they were dead just moments ago." Cullen couldn't figure it out; how were the dead now standing? They'd been placid before; why would they rise now? What would make them do it? Now, their attempt to find Edith and any of the others was all the harder. They'd have to battle for every step they'd make from here on out.

Tiatria furrowed her brow in confusion, peering over Cullen's shoulder to get a better look. It was true; the guards were clearly deceased but somehow still standing upright, defying all logic and reason. Their presence sent a chill down her spine, as if some dark magic was at work here. "How is this possible?" she whispered in disbelief.

Cullen let out a shaky sigh, his mind racing for a solution. "We have to go through there," he said reluctantly, gesturing towards the undead guards. "The dungeon is the most fortified place in the castle. There is only one way in and one way out. If any survivors remain, that's the only place they'd be." Tiatria's heart sank at the thought of facing such powerful dark magic, but she knew they had no other choice if they were to find anyone else alive. They'd have to get past the soldiers of undead. "Then we'll have to be careful," she replied firmly, steeling herself for the challenge ahead.

Cullen wished he had his sword with him as they cautiously stepped away from the wall and towards the undead guards, their eyes scanning for any signs of danger. Cullen took a breath before looking back at Tiatria, and every step felt like walking into a trap. "Any suggestions?" he asked nervously, feeling a knot form in his stomach. She shook her head, her expression troubled as she tried to think of a plan to defeat the foul magic before them.

Cullen charged forward, his shield raised high in front of him like a bulwark against the onslaught of soldiers. He braced himself, digging his feet into the ground as he used the weight of his body to bash into the enemy with his shield. Tiatria, her hands glowing with an icy aura, stood by his side and unleashed a flurry of sharp ice shards at their opponents. Each shard varied in size and shape, some thick and jagged while others were thin and needle-like.

As Cullen fought on, he spotted a spear lying on the ground nearby. Without hesitation, he planted his left foot on it and lifted it up into his hand. With precise movements, he turned his forearm to flatten his shield and then rested the spear on top at its center. With this improvised weapon in hand, Cullen let out a mighty war cry and charged towards the soldiers. His attack was ferocious and powerful, skewering two enemies and pinning them against the wall with his spear. He used his shield to cleanly sever the heads off of two more soldiers before pulling his weapon back out from their bodies with a loud thud.

Meanwhile, Tiatria moved with grace and fluidity as she conjured up frozen spells that immobilized or threw back their enemies. She seemed to glide effortlessly across the battlefield, her hands weaving intricate patterns as she controlled the ice around her. The pinned soldiers screamed and moaned as they struggled to break free from their icy prisons.

Together, Cullen and Tiatria fought valiantly against their opponents, leaving behind a trail of fallen enemies with each strike. Their coordinated attacks were like a dance, each one perfectly complementing the other's moves. And as they continued to fight side by side, it was clear that they were an unbeatable duo.

Tiatria danced with fluid, effortless grace, her hands weaving through the air with precision as she summoned shards of ice to shoot out in all directions. Cullen's heart raced in his chest as he frantically tried to open the locked door, his fingers fumbling with the handle. "It won't budge!" he shouted, desperation and panic creeping into his voice. Beads of sweat formed on his forehead as he turned to Tiatria for guidance. "What do we do now, Tia?" he pleaded, fear and urgency evident in every line of his face. The air crackled with energy as Tiatria surveyed their surroundings; her ears picked up noises coming from the other side of the door.

With a fierce shout, Tiatria launched an ice shard at the wooden door, causing it to splinter and crack. The sound of terrified screams echoed from within, making Cullen realize there were still live people trapped on the other side. "Open the door!" he cried out, desperation creeping into his voice. "How do we know you won't kill us?" A voice from behind the door questioned, filled with fear and uncertainty. As another wave of undead creatures rose up around them, Cullen knew that their chances of survival were dwindling. He watched in horror as the undead creatures continued to rise despite their icy obstacles, their hungry moans growing louder by the second.

He frantically banged on the door, pleading for someone to let them in. "Because I'm not an undead creature!" Tiatria's movements were slowing, exhaustion taking its toll as she continued to fend off the relentless horde with her magic. "Please, for the love of God, open up!" Cullen's pleas became more urgent as he feared they would meet their end at the hands of the undead if they couldn't find shelter soon.

The sound of movement behind the door echoed through the dimly lit hallway, which gave Cullen a sign of hope. His heart raced as he watched with bated breath, knowing that they were not alone in this abandoned castle. Suddenly, a board was heard as it was removed from the door, and it creaked open slightly, revealing another knight of the order. Cullen's amazement quickly turned into determination as he called out to Tiatria, "Tia! Let's go!" Tiatria, who had been spinning gracefully in an effort to ward off any danger, immediately snapped to attention and ran for the door. With impressive agility, she evaded the grasping hands of undead creatures and made her way to freedom. In a matter of moments, she slipped through the doorway just before it was slammed shut and secured with a wooden board again, barring any further entry from the outside world. The relief and sense of accomplishment filled Cullen's chest as they both stood on the other side of the door, safe from whatever else lurked in the darkness of the castle halls.

Chapter 26

Cullen's body pressed firmly against the sturdy oak door, his muscles tense and ready for whatever may come. The frantic scratching and clawing from the other side caused his heart to pound heavily in his chest, but he forced himself to take slow, calming breaths as he leaned back against the solid wood. Standing beside him were a group of knights, their faces familiar from years of training together. Their expressions mirrored Cullen's determination and readiness for battle.

Before he could speak, a figure launched itself at him with an almost childlike eagerness. Cullen flew and thud against the door as he was being tightly squeezed around the chest and neck. It was Edith, her arms wrapping tightly around his neck in an exuberant hug. Cullen gasped for air since she knocked the wind out of him. She squeezed him fiercely, but a genuine smile spread across Cullen's face as he was happy to see her alive. Thankful that the King's daughter survived all this horror. "CULLEN!!!!" She almost screamed. "I knew you would save us!" Edith exclaimed with pure joy shining in her eyes.

After a moment, Cullen managed to catch his breath and gently pushed Edith back by her shoulders. "Edith," he gasped out, his voice filled with relief and gratitude, "you're alive!"

Tears glistened in Edith's eyes as she looked up at him. "It was horrible," she told him shakily, "that evil woman forced these knights to capture me along with my ladies in the chapel. She forced them to put us into the dark, cold dungeons."

Cullen's jaw tightened thinking about Edith and her companions being held captive by Amalia. He vowed to himself that he would do everything in his power to protect her and all those who were left in the castle and the kingdom from Amalia and Nimriar, no matter what it took. Cullen looked at Tiatria and the others as he looked at the soldiers, "How did you guys get here?" he questioned.

One of the guards looked at Cullen and told him what happened.

)o(

Amalia's cruel eyes scanned the remaining men left in the castle, a wicked and twisted smile creeping onto her lips. The Knight Commander stood tall and proud, surrounded by his loyal men who stood in a defiant stance. "What do you want with us, witch?" he demanded, his voice filled with determination.

A hush fell over the upper courtyard as Amalia's piercing gaze shifted from the Knight Commander to each of his men in turn. A malicious smirk played on her lips, reveling in their fear and desperation as she spoke with a vile tone, relishing in her power. "I have killed your King," she sneered, her voice dripping with venom. "I have taken your castle." The air was thick with tension and terror as she paused for dramatic effect, drinking in the fear and uncertainty of those around her. "You have a choice," she continued, her words laced with malice. "Either you serve me or you die the same way as your King, by dragon fire." The wind carried the scent of burning embers and smoke, a reminder of the destruction that had been unleashed upon the kingdom. Standing amidst it all was Amalia, a wicked Queen basking in her newfound power.

The Knight Commander loomed over what was left of the battlefield of the upper courtyard. His body stood tall amidst the chaos and destruction. His broad shoulders were squared, displaying a sense of strength and determination; even in the face of the witch's impressive display of power, he did not flinch even as he felt her powerful magic crackled around him. He remained unfazed, his expression a mask of steel. He drew in a deep breath; his grip tightened on the hilt of his sword as he steeled himself before addressing Amalia with a voice that was steady and unwavering. "If my King chose to meet his end by dragon fire, then it is an honorable fate for any knight loyal to both the crown and the Order," he declared boldly, a fierce glint in his eyes. With a swift motion, he unclasped his sword belt and let it fall to the ground with a resounding thud, a symbolic gesture of his unwavering loyalty and bravery in the face of such formidable danger. The clash of metal and roar of flames filled the air, but the Knight Commander stood strong, ready to defend his kingdom until the very end.

Amalia's bright eyes, reminiscent of precious cerulean jewels, flickered with an eager excitement as she intently observed the others around her. Anticipation and curiosity danced in her gaze as she awaited to see which brave soul would join their Commander in open defiance. The air was charged with tense energy, thick and weighty like an impending storm cloud, as they all braced for what was to come. Yet among the chaos, Amalia couldn't help but feel a sense of pride as she watched the seasoned knights, their polished armor reflecting the golden rays of sunlight, stand tall beside their fearless leader. They were a united front, unyielding to the will of a cruel tyrant and her ferocious beast.

A cruel smirk danced across Amalia's face. The thrill of victory sent shivers down her spine. She reveled in the sight before her - more than half of these pathetic humans had chosen death rather than bow to her will. Their screams would echo in her twisted mind like a symphony of suffering, as this brought a wicked delight to her heart. And soon, she would watch them burn in the merciless flames of the dragon she controlled, a glorious spectacle of destruction and power.

Amalia didn't spare a glance at her dragon as he rose onto his feet, his massive body towering over them all. The Commander and his men stood their ground, unflinching as they watched the beast open his jaws. A flicker of fire danced in the back of his throat, a sign of the destruction to come. Those who chose life wisely backed away, fear displayed on their trembling bodies. In an instant, the dragon unleashed a torrent of flames upon the traitors, engulfing them in an inferno. Amalia's eyes followed the horrifying scene before her, watching as the skin melted from their bodies and their armor disintegrated into pools on the floor.

Her lips curled into a satisfied smile as she turned to address those who remained loyal to her. "Search the palace," she commanded, her voice dripping with power and authority. "Bring anyone left alive to me."

Without another word, she strode confidently into the castle, her long white hair billowing behind her like a cloak. "You'll find me in my new throne room," she declared, already picturing herself sitting upon a grand throne as ruler of all she surveyed. The taste of victory was sweet on her tongue, and she reveled in it and made her way towards her newfound kingdom.

Edith huddled with her maids in a far corner of the chapel, the only shelter in the midst of chaos. Dust and debris littered the floor, the once-beautiful stained glass windows now shattered and scattered across the ground. Moving around was dangerous, but they had no choice. The priests continued to pray at the altar, their voices a steady hum amidst the chaos. Edith clutched her rosary tightly, praying fervently for Cullen to come and save her from this nightmare.

Suddenly, pounding could be heard against the chapel's door, causing Edith and her ladies to jump and scream. A commanding voice shouted, "Open up!" The Cardinal turned from the altar to look at the door, and a brave priest dashed over to open it. Relief flooded through everyone as they saw it was knights standing on the other side.

"Thank God!" exclaimed the priest as he swung open the heavy doors. The Cardinal approached cautiously, his eyes filled with concern. The knight's face betrayed nothing as he delivered his message.

"You're ordered to the throne room with immediate effect," he said firmly, leaving no room for questions or hesitation. The gravity of the situation weighed heavily on everyone present as they followed the knight out of the safety of the chapel and into unknown danger.

As they walked through the lavish halls towards the throne room, Edith's eyes darted nervously to one of the soldiers beside her. "Where is my Father? Is he safe?" she whispered, her heart thumping in her chest. The knights remained tight-lipped and forced them to keep walking. Fear began to gnaw at Edith as they approached the grand door of the throne room.

Once inside, Edith gasped in horror at the sight before her. Amalia, a woman she had never seen before, sat casually on her Father's ornate throne. Her legs were crossed, and her arms rested confidently on the armrests. A wave of rage and confusion swept over Edith as she demanded, "Who are you? And why are you sitting on my father's throne?"

Amalia's lips curled into a malicious smile as she spoke with venom in her voice, "I am your new Queen, little one." The weight of her words and the betrayal of seeing a stranger sitting on her Father's throne hit Edith like a blow to the stomach. She could feel everything crumbling around her as she stared in disbelief at this usurper who dared to disclaim her rightful place as Princess and heir to the throne.

Edith and the others exchanged worried glances before Edith squared her shoulders and turned to face Amalia. "Who are you, and where is my Father?" she demanded, her voice trembling slightly. Amalia slowly stood up from her throne and descended the marble steps until she was standing in front of the young Princess. With a sudden, swift motion, Amalia's hand connected with Edith's cheek in a resounding slap. "Your Father is dead," she answered, her tone filled with morbid satisfaction. "My dragon set him and his friends on fire." Edith's eyes widened in horror as she stared at Amalia in disbelief. "You lie! My Father wouldn't die like that!" she argued back, her voice rising in anger. But Amalia only looked at her with disdain, giving a signal to one of her soldiers who stepped forward to grab the Princess by the arm. "Take this insolent Princess to the courtyard," she ordered coldly before turning back to sit on her throne. "Once she learns the truth, have her whipped for her insubordination and locked away in confinement." The soldier dragged Edith away as she struggled against them, tears streaming down her face at the cruel fate that had befallen her beloved Father.

"You're wrong, you heretic witch!" Edith's words tore through the air like a sword slicing through flesh. Her eyes blazed with rage as she struggled against the knight who held her in a fierce grip. "Cullen would have protected my Father," she spat, her voice trembling with emotion. "He wouldn't have let him die in such a horrid manner!" The tears streaming down her face mingled with the dirt and blood on her cheeks, creating a hauntingly beautiful image of desperation and fury.

The sun beat down mercilessly through the windows, intensifying the heat of their heated exchange. The scent of burnt wood and charred flesh permeated the air, a grim reminder of the destruction that had taken place just moments before. Edith's heart pounded in her chest, fueling her determination to break free and unleash her wrath upon the one who dared speak ill of her beloved Cullen.

Amalia's lips curved into a quiet smile as she recalled the encounter. "There was a knight, a warrior mage and a mage of your Order," she began, her voice laced with amusement. "They bravely attempted to stop me, but I made short work of one of them and the others before the knight and the warrior mage fled with their tails tucked between their legs." Her eyes twinkled mischievously, remembering the swift and effortless victory over her opponent. The memory brought a surge of adrenaline and satisfaction, knowing her skills were unmatched.

"You're a liar!" Edith screamed, "You're a liar!"

)o(

Cullen's heart ached as he watched the tears well up in Edith's eyes, her pain evident in her trembling voice. "I was forced to look at a smoldering black patch that showed the remains of three bodies, burned beyond recognition. They claimed one of them was my Father," she choked out, her hand trembling as she gestured towards a pile of rubble in the distance. Cullen's jaw clenched at the thought of what she must have endured. "And then they dragged me here and locked us in. I'm afraid that witch would come after us again."

Cullen's grip on Edith's shoulders tightened as he recalled the horrifying scene he had witnessed earlier. The screams, the flames, the chaos...it was all too much to bear. But he couldn't let her see his own emotions crumbling under the weight of it all. Cullen then guided her to a nearby chair and knelt in front of her.

Edith looked up at him with pleading eyes, hoping against hope for some kind of reassurance. "Is it true?" she asked quietly, her voice barely above a whisper. "Is my Father really gone?"

Cullen turned away, not wanting to meet her gaze as he spoke the harsh truth. "Yes," he said softly, his voice heavy with sorrow. "He's gone."

Tears streamed down Edith's face in a torrent of grief as she buried her head in Cullen's chest, seeking comfort and solace in his embrace. They both knew that their lives would never be the same after this tragic event. The weight of the moment pressed heavily upon them as they stood locked in a heartbreaking embrace.

Edith's shoulders shook violently as she broke down in a full blown sob, her body wracked with the intensity of her emotions. She screamed at the unfairness of it all, at the profound loss that now consumed her.

In the background, Tiatria could hear everything that ran through the Princess' mind. Her thoughts seemed to revolve around Cullen killing the heretic witch, saving the kingdom, and marrying Edith to rule together. But Tiatria also noticed something else - Edith's gaze lingering on her ears, which were strikingly similar to those of the usurper's. Not to mention, her clothes were too revealing. After a moment, realization dawned on Edith as she turned to Cullen with fiery eyes and demanded answers: "Who is she? What is she?" she huffed, pointing at Tiatria. "Her ears are just like the other woman's!"

Cullen quickly stood up from where he had been kneeling and positioned himself between Edith and Tiatria. The elf's long, pointed ears twitched as she regarded them calmly. "Edith, relax," Cullen said firmly, trying to ease the tension in the room. "She is what's known as an elf." But the words seemed to do little to calm Edith or anyone else, who looked back at Cullen with wide, fearful eyes.

"The woman who killed my father looked just like her!" Edith screamed, her voice rising in panic. Several of the knights drew their swords, ready to defend against this potential threat. Cullen could feel his own hand tightening around the hand straps of his shield, prepared to use it if necessary. Honestly, Cullen knew he couldn't fight properly with just a shield, but he had practiced with his instructors to know how to make his shield not only a defensive weapon but also an offensive one, as well. "Tiatria may resemble our enemy, but she is not our enemy," he tried to reason with them.

"But she is one of them!" Edith yelled, her fury and grief evident in every word. "And now she sits on my Father's throne."

The Cardinal marched up to where Edith stood, his face twisted with disgust. The deep lines on his forehead and the quiver in his lip revealed his intense distaste for what lay before him. "You can't seriously be suggesting that we tolerate her presence?" he spat out, his voice dripping with venom. His piercing gaze bore into Tiatria as if she were a vile creature that did not deserve to walk among them. Cullen's jaw tensed as he tightened his grip on his shield, ready to defend Tiatria at all costs. The muscles in his arms bulged as he braced himself for any confrontation. His eyes burned with determination and anger, daring anyone to try and harm her while he still drew breath. The Cardinal's cold gaze then turned towards Cullen, "If you have any love or loyalty to God," he sneered, "you'll arrest that creature!" With a pointed finger, he gestured towards Tiatria, his hatred for her apparent. Cullen's heart raced as he stood there, torn between his faith and his conscience. "Or even better yet," the Cardinal continued with a sick grin, "kill her yourself!" The words hung in the air like a death sentence, sending shivers down Tiatria and Cullen's spines. But Cullen refused to let fear cloud his judgment - he would protect Tiatria until the very end.

With graceful, measured steps, Tiatria glided forward, her hands held out in a calming gesture towards the others. The golden light of the torches in the dungeon caught in her hair, highlighting its rich, red tones and casting her regal bearing in an ethereal glow.

All around her, the knights were drawn to her presence, their eyes fixated on her with a mix of awe and respect.

"I offer my most sincere apologies for the suffering you have endured, Princess," Tiatria spoke with a calm yet commanding voice that carried weight and authority. Her words were like a soothing balm, easing the tension and fear that had gripped them all. "Your suspicions are not unfounded; I myself and my people felt similarly when we first encountered Cullen and his friends. But in time, we came to understand one another and realize that we were not enemies."

She paused for a moment before continuing, her gaze locked with each knight's in turn. "I know that my appearance may bear resemblance to your enemy," she said softly but firmly, "but I assure you, I am not your enemy. I am here to stop Amalia and the dragon from causing any more harm to your land or your people." With her every word, Tiatria exuded strength and determination, making it clear that she was a force to be reckoned with in this battle for peace and justice.

Tiatria's words were laced with determination and a quiet power. She willed her words to carry their message of peace and resolution, her eyes locked with those of her opponents. "Once my task is done," she proclaimed, "I will return to my own realm and leave you to live in peace." The other knights watched on with awe and admiration, marveling at Tiatria's poise and grace under the tense circumstances. Her stance was unwavering, every move deliberate and filled with purpose. As she spoke, the weight of her words seemed to carry themselves to every corner of the dungeon.

Edith's eyes flicked with a mix of emotions as she looked at Cullen, her lips pursed in a deep frown. "How can you trust her?" she asked, her voice dripping with doubt and anger, "Or even tolerate her after all that her kind has done?" Cullen felt the weight of her words like a physical blow, knowing that she had no idea about the complicated history between humans and elves. His throat tightened as he struggled to find the right words to defend Tiatria, to explain the depth of their bond and the truth of her actions. But there was no time for such discussions now. The battle ahead loomed over them like a dark cloud, pushing aside any personal conflicts or prejudices.

"Edith, we don't have time for this," he told her and looked at the others, "We don't have time for any of this!" He couldn't blame Edith or the others, really. They were facing a serious threat to their kingdom, and any personal grievances would only hinder them. With a sigh, Cullen turned to address the other knights. "Those who wish to avenge our fallen king, come with me," he commanded, his voice firm and determined. "Any who choose to stay behind must protect the Princess with their lives."

The knights stood in a circle, their eyes focused intently as they made their choices and began to gather their weapons. The powerful aura of determination filled the air, swirling around them like a cloak of courage. The Cardinal's sharp, calculating eyes darted back and forth between the young knight Cullen and the delicate elven warrior Tiatria. He couldn't help but be intrigued by this unlikely pair. What could have brought them together? And then it dawned on him – Cullen had feelings for this elf, and perhaps she reciprocated.

The realization caused a flicker of annoyance to cross the old man's weathered face. How dare this inexperienced boy claim to protect such an exquisite creature? But he couldn't deny the underlying admiration he felt for Cullen's bravery. With a subtle clench of his jaw, he looked at the young knight with narrowed eyes.

"You're in love with her aren't you, boy?" His voice was laced with skepticism as he stroked his chin with his right hand and supported his elbow with his left arm.

A wave of shock and disbelief washed over Edith, causing her once rosy cheeks to turn deathly pale. Her heart stopped as she felt sharp, icy daggers pierce through her chest at the sight before her - The Cardinal standing in front of Cullen. She could see the truth in Cullen's eyes as he froze upon hearing those words. With trembling lips, she looked at Cullen, her eyes searching for an explanation.

"You're...in love with her?" She choked out the words in a cold, pained tone, unable to hide the hurt in her voice. But even as she spoke, the realization dawned on her like a bolt of lightning. It was clear in her tone and her expression - she already knew the answer.

Cullen's face flushed with embarrassment as he avoided meeting her gaze. He had never intended for things to happen this way, but his heart had led him to where it truly belonged. "We were supposed to be married," Edith whispered in disbelief and confusion, which was evident in every word she spoke. As she looked between Cullen and the Cardinal, she couldn't help but wonder how everything could fall apart so quickly.

Without warning, Edith's body tensed, and she lunged at Cullen with a primal ferocity. The sound of her sharp intake of breath was like a predator preparing to strike. Her fingers curled into claws as she swiped at his cheek with all her might, the impact resonating through the air like a thunderclap. Cullen reacted swiftly, catching her flailing arms in a firm grasp as she thrashed against his chest plate. Her screams were guttural, reverberating off the stone walls like a trapped animal fighting for its life.

"You promised to marry me! We were supposed to rule this kingdom together!" Edith's words were filled with desperation and betrayal, tears streaming down her flushed cheeks.

Cullen's face contorted with anger as he looked down at her, his expression raw and honest. "I didn't promise to marry you!" he snarled, his voice laced with bitterness and resentment. "My father told me I had to." His own fists clenched at his sides, the weight of his duty heavy on his shoulders.

Edith's gaze burned with anger as she stared at Cullen, her fists clenched tightly at her sides. "Of course he did!" she exclaimed, her voice sharp and filled with bitterness. "I told my Father I wanted to marry you, and he in turn, told your Father to make it happen!" Her eyes then shifted to Tiatria, and they were filled with piercing green jealousy. "How could you betray me like this?" Her voice cracked, revealing the raw emotion of disbelief and hurt that had taken hold of her. She shook her head in disbelief, unable to comprehend how Tiatria could have fallen for someone who wasn't even human. Tears streamed down her face, mixing with sweat and dirt as she continued to fight against him in a wild frenzy fueled by the pain and betrayal of their once close relationship.

Cullen shook his head, his inner turmoil reflected in the deep creases of his brow. He felt as though he were being pulled in two different directions - one towards duty and responsibility, the other towards the desires of his heart. His mind was a swirling storm of conflicting emotions, and it showed on his face. "Edith," he began, his voice strained with raw emotion, "if this journey has taught me anything, it is that matters of the heart cannot be dictated by others." His words hung heavily in the air, causing the Princess to pause and turn to face him. And then, as if a switch had been flipped, Cullen's eyes softened into warm pools of melted honey. "I have always cherished our friendship," he continued, his hand reaching out to gently caress her cheek, "but I cannot force myself to love you in a way that I am not capable of." The walls seemed to soak in Cullen's gentle words, leaving only the weight of unspoken truths between them.

Cullen then looked at the Cardinal and the others, "We don't have time for this," he said, "We have bigger problems to deal with." And with that, he turned and opened the door as he and Tiatria left the room, leading his men into battle, leaving Edith alone with the Cardinal to process her conflicting emotions.

)o(

Maxwell stood in the smoky, dimly lit blacksmith's shop, watching intently as the skilled craftsman put the finishing touches on the chains. The fire from the hearth cast flickering shadows across the walls and floor, adding an eerie ambiance to the scene. Maxwell couldn't help but nod with approval at the completed work, admiring the expert craftsmanship of the man before him.

Leaning forward over the flames, Maxwell addressed the blacksmith with a serious tone. "Excellent," he said, his eyes never leaving the chains. "Now, I need you to do one more thing."

The blacksmith gave a respectful nod, waiting for further instruction. "I need you to carefully pack these chains into a cart or box and transport them as close as possible to the dragon's location," Maxwell explained, his voice low and urgent. "But be careful not to wake it." A sense of tension filled the air as both men understood the danger of their mission. But they also knew it was necessary in order to defeat the powerful dragon that threatened their kingdom.

The Blacksmith's weathered face was contorted in anger, his rough hands clenched into fists at his sides. Normally, he would have cursed at Maxwell and knocked him out with a single punch to the face for his reckless actions. But in that moment, all he could think about was stopping the witch and her fire breathing beast from destroying their land.

"I'll see it done," he growled, determination shining in his eyes as he met Maxwell's pleading gaze. "Just stop that witch and her fire-breathing lizard of hers."

Maxwell nodded, grateful for the blacksmith's pledge of assistance. He held out his trembling hand as the blacksmith took it firmly in his own calloused grip. "Thank you," he said before tearing himself away and running out of the building, his mind racing to figure out what to do next. The sound of the blacksmith's hammer pounding against hot metal echoed behind him as he raced towards the looming threat, heart pounding in his chest.

Maxwell walked away slowly from the smith's building, and as he turned a corner, his eyes widened in shock at the sight before him. Dead soldiers stood around, their lifeless bodies seemingly frozen in time. Each one was standing attentive, as if still under orders from their commanders. Maxwell had never seen anything like it in all his years of battle. He took a deep breath and steeled himself for whatever fate was to come his way. With determination in his heart, he drew his swords and channeled electricity into them, causing them to crackle with power. His senses were heightened, ready to face this new enemy.

The soldiers moved towards him with surprising speed, their attacks wild and sloppy but still dangerous. Maxwell cried out as he swung his swords with precision and strength, each strike taking off heads or cutting off limbs. One unfortunate soldier met its end as Maxwell's blades pierced through its armor, the electricity coursing through its body until it was nothing more than a charred shell. But even in death, these soldiers showed no signs of pain or fear. They simply continued to attack, driven by some unknown force. Maxwell grimaced as he effortlessly sliced through them, the sound of metal against metal filling the air like a macabre symphony.

Finally, with one swift movement, Maxwell used both swords to slice a soldier clean in half. His eyes held no emotion or recognition of what was happening, just an empty stare as the soldier fell to the ground. Maxwell couldn't help but feel a twinge of sadness for these undead soldiers who were once brave warriors like himself. But there was no time for sentimentality in the midst of battle.

With a determined stride and a steadfast gaze, he moved on, resolute in his determination to face whatever challenges lay ahead. His mind was focused, and his heart was brave as he braced himself for the unknown. There was no turning back now, but he felt ready to take on whatever the future held in store for him and the others.

Chapter 27

With gritted teeth and a fearless determination, Maxwell carved his way through the castle's undead soldiers. Each swing of his sword was precise and deadly, aimed at their legs to prevent them from following him. His heart raced as he thought about Cullen and the others, hoping they were safe amidst the chaos. The sprawling castle was a maze of hallways and stairs; Maxwell had no idea where any of his comrades might've gone. But he ran on, driven by a burning need to find them.

After what felt like an eternity of twists and turns, Maxwell caught a glimpse of movement up ahead. Relief flooded through him as he recognized Cullen and Tiatria leading a small group of surviving members from the order. "There you are, Branson!" Maxwell called out as he joined them in their frantic escape.

As they kept running, Cullen turned to Maxwell with urgency in his eyes. "The men told me Amalia is in the throne room! I know where it is; follow me!" With a renewed sense of determination, they followed Cullen's lead towards the heart of the castle, praying that they would reach Amalia before it was too late.

After several minutes of fighting the undead, Ásbjǫrn's sharp, piercing eyes took in another scene. He noticed Amalia's delicate features twisted in shock and she gasped for breath, her chest heaving with each ragged intake of air. Thamyris, on the other hand, seemed to visibly release his tense stance and take a deep, relieved breath. But in an instant, everything changed. Amalia fell to her knees with a loud thud, her once graceful movements now clumsy and uncoordinated as she clutched at her stomach. A wave of confusion and alarm washed over Ásbjǫrn as he watched

Thamyris step back from his sister, the truth slowly dawning on him. His eyes caught sight of a glint of metal and he realized with horror that there was a small dagger buried in Amalia's stomach. Black tendrils snaked their way across her body, spreading like a dark poison as her eyes widened in shock and pain.

Without hesitation, Ásbjǫrn extended his right hand and summoned vines from the earth, their strong grasp quickly wrapping around Amalia's trembling body and preventing her from causing any further harm to herself or others. Meanwhile, Thamyris pulled out the dagger with a shaking hand, his gaze filled with tears and regret as he looked upon his sister.

"Iron," he gasped through choked sobs, "I took it from one of these corpses before I ran to put myself between you two." A wave of empathy washed over Ásbjǫrn as he realized the desperate measures Thamyris had taken to deceive and stop his own sister. "I just needed you to get close enough to me," Thamyris explained, his voice filled with sorrow and guilt at what he had done. "So I had to let you think you had the upper hand."

Ásbjǫrn pounded his massive paws into the ground, causing the vines to sprout from the ground and take hold of the undead. The vines blanketed the floor, preventing any undead from rising to their feet. Others were ensnared by vines like ropes, which crushed them as they tightened their grip.

The ancient castle was shaken to its foundations as Nimriar roared in fury, his powerful voice reverberating off the stone walls and rattling the windows. Amalia's pained cries only fueled his rage, igniting a fire within him that threatened to consume everything in its path. Meanwhile, Tiatria stood frozen in shock, her heart pounding in her chest as she watched the men rush past her toward the throne room.

But instead of following them, she turned and ran towards the courtyard. The cool, marble tiles beneath her feet echoed with each step as she made her way towards the dragon, determined to face him on her own terms.

Finally, Cullen and the others pushed open the heavy doors of the throne room to find Thamyris and Ásbjǫrn battered and bruised but miraculously alive. Amalia lay tangled in a web of vines, controlled by Ásbjǫrn's powerful abilities. The two friends looked up at their rescuers with a mix of relief and amusement. "Took you long enough," Thamyris teased with a smirk, "Where's Tiatria?" His voice was gravelly from hours of shouting and fighting, but there was still a hint of humor in it despite their dire situation. The flickering torches cast shadows across their faces, making them look even more battle-worn and determined as they prepared for their next move against Nimriar.

Cullen and Maxwell frantically scanned their surroundings, searching for the elusive elf. But she seemed to have vanished into thin air. "She was just here," Cullen muttered, his heart racing as a sense of foreboding washed over him, chilling his blood and sending shivers down his spine.

Maxwell's heart raced as he cautiously approached Thamyris and the others, his feet dragging through the underbrush of vines as he walked up to the three he noticed the blood seeping and dripping from the tightly bound vines that held Amalia captive. His hands shook with fear and rage, his voice betraying his emotions as he gruffly asked, "Is she dead?"

Amalia's once beautiful face was now twisted and contorted with malice, her eyes cold and lifeless. As she slowly turned to face Maxwell, a cruel smile stretched across her lips, revealing white teeth like a predator ready to strike. With venomous words, she taunted him, relishing in his pain and suffering. "I took great pleasure in seeing the one you loved writhe in agony as his flesh burned." Each word felt like a sharp dagger piercing Maxwell's already wounded heart.

In a fit of blind rage, Maxwell lashed out and slapped Amalia across the face. His eyes blazed with steel determination and danger as he snarled at her through gritted teeth, "You have no idea what you took from me!" The pain and anguish in his tone echoed the depth of his loss, his fists trembling as he fought back tears of anger and sorrow. Maxwell's face reacted to being caught by surprise as Ásbjǫrn put his right hand on his shoulder. Maxwell's eyes softened as he could see the compassion in Ásbjǫrn's eyes.

Amalia's intense gaze suddenly shifted, causing Maxwell's eyes to follow her line of sight. There, nestled on a nearby table, was a book. It seemed to emanate an otherworldly aura, drawing Maxwell in. As he approached the book, his heart skipped a beat when he realized it was the same one the elven Queen had gifted to Dorian. Its magic was undeniable; not even dragon fire could extinguish such a powerful relic. Tears welled up in Maxwell's eyes as he reverently took the book into both hands.

But then something caught his eye, causing him to stagger backwards in disbelief. In the corner of the room stood a full length mirror, reflecting back a scene that left Maxwell and Cullen speechless. Inside the mirror stood their loved ones - Dorian and Cullen's Father - looking just as they did before their tragic deaths.

Cullen stepped forward, unable to believe what he was seeing. Was this some kind of illusion? But as he looked closer at his Father inside the mirror, he knew deep down that it was real. Maxwell approached cautiously, his shock turning to awe and wonder at the sight of his love alive inside the mirror.

Turning to Amalia, Cullen saw a dark gleam in her eyes, a wicked grin on her face that sent chills down his spine. This wasn't just any mirror - it was a magical portal, created by Amalia's twisted mind for her own sadistic enjoyment.

Cullen's voice was sharp with accusation as he demanded an answer, eyes narrowed and fists clenched. Maxwell slowly approached the mirror, his heart sinking as he caught sight of Dorian on the other side, his reflection almost mocking in its perfection. His trembling fingers reached out to touch the cold surface of the glass, as if hoping for some kind of connection. Maxwell fought back a wave of tears, knowing that Dorian would see it as weakness. He could sense the weight of Dorian's disapproving gaze, silently telling him that enough tears had been shed already, there was no use wasting any more now. The room felt heavy with unspoken emotions as the two men stood on either side of the mirror, their reflections a stark reminder of everything they had lost.

A cruel smirk played on Amalia's lips as Cullen's anger fueled her twisted pleasure. She reveled in the pain she had given, savoring every moment of his rage like a fine wine. "I bound their souls, trapped them within the mirror," she sneered, her voice dripping with malice. "I ground their charred remains into dust after the Princess saw what remained of her Father." she giggled maniacally, "I knew you would love one final reunion with your loved ones before you meet your own death."

Maxwell could only watch helplessly as Dorian pressed his hand against the unforgiving glass, his captivating smile never faltering. The scene before him was both disturbing and mesmerizing.

"It is a perversion against nature itself!" Ásbjǫrn bellowed, his fists clenching so tightly that even the vines around him seemed to constrict further. "To deny a soul, any soul, from its natural rest is an affront to nature itself! How could you do such a thing?"

Amalia giggled at the outburst. "Fool," she taunted, "toying with one's prey is only natural! I am relishing every delicious moment that your friends are enduring." Cullen shook his head in defiance. "I will not give you anything!"

Amalia chuckled darkly. "You may not be willing to give me what I desire, but your friend certainly is." Amalia's lips curled into a wicked smile as she leaned back, savoring every moment of their excruciating pain. Cullen couldn't tear his eyes away as he watched her, feeling a mixture of fear and fascination. He turned to the mirror beside him, where his Father stood with his usual air of pride. His strong hand rested casually on the pommel of his sword, but this time there was something different in his expression. It was a look that Cullen had never seen before - pride. As he met his Father's gaze, a small smile tugged at the corners of his lips and he gave a subtle nod of approval. It was a feeling he had never experienced before, to be seen as a man by his own father. And in that moment, Cullen knew that he had made him proud.

A sharp, piercing whistle sliced through the air, followed by a deafening crash as the mirror shattered into a thousand pieces, jolting Maxwell out of his thoughts. Maxwell spun around, his eyes wide with shock and fear, to see Thamyris lowering his bow with a placid expression on his face. Meanwhile, Amalia stood nearby, her laughter ringing out in a half-mad tone that sent chills down everyone's spine. "We need to leave," he urged the others before turning to walk away.

Maxwell turned his head back at the pieces of the mirror, he fell to his knees as tears threatened to burst from his eyes. A knot formed in his throat as he felt a gentle touch on his shoulder, as he turned his head, Ásbjǫrn stood beside him, looking at him with compassionate eyes. Maxwell's gaze fell upon the broken fragments of the mirror, its once pristine surface now reflecting only the chaos of the room and the destruction around it.

"Come," Ásbjǫrn said softly, "what you were seeking was never here."

With those words, Maxwell watched Ásbjǫrn turn and walk towards Thamyris, leaving Maxwell to follow behind in a daze of confusion and loss. The scene around them was filled with shards of glass glinting in the light, their sharp edges gleaming like knives in the fading sunlight. It was a befitting reflection of the turmoil within Maxwell's own mind as he struggled to make sense of what had just transpired.

)o(

With the warmth of the sun on her face, Tiatria burst out into the open courtyard. The rays danced across her skin, welcoming her with a gentle caress. She stood before Nimriar, his powerful form towering over her, as he laid in front of her with his front legs crossed. As she looked up at the dragon, she could feel the heat radiating from his massive body. His jaw was still dripping with a fiery ooze, and his eyes glinted with amusement as he spoke.

"So you have come to me at last, little one," boomed the beast. Tiatria's heart pounded in her chest as she gazed up at him, unable to tear her eyes away. "Come to command me then?" he questioned.

Summoning all strength Tiatria's body took on a golden glow, revealing her newly anointed status. "I am your new Priestess, and I command you to return to your home in the forest. Go back to your slumber until the day when you are truly needed." The words rang out with a commanding tone, echoing through the courtyard. Tiatria could feel the weight of her destiny upon her shoulders, her eyes then took on the same golden glow as she stared into the fierce gaze of Nimriar. She prayed that her faith and power would be enough to tame the mighty creature before her.

The dragon let out a deep, rumbling bellow of a laugh, as he was clearly unimpressed, his voice reverberating through the air. "You are not the one who summoned me," he retorted, "you are not the one who commands me." Tiatria's expression turned disapproving as she stared up at the mighty creature before her. "Your Priestess has been stripped from her title, by our Goddess!" she declared as her voice echoed, determined to stand her ground. Nimriar snorted and stomped his right front leg, causing the ground to tremble beneath them. "I will not take orders from you!" he roared, his fiery breath causing the air to sizzle with heat. "How do you propose to stop me?" Tiatria's lips curled into a sly smile as she spoke confidently, "By summoning those who are loyal to me." The dragon's eyes narrowed in amusement as he felt pretty confident in handling any of her companions, who were mere ants in his view. "Like who?" he challenged with a smirk on his face.

The deafening roar that echoed across the wind, "Like me!" The familiar voice sent delicious shivers down Nimriar's spine, the sound reverberating through his bones. He could feel the ground beneath him tremble with each powerful gust of wind as a massive force approached. Suddenly, tons of thick, mud-like sludge rained down on him as Myrae flew over the beast, her enormous jaws and fluid-like body unleashing their strength upon him in a ferocious attack. As the earth shook and the air filled with dust and tumultuous noise, Nimriar couldn't help but let out a deep laugh, feeling alive and exhilarated by the thrilling challenge before him. It was a battle for dominance, a dance between two mighty creatures that reignited his primal instincts and ignited a fire within his soul.

With a roar that matched Myrae's in both volume and intensity, Nimriar opened his own formidable jaws, unleashing a stream of fiery breath that narrowly missed its target. As he beat his powerful wings, lifting himself into the air, the two dragons engaged in a chaotic dance in the sky. Tiatria watched in awe as they clashed, their movements swift and graceful despite their massive size.

Their breaths collided in a dazzling display of power and skill, mud-like and fiery streams mixing together and lighting up the sky. Claws and teeth clashed, each combatant fiercely determined to gain an advantage over the other in this epic aerial battle. Their resounding roars shook the very ground beneath them, captivating all who witnessed the thrilling scene unfolding before them. It was a magnificent display of strength, agility, and primal power that left all who saw it speechless with wonder and awe.

As Cullen and his companions burst into the open courtyard, a sudden cascade of shimmering ice rained down from the sky, showering Nimriar in a freezing torrent. The once-fierce fire dragon was caught off guard, unable to withstand the sudden onslaught of cold. In a flash, Myrae, with her powerful jaws and sharp claws, was upon him, her body exuding a palpable aura of sheer strength and determination. She latched onto Nimriar's neck with a ferocious grip, determined to take him down. But she was not alone in this battle.

Naga, the magnificent ice dragon with sleek icy pale scales that reflected the sun's rays, also joined the fray, his immense size and power causing even more chaos within the courtyard. As he flew through the air, his wings created a gust of wind that whipped around them all. Nimriar let out an angry roar as Naga's icy breath hit him square in the chest, cooling the molten fire that coursed through his body and sending waves of pain through his being.

The clash of elements filled the air as these two mighty dragons battled for dominance over both the sky above and the land below. Sparks flew as their powers clashed, each trying to gain the upper hand in this epic aerial duel. Amidst it all stood Cullen and his companions, watching in awe and fear as the fate of their world hung in the balance.

Maxwell's keen eyes scanned the courtyard, taking in the scene of chaos and destruction. The air was thick with the stench of death and decay as the undead roamed around. The blacksmith stood there, gasping for breath and clung onto the handles of a wheelbarrow filled with heavy chains. His body was covered in cuts and bruises, evidence of his desperate struggle to escape the grasp of the undead.

With a determined look on his face, Maxwell wasted no time barking out orders to his men who quickly fell into formation behind him. They moved swiftly towards the blacksmith, their weapons at the ready.

But amidst all the chaos and commotion below, Tiatria couldn't tear her gaze away from the fierce battle happening above her. Naga, the powerful fire dragon, had Nimriar's fragile wing clamped between his razor-sharp jaws, causing blood to pour from the torn membranes. In retaliation, Nimriar used his hind legs to slash at Naga's belly, leaving behind a deep gash that caused the ice dragon to roar in pain and release his hold on Nimriar.

Seizing this opportunity, Nimriar swiftly turned and engaged Myrae in a deadly dance. His front legs clawed at her neck while she fought back by sinking her teeth deeper into his fiery scales. The clash of two mighty dragons echoed through the sky as they battled for dominance, their roars reverberating through every inch of the courtyard.

Naga's majestic wings beat against the wind as he soared through the skies, his regal form illuminated by the golden rays of the sun. But Tiatria's keen eyes immediately spotted a deep wound on his side, and her heart clenched with fear and concern. Closing her eyes in intense concentration, she spread out her slender fingers in a prayer-like gesture and began to speak soothing elvish words. The air seemed to be still around them as she channeled her healing powers towards Naga's injury. The golden light radiating its power from her body grew brighter with each passing moment. Cullen could only watch in amazement when the incredible magic of his elven love worked its wonders. The very fabric of nature seemed to respond to Tiatria's powerful magic, the gentle breeze carrying the sweet fragrance of wildflowers and adding to the mystical atmosphere that surrounded them.

Ásbjǫrn and Thamyris quickly noticed a horde of undead surging towards them. The sound of their decayed limbs dragging against the ground echoed through the courtyard, sending shivers down their spines. Without hesitation, Thamyris swiftly notched arrows onto his bowstring and let loose a barrage of shots, taking down any creature that dared get too close to Maxwell or his men, who were busy pulling heavy iron chains out of a nearby wheelbarrow. Meanwhile, Ásbjǫrn brought Amalia with him, her body still tightly bound by thorny vines. Gently setting her aside, he looked into her eyes with sadness as he could see the vines and the stab wound taking a toll on her strength. His eyes softened as he saw her struggling to breathe.

But there was no time to tend to her now. With a determined look, Ásbjǫrn's body morphed into that of a large bear and he charged towards the oncoming army of undead. His massive paws swiped and crushed any undead in his path, while his ferocious roars filled the air and struck fear into their decaying hearts.

As much as he wanted to go back and help Amalia, Ásbjǫrn knew that his priority was to protect his comrades and defeat their enemies. "I will come back for you," he promised silently, before turning back to the battle at hand with renewed vigor and determination.

Cullen's eyes widened in awe as he watched Tiatria's light grow brighter, almost blinding in its intensity. Naga could feel the surge of healing power coursing through his body, repairing his wounds and restoring his strength with each passing moment. The radiant energy washed over him, filling him with renewed vigor and vitality. With a fierce roar of rejuvenation, he took to the air once more, his wings beating strong against the wind as he soared towards Nimriar. As he closed in on his fiery foe, he could feel the familiar rush of adrenaline and excitement building within him.

With expert precision and agility, Naga grabbed onto Nimriar's left wing and spun the beast around, causing it to lose balance and momentum. Sensing an opportunity, both Naga and Myrae entwined their powerful tails around Nimriar's massive body, adding to its weight and causing all three dragons to crash to the ground in a thunderous collision.

The impact was so forceful that it uprooted trees and sent dirt flying into the air as they slid across the earth in a chaotic display of strength and power. The ground trembled beneath their massive forms as they continued to battle, their roars echoing through the surrounding landscape like thunder in a stormy sky.

Maxwell, Cullen and their companions strained against the weight of the massive chain, their muscles bulging and straining as they fought to haul it over to where the dragons had landed. Their arms burned with exertion as they pulled and tugged, sweat glistening on their brows. Myrae, her jaw gaping wide, pinned Nimriar to the ground with her enormous claws, her gleaming scales glittering in the sunlight. As she did, a deluge of thick mud rained down upon him, coating everything in its path.

Naga's urgent voice pierced through the chaos, "Hurry, little ones! We cannot hold him forever!" He too was struggling against Nimriar's immense strength, his own scales flashing in the light as he fought to keep the enemy at bay. The ground shook and trembled beneath their feet as the two powerful creatures clashed, their roars thundering through the air like an earthquake. Maxwell could feel the weight of their mission pressing down on them, knowing that they had only moments before Naga and Myrae would lose their advantage over Nimriar's.

With gritted teeth and full force, he and his companions pushed forward with all their might. Every step felt like trudging through quicksand, but they refused to give up. They were determined to protect their dragon allies and defeat this formidable foe. As they strained against the chain, Maxwell could feel his heart beating rapidly in his chest, a mixture of fear and adrenaline coursing through his veins. But he refused to let it slow him down - failure was not an option.

Maxwell and Cullen's eyes widened in awe as they watched the mighty dragon fight with Myrae against Nimrair. The massive creatures' scales glistened under the sunlight, each one reflecting a different color of the rainbow. "It would go faster with your help!" Maxwell exclaimed, straining to walk towards them against the powerful gusts of wind created by the fighting dragons. They were only a few hundred yards away, but it felt like miles. Naga turned her head briefly to look at Nimrair, who was struggling to keep the dragon pinned down into the earth. "I would if I could," Naga called back to Maxwell over the deafening roars and bursts of fire, "but I too am occupied!" Flames continued to spout from Nimriar's jaws as he fiercely battled against the other two dragons, each using their own unique breath weapons to try and subdue him. Meanwhile, Thamyris had heard the commotion so he swiftly turned around to face the direction of the fight. Within a moment of intense concentration, he sensed the source of the heat emanating from. With a quick motion, he pulled back his bowstring and called forth divine energy that swirled around him as he charged his arrow.

"Ásbjǫrn!" he cried out, Ásbjǫrn gave a massive swipe of his large paw to swipe an undead soldier a cross the ground. He then turned around to look at Thamyris, "I need your eyes!" Ásbjǫrn ran as fast as he could towards the dragons, with Ásbjǫrn looking in the dragons' general direction. He was able to pinpoint Nimriar's location, Thamyris let go of the arrow, sending it whistling through the air at blinding speed towards its target.

As Nimriar tilted his head to look at Thamyris, he let loose a torrent of fiery breath in an attempt to incinerate the oncoming arrow. But it passed through the flames unscathed, gaining speed with each passing second. A burst of light radiated from the arrow as it closed in on its target. Nimriar's heart raced as he desperately fought against the two dragons perched on top of him, his adrenaline finally kicking in as he managed to strike Naga in the jaw with his powerful tail. In a sudden surge of strength, he lurched upwards and snatched Myrae by the neck, throwing her to the ground before rolling onto his feet.

Meanwhile, Tiatria raised her left hand, still engulfed in a dazzling golden light. With her heightened senses, she could see that the arrow was now poised to strike Myrae instead of Nimriar. Acting quickly, she caused the arrow to disintegrate into nothingness before it could do any harm. As Nimriar used his massive claws to pin Myrae down, his fierce eyes locked onto Maxwell and the others with a deadly grin. Fire seemed to flicker between his teeth as he prepared for his next move.

Maxwell's voice rang out in panic, "Run, run, run!" And they all dropped the chain scattered around them, scrambling away from Nimriar's terrifying presence. But even as they fled, the dragon unleashed his fire with deadly precision, scorching everything in its path. The intense heat and flames claimed several of the knights' lives as they were caught in its destructive wake.

While holding Myrae's slender neck firmly in his razor-sharp claws, Nimriar summoned all of his dragon strength and unleashed a ferocious torrent of fiery lava onto the emerald dragon. She thrashed and roared in agony as her once vibrant scales sizzled and blackened under the intense heat. But despite the pain, she refused to back down, her determination shining through her desperate cries. "Give up, Nimriar!" she bellowed bravely. "You cannot win this battle!"

Before Nimriar could even muster a response or catch his breath, Naga appeared with a mighty swoop from above, followed by a deafening crash. She slammed into Nimriar with incredible force, sending both dragons hurtling towards one of the castle's towering turrets. The impact shook the ground beneath them, causing a massive cloud of dust to billow into the air and adding to the chaos of their fierce battle. As they tumbled and struggled amid the debris, bricks and rubble rained down around them like a violent storm. It was a clash of epic proportions between two dragons locked in an unyielding struggle for dominance.

The great dragon, Naga, abruptly halted his flight, his massive wings continuing to beat with such force that the air around them seemed to freeze. Nimrair's body was covered in rubble from the castle's debris, and Myrae struggled to break free as Nimriar's jaws grip loosened. Naga's icy breath froze the ground, as to make it harder for the dragon to rise from frozen earth. Myrae used all her strength to rise to her feet as Nimriar's grip on her neck finally released her, turned to face Maxwell and the others. Urgency filled her voice as she cried out to them: "Quickly! Now! Hurry!" The group wasted no time and grabbed the chain that would hopefully weaken the beast, running as fast as they could towards the buried dragon.

Their feet pounded against the ground, their muscles straining under the weight of fear and determination. Each step was a battle against the intense heat emanating from Nimriar's body, radiating outward like waves from a scorching sun. But they pushed forward, risking everything for this one gamble.

With every step closer to Nimrair's body, their senses were assaulted by a mix of sensations - the overwhelming heat, the stench of burnt flesh and singed hair, and the deafening roar of Naga's rage. But amidst all of it, Myrae's emerald scales shone like gems in the sunlight, reflecting the colors of the surrounding landscape in dazzling hues. She used her powerful mud breath to add onto the debris piled atop Nimrair, adding an earthy scent to the air as she coated the ground in thick layers of protective muck.

As they closed in on their goal, their hearts pounded with adrenaline and fear; they knew that their success would only come down to luck. But they didn't let that stop them - they were warriors on a mission, and nothing would stand in their way now.

Slowly, Nimriar began to awaken from his unconscious state. Maxwell's body jolted and trembled as he dropped his section of the chain as if it were searing hot causing the others to do the same which caused a loud clang that reverberated through the air. The others mirrored his actions, their eyes wide with fear as they backed away in unison. "Back up!" Maxwell bellowed, sprinting back with his men several feet away from the towering beast that had burst out of the rubble.

Nimriar, the dragon, roared with such force that it shook the ground beneath their feet. His eyes glowed with a dangerous rage, while flames erupted from his massive jaws like a volcano about to erupt. With a swift motion, Maxwell and his men grabbed the chain and used it as a makeshift rope, leaving enough slack for them to maneuver with it. The dragon's tail whipped around wildly, smashing into boulders and sending them hurtling towards Maxwell and his men. Reacting quickly, Maxwell dodged and weaved alongside Cullen and a handful of others, narrowly avoiding being crushed by the flying rocks. However, two unfortunate knights weren't as lucky and were mercilessly crushed under the weight of the debris. Maxwell hit the ground hard, skidding across the dirt before coming to a stop. He shook his head to clear it, using his arms to push himself back up onto his feet. Without hesitation, he charged towards the chains once more with a determined group of men at his heels, ready to end this battle once and for all.

As Tiatria looked on, suspended in the air by her powerful magic, she extended her right arm, and the chains glowed with a blinding white light. Maxwell and the others, their muscles bulging with effort, lifted the heavy chains as if they weighed nothing at all. Myrae, with her enormous body and glistening scales, whipped around and used her powerful tail to strike Nimriar across the face, catching him in his fiery eye. He let out a guttural roar of pain and anger as Naga swooped down once again to blast him with a freezing breath.

The fires within Nimriar's jaws smoldered as he let out another deafening roar. Suddenly, the iron chains shot and wrapped tightly around his massive jaws, snapping them shut. The dragon's power was immense, and it took all of Maxwell and his companions' strength to hold onto the dragon that felt like a searing hot chain and keep Nimriar restrained. The iron burned. It burned worse than any fire, anything that could have ever been conceived, through the dragon's scales as it tightly bound his mouth shut. Myrae and Naga continued their relentless attacks, slowly wearing down the mighty dragon as they circled each other in a dance of ice and earth.

Maxwell's muscles rippled and bulged beneath his skin as he poured all of his energy into pulling the thick, heavy chain. A fierce roar erupted from deep within his chest, matching the sparks that shot from his hands and up the links of the chain. The powerful electrical currents coursed through his body, crackling and hissing with a life of their own. The dragon's massive body was engulfed in a blinding light, its once mighty form now writhing in agony as it faltered and collapsed to the ground at Maxwell's feet.

But this was not yet the end - Maxwell could feel it in his bones. He knew that if he stopped channeling the electrifying energy, the dragon would rise again and continue its rampage, surely killing them all. So he gritted his teeth, tightened his grip on the chain, and steeled himself for the final strike against their formidable foe.

With a fierce determination burning in his eyes, Maxwell raised the chain high above his head, ready to deliver the ultimate blow. He would protect his comrades at any cost and defeat this terrifying creature once and for all. He reached for Ka'imil but discovered that it was missing from his belt.

"SHIT!" he cried in frustration, "Where did it go?"

Maxwell watched as Cullen ran past him, his feet barely touching the thick chain as he balanced effortlessly. His shining sword, Ka'imil, caught the sunlight and reflected it back like a beacon as he held it tightly in his right hand. Pure white light burst from the blade, swirling around Cullen's arm and the blade itself. His left hand gripped onto the shield for balance as he traversed the precarious path.

"CULLEN! NO!" Maxwell's desperate cry echoed through the air, "LET ME DO IT!" he pleaded, but it was already too late. Cullen was already consumed by his determination to reach his enemy and end the fight once and for all. In his fervor, Maxwell hadn't even noticed that his sword had slipped from its holster when it fell to the ground after the dragon's last assault. The wind whipped through Cullen's hair, clearing sight from his determined face as he charged towards his destiny, willing to pay any price for victory. Every step felt like an eternity as he closed the distance between himself and his opponent, sparks flying from under his feet with each powerful stride.

As Maxwell's voice echoed in the distance, urging Cullen to return, the young warrior sprinted through the battlefield as he ran across the chain with his shield held firmly in front of him and his sword clutched tightly in hand. The sound of his heartbeat thundered in his ears with every step - a constant reminder of the danger that lurked ahead. As he approached the end of the chain's length, Cullen leaped into the air, his muscles straining as he raised his weapon above his head.

All eyes were fixed on him as he descended towards the dragon, like a mighty avenger descending from the heavens. With a resounding clang, Cullen's blade pierced through Nimriar's skull, effortlessly slicing through flesh and bone like a knife through hot butter. The dragon let out one final roar before succumbing to death, its massive head crashing to the ground and causing Maxwell and the others to release their grip on the chain as a massive dust cloud rose around them.

Cullen stood there, still and victorious, his sword buried into the dragon's skull, as he whispered a prayer of protection for all those he loved. Tears streamed down Tiatria's cheeks as she watched from above, her heart filled with both fear and admiration for Cullen all the more. It was over; the most formidable threat to Amalthea and humanity lay defeated at their feet. And it was all because of Cullen's unwavering courage and selflessness in battle.

Chapter 28

as the dust settled and silence hung heavily in the air, every eye was fixed on the scene before them. Thamyris, Ásbjørn, and Maxwell cautiously made their way towards the dissipating cloud, hoping to catch a glimpse of Cullen and the dragon. Naga and Myrae had landed nearby, their wings folded neatly at their sides as they observed the unfolding events. Tiatria gracefully descended from above, her feet touching the ground with a soft thud as she rushed over to Cullen's side. Slowly, Cullen's trembling hands released their grip on the sword and shield before he stumbled backward, his face pale and filled with confusion. In an instant, Maxwell was by his friend's side, concern etched onto his features as he knelt down to get a closer look at Cullen. "Cullen?" Maxwell's voice was filled with worry and urgency as he tried to rouse his friend from his dazed state. "Cullen?" His pleas went unanswered as Cullen remained lost in a world of uncertainty and disorientation

Cullen's eyes scanned the area desperately to find that one person. And then they landed on her - Tiatria - holding herself as if she could protect herself from the fear that radiated off of Cullen. Without hesitation, he reached out his left hand to her, seeking comfort and solace. She took it gently, her fingers intertwining with his as she held onto him like a lifeline. Maxwell watched in awe as Cullen's head lowered onto Tiatria's chest, his body seeking the warmth and safety of her embrace. She instinctively cradled his head with her right hand, her tears falling freely now. But there was something more - a soft glow emanating from her hand, casting a warm light over the two of them. As Cullen's breathing became erratic and his grip on her hand tightened in fear, Tiatria knew what she had to do, she had to be with him, till the very end.

Maxwell noticed a rose quartz rosary not far on the ground; he recognized them as Cullen's. He remembered Cullen praying with them in Bestla's church. They must have fallen from Cullen's belt at some point. Tiatria noticed Maxwell's hand in front of her with the beads intertwined with his fingers. "Give these to him," he told her gently.

With trembling fingers, she placed Cullen's rosary into his left hand. Tiatria watched as Cullen's fingers fiercely held onto the beads of his rosary as he held her hand. A gentle smile graced her lips; Tiatria began to sing an enchanting elvish tune, filling the air around them with magic, sorrow, and love. Her voice wove through the air, wrapping itself around Cullen and bringing him peace in the midst of his fear. In that moment, they were both lost in the music and each other, finding solace in the darkness together.

Cullen's heart was heavy with emotion. His eyes locked onto Tiatria's tear-filled gaze. The weight of the moment hung heavy in the air, each second ticking by at an excruciatingly slow pace. His throat felt constricted, unable to form the words that he so desperately wanted to convey to her. Instead, he poured all of his love and devotion into his gaze, hoping she could feel it radiating from him.

(I love you) she told him in his mind

(I love you too, I don't regret dealing the final blow. I wasn't going to let Maxwell commit suicide.)

Tiatria's right hand gently tightened its hold on Cullen's. (I know, and as hard as it is to admit. This fate was meant for you, not him.)

Tears fell from Cullen's eyes (I wish we had more time together)

(I know) she told him as tears dripped down her cheeks.

Slowly but reluctantly, Cullen released her hand, and a cold emptiness settled in its place, reminding him of the warmth and comfort it once provided. Maxwell, with a bowed head and trembling hands, placed a gentle hand on Cullen's. His voice trembled as he spoke in a hushed tone,

"Dominus regit me, et nihil mihi deerit:

in loco pascuae ibi me collocavit. Super aquam refectionis educavit me,

animam meam convertit. Deduxit me super semitas justitiae, propter nomen suum.

Nam, etsi ambulavero in medio umbrae mortis, non timebo mala, quoniam tu mecum es. Virga tua, et baculus tuus, ipsa me consolata sunt.

Parasti in conspectu meo mensam, adversus eos qui tribulant me; impinguasti in oleo caput meum; et calix meus inebrians quam praeclarus est!

Et misericordia tua subsequetur me omnibus diebus vitae meae; et ut inhabitem in domo Domini, in longitudinem dierum."

Cullen could have sworn he felt tear drops touch his hand. "You have made the Order proud, my friend."

With trepidation and fear coursing through their veins, Edith and her companions emerged into the courtyard. The deafening roars and rumbling had finally subsided, leaving a thick silence in its wake. As they stepped closer, their eyes widened in disbelief at the sight before them. The once fearsome red dragon now lay lifeless on the ground, its massive body growing cold. Two other dragons stood behind a small group of people. The dragons' scales glistened in the sunlight, their eyes sharp and intelligent as they surveyed the scene before them.

Driven by a mix of curiosity and desperation, Edith pushed her way through the shocked crowd to reach the small group. Her heart sank as she saw Cullen in Tiatria's arms. Without a second thought, she ran over and possessively snatched his body from Tiatria's grasp.

"CULLEN!" she cried out, her voice filled with grief and terror as she shook him desperately, hoping for any sign of life. "WAKE UP! WE WERE SUPPOSED TO GET MARRIED!"

But it was too late. His face was already pale and his eyes were dilated, seemingly trying to focus on her one last time before he let out a final long breath. In that moment, all sound seemed to fade away as Edith let out a mournful cry, holding onto Cullen's lifeless body.

Her gaze shifted to Tiatria, her voice filled with accusation and anger. "WHAT DID YOU DO TO HIM?" she demanded, her grip tightening on Cullen's body. But as she turned her head back to him, her heart shattered into a million pieces at the realization that he was truly gone. Tears streamed down her face as she mourned the loss of her beloved and best friend.

In a sudden burst of energy, the majestic sword Ka'imil disintegrated into a flurry of shimmering particles, vanishing into the wind as it left behind a trail of fading light. The ground beneath Nimriar's body trembled violently before it also crumbled to dust, carried away by the powerful force of the wind. Tiatria, Edith and the others felt their hearts race and their breath caught in their throats as they watched in awe and horror. The air was filled with tension and anticipation as they tried to make sense of what had just happened.

But before they could fully comprehend, another explosion shook the ground beneath them. Cullen's body seemed to emit a blinding burst of pure white light, engulfing everything around him and throwing all who were standing near him back several feet. A circle of space formed around him as they gazed upon his transformation in both fear and fascination.

His voice let out a harrowing shriek that pierced the air and sent chills down their spines. His body began to shake uncontrollably, muscles rippling and shifting under his skin as he struggled to contain an unimaginable power within. It was a sight both terrifying and mesmerizing, leaving those who witnessed it unable to look away despite their fear and confusion. The air crackled with energy and magic, swirling around Cullen like a vortex as he underwent his transformation.

All eyes were fixed on him as his body convulsed and he fell to the ground, writhing in agony. His screams echoed through the air, sending chills down the spines of all who heard them. Claws erupted from his fingertips, ripping through his once sturdy armor like paper. The transformation began at his arms, where elongated appendages sprouted and shimmered in the sunlight with crimson scales. Suddenly, his boots burst apart as his feet underwent a similar change, growing in size and taking on a reptilian appearance. "WHAT IS HAPPENING TO ME?" he cried out, his voice distorted and filled with immense pain. With wild eyes, he turned to his friends. Their faces now twisted with fear as they bore witness to the changes overtaking him. His own eyes glowed with an otherworldly intensity, gaining a reptilian quality that seemed to pierce into their very souls. As his mouth contorted in agony, his teeth lengthened and sharpened into pointed fangs, his nose and jaws elongated outward as the others watched in horror.

With a deafening crunch, the last remnants of Cullen's armor broke off, revealing a body in the midst of transformation. The sound of bones cracking and breaking echoed through the air as Cullen's form grew larger and larger until he towered over all of them. His once-human features twisted and contorted, giving way to scales that shimmered in the sunlight. A long and powerful tail emerged from his now-scaled back, swaying back and forth with each movement like a pendulum. And then, with one final burst of energy, a magnificent red dragon stood before them - its scales caught every color of the rainbow in the sun's light as its towering size was identical to Nimriar, it seemed to exude an air of regality and strength.

But this was no ordinary dragon - there was a familiarity to its features that set it apart from any other creature they had seen before. This was not Nimriar standing before them now - it was something else entirely, something unique and breathtaking. It was Cullen, reborn as a majestic dragon before their very eyes.

Edith's scream echoed through the air, piercing the thick air of the courtyard. The man she had known all her childhood was now an enormous dragon towering over her, his scales shimmering in hues of deep red and vibrant gold. Cullen's eyes, once friendly and warm, were now blazing amber orbs that seemed to hold a mesmerizing power. They glistened like melted pools of honey, drawing Tiatria's gaze towards them. Unlike Edith, she remained calm and saw past the dragon's exterior to the soul of the man she loved. But Edith couldn't look away from the monstrous form in front of her, terror gripping her heart at the sight of Cullen in such a state.

In a swift move, Maxwell appeared by their side and grabbed Edith by the shoulders, forcefully turning her around to face him. "Princess, stop it!" His voice was stern and commanding, trying to get through to her panicked mind. "You're not helping the situation by screaming!"

But Edith couldn't control her fear, tears streaming down her face as she trembled in Maxwell's grasp. She could only watch in horror as her childhood friend stood before her as a fearsome dragon. And she couldn't shake off the feeling that this was all somehow her fault.

There was a sharp, resounding crack as Edith's hand collided with Maxwell's face. Her voice, filled with a potent mix of anger and fear, seethed through clenched teeth. "Are you insane?" she demanded, her eyes blazing with fury. "The man I love has been transformed into a beast, a monstrous creature!" She pointed accusingly at the creature before them, its giant scaly body glistening in the bright sunlight. Tiatria watched on helplessly as Edith lashed out at Maxwell, her own hand twitching with the urge to intervene. But when Edith turned to face her, her wild and desperate eyes pleading for help, Tiatria could no longer stand idly by. With a determined motion, she brought her palm down on Edith's cheek, the force causing the princess to stumble back in shock. As they stood facing each other, their cheeks stinging from the impact, the dragon let out a deafening roar that reverberated through the air and sent tremors through the ground beneath their feet. Cullen didn't like to see the tension or the fighting.

A blinding, white light burst forth with a deafening force from Tiatria's body, causing all around her to shield their eyes in shock and awe. As the light slowly dimmed, they saw that Tiatria was now floating in the air, her once bright blue eyes now glowing with an ethereal white light. It was as if she was channeling the very essence of the Goddess herself. A powerful yet soothing voice echoed through the clearing, emanating from Tiatria - it was the Goddess speaking through her vessel. Thamyris and Ásbjǫrn couldn't believe what they were witnessing - the physical manifestation of their divine Mother intervening in the bickering between her children.

"I will not have my children fight again!" Her voice boomed, commanding attention and reverence from all those present. The weight of her words hung heavy in the air, as everyone listened intently to what she had to say. "I am sorry, little princess," she continued, addressing Edith directly with a sympathetic tone. "But in order for this evil to be vanquished, the dragon must be struck from this earth. And in doing so, Cullen's life must be given in exchange."

The gravity of the situation hit them like a ton of bricks as they realized the true cost of victory over their powerful foe. The daunting realization that there must always be a balance - for every element taken away, a life must be given in return - weighed heavily on their hearts and minds.

Edith couldn't bear to listen any longer, her heart heavy with sorrow. She turned away from the scene and retreated into the castle alone, tears streaming down her face. The weight of her grief bore down on her, making each step a struggle. As she walked, Ásbjǫrn's sharp eyes followed her, causing Thamyris to take notice of something. He gently placed a hand on Ásbjǫrn's shoulder, prompting him to turn and meet his concerned stare.

"Is that my Sister?" Thamyris asked in a hushed tone, his eyes pleading for confirmation. Thamyris' eyes saw through Ásbjǫrn's as he looked back towards her and saw Amalia's still figure lying on the ground, entwined by the vines. His heart stopped at the sight of her, his mind racing with worry and fear for her as she remained motionless. The vines were still wrapped around her body.

Thamyris raced towards her, his feet pounding against the ground in a desperate attempt to reach her. His mind struggled to keep up with his movements as he skidded to a stop beside her. A sense of dread consumed him as he took in the sight before him. Her once bright and lively blue eyes now gazed back at him, half-open and devoid of life. The iron veins that had been slowly creeping across her body had finally reached her face, transforming it into a deadly mask with a metallic sheen. It was like watching a beautiful statue turn to stone before his very eyes.

Thamyris could feel desperation clawing at his chest as he frantically tried to untangle the thick, pulsing vines from Amalia's body. His trembling fingers fumbled and slipped, coated with a palpable layer of fear and grief that seemed to linger on his skin. The taste of it filled his mouth, bitter and metallic, driving him to work faster and more frantically. With each passing second, his sense of urgency grew, almost bordering on panic as he fought against the vines in a desperate attempt to release her from their grasp.

Seeing Thamyris struggle, Ásbjǫrn stepped in to help with his large, powerful hands, deftly breaking off the vines and freeing Amalia's body. But it was all in vain. As her limp form fell into Thamyris' arms, he knew with a sinking feeling in his gut that she was gone, never to return, no matter how desperately he wished for it. The cold hand of death had claimed her at last and in that moment, Thamyris couldn't deny that it was his fault for not being able to save her and being the one who did it. The weight of regret settled heavily on his heart and shoulders as he held her lifeless body, surrounded by the haunting silence of a sibling's love lost too soon.

Thamyris' face was a torrent of tears as he cradled his beloved sister in his arms, desperately trying to bring this nightmare to an end. His body swayed back and forth in a haunting rhythm, a silent plea for her to come back to him. But with every passing moment, the reality of her death grew heavier and heavier, threatening to crush him under its weight. His shoulders began to shake violently with uncontrollable sobs, the sound muffled as his face pressed against her chest. The world around Thamyris faded away as he clung to his Sister's lifeless body, unable to accept that his family was truly gone. In that moment, all that remained was the terrible ache in his heart and the emptiness that consumed him.

The ethereal voice of the Goddess was like a gentle breeze, soothing and comforting. As she spoke, "Take heart, my child," a warm light radiated from her hand and enveloped Amalia's body, slowly lifting her into the air. The onlookers gasped in awe as they watched the miracle unfold before them. "She has suffered for the last time, I promise you," she vowed as Amalia's body floated to her.

Tiatria's gaze softened as she looked at Amalia with an expression of pure love and compassion. Within moments, Amalia's tattered clothes transformed into a flowing white chiffon gown that seemed to emit its own radiant light under the sun's rays. It had a sweetheart neckline with long sleeves that had split up the middle all the way up to the shoulder, which caused the delicate and lightweight fabric to float easily. The fabric looked almost translucent as it fluttered in the gentle breeze.

As Amalia's hair floated around her back and shoulders in waves, it, too, took on a brilliant white hue and glimmered with a celestial glow. A crown of ivy and jasmine materialized on her head, adding to her ethereal appearance. A delicate crown of ivy and jasmine adorned her head, adding to her ethereal beauty.

As Amalia's body disappeared from sight, a magical portal appeared, revealing a majestic weeping willow tree. Its thick trunk was covered in moss and ivy, creating a lush and enchanting setting. Amalia reappeared beneath the tree, resting peacefully with the left side of her face against a massive root with a generous amount of soft moss on it to cushion her head as her hand gently rested upon it.

For the first time since leaving the forest, Amalia was home. A serene look graced her face - one that brought tears to Thamyris' eyes as he saw his sister at peace. The foliage around her body shifted and transformed, creating a soft and cozy bed of ivy and jasmine flowers for her to rest upon.

Thamyris' throat caught as a lump formed, the weight of memories crashing over him as he gazed upon the tall tree in front of them. "I know that tree," he whispered, his voice trembling with emotion. "Lia and I used to play on it all the time when she was just a little." The Goddess smiled warmly, her serene expression adding to the already magical aura surrounding them. "There she shall remain," she said, gesturing towards the tree with a graceful hand. "Under my watchful eye and the spirits of nature, until her heart and soul have fully healed and she can be reunited with those who were taken from her." Thamyris couldn't hold back the tears that now streamed down his face, a mixture of relief and overwhelming happiness flooding through him. For so long, all he had wanted was to know that his Sister was safe. And now, in this sacred place filled with hope and healing, he finally had that reassurance. The sun's rays filtered through the leaves above, casting dappled light on the ground below and adding a sense of divinity to the moment.

As the portal slowly dissipated, Amalia was left to slumber undisturbed, her tranquil form cocooned in a soft bedding of ivy and moss. The Goddess turned her gaze towards Myrae and Naga, who both bowed their heads respectfully in recognition of their Mother and the arrival of their new brother. "Welcome, Brother," Naga yawned as he lifted his head, his golden eyes sparkling with warmth. "Our time is done for now, and it is time for us to slumber until we are needed once more."

Cullen looked on curiously at the other dragons before turning back to his human friends. The Goddess smiled at him before slowly departing from Tiatria's body, her feet gently touching the ground before settling firmly on the earth. Cullen lowered his head towards Tiatria, who placed her hands tenderly on the dragon's snout. "I will always love you," she spoke softly.

With a slow and graceful movement, Cullen raised his head and began making his way towards the other dragons. Tiatria watched with bittersweet emotions as three portals appeared, each one a pathway for the individual dragons to return to their own realms and slumber once again. Myrae and Naga wasted no time in passing through their respective portals and disappearing into the unknown.

But Cullen hesitated, torn between staying with his human companions or following his instinctual desire to be with his kind.

Maxwell slowly made his way towards his friend, his footsteps echoing on the rocky ground as he approached. He reached out and placed his left hand gently on one of Cullen's massive toes, offering words of reassurance. "It's alright to be frightened," he told him, his voice steady and calm, "We'll be alright, we'll *all* be alright." The dragon let out a deep sigh as he turned to look back at Tiatria, his golden eyes filled with determination. "Don't worry about her," he assured, "I'll watch over her and anyone else you may have left behind with her." A sense of pride swelled within him as he spoke these words, knowing that he had a duty to protect those he cared for.

Cullen gave a snort of approval before turning back to Tiatria. Despite the tense situation, there was a sense of peace between them. "Y-you...are..." the dragon struggled to speak, still getting used to his permanent form, "mmyy...ro-rose." His voice was soft but filled with love and adoration for the woman in front of him. Tiatria managed to give a weak smile in return, holding back tears that threatened to spill down her cheeks as she watched Cullen prepare to enter the portal and disappear.

As Tiatria struggled to keep the tears bursting from her eyes while her emotions ran high, Thamyris stepped forward and placed a comforting hand on Tiatria's shoulder. She turned to face him and broke down into sobs, unable to hold back any longer. Thamyris held her close as she wept, both of them experiencing bittersweet moments with their loved ones who were now gone from their lives forever. The air was heavy with sorrow and longing as they stood together, taking comfort in each other's embrace during the difficult moment.

Ásbjǫrn's heart felt heavy, as he embraced his friends. Tears streamed down their faces, mingling with the dirt and blood that adorned them after the fierce battle they had just faced. He held on to them tightly, offering whatever comfort he could through his touch and words. "You will see them again, my dear friends," he promised softly, trying to infuse hope into his own voice. As he gently lowered Tiatria to the ground, she opened her eyes and looked at the remaining knights with a mixture of exhaustion and determination. "It's time for us to go home as well," she said, her tone filled with both resignation and sadness. "The Goddess has extended an invitation for all who have witnessed today's events to live in the forest under her protection." She turned to face Maxwell directly, her eyes full of compassion and understanding. "And that includes you, my friend," she continued, placing a hand on his shoulder. "You will always have a place among us." As they stood together in the courtyard, the sun began to set behind them, casting a warm orange light over the scene. The sound of birds singing and leaves rustling filled the air, a peaceful reminder of the serenity that awaited them in the forest.

Maxwell stood at a crossroads, his heart torn between the familiar call of duty he'd always known in Amalthea and the peaceful life of the forest. The weight of his decision pressed heavily upon him, like a heavy stone. His old life beckoned to him with its comforting routines and familiar faces, but he had made a promise to Cullen and knew he must honor it. With a small smile at Tiatria, who stood beside him with determination in her eyes, he gathered his resolve and spoke, "Let us return home."

As they stood in the once-grand courtyard, now broken in debris and torn-up earth, Tiatria's eyes lit up with excitement. Her slender hand glided through the air in a graceful wave, summoning a shimmering portal before them. Thamyris and Ásbjǫrn were the first to step through, their figures disappearing into the rippling light as they were eager to get home. Maxwell turned to face the remaining members of their Order, feeling a pang of sorrow for all they had lost in this tumultuous battle.

But he straightened his shoulders and addressed his comrades with determination, "Well men," he declared, "who among you will be the first to follow?" The men looked at Maxwell, their expressions reflecting both uncertainty and trust. They then looked at the castle looming behind him, its walls marred by battle scars and memories of their fallen brethren. And within a moment or two, they dropped their swords and walked into the portal without so much as a word.

Maxwell smiled sadly, as he followed suit, knowing that this was not just another mission or quest. It was a new beginning for all of them, a chance to leave behind the pain and darkness of their past and embrace the hope and light of their future together. As they passed through the portal one by one, with Tiatria being the last, it closed behind them with a soft whoosh, sealing their decision to start anew.

)o(

Edith watched from a hidden doorway, her heart heavy with disappointment as she heard Cullen's last words that were meant for another. Tears streamed down her cheeks as she turned away in a huff. It was the first time in Edith's privileged life that she had been denied what she wanted. The Cardinal emerged from the dungeon, the sound of falling debris still echoing behind him. He made his way through the castle towards the courtyard but stopped when he saw Edith approaching. Without a word, he walked to her and followed the Princess to the throne room.

As they entered, the stench of death and destruction filled their senses. The once grand room was now littered with corpses and debris from the recent battle. Edith wrinkled her nose in disgust before commanding, "Clean all of this up immediately."

The Cardinal bowed his head in acknowledgement before replying, "Yes, your Grace." His eyes took in the gruesome scene before him, but he quickly averted his gaze and focused on the task at hand.

Edith strode confidently to the throne and sat upon it, already envisioning her coronation as queen. "I want everything prepared for my coronation as soon as possible," she declared.

"As you wish," replied the Cardinal, his voice strained with the weight of what they had just witnessed. Together, they began to make plans for Edith's ascension to the throne, determined to leave behind the horrors of war and create a new era of prosperity for their kingdom.

The Cardinal's eyes followed Edith as she suddenly stood from her throne as she noticed Dorian's book of spells still lay where Maxwell had left it. The weight of the ancient tome surprised her as she lifted it from its resting place. She could tell this book was not of her world and that it still may hold some value in it. Her eyes then drifted to the shattered mirror, its pieces scattered haphazardly across the floor. As she bent down for a closer look, she caught a glimpse of something shimmering within the shards.

Gasping in shock, Edith rose to her feet and covered her mouth with trembling hands. The sound drew the attention of the Cardinal, who hurried over to her side. "What is it, child?" he asked in concern. But Edith couldn't form words, for in one of the broken pieces of mirror, she could see her father's face staring back at her.

The Cardinal's own gasp resounded through the room as he, too, caught sight of the King trapped within the mirror fragments. "God help us," he whispered.

Edith gingerly picked up one of the shards and turned to face the Cardinal, confusion etched upon her features. "How can this be?" she asked, desperate for an explanation.

The Cardinal's expression grew grave as he replied, "Witchcraft."

Edith let out a determined sigh, frustration and anger bubbling within her. "These vile elves have taken everything from me," she seethed, her eyes blazing with fury. "First, the man I loved, and now my own father!" Her gaze then shifted to the book that lay on the floor, its ancient pages filled with secrets and answers. "Take this book to one of our most skilled archivists," she demanded, her voice laced with determination. "It must be studied to uncover their whereabouts and how to defeat them!" The Cardinal reverently picked up the book with both hands, his expression serious and focused.

"I do not know what lies within these pages," he replied, his tone grave. "But it is our best chance at defeating those blasphemous heretics." Edith's fists clenched at her sides as she struggled to contain her rage. She would not rest until those treacherous elves paid for their crimes against her loved ones.

The Cardinal bowed low before her. "I will see to it immediately, Princess," he said, quickly correcting himself. "My Queen." With one last respectful nod, he hurried off to carry out her orders.

Edith turned back to her father, who could only look back at her through the shard. "I swear on our kingdom," she whispered fiercely, her hand squeezing the shard. "They will pay for all they have done." Her resolve was unshakable as the shard cut into her skin, causing blood to trickle down her wrist and arm.

Chapter 29

The forest was alive in the confident strides of Thamyris and Ásbjǫrn, their feet barely making a sound on the thick carpet of moss and fallen leaves. Behind them, their group of soldiers followed closely, their eyes wide in awe as they took in the lush surroundings. The soldiers, who were used to the cold stone walls and strict regulations of castle life, were stunned into silence by the abundance of greenery and vibrant plant life surrounding them.

As they approached the large tree with its ornate doors, Thamyris and Ásbjǫrn looked back at their men, who were starting to look a little panicked. Never before had they seen such an enchanted place. The air was thick with anticipation and a sense of magic that seemed to emanate from every leaf and blade of grass.

With Thamyris leading the way, they entered through the grand doors and found themselves inside a magnificent palace. The walls were adorned with intricate tapestries depicting scenes of elven folklore and the floors had polished wood that shone in the sunlight streaming through intricate glassless windows. The light played through the air, casting colorful reflections across the room like dancing fairies.

The elves walked in a graceful silence, their ethereal beauty mesmerizing to the newcomers. Maxwell, sensing their unease, walked to the front of the group and raised his hands reassuringly. "Do not be afraid," he said in a soothing tone. "This place may seem intimidating at first, but it is also full of wonder and magic." The soldiers relaxed slightly at his words, comforted by his calm demeanor and confident assurance. In this place, surrounded by enchanting beauty and mystical creatures, they realized that anything was possible.

Thamyris placed his hand gently on Maxwell's shoulder, a silent reassurance as he took a step forward. The men stood in stunned silence, unsure of what to say or think as they watched the elegant elf before them. His graceful movements and regal presence commanded their attention.

"You are all welcome to stay in my palace as you get settled," Thamyris announced, gesturing towards the grand staircase that led to the castle's interior. "You will be given ample time to rest and recover, along with new clothes and the opportunity to pursue a new purpose. Whether that means becoming a soldier in my kingdom or learning a new trade, the choice is yours."

He paused, his gaze sweeping over the group of men. "I do not require you to worship our God and Goddess, but I do ask that you show respect to those who do." His words held a weight of authority and sincerity, leaving no room for argument. As he spoke, the warmth and richness of the palace enveloped them, a stark contrast to their previous life in the castle. Thamyris' offer was both generous and unexpected, filling them with hope for a better future under his rule.

Ásbjǫrn gave a solemn nod, his eyes glinting with determination. "Right, now follow me as I show you to your new quarters," he announced, his voice ringing out across the courtyard. Maxwell watched with keen interest as the soldiers made a queue and followed Ásbjǫrn towards their destination.

Thamyris' head turned towards Maxwell, a small smile playing on his lips. "Your room is now yours, permanently," he stated, gesturing towards the grand castle walls. As they walked, Thamyris lightly trailed his fingers along the walls as if in reverence. "Clothes have been placed in your armoire, and you will find everything you need here." He then motioned for Maxwell and Tiatria to follow him further into the castle.

"I have decided to make you one of my advisors," Thamyris suddenly declared, causing Maxwell's eyes to widen in shock. The elf's ears twitched slightly at the sound of Maxwell's sharp intake of breath. Thamyris turned his head slightly, his expression serious. "I can feel what's coming. That Princess will not let this go."

Silence fell between them before both Tiatria and Maxwell exchanged a meaningful look and continued following Thamyris down the winding corridors of the castle. Maxwell couldn't deny that he wasn't surprised by Thamyris' decision. After all that had transpired - Cullen's transformation, the destruction of the castle, and the loss of innocent lives and even their king - it was only natural for tensions to rise and for war to be on the horizon. Perhaps even a holy war, if pushed far enough.

Thamyris' fingers slowly left the intricate designs on the smooth walls of his throne room as he counted his steps. Slowly and easily, he reached out with his right hand as he counted his steps and when his left foot tapped against the edge of his throne, he turned around before settling into it. His blank eyes seemed fixed on the entrance, his posture tense with anticipation. "How do you even know they will come here?" Maxwell's voice broke through the silence, his arms folded across his chest in a defensive stance. "You have to enter through a portal or through the forest itself. You can't just walk in."

Thamyris' left finger continued tapping on the armrest, a sign of his deep contemplation. "I'm fully aware the forest can open again," he responded with a sigh, "but after this, I'm fairly sure it has closed itself off as a defensive measure. Still, we don't know how long that may be." The weight of their situation hung heavy in the air, thick like the ominous clouds gathering above them. "Do you have the book my Mother gave Dorian?" The question hung heavy in the air, its implications sending shivers down Maxwell's spine. He could feel his heart stop and blood turn to ice as he remained silent. "That means they have it," Thamyris spoke gravely, "and it will only be a matter of time." The gravity of their predicament settled heavily upon them both, weighing down their spirits and filling the room with an unshakeable sense of dread.

"Can they even read it?" Tiatria questioned, her voice laced with worry as she held her chin with her right hand. "The book could only be read by Dorian," she then looked at Thamyris, her brows furrowed in concern. "With Dorian gone, how can they possibly unlock its secrets?"

Maxwell and Tiatria exchanged a worried glance as they watched Thamyris's face grow old and tired, his features drawn along with the weight of their predicament. "The book will not give up its secrets easily to any who seek harm upon this realm," Maxwell spoke solemnly. "But sooner or later, it will speak to them and they will find us. We must be ready."

Heaving a heavy sigh, Maxwell gave a determined nod. "I'll help you prepare for whatever comes our way. We can start immediately." For him, this place had become his home, and he was well aware that Dorian would never forgive him if anything were to happen to the library.

Thamyris raised his hand before resting it on the armrest of his throne. "We still have some time before we must face them again," he said with a weary tone. "The humans will need to rebuild their numbers in the Order, reconstruct the castle, bury their dead, and crown a new Queen." At these words, Maxwell visibly relaxed; he still knew better than to grow complacent.

Turning to Tiatria, he noticed that she seemed unusually pale and drawn. Concern etched his features as he asked softly, "Are you alright?"

Tiatria's mind was racing, trying to process all of the new information and challenges that lay ahead. The possibility of war hung heavily in the air, adding an extra layer of urgency to their situation. She couldn't help but feel overwhelmed by the weight of responsibility on her shoulders - not only for her own people but also for these newcomers who needed to be settled and acclimated to their new home. There was so much to consider and even more to do. Slowly, she turned to Maxwell and nodded in agreement with his statement. "Yes," she said wearily, "just a lot to think about." Both Thamyris and Maxwell shared the same feeling of exhaustion; the day had been long and filled with difficult decisions. But they knew there was no time to rest - their people were counting on them to lead them through what would soon be a tumultuous time.

Thamyris gazed intensely in Tiatria's direction, his eyes deep in thought as he rested the right side of his head on top of the knuckles of his right hand. His words were deliberate and purposeful as he spoke, capturing Tiatria's full attention. "There is something I need to make clear," he began, causing a knot of anxiety to form in Tiatria's stomach. Maxwell watched from the sidelines, aware of the tension in the air.

"I know about you and Cullen," Thamyris continued, his voice unwavering. "I know what happened between you two before we returned to his realm." Tiatria's heart froze as tears welled up in her eyes. She braced herself for the anger and disappointment she expected from Thamyris. But instead, he stood up from his seat and used his ears to hear where she was standing. He slowly put his hands on her shoulders.

"I understand that as a Queen, you have certain responsibilities, as do I." Thamyris said, his face softened slightly. "And that I cannot fulfill those duties with you, such as creating children and giving you a family life." Maxwell knew all too well the importance of a Queen's role in continuing the royal line. However, with Thamyris' preference for men, it seemed impossible for them to have children together.

"But I want you to know," Thamyris said gently, reaching out to wipe away Tiatria's tears, "that if you are with a child from your nights with Cullen, I will accept and adopt this child without question." The tears streamed down Tiatria's cheeks as she felt an immense weight lifted off her shoulders. Thamyris' sensitive ears could pick up on her quiet sobs as she struggled to hold back her emotions.

"And based on your reaction," he added with a small smile, "I'd say that the chances are very high." His words filled Tiatria with a sense of hope and gratitude towards Thamyris. Despite his own desires, he was willing to accept her and any child she may carry. This only deepened Tiatria's love for him, and she couldn't believe her luck in finding such a kind and understanding husband.

Before the Goddess departed from her mortal vessel, she made a solemn promise to Tiatria that she would ensure Cullen would leave behind something incredibly precious for her. As Maxwell placed his right hand gently on Tiatria's trembling shoulder, he spoke in a soft, soothing voice. "I gave Cullen my word that I would be here for you and anyone else he leaves behind." Tiatria then watched as Maxwell gently put Cullen's rose quartz rosary into her hands.

Tiatria looked at Maxwell in shock, "And I intend to keep that promise." A single tear glistened in Tiatria's eye as she gazed up at Maxwell. She could see the sincerity in his warm brown eyes, and it brought a sense of calm to her grieving heart. Without hesitation, she fell into Maxwell's comforting embrace, holding onto him tightly as if he was a lifeline in this sea of sorrow. Thamyris listened from the sidelines, a small smile playing on his lips as he observed the deep bond between these two dear friends. The weight of their grief seemed to ease in each other's presence, finding solace in their shared memories of Cullen.

With a steady stride, Ásbjǫrn entered the grand throne room. The air was thick with anticipation and the sound of his heavy footsteps echoed off the walls. "There you all are," he announced, his voice booming through the hall. "All the soldiers have been shown their quarters and seem settled." His eyes scanned the room before settling on Thamyris, who stood confidently with his hand on his hip.

"What's happening here?" Ásbjǫrn's curiosity was piqued.

Thamyris gestured towards Tiatria, who stood between Maxwell and him."It seems there is going to be an addition to the family," Thamyris replied with a sly smile.

Ásbjǫrn's face lit up with joy, "That is wonderful!" he exclaimed, spreading his arms wide in excitement. "Nature has surely blessed us!" With a warm smile, he walked over to Tiatria and enveloped her in a hug full of love and happiness.

A warm, gentle smile slowly spread across Maxwell's face, his entire being filled with hope and wonder as Veronna's words rang through his mind. It was as if a weight had been lifted from his shoulders, a weight he hadn't even realized he had been carrying. The prophecy the elves had been waiting for, praying for, was finally unfolding before their very eyes - a child born out of two worlds destined to bring peace and unite their divided people.

Maxwell's gaze drifted upwards towards the sky visible through a large window in the ceiling. The golden sunlight poured into the room, illuminating everything in its warm embrace. It felt like a sign, a divine blessing, as he whispered a prayer under his breath. His heart overflowed with emotion, pleading for this new life to be the bridge that would finally connect their divided worlds and usher in an era of harmony.

In that moment, Maxwell's mind was flooded with images of what this child could mean for their worlds. A future filled with endless possibilities and wonders unfolded before him. He couldn't help but feel a sense of overwhelming anticipation and excitement, knowing that this child held the key to their future. It was a moment he would never forget, one that he knew would change everything for good, forever.

)o(

Deep in the mystical forest, the air was filled with the intoxicating scent of jasmine blossoms. A gentle breeze delicately carried the fragrance through the trees, creating a dreamlike atmosphere around Amalia as she slept. Sunlight filtered through the lush leaves of the willow tree above, casting a warm glow upon her peaceful face.

In her slumber, Amalia dreamed of Tahl'rail and their children frolicking in the royal courtyard. Her heart swelled with joy as she watched them play under the loving gaze of her parents. This was all she had ever wanted – a happy family to call her own.

Suddenly, the sound of heavy footsteps interrupted her blissful reverie. A large bear emerged from the shadows, cautiously approaching Amalia. She stirred slightly as it sniffed at her hair, seemingly checking on her safety and surroundings. It was Ásbjǫrn, a loyal protector appointed by Thamyris himself. He made sure to visit Amalia regularly at Thamyris's request, knowing he couldn't always be there to watch over her.

Although Thamyris would occasionally come to visit Amalia, his duties as ruler kept him from spending as much time with her as he would have liked. As an extra precaution, he had declared that no one in his kingdom's borders was allowed near Amalia – earning her the nickname "The Sleeping Maiden". But in this secluded corner of the forest, surrounded by nature and guarded by Ásbjǫrn, Amalia could sleep peacefully without any worries or fears.

The End

For Now....

Appendix

Latin language translation

Pater noster, qui es in caelis,

sanctificetur nomen tuum. Adveniat regnum tuum.

Fiat voluntas tua, sicut in caelo et in terra.

Panem nostrum quotidianum da nobis hodie,

et dimitte nobis debita nostra sicut et nos dimittimus debitoribus nostris.

Et ne nos inducas in tentationem, sed libera nos a malo.

Amen.

English Translation

Our Father, who art in heaven, hallowed be Thy name.

Thy kingdom come.

Thy will be done on earth as it is in heaven.

Give us this day our daily bread and forgive us our trespasses as we forgive those who trespass against us.

And lead us not into temptation, but deliver us from evil.

Amen.

Latin Version

Dominus regit me, et nihil mihi deerit:

in loco pascuae ibi me collocavit. Super aquam refectionis educavit me, animam meam convertit. Deduxit me super semitas justitiae, propter nomen suum.

Nam, etsi ambulavero in medio umbrae mortis, non timebo mala, quoniam tu mecum es. Virga tua, et baculus tuus, ipsa me consolata sunt.

Parasti in conspectu meo mensam, adversus eos qui tribulant me; impinguasti in oleo caput meum; et calix meus inebrians quam praeclarus est!

English Translation

The LORD is my shepherd; I shall not want.

He maketh me to lie down in green pastures: he leadeth me beside the still waters.

He restoreth my soul: he leadeth me in the paths of righteousness for his name's sake.

Yea, though I walk through the valley of the shadow of death, I will fear no evil: for thou art with me; thy rod and thy staff they comfort me.

Thou preparest a table before me in the presence of mine enemies: thou anointest my head with oil; my cup runneth over.

Surely goodness and mercy shall follow me all the days of my life: and I will dwell in the house of the LORD for ever.

Latin words Translated

Evanescere: Vanish

Scutum: Shield

French Word Translation:

Amant: Love/ Lover